Alexander Jamieson

A Grammar of Logic

and intellectual philosophy - Vol. 2

Alexander Jamieson

A Grammar of Logic
and intellectual philosophy - Vol. 2

ISBN/EAN: 9783337370442

Printed in Europe, USA, Canada, Australia, Japan

Cover: Foto ©Andreas Hilbeck / pixelio.de

More available books at **www.hansebooks.com**

A

GRAMMAR OF LOGIC

AND

INTELLECTUAL PHILOSOPHY,

ON

DIDACTIC PRINCIPLES;

FOR THE USE OF

COLLEGES, SCHOOLS, AND PRIVATE INSTRUCTION.

BY ALEXANDER JAMIESON,

AUTHOR OF A TREATISE ON THE CONSTRUCTION OF MAPS, A GRAMMAR OF RHETORIC
AND POLITE LITERATURE, CONVERSATIONS ON GENERAL HISTORY, EDITOR
OF THE FIFTH AND IMPROVED EDITION OF ADAMS'S ELEMENTS
OF USEFUL KNOWLEDGE, &C. &C.

Understanding is a well-spring of life to him that hath it.
Prov. xvi. 22

Tenth Edition, Stereotyped.

NEW YORK:
KIGGINS, TOOKER & CO.,
123 & 125 WILLIAM STREET.

INTRODUCTION.

GRAMMAR, LOGIC, and RHETORIC are the handmaids of LITER-
ATURE, SCIENCE and PHILOSOPHY. The study of grammar is the
study of LANGUAGE, and MEMORY is the faculty which it chiefly
employs and exercises. But in proceeding towards the cultivation of TASTE and GENIUS, the acquisition of SCIENCE, and other
ulterior objects of education, the faculties most susceptible of
improvement and refinement are the IMAGINATION and the
UNDERSTANDING.

· POLITE LITERATURE is addressed to the IMAGINATION and
the UNDERSTANDING in conjunction; SCIENCE is addressed to the
UNDERSTANDING alone.

With the view, therefore, of conducting youth from the mere
exercise of memory, in the study of language, towards investigations on the powers of the understanding, in the regions of science, my GRAMMAR of RHETORIC and POLITE LITERATURE professes, by a proper gradation, to occupy the mind, for some time,
in those agreeable prospects exhibited to the imagination, and in
those interesting speculations, also, addressed to the understanding, with which the arts of speaking and writing so amply
abound.

But the most successful initiation and discipline into the researches of philosophy, are disquisitions about the objects with
which we are familiar, and inquiries into the operations of the
human mind, which we every day experience. And LOGIC has
been justly styled *the history of the human mind,* inasmuch as it
traces the progress of our knowledge, from our first and simple
perceptions, through all their different combinations, and all those
numerous deductions, that result from variously comparing them
one with another. For it is thus, only, that we are let into the
frame and contexture of our own minds,—that we learn in what
manner we ought to conduct our thoughts, in order to arrive
at truth, and avoid error,—that we see how to build one discovery
upon another, and, by preserving the chain of reasoning uniform and unbroken, to pursue the relations of things through
all their labyrinths and windings, and at length exhibit them
to the view of the soul with all the advantages of light and
conviction.

I, therefore, trust that this GRAMMAR OF LOGIC AND INTEL-
LECTUAL PHILOSOPHY will be found adequate to initiate youth in
that history, and to resolve such inquiries respecting the operations of their own minds, as they daily experience.

The plan of the volume is briefly as follows:—

The FIRST BOOK is devoted exclusively to the Definition of
terms — Preliminary explanations — Enumeration of principles
which are taken for granted — Inquiries into the nature and value
of hypotheses — The doctrine of analogy — The proper means of
knowing the operations of our own minds — The difficulty of
attending to these operations, with observations which may assist
us in overcoming this difficulty, — and, finally, A comprehensive
division of the powers of the human mind.

The SECOND BOOK embraces *Elements of Intellectual Philosophy*, calculated to instruct youth in a knowledge of those principles to which the development of the mental faculties may be
traced, and upon which we rest all our knowledge of legitimate
logic. These elements comprise analyses of the faculties, Consciousness — Sensation — Perception — Attention — Conception —
Abstraction — Association — Memory — Imagination — Judgment
— Reason — Moral Perception.

The THIRD BOOK treats on *Subjects of collateral Inquiry with
the Intellectual Powers,* — such, for example, as the Primary and
Secondary qualities of bodies — Natural language and signs — Matter and Space — Duration, Extension, and Number — Identity —
The train of thought in the Mind — and Prejudices.

The FOURTH BOOK — *The Grammar of Logic* — unfolds the
doctrines of Ideas — Propositions — Sophisms — Reasoning and
Syllogism.

The FIFTH BOOK concludes the volume, with a brief sketch
of *The Philosophy of Human Knowledge*, as it is addressed to the
MEMORY, the UNDERSTANDING, and the IMAGINATION.

The foregoing arrangement was dictated by motives which the
following observations pretend to explain.

In a work that treats of Logic and Intellectual Philosophy, and
where selection is so imperiously required, there must be an
equal necessity that certain fixed and intelligible principles should
be preëstablished. Nor, in handling subjects that have been
controverted, and which, from their very nature, are ever liable
to discussion, is there any thing of more consequence than agreement, at the outset, about the language we use; for, when, in
philosophical disquisitions, we are once agreed respecting the
signification of the words and terms we employ, it is unlikely
that we shall differ about their application, provided we continue
to use them in the sense which we had already affixed to them:
hence the position and division of *Book First.*

A knowledge of the powers of the human mind, and of the
science of Intellectual Philosophy, furnishes the proper basis
upon which every other science is grounded, because the human

faculties are the instruments by which alone invention in all the sciences can be accomplished.

The examination and analysis of these faculties reciprocally open sources of intellectual improvement, and exercise the student in habits of thinking, judging, reasoning, and communication, upon which depend, not merely the study of logic, and the further prosecution of science, but almost entirely the active business of life. Nor does it appear to me that any other process could, with equal certainty of success, be adopted, by which the mind of youth, launching into a new and pleasing field of speculation, might be enabled to form an estimate of its own powers, of the acquisitions it has made, of the habits it has formed, and of the further improvements of which it is susceptible. For, when the student has acquired those habits of attention, and that capacity of observation, which the study of his intellectual powers must necessarily give him, it is then, and not till then, I have no hesitation in affirming, that he is qualified to enter upon a philosophical, but popular course of LOGIC.

Besides, as the progress of the intellectual powers is not prematurely quickened, an acquaintance with the phenomena of the human mind, arranged so as to enable us to profit by our personal experience, cannot be a subject of abstract speculation, but must be the channel through which we advance to the highest endowments of the understanding.

But the professed object of Logic is to teach us the RIGHT USE OF REASON, both in the investigation and in the communication of TRUTH.

I have already pointed out the relation in which I conceive RHETORIC to stand to GRAMMAR and LOGIC, and, without arrogating pretensions to superior discernment, which would only lay me open to the suspicion of a particular prejudice, I do not see how it is possible to conduct ingenuous youth upwards from the *correctness* of their *taste* to the *cultivation* of their *understanding*, but by previously explaining to them the faculties of the mind, and their various operations with which we are immediately or remotely conversant, the circumstances favorable or unfavorable to the development of those faculties, and the means by which their improvement may be most successfully undertaken.

In the execution of this task, I was also laid under an imperious necessity of banishing from my work all the trifling subtilties of the ancient Logicians, all the logomachy of the schools, all the puzzling distinctions which perplex us in most of the popular treatises of our modern philosophers. But I do not thence lay claim to any new discoveries either in the science of mind, or in the art of Logic.

It has been with me a principle of paramount importance, to endeavor to select the most unexceptionable materials from the most approved works of my predecessors' or contemporaries,

A *

employed, like myself, in extending the elements of science. And those subjects which seemed best adapted for the employment of youth at the commencement of their philosophical studies, I have labored to present to them in this BOOK with faithfulness and assiduity in their selection, and with simplicity and intelligibility in their form and arrangement.

Of the difficulty of executing an acceptable compilation of the ELEMENTS OF THE SCIENCE OF MIND with analyses of the intellectual powers, in the order of their connection and dependence, it would be superfluous to reason with empirics who have not added one iota to literature or to science. But the philosopher and the critic know that judgment in selection, perspicuity of style, and compression of argumentation, the great requisites of every writer who would not become dull from crudity of conception, nor obscure from prolixity of reasoning, are indispensable to give anciently-received truths and established modern discoveries those charms which shall fascinate readers in the purple bloom of youth. And in pleasing satisfaction will my mind now repose, if, among the unambitious pretensions of a compiler, the reasonings which support those truths shall be found to possess conciseness, and the illustrations of those discoveries no more expansion of proof than the different steps of their relative processes required; for, with youth whose mental faculties we would, by active discipline, invigorate, improve, and embellish, brevity is not less the soul of reasoning than of wit. Their knowledge, however, is not to rest on tarnished fragments struck off from splendid systems, nor on defective models the relics of doubtful institutes; but on the details of human knowledge, and such discipline of education as shall accustom them to exert their intellectual faculties, without preparation, and render them prompt in expedient, and active in resource.

Sufficient, however, has been said on *Book Second*, as well to show its high importance, as to satisfy every impartial reader, that, to have omitted it, or assigned to it any other place in the volume, would have evinced culpable neglect or capricious arrangement.

To have blended with the subjects in the SECOND BOOK those which constitute the *Third*, would have created a species of confusion, which, in elementary works, should always be avoided; and, besides, the relative importance this BOOK bears to the *Second* and the *Fourth* reciprocally, allotted to it that neutrality which makes it of easier reference to the numerous subjects that it may collaterally illustrate, or with which, in many instances, its materials may be directly conjoined. Nor is this the only light in which Book Third may be viewed. If the subjects of which it is composed be considered abstractedly, then does the student enter upon disquisitions and analyses of separate branches of INTELLECTUAL PHILOSOPHY, of primary importance on his entrance upon philosophical studies. But it is unnecessary to offer proofs for that which is clear as sunshine.

Of Book Fourth, assigned to Pure Logic, I shall say a few words. But I premise, that of all arts, that surely is entitled to attention which pretends to tell us how we may improve and properly employ the understanding,—the faculty by which man is most eminently distinguished above the other creatures of this world, and by which, perhaps, he partakes most of the constitution of superior natures. Now, Logic is that art. Its professed purpose, as we have observed above, is to teach us the right use of reason, both in the investigation and in the communication of truth;—to inform us how to introduce clearness and good order among our ideas;—to explain the operations of the mind which are conversant about those ideas; and by the proper exercise of which operations, we shall be least in danger of deviating into error.

The understanding is occupied entirely with knowledge—the end of all science is to instruct us in knowledge; and the same end is pursued by all study, whether prudential, political, moral, or mechanical. In what way soever we exert and exercise our understanding, it is to obtain some information that we did not before possess; and the design of logic, considered as an art, is to hold forth the manner of attaining that knowledge with the greatest ease and expedition.

From these views of the nature and end of Logic, it is apparent, that it claims our attention as one of the first arts to which we should apply, in our progress towards knowledge, either as the best means of fortifying or of improving the understanding. The more acute the understanding is, the more successful will it be in the investigations of science. The less it is liable to err, the more certain and expeditious will be its progress in new and untried pursuits. The more we are acquainted with those sophistries which have misled other reasoners, the less liable shall we be to fall into similar mistakes. The better we understand the nature of the instrument which we employ, we may reasonably expect to be more expert and successful in its use. Every thing, then, in Logic, that does not contribute to improve the understanding, and to promote our progress in useful knowledge, deserves no attention; but every thing, on the other hand, that promotes these ends, cannot obtain more attention than it deserves.

Though no art ever gave occasion to so much idle research and fanciful refinement as Logic; though none ever so much bewildered the human mind, and repressed every useful exertion of the understanding, as that which pretended to enlighten and improve this faculty, and to guide it in the road to truth; though all the syllogism of the schools, after the thousand volumes that have been written on it, and after the employment of a series of ages to bring it to perfection, never enriched science

or art with one useful discovery,—we must not rashly conclude
that these abuses furnish proofs of the general inutility, or insignificance, of Logic as an art.

As, then, the sophistry and absurdity with which Logic has
been disgraced, are no valid objections against its use in a philosophical course of education, so neither is it to be contemned because we hear some men reason very justly without any acquaintance with its rules.   There is in all mankind some natural logic,
for it is one of those arts which may be learned by practice, with
out the knowledge of theory.

One of the best methods of making progress in the art of
reasoning, is actual practice, or the acquisition of the habit of
examining a train of ideas constituting an argument; and of this
branch of the art all men acquire some share by experience—
many men acquire a great deal; but though long experience in
sound reasoning may render us expert logicians, in the same manner as practice, without the knowledge of principles, may form
eminent practitioners in any other art, yet this success will not
justify any inference against the utility, or even the propriety of
the theory.   The end of all theory in the arts, is, to render us
more methodical and reputable in their performance; and a
knowledge of the principles on which, in this volume, the art of
Logic is founded, can scarcely fail to facilitate the progress of
youth in becoming good reasoners.

Of this they may be assured, if they have sufficient candor to
admit there is such a thing as good reasoning, that there is
no accomplishment or qualification any man can acquire more
important than the art of reasoning well.   Whether, then, youth
shall become, in life, men of speculation or men of business, in
every step they take, their rational faculties must be constantly exercised; and the subject of which we now speak is
calculated entirely to render them expert and successful in
that exercise.

The FIFTH BOOK, which offers a sketch of "The Philosophy of Human Knowledge," seemed a necessary Appendix to
the volume; but it was not my object, in the compass of a
few pages, to enter upon a subject which I intend to publish
in a separate work, as a sequel to my Grammars of Rhetoric
and Logic.

And, for the purpose of initiating youth in the doctrines
of the Philosophy of Mind, I have constructed, on this Grammar
of Logic, a Book of "Questions and Exercises," with a "Key" to
the same; as, in my humble judgment, no discipline is more successful in accomplishing its end, than that which reduces literature, philosophy, and science, to interlocutory discourse, conducted in the style and manner of a spirited dialogue. The ease with
which the entire volume may be converted into "Dialogues on
Logic and Intellectual Philosophy," by means of its companion,
the "Book of Questions," can only be equalled by the advantages

which youth ever derive from catechetical instruction, possessing the sprightliness of living language, and familiarizing the speakers to unpremeditated extempore discussion. If any thing can verify the observations contained in this Introduction, it must be the practice of the catechetical method which I now recommend —a practice which distinguished the instructions of Socrates, which Plato has preserved in his Dialogues, and to which Cicero has reduced almost all his philosophical writings.

ALEXANDER JAMIESON

LONDON, *March*, 1819.

CONTENTS.

BOOK I.

CHAPTER.   PAGE.
  I. TERMS DEFINED AND EXPLAINED...................... 17
 II. PRINCIPLES TAKEN FOR GRANTED...................... 27
III. OF HYPOTHESES..................................... 32
 IV. OF ANALOGY.. 35
  V. OF THE PROPER MEANS OF KNOWING THE OPERATIONS OF
       OUR OWN MINDS.................................. 38
 VI. OF THE DIFFICULTY OF ATTENDING TO THE OPERATIONS
       OF OUR OWN MINDS, INTERSPERSED WITH OBSERVATIONS
       WHICH MAY ASSIST US IN OVERCOMING THIS DIFFICULTY 40
VII. DIVISIONS OF THE POWERS OF THE MIND.............. 42

BOOK II.

OF THE INTELLECTUAL POWERS.

   I. OF CONSCIOUSNESS.................................. 45
  II. OF SENSATION..................................... 46
 III. OF PERCEPTION.................................... 50
  IV. OF ATTENTION..................................... 53
   V. OF CONCEPTION.................................... 61
  VI. OF ABSTRACTION................................... 66
        Of Abstract or General Terms................... 67
        Of General Conceptions........................ 70
        Of General Conceptions formed by analyzing Objects..... 73
        Of the Operation of Generalizing............... 75
        General Conceptions formed by Combinations..... 77
 VII. OF THE ASSOCIATION OF IDEAS, OR COMBINATION....... 84
        Association by essential Relations............. 86
        Accidental Relations or Sources of Association.......... 93
        Of the Influence of Association on our various Judgments 96
        As it affects the Decisions of Taste........... ib.
        As it affects the speculative Opinions of Mankind........ 97
        The Influence of arbitrary Association, as it affects our
          Moral Judgment............................... 101
VIII. OF MEMORY.. 102
        Things obvious with regard to Memory........... ib.

CHAPTER.	PAGE.
Memory an original Faculty	104
Analysis of the Faculty of Memory	105
Varieties of Memory in different Individuals	107
Of the Decay of Memory in old People	109
Of the Improvement of Memory	110
IX. OF IMAGINATION	112
Analysis of the Operations of Imagination	113
Of Imagination in its Relation to some of the Fine Arts	120
The Relation of Imagination and of Taste to Genius	122
Of the Influence of Imagination on Human Character and Happiness	123
On the Culture of the Imagination	125
X. OF JUDGMENT	127
Analysis of this Faculty in general	ib.
Of the Exercise of Judgment in the Formation of Abstract and General Conceptions	131
Of the Objects of Sense	134
XI. OF REASON	136
Definition and Analysis of this Faculty	ib.
Of Demonstrative Reasoning	139
Of Probable Reasoning	141
Division of Probable Evidence into different Kinds	143
XII. OF MORAL PERCEPTION	149
The Rational Principles of Action in Man	ib.
Of Regard to our Good on the whole	150
Analysis of Conscience, or the Moral Principle	153
Analysis of Duty, Rectitude, and Moral Obligation	156
Analysis of the Sense of Duty	158
Of Moral Approbation and Disapprobation	160

BOOK III.

SUBJECTS OF COLLATERAL INQUIRY WITH THE INTELLECTUAL POWERS.

I. OF THE PRIMARY AND SECONDARY QUALITIES OF BODIES	162
II. ON NATURAL LANGUAGE AND SIGNS	165
III. OF MATTER AND SPACE	168
IV. OF DURATION	171
V. OF IDENTITY	173
What is meant by Identity in general	ib.
Of Personal Identity	174
VI. OF THE TRAIN OF THOUGHT IN THE MIND	177
VII. OF PREJUDICES	187
Prejudices of the first Class, or Idola Tribus	188
Prejudices of the second Class, or Idola Specus	193
Prejudices of the third Class, or Idola Fori	194
The Prejudices of the fourth Class, or Idola Theatri	198
Rules to prevent Prejudices, and direct our Judgments	200
Concluding Remarks	206

BOOK IV.

GRAMMAR OF LOGIC.

CHAPTER.   PAGE.

I. OF IDEAS.. 207
Of simple and complex Ideas............................... 208
Of distinct and confused Ideas............................ ib.
Of adequate and inadequate Ideas.......................... 209
Of particular or abstracted Ideas......................... 210
Rules for the Acquisition and Examination of Ideas and
    Words.. 211
Of the Ambiguity of Words................................. 215
Of Enumeration, Description, and Definition............... 219
II. OF PROPOSITIONS.. 223
Knowledge and Truth....................................... ib.
Different Kinds of Propositions........................... 225
Sources of Human Knowledge................................ 228
Of mathematical, moral, political, and prudential Reason-
    ing.. 232
Different Species of Reasoning............................ 238
Examples of Reasoning a Priori............................ 240
Example of Reasoning a Posteriori......................... ib.
Analytic and Synthetic Reasoning.......................... 241
Example of Analytic Reasoning............................. 242
III. OF SOPHISTRY.. 243
IV. OF REASONING AND SYLLOGISM................................ 249
Of the Constitution of Syllogisms......................... 250
Of plain, simple Syllogisms, and their Rules.............. 253
Of the Modes and Figures of simple Syllogisms............. 255
Of complex Syllogisms..................................... 259
Of conjunctive Syllogisms................................. 261
Of compound, imperfect, or irregular Syllogisms........... 265
Of the Merit of Syllogistic Reasoning..................... 272

BOOK V.

THE PHILOSOPHY OF HUMAN KNOWLEDGE.

I. HUMAN KNOWLEDGE ADDRESSED TO THE MEMORY...... 278
II. HUMAN KNOWLEDGE ADDRESSED TO THE UNDERSTAND-
    ING... 285
III. HUMAN KNOWLEDGE ADDRESSED TO THE IMAGINATION.. 295

A

GRAMMAR OF LOGIC

AND

INTELLECTUAL PHILOSOPHY.

BOOK I.

CHAPTER I.

TERMS DEFINED AND EXPLAINED.

1. The professed end of LOGIC is to teach men to *think*, to *judge*, to *reason*, and to communicate their thoughts to each other with precision and accuracy.

Observation 1. This, then, being the design of logic, it has justly been styled the history of the human mind; inasmuch as it traces the progress of our knowledge from our first and simple perceptions, through all the different combinations, and all those numerous deductions, which result from variously comparing these perceptions one with another.

2. It is thus that we are let into the frame and contexture of our own minds, and learn in what manner we ought to conduct our thoughts, in order to arrive at truth and avoid error. We see how to build one discovery upon another, and, by preserving the chain of reasoning uniform and unbroken, to pursue the relations of things through all their labyrinths and windings, and at length exhibit them to the mind with all the advantages of light and conviction.

2. By the MIND of man, we understand that in him which *thinks*, and *feels*, and *wills*, and which is conscious of its actions or operations.

3 The essence of body, as well as that of mind, is unknown to us. We know certain *properties* of the first, and

1

certain *operations* of the last, and by these properties and operations we define or describe both body and mind.

4. We define *body* to be that which is extended, figured, colorable, movable, divisible, hard or soft, rough or smooth, hot or cold ; that is, we define it in no other way than by enumerating its sensible qualities.

5 In like manner we define *mind* to be that which *thinks.* We are not immediately conscious of its existence, but we are conscious of sensation, thought, and volition— operations which imply the existence of something that feels, thinks, and wills. Every man, too, is impressed with an irresistible conviction, that all these sensations, thoughts, and volitions, belong to one and the same being, which he calls *himself;* a being which he is led, by the constitution of his nature, to consider as something distinct from his body, as not liable to be impaired by the loss or mutilation of any of his organs ; and this being, this principle of intelligence, we call the *mind* or *soul* of man.

6. When we witness the effects of similar operations or actions performed by our fellow-men, we have sufficient evidence that all human beings have minds.

Obs. 1. The conduct of brute animals, too, proves that they have a thinking principle, though of a nature very inferior to that of man, insomuch that its principal qualities are included in those of the human intellect.

2. The proofs of intelligence and of superintending providence, which are amply furnished by a survey of nature's works, lead us to a firm belief in the existence of a supreme and all-governing Mind, of a nature infinitely superior to that of the minds of men.

3. Many speculative men, both ancient and modern, have conjectured that those natural phenomena which cannot be easily explained by mere matter and motion, are the operations of various orders of intelligent beings, in the universe, of various rank and dignity. Others have been inclined to explain these phenomena by the agency of beings that are active without intelligence, so as to perform their destined work without any knowledge or intention. But we may safely say, that, whatever may be the result of future investigations or discoveries, we have, as yet, no certain evidence with respect to either of these conjectures.

7. By the OPERATIONS of the mind, we understand every mode of thinking of which we are conscious.

In all languages, as far as we know, the various modes of thinking have always been called operations of the mind, or by names of the same import.

8. We ascribe to body various *properties,* but not operations : it is extended, divisible, movable, inert ; it contin-

ues in any state in which it is put; every change of its state is the effect of some force impressed upon it, and is exactly proportional to the force impressed, and in the precise direction of that force.

These are the general properties of matter, and these are not operations; on the contrary, they imply its being a dead, inactive thing, which moves only as it is moved, and acts only as it is acted upon.

9. But the mind is, from its very nature, a living and active being. Every thing we know of it implies life and active energy; and the reason why all its modes of thinking are called its operations, is, that in all, or in most of them, it is not merely passive, as body is, but is really and properly active.

10. In all ages, and in all languages, ancient and modern, the various modes of thinking have been expressed by words of active signification; such as *seeing, hearing, reasoning, willing*, and the like.

Corollary. It seems, therefore, to be the natural judgment of mankind, that the mind is active in its various ways of thinking; and for this reason they are called its operations, and are expressed by active verbs.

11. Every operation supposes a *power* in the being that operates; for to suppose any thing to operate, which has no power to operate, is manifestly absurd. But, on the other hand, there is no absurdity in supposing a being to have power to operate, when that being does not operate.

Illustration. Thus, I may have power to walk, when I sit; or to speak, when I am silent.
Corol. Every operation, therefore, implies power; but the power does *not* imply its being always exerted to produce an operation.

12. The terms *faculty* and *power*, as applied to the mind, are not exactly synonymous, though they are often taken in the same radical meaning. The latter is of more extensive import than the former, since it may be used in relation to *material* as well as *mental* objects.

13. From observing the changes which are made, or the effects which are produced, by one external object upon another, as well as by these objects upon the mind, through the medium of the senses, we derive our first notion of *power*.

Illus. 1. Thus, if a needle be placed on a table, standing horizontally, it lies at rest; but if a magnet be brought within a certain distance of the needle, motion instantly commences, and the needle rushes to the magnet. You have witnessed the change; you contemplate the effect—the two objects are conjoined Remove the mag net, leave the needle on the table at rest, and place a piece of flint where the magnet lay when it attracted the needle, no motion takes place, the needle remains at rest.

2. Now, *that* in the magnet which produced motion in the needle, is not perceivable by the senses; for it is neither in the shape, nor in the color, nor in the weight of the substance called magnet that this singular property resides. But to that unknown something, to that unperceived energy in the *magnet*, the term power is given; and when we speak of this energy or property in relation to the effect—that is to say, the conjunction of the two objects—we call it the *cause* of the motion that we witnessed in the needle rushing to the magnet.

3. This is an apt illustration of the connection, or relation, that subsists between *cause* and *effect*.

14. By observing the changes of motion and direction in the several members of the body, arising from an act of the will, we arrive at a similar conclusion. We are conscious of an exercise of that faculty, and we observe, at the same instant, that a change in the members of the body has taken place. We are likewise conscious of certain acts of the will directing the motions of the mind. The act of the will and the corresponding change are, in all those cases, so closely conjoined, that they naturally force themselves upon our observation, and, ever after, remain associated in the particular relation of cause and effect. What did we observe more than the change? Nothing.—We saw indeed a fact, in a particular circumstance, resulting as a consequent from an antecedent; but of the *cause*, that is to say, the *power*, considered metaphysically, we can form no distinct notion.

15. We can entertain clear and distinct notions of an effect, while we find it impossible to penetrate into the nature of the cause whence that effect proceeds. Of the effects, for instance, which spring from the union of mind and body, in the human constitution, we have a lively perception; but of the principle upon which that union is founded, we cannot form the most remote conception.

Illus. 1. But to illustrate that our purest and most correct notions of power are derived from mind, lay a ball on a billiard table, and it lies at rest; but bring a mace in contact with the ball, and it is instantly put in motion. In this case, though the hand of a human being moved the mace—though the mace, hitting the ball, put it in motion—the source of that motion is traced up to the mind, which, by an act of the will to move the ball, stretches forth the bodily organ that grasped the mace.

2. Again, let us conceive a painter painting his own likeness. The brush which he uses, and which comes in contact with the canvass, possesses no power of forming a likeness of itself, far less

of the human countenance. Nor is the power in the hand of the artist, which, as in the former example, obeys the will; nor in his eye, though it be the chief organ on which the correctness of the likeness depends; and it resides not in the mirror, which takes no part in the operation of painting; but the source of motion in the eye and in the hand, is in the mind, which, by an act of the will, exerts the eye in viewing one object, and in conveying back to the mind its view of another object, that the hand delineates.

16. It is said above, that the terms faculty and power have nearly the same radical meaning. The term *power* is used in relation both to material and mental objects. Thus a stone has the power of falling to the ground. The term *faculty* is used in reference to the understanding and volition of the human mind. The terms now defined are not applied to the passions of the soul of man; for to those active energies, or principles, as desire, hatred, joy, love, anger, revenge, &c., we never use such expressions as the " faculty of desire," or the " power of hatred."

17. There is a distinction between things *in the mind* and things *external* to the mind. The powers, faculties, and operations of the mind, are things in the mind. Every thing is said to be in the mind of which the mind is the *subject*.

18. It is evident, that there are some things which cannot exist without a subject to which they belong, or of which they are attributes.

Illus. Thus, color must be *in* something colored; figure *in* something figured; thought, being an act of mind, can only belong to something that acts or thinks; and volition cannot exist but in some being that wills. When, therefore, we speak of things in the mind, we understand by this, things of which the mind is the subject.

19. Excepting the mind itself, and things within the mind, all other things are said to be external, or without the mind.

20. There is a figurative sense in which things are said to be in the mind.

Illus. Thus we say, such a thing is not in our mind, meaning no more than that we had not the least thought of it. For, by a figure, we put the *thing* for the *thought* of it. In this sense, external things are in the mind as often as they are objects of thought.

21. *Thinking* is a very general word, that includes all the operations of our minds.

22. To *perceive,* to *remember,* to be *conscious,* and to *conceive* or *imagine,* are words that signify different operations of mind, which are distinguished in all languages, and by all men that think.

1 *

Illus. 1. We are never said to *perceive* things, of the existence of which we have not a full conviction. We may *conceive* or imagine a mountain of gold, or a winged horse; but no man says that he *perceives* such a creature of imagination as a winged horse. Thus, *perception* is distinguished from *conception*, or imagination.

2. Perception is applied only to external objects, not to those that are in the mind itself. When I am pained, I do not say, that I perceive pain, but that I *feel* it, or that I am *conscious* of it. Thus, *perception* is distinguished from *consciousness*

3. The immediate object of perception must be something *present*, and not what is past. We may *remember* what is past, but we do not perceive it. I may say, I perceive such a person has had the small-pox; but this phrase is figurative, although the figure is so familiar that it is not observed. The meaning of it is, that I perceive the pits in his face, which are certain *signs* of his having had the small-pox. We say that we perceive the thing signified, when we perceive only the *sign*. But when the word *perception* is used properly, and without any figure, it is never applied to things past; and thus it is distinguished from *remembrance*.

23. Perception is most properly applied to the evidence which we have of external objects by our senses. Seeing, hearing, smelling, tasting, and touching or feeling, are words that express the operations proper to each sense ; perceiving expresses that which is common to them all.

24. *Consciousness* signifies that immediate knowledge which we have of our present thoughts and purposes, and, in general, of all the *present* operations of our minds. To apply consciousness, therefore, to things past, is to confound it with memory.

Consciousness is only of things *in the mind*, and not of things external, or without the mind.

25. *Conceiving, imagining,* and *apprehending,* are commonly used as synonymous in our language, and signify the same thing which the logicians call *simple apprehension.*

Ilus. Simple apprehension is an operation of mind different from all those we have mentioned. Whatever we perceive, whatever we remember, whatever we are conscious of, we have a full persuasion or conviction of its existence. But we may conceive or imagine what has no existence, and what we firmly believe to have no existence. What *never* had an existence cannot be remembered; what has no existence *at present* cannot be the object of perception or of consciousness ; but that which never had existence, or that which has no existence, may be conceived. Every man knows, that it is as easy to conceive a winged horse, or a centaur, as it is to conceive a horse, or a man

Corol. Let it be observed, therefore, that to *conceive,* to *imagine,* to *apprehend,* when taken in the proper sense, signify an act of the mind which implies no belief or judgment at all. It is an act of the mind by which nothing is affirmed or denied, and which therefore can be neither true nor false.

26. When these words are used, as above, to express simple apprehension, they are followed by a noun in the accusative or *objective case*, which signifies the object conceived; as, I conceive an Egyptian pyramid. This implies no judgment.

27. But there is another and a very different meaning of those words, so common and so well authorized in language, that it cannot easily be avoided; and, on that account, we ought to be the more on our guard, that we be not misled by the ambiguity.

Illus. Politeness and good-breeding lead men, on most occasions, to express their opinions with modesty, especially when they differ from others whom they respect. Therefore, when a man would express his opinion modestly, instead of saying, "This is my opinion," or, "This is my judgment," which has the air of dogmaticalness, he says, "I conceive it to be thus, I imagine. or I apprehend, it to be thus," which is understood as a modest judgment. In like manner. when any thing is said which we take to be impossible, we say, "We cannot conceive how it could be," thereby intimating, that we cannot believe it.

28. But when the words *conceive, imagine,* or *apprehend,* are used to express opinion or judgment, they are commonly followed by a verb in the *infinitive mood;* as, I conceive the Egyptian pyramids *to be* the most ancient monuments of human art.

Illus. This implies judgment. When the words are used in this last sense, the thing conceived must be a proposition, because judgment cannot be expressed but by a proposition. When they are used in the first sense (26.), the thing conceived may be no proposition, but a simple term only; as a pyramid, an obelisk. Yet even a proposition may be simply apprehended, without forming any judgment of its truth or falsehood; for it is one thing to conceive the meaning of a proposition; it is another thing to judge it to be true or false.

29. Most of the operations of mind, from their very nature, must have *objects* to which they are directed, and about which they are employed He that perceives must perceive *something;* and that which he perceives is called *the object of his perception.*

Corol. It is, therefore, impossible to perceive without having some object of perception. The mind that perceives, the object perceived, and the operation of perceiving that object, are distinct things, and are distinguished in the structure of all languages.

30. In his sentence, *I see, or perceive the moon;* I is the person or *mind;* the active verb *see,* denotes the operation of that mind; and the *moon* denotes the object.

31. What we have said of perceiving, is equally applicable to most operations of mind, which are, in all languages, expressed by *active transitive verbs ;* and such verbs require an agent and an object.

Corol. Whence it is evident, that all mankind, both those who have contrived language, and those who use it with understanding, have distinguished these three things as different; to wit, the *operations* of the mind, which are expressed by active verbs, the *mind* itself, which is the nominative to those verbs; and the *object*, which is the oblique case governed by them.

32. The word *idea*, in popular language, signifies precisely the same thing that we commonly express by the active participles *conceiving* or *apprehending*.

Illus. 1. Thus, to have an *idea* of a thing, is to conceive it. To have a *distinct idea* of it, is to conceive it distinctly. To have *no idea* of it, is not to conceive it at all.

2. *Idea*, therefore, signifies the same thing as *conception, apprehension, notion*.

33. When the word idea is taken in this popular sense, no man can possibly doubt whether he has ideas; for he that doubts must think, and *to think is to have ideas.*

34. The term *idea*, coming from the Greek verb ἰδεῖν, properly signifies a thought, representative of such objects as have been perceived by the sense of sight.

Obs. It is solely owing to the poverty of language that this word is also used for the notions which we have of things received by means of the other senses; and, further still, to those primary notions or elements of abstract thought, which compose trains of argument and chains of reasoning, in the mind of the philosopher or the statesman.

35. When, therefore, in common language, we speak of having an idea of any thing, we mean no more by that expression than to conceive of it.

Illus. But as we cannot conceive, or have a notion of any thing, without thinking of it, to constitute an idea implies a mind that thinks; an act of the mind which we call thinking; and an object about which we think.

36. The word idea, however, in a philosophical sense, means some image, or representative of an external object present to the mind.

Illus. 1. The idea is in the mind itself, and can have no existence but in a mind that thinks; but the remote or mediate object may be something external, as the sun or moon; it may be something past or future; it may be something which never existed; and we may observe that this meaning is built upon a philosophical opinion.

2. For, if philosophers had not believed that there are such im-

mediate objects of all our thoughts in the mind, they would never have used the word idea to express them.

3. But the term *idea*, taken in this sense, is to be considered a mere fiction of philosophers; and use, the arbiter of language, hath now in all popular discussions, authorized as synonyma the words *thought, notion, apprehension,* and *idea.*

37. When a figure is stamped upon a body by pressure, that figure is called an *impression*, as the impression of a seal on wax, or of printing-types, or of a copper-plate, on paper. This seems now to be the literal sense of the word; the effect borrowing its name from the cause.

Obs. But by metaphor or analogy, like most other words, its meaning is extended to signify any change produced in a body by the operation of some external cause. A blow of the hand makes no impression on a stone wall; but a battery of cannon may. The moon raises a tide in the ocean, but makes no perceptible impression on rivers and lakes.

38. When we speak of making an impression on the mind, the word is carried still farther from its literal meaning; use, however, which, as we have observed above, is the arbiter of language, authorizes this application of it; as when we say that admonition and reproof make little impression on those who are confirmed in bad habits. The same discourse delivered in one way makes a strong impression on the hearers; delivered in another way, it makes no impression at all.

Illus. 1. Now, in such examples, an impression made on the mind always implies some change of purpose or will; some new habit produced, or some former habit weakened; some passion raised or allayed. When such changes are produced by persuasion, example, or any external cause, we say that such causes make an *impression* upon the mind. But when things are seen, or heard, or apprehended, without producing any passion, or emotion, we say that they make no impression.

2. In the most extensive sense, an impression is a change produced in some passive subject by the operation of an external cause. If we suppose an active being to produce any change in itself by its own active power, this is never called an impression. It is the act or operation of the being itself, not an impression upon it. From this it appears, that to give the name of an impression to any effect produced in the mind, is to suppose that the mind does not act at all in the production of that effect.

3. If seeing, hearing, desiring, willing, be operations of the mind, they cannot be impressions. If they be impressions, they cannot be operations of the mind. In the structure of all languages, they are considered as acts or operations of the mind itself, and the names given them imply this. To call them impressions, therefore, is to trespass against the structure, not of a particular language only, but of all languages.

Corol. The term *impression*, consequently, in the department of logic and mental science, merely denotes whatever produces that change in the mind which is necessary to perceive an object, or to form a thought.

39. *Sensation* is a name given by philosophers to an act of mind which may be distinguished from all others by this, that it hath no object distinct from the object itself.

Illus. Pain of every kind is an uneasy sensation. When I am pained, I cannot say, that the pain I feel is one thing, and that my feeling it is another thing. They are one and the same thing, and cannot be disjoined even in imagination. Pain, when it is not felt, has no existence. It can be neither greater nor less in degree, or duration, nor any thing else in kind, that it is felt to be. It cannot exist by itself, nor in any subject, but in a sentient being. No quality of any inanimate and insentient being can have the least resemblance to it.

40. What we have said of pain may be applied to every other sensation ; some of them are agreeable, others uneasy, in various degrees.

Obs. These, being objects of desire or aversion, have some attention given to them; but many are indifferent, and so little attended to, that they have no name in any language.

41. Most operations of the mind, that have names in common language, are complex in their nature, and made up of various ingredients, or more simple acts; which, though conjoined in our constitutions, must be disjoined by abstraction, in order to our having a distinct and scientific notion of the complex operation. In such operations, sensation, for the most part, makes an ingredient. Those who do not attend to the complex nature of such operations, are apt to resolve them into some one of the simple acts of which they are compounded, overlooking others.

Obs. Nothing, therefore, is of so much importance as to have a distinct notion of that simple act of the mind which we call sensation, without puzzling ourselves about the particular nature of the change effected in the organ, in the nerves, or in the brain, by the secondary qualities of matter, in the process which constitutes sensation, and of which we can have no clearer knowledge than if we ourselves were not the subjects of that mysterious operation.

42. The word *feeling* hath two meanings.

First, It signifies the perceptions which we have of external objects, by the sense of touch. When we speak of feeling a body to be hard or soft, rough or smooth, hot or cold ; to *feel* these things, is to perceive them by touch.

Secondly, The word *feeling* is used to signify the same thing as *sensation*, which we have just explained; and in this sense, it has no object ; the feeling and the thing felt, are one and the same.

Obs. Perhaps betwixt feeling, taken in this last sense, and sensation, there may be this small difference, that sensation is most commonly used to signify those feelings which we have by our external senses and bodily appetites, and all our bodily pains and pleasures. But there are *feelings* of a nobler nature accompanying our affections, our moral judgments, and our determinations in matters of taste, to which the word sensation is less properly applied.

Note. Other words that need explication, shall be explained as they occur.

CHAPTER II.

PRINCIPLES TAKEN FOR GRANTED.

43. A GENERAL rule, when applied to regulate particulars, is termed a *principle;* and explanations or injunctions from principle are termed *theory,* or *system.* The particulars to be explained are termed *phenomena.*

Obs. As there are words common to philosophers and to the unlearned, which need no explication ; so there are principles common to both, which need no proof, and which do not admit of direct proof.

44. Such principles, when we have occasion to use them in science, are called *axioms.*

Illus. Thus, mathematicians, before they attempt to prove any proposition in mathematics, lay down certain axioms or common principles, upon which they build their reasonings. And although those axioms be truths which every man knew before ; such as, " That the whole is greater than a part"—" that equal quantities added to equal quantities make equal sums ;" yet, when we see nothing assumed in the proof of mathematical propositions, but such self-evident axioms, the propositions appear more certain, and leave no room for doubt or dispute.

45. In every other science, as well as in mathematics, it will be found that there are a few common principles, upon which all the reasonings in that science are grounded, and into which they may be resolved. If these principles were pointed out and explained, we should be better able to judge what stress may be laid upon the conclusions in that science. If the principles be certain, the conclusions justly drawn from them must be certain. If the principles be only probable, the conclusions can only be probable. If the princi-

ples be false, dubious, or obscure, the superstructure that is built upon them must partake of the weakness of the foundation.

Illus. Thus, Sir Isaac Newton, by laying down the common principles or axioms, on which the reasonings in natural philosophy are built, laid a solid foundation in that science, and reared on it a noble superstructure, about which there is no more dispute or controversy among men of knowledge, than there is about the conclusions of mathematics. Yet are the first principles of natural philosophy of a nature quite different from mathematical axioms. They have not the same kind of evidence, nor are they necessary truths, as mathematical axioms are. They are such as these—" that similar effects proceed from the same or similar causes; that we ought to admit of no other causes of natural effects, but such as are true, and sufficient to account for the effects." These are principles, which, though they have not the same kind of evidence that mathematical axioms have; yet have such evidence, that every man of common understanding readily assents to them, and finds it absolutely necessary to conduct his actions and opinions by them, in the ordinary affairs of life.

46. In like manner, there are some things which we shall take for granted, as first principles in treating of the mind and its faculties; or of a rational and useful logic.

47. The evidence of first principles is not demonstrative, but intuitive. They require not proof, but to be placed in a proper point of view.

48. *First,* then, we shall take it for granted, that man *thinks, remembers, reasons,* and, in general, that he really performs all those operations of mind, of which he is conscious.

Illus. The operations of our minds are attended with consciousness; and this consciousness is the evidence, the only evidence which we have, or can have, of their existence. Every man finds himself under a necessity of believing what consciousness testifies, and every thing that hath this testimony is to be taken as a first principle.

49. As by consciousness we know certainly the existence of our present thoughts and passions; so we know the past by *remembrance.* And when they are recent, and the remembrance of them fresh, the knowledge of them, from such distinct remembrance, is, in its certainty and evidence, next to that of consciousness.

50. When we make our own thoughts and passions, and the various operations of our minds, the objects of our attention, either while they are present, or when they are recent and fresh in our memory, this act of the mind is called *reflection*

Corol. We take it for granted, therefore, that by attentive reflection, a man may have a clear and certain knowledge of the operations of his own mind ; a knowledge no less clear and certain, than that which he has of an external object when it is set before his eyes.

51. This *reflection* is a kind of intuition ; it gives a like conviction with regard to internal objects, or things in the mind, as the faculty of seeing gives with regard to the objects of sight.

Corol. A man must, therefore, be convinced, beyond the possibility of doubt, of every thing with regard to the operations of his own mind, which he clearly and distinctly discerns by attentive reflection.

52. We shall take it for granted, that all the thoughts which a man is conscious of, or remembers, are the thoughts of one and the same thinking principle, which he calls *himself*, or his *mind*.

Illus. 1. Every man has an immediate and irresistible conviction, not only of his present existence, but of his continued existence and identity as far back as he can remember.

2. Every man of a sound mind feels himself under a necessity of believing his own identity and continued existence. The conviction of this is immediate and irresistible ; and if he should lose this conviction, it would be a certain proof of insanity, which is not to be remedied by reasoning.

53. We shall take it for granted, that there are some things which cannot exist by themselves, but must be in something else to which they belong, as qualities, or attributes.

Illus. Thus, motion cannot exist but in something that is moved. For to suppose that there can be motion while every thing is at rest, is a gross and palpable absurdity. In like manner, hardness and softness, sweetness and bitterness, are things which cannot exist by themselves. They are qualities of some thing which is hard or soft, sweet or bitter. That thing, whatever it be, of which they are qualities, is called their *subject*, and such qualities necessarily suppose a subject.

54. Things which may exist by themselves, and which do not suppose the existence of any thing else, are called *substances ;* and with relation to the qualities or attributes that belong to them, they are called the *subjects* of such qualities or attributes. And, in respect to material objects, we give the name of *body* to that which is the subject of these qualities or attributes.

55. In like manner, those operations of which a man is conscious, such as thought, reasoning, desire, necessarily suppose something that thinks, reasons, and desires. We do not give the name of *mind* to thought, reason, or desire,

2

but to *that being* which thinks, which reasons, and which desires.

56. That every act, or operation, therefore, supposes an agent, that every quality supposes a subject, are things which we do not attempt to prove, but take for granted. Every man of common understanding discerns this immediately, and cannot entertain the least doubt of it.

57. In all languages, we find certain words which, by grammarians, are called adjectives. Such words denote attributes; and every adjective must have a substantive to which it belongs, because every attribute must have a subject.

58. In all languages, we find active verbs, which denote some action or operation; and it is a fundamental rule in the grammar of all languages, that such a verb supposes a person; that is, in other words, every action must have an agent.

Corol. We take it, therefore, as a first principle, that goodness, wisdom, and virtue, can only be in some being that is good, wise, and virtuous; that thinking supposes a being that thinks, and that every operation of which we are conscious supposes an agent that operates, which we call *mind.*

59. We take it for granted, that in most operations of the mind, there must be an *object* distinct from the operation itself.

Illus. 1. I cannot see, without seeing something. To see without having an object of sight is absurd. I cannot remember, without remembering something. The thing remembered is past, while the remembrance of it is present; and therefore the operation and the object of it must be distinct things.
2. I remember the comet of 1811. Here the act of remembering is present, but the comet, which is the object of this act, is absent; whence the operation and the object of that operation are distinct things.

60. We ought likewise to take for granted, as first principles, things wherein we find an *universal agreement* among the learned and unlearned, in the different ages of the world.

Obs. A consent of ages and nations, of the learned and unlearned, ought, at least, to have great authority, unless we can show some prejudice, as universal as that consent is, which might be its cause. Truth is one, but error is infinite.
Corol. An universal consent in things gives the greatest presumption that can be, that such a consent is the natural result of the human faculties, and must have great authority with every sober mind that loves truth.

61. Though it may be impossible to collect the opinions of *all men* upon all points, there are many cases in which it is otherwise ; so that the foregoing postulate will still hold good.

Obs. Who can doubt, for instance, whether mankind have, in all ages, believed the existence of a material world, and that those things which we see and handle are real, and not mere illusions and apparitions ? Who can doubt whether mankind have universally believed that every thing that begins to exist, must have a cause ? Who can doubt, whether mankind have been universally persuaded that there is a right and a wrong in human conduct? some things, which, in certain circumstances, they ought to do, and other things which they ought not to do?

Corol. The universality of these opinions, and of many such that might be named, is sufficiently evident, from the whole tenor of men's conduct, as far as our acquaintance reaches, and from the records of historians of all nations, transmitted to us from the remotest ages.

62. There are other opinions that appear to be universal, from what is common in the structure of all languages, ancient and modern, polished and barbarous. Language is the express image and picture of human thoughts ; and from the picture we may often draw certain conclusions with regard to the original.

Illus. 1. We find in all languages the same parts of speech, noun, substantive and adjective ; verbs active and passive, varied according to the tenses of past, present and future ; we find adverbs, prepositions, and conjunctions. There are general rules of syntax common to all languages. This uniformity in the structure of language, shows a certain degree of uniformity in those notions upon which the structure of language is founded.

2. We find in the structure of all languages, the distinction of acting and being acted upon, the distinction of action and agent, of quality and subject, and many others of the like kind ; which shows that these distinctions are founded in the universal sense of mankind.

Corol. There are many occasions on which it is necessary to argue from the sense of mankind expressed in the structure of language ; and therefore it was proper at the threshold to take notice of the force of arguments drawn from this topic.

63. We shall also take for granted, as first principles, such facts as are attested to the conviction of all sober men, either by their senses, by memory, or by human testimony.

Obs. 1. For, though skepticism may endeavor to discredit the testimony of the senses, we never heard of any skeptic who struck his head against a post, or stepped into a kennel because he did not believe his eyes.

2. Let us, however, be cautious, that we do not adopt opinions

as first principles, which are not entitled to that character. Let us deal with every thing offered as a first principle, as an upright judge does with a witness who has a fair character. He pays a regard to the testimony of such witness, while his character is unimpeached ; but if it can be shown that he is suborned, or that he is influenced by malice or partial favor, his testimony loses all credit, and is justly rejected.

CHAPTER III.

OF HYPOTHESES.

64. EVERY branch of human knowledge hath its proper principles, its proper foundation and method of reasoning; and if we endeavor to build upon any other foundation, the fabric we raise will never stand firm.

Illus. 1. Thus, the historian builds upon testimony ; and rarely indulges conjecture.

2. The antiquary mixes conjecture with testimony ; and the former often makes the larger ingredient.

3. The mathematician pays not the least regard either to testimony or conjecture, but deduces every thing, by demonstrative reasoning, from his definitions and axioms.

Corol. Whatever, therefore, is built upon conjecture, is improperly called science ; for though conjecture may beget opinion, it cannot produce knowledge. Natural philosophy must be built upon the laws of the material system, discovered by observation and experiment.

65. When men began to philosophize, or to carry their thoughts beyond the objects of sense, and to inquire into the causes of things, their ignorance of a scientific way of proceeding in such philosophical disquisitions, gave birth to conjecture.

Illus. Accordingly we find that the most ancient systems, in every branch of philosophy, were nothing but the conjectures of men famous for their wisdom, whose fame gave authority to their opinions.

Example. Thus, in early ages, wise men conjectured that the earth was a vast plain, surrounded on all sides by a boundless ocean ; that from this ocean, the sun, moon, and stars, emerged at their rising, and plunged into it again at their setting.

66. With regard to the mind, men in their rudest state are apt to conjecture that the principle of life in man is his breath ; because the most obvious distinction between a liv-

ing and a dead man is, that the one breathes, and the other does not.

Obs. To this it is owing that, in ancient languages, the word which denotes the *soul*, is that which properly signifies *breath*, or *air*.

67. As men advance in knowledge, their first conjectures appear silly and childish, and give place to others which agree better with later observations and discoveries. Thus, one system of philosophy succeeds another, without any claim to superior merit, but this, that it is a more ingenious system of conjectures, and accounts better for common appearances.

Illus. *Des Cartes* thus conjectured, that the heavenly bodies are carried round by a vortex or whirlpool of subtile matter, just as straws and chaff are carried round in a tub of water. He conjectured also, that the soul is seated in a small gland in the brain, called the pineal gland; that there, as in her presence chamber, she receives intelligence of every thing that affects the senses, by means of a subtile fluid contained in the nerves, and called *animal spirits;* and that she despatches these animal spirits as her messengers, to put in motion the several muscles of the body, as there is occasion. By such conjectures as these, *Des Cartes* could account for every phenomenon in nature, in such a plausible manner as gave satisfaction to a great part of the learned world for more than half a century.

68. Such conjectures, in philosophical matters, have commonly received the name of *hypotheses*, or *theories*.

Obs. 1. And the invention of any hypothesis which, founded on some slight probabilities, accounts for many appearances of nature, has been considered as the highest attainment of a philosopher. If the hypothesis hangs well together, is embellished by a lively imagination, and serves to account for common appearances, it is considered by many as having all the qualities that should recommend it to our belief; and all that ought to be required in a philosophical system.

2. There is such proneness in men of genius to invent hypotheses, and in others to acquiesce in them, as the utmost that the human faculties can attain in philosophy, that it is of the last consequence to the progress of real knowledge, that men should have a clear and distinct understanding of the nature of hypotheses in philosophy, and of the regard that is due to them.

69. Although some conjectures may have a considerable degree of probability, yet it is evidently in the nature of conjecture to be uncertain. In every case, the assent ought to be proportioned to the evidence; for to believe firmly what has but a small degree of probability, is a manifest abuse of our understanding.

Obs. If a child were to conjecture how an army is to be formed in

2 *

the day of battle; how a city is to be fortified, or a state governed; what chance has he to guess right? As little chance would a thousand of the greatest wits whom the world ever produced, have, without any previous knowledge in anatomy, to contrive how and by what internal organs the various functions of the human body are carried on ; how the blood is made to circulate, and the limbs to move.

70.   Of all the discoveries that have been made concerning the inward structure of the human body, never one was made by conjecture.

Illus. Accurate observations of anatomists have brought to light innumerable artifices of nature in the contrivance of this machine of the human body, which we cannot but admire as excellently adapted to their several purposes. But the most sagacious physiologist never dreamed of them till they were discovered. On the other hand, innumerable conjectures, formed in different ages, with regard to the structure of the body, have been confuted by observation, and none ever confirmed.

71.   What we have said of the internal structure of the human body, may be said, with justice, of every other part of the works of God, wherein any real discovery has been made.

Obs. Such discoveries have always been made by patient observation, by accurate experiments, or by conclusions drawn by strict reasoning from observations and experiments ; and such discoveries have always tended to refute, but not to confirm, the theories and hypotheses which ingenious men had invented.

Illus. 1.   The finest productions of human art are immensely short of the meanest productions of nature. The nicest plumasier cannot make a feather. Nor could any society of chemists and meteorologists cover the hills with mists, and the face of the sky with clouds. Human workmanship will never bear a comparison with the workmanship of nature.

2.   The Indian philosopher, being at a loss to know how the earth was supported, invented the hypothesis of a huge elephant, on whose back it rested ; and the elephant he supposed to stand on a huge tortoise. This hypothesis, how ridiculous soever it appears to us, might seem very reasonable to other Indians, who knew no more of it than the inventor, and never inquired, What did the tortoise stand on ?

72.   Let us, therefore, lay down this as a fundamental principle in our inquiries into the structure of the mind, and its operations, that *no regard is due to the conjectures or hypotheses of philosophers,* how ancient soever, however generally received. Let us accustom ourselves to try every opinion by the touchstone of fact and experience. What can fairly be deduced from facts duly observed, or sufficient-

iy attested, is genuine and pure; it is the voice of Nature, and no fiction of human imagination.

73. The first rule of philosophizing laid down by the great Newton, is this :—" No more causes, nor any other causes of natural effects, ought to be admitted, but such as are both true, and are sufficient for explaining their appearances." This is the golden rule; it is the true and proper test, whereby what is sound and solid in philosophy may be distinguished from what is hollow and vain.

Corol. If a philosopher, therefore, pretend to show us the cause of any natural effect, whether relating to matter or mind, let us first consider whether there be sufficient evidence that the cause he assigns does really exist. If there be not, reject it with disdain, as a fiction which ought to have no place in genuine philosophy. If the cause assigned really exist, consider, in the next place, whether the effect it is brought to explain necessarily follows from it. Unless it have these two conditions, it is good for nothing.

CHAPTER IV.

OF ANALOGY.

74. It is natural to men to judge of things less known, by some similitude which they observe, or which they think they observe, between them and things more familiar or better known. This method of judging is called *Analogy;* and in many cases we have no better way of judging. And where the things compared have really a great similitude in their nature, when there is reason to think that they are subject to the same laws, there may be considerable degrees of probability in conclusions drawn from analogy.

Illus. Thus we may observe a very great similitude between this Earth which we inhabit, and the other planets, Herschel, Saturn, Jupiter, Mars, Venus, and Mercury. They all revolve round the Sun, as the Earth does, although at different distances, and in different periods of time. They all borrow their light from the Sun, as the Earth does. They revolve round their axes like the earth round her axis, and, by that means, must have a regular succession of day and night. Some of them have moons, which serve to give them light in the absence of the Sun, as our Moon does to us. They are all, in their motions, subject to the same law of gravitation as the Earth is. From all this similitude, it is not unreasonable to think, that those planets may, like our Earth, be the habitation of various orders of living creatures; nay, of sentient natures. There is some probability in this conclusion from analogy.

75. In medicine, physicians must, for the most part, be directed in their prescriptions by analogy.

Illus. The constitution of one human body is so like to that of another, that it is reasonable to think, that what is the cause of health or sickness to one, may have the same effect upon another. And this is generally found true, though not without some exceptions.

76. In politics we reason, for the most part, from analogy. The constitution of human nature is similar in different societies, or commonwealths; hence we conclude, that the causes of peace and war, of tranquillity and sedition, of riches and poverty, of improvement and degeneracy, are much the same in all.

Corol. Analogical reasoning, therefore, is not, in all cases, to be rejected. It may afford a greater or a less degree of probability, according as the things compared are more or less similar in their nature. But it ought to be observed, that, as this kind of reasoning can afford only probable evidence, at best, so, unless great caution be used, we are apt to be led into error by it. For we are naturally disposed to conceive a greater similitude between things than there really is.

77. To give an instance of this. Anatomists, in ancient times, seldom dissected human bodies; but very often the bodies of those quadrupeds whose internal structure was thought to approach nearest to that of the human body. Modern anatomists, by the actual dissection of human bodies, have discovered many mistakes into which the ancients were led, by their conceiving a greater similitude between the structure of men and of some beast, than there is in reality.

Corol. By this, and many other instances that might be given, it appears that conclusions built on analogy stand on a slippery foundation; and that we ought never to rest upon evidence of this kind, when we can have more direct proof.

78. We form an early acquaintance, by means of our senses, with material things, and are bred up in a constant familiarity with them. Hence we are apt to measure all things by them; and to ascribe to things most remote from matter, the qualities that belong to material things.

Corol. It is for this reason that mankind have, in all ages, been so prone to conceive the mind itself to be some subtile kind of matter; that they have been disposed to ascribe human figure and human organs not only to angels, but even to the Deity!

79. We are conscious of the operations of our own minds, when they are exerted; we are even capable of attending to them, so as to form a distinct notion of them, but this is so

difficult a work to men, whose attention is constantly solicited by external objects, that we give them names from things that are familiar, and which are conceived to have some similitude to those operations ; and the notions we form of them are no less analogical than the names we give them.

80. Almost all the words, by which we express the operations of the mind, are borrowed from material objects.

Illus. To *understand,* to *conceive,* to *imagine,* to *comprehend,* to *deliberate,* to *infer,* and many other words, are of this kind; so that the very language of mankind, with regard to the operations of the mind, is *analogical.*

81. Because bodies are affected only by contact and pressure, we are apt to conceive that what is an immediate object of thought, and affects the mind, must be in contact with it, and make some impression on it.

82. When we *imagine* any thing, the very word leads us to think that there must be some image in the mind of the thing conceived.

Corol. It is evident that these notions are drawn from some similitude conceived between body and mind, and between the properties of body and the operations of mind.

83. When a man is urged by contrary motives, those on one hand inciting him to do some action, those on the other to forbear it, he deliberates about it, and at last resolves to do it, or not to do it. The contrary motives are here compared to weights in the opposite scales of a balance ; and there is not, perhaps, any instance that can be named of a more striking analogy between body and mind.

Corol. Hence the phrases *weighing* motives, *deliberating* upon actions, and the like, are common to all languages.

84. From this analogy, some philosophers draw very important conclusions. They say, that as the balance cannot incline to one side more than the other, when the opposite weights are equal, so a man cannot possibly determine himself, if the motives on both hands are equal ; and as the balance must necessarily turn to that side which has most weight, so the will of the man must necessarily be determined to that hand where the motive is strongest.

Obs. And on this foundation, some of the schoolmen maintained, that if a hungry ass be placed between two bundles of hay, equally inviting, the beast must stand still and starve to death, being unable to turn to either, because the unfortunate animal has equal motives to both the bundles.

85. This is an instance of that analogical reasoning which

Dr. Reid conceives ought never to be trusted ; for the analogy between a balance and a man deliberating, though one
of the strongest that can be found between matter and
mind, is too weak to support any argument.   A piece of
dead, inactive matter, and an active and intelligent being,
are things very unlike ; and because the one would remain
at rest in a certain case, it does not follow that the other
would be inactive in a case somewhat similar.

Illus. The argument is no better than this, that, because a dead
animal moves only as it is pushed, and, if pushed with equal force
in contrary directions, must remain at rest, therefore the same
thing must happen to a living animal; for surely the similitude between a dead animal and a living, is as great as between a balance
and a man.

Corol. The conclusion which results from all that has been said on
analogy, is, that, in our inquiries concerning the mind and its operations, we ought never to trust to reasonings drawn from some supposed similitude of body to mind ; and that we ought to be very much
upon our guard, that we be not imposed upon by those analogical
terms and phrases by which the operations of the mind are expressed
in all languages.

CHAPTER V.

OF THE PROPER MEANS OF KNOWING THE OPERATIONS
OF OUR OWN MINDS.

86. SINCE we ought to pay no regard to hypotheses, and
to be very suspicious of analogical reasoning, it may be
asked, from what sources must the knowledge of the mind,
and its faculties, be drawn ?   I answer, from the three following.   The *first* is attention to the structure of language ;
because the language of mankind is expressive of their
thoughts, and of the various operations of their minds.

Illus. 1. Those operations which are common to mankind, have
various forms of speech corresponding to them in all languages.
These various forms of speech are the signs of the various operations of the understanding, will, and passions; and by those signs
these operations are expressed.   A due attention, therefore, to the
signs, may, in many cases, give considerable light to the things
signified by them.

2. But languages, from their imperfections, can never be adequate
to all the varieties of human thought.   There may, therefore, be
things really distinct in their nature, and capable of being distinguished by the human mind, which are not distinguished in common

language. There may also be peculiarities in a particular language, of the causes of which we are ignorant, and from which, therefore, we can draw no conclusion. But whatever we find common to all languages, must have a common cause ; must be owing to some common notion or sentiment of the human mind.

87. The *second* source of information on this subject, is a due attention to the course of human actions and conduct. The actions of men are effects ; their sentiments, their passions, and their affections, are the causes of those effects ; and we may, in many cases, form a judgment of the cause, by observing the effect.

Illus. 1. Thus, the behavior of parents towards their children gives sufficient evidence, even to those who never had children, that the parental affection is common to mankind. The general conduct of men, too, shows us what are the natural objects of their esteem, their admiration, their love, their approbation, their resentment, and of all their original dispositions. From the conduct of men in all ages, it is likewise obvious, that man is, by his nature, a social animal ; that he delights to associate with his species ; to converse, and to exchange good offices with them.

2. Not only the actions, but even the opinions of mankind, may sometimes give light into the frame of the human mind. The opinions of men may be considered as the effects of their intellectual powers, as their actions are the effects of their active principles. Even the prejudices and errors of mankind, when they are general, must have some cause no less general ; the discovery of which will throw some light upon the frame of the human understanding.

88. The *third*, and main source of information, respecting the mind and its faculties, is accurate and attentive reflection upon the operations of our own mind. The power of the understanding to take notice of its own operations, to attend to them, and examine them on all sides, is the power of *reflection ;* and all the notions we have of mind, and of its operations, have been called *ideas of reflection.*

Illus. 1. The term reflection implies nothing more than the deliberate and mature exercise of consciousness. But to acquire a habit of reflection upon the powers of our own minds, or of the deliberate exercise of consciousness, is a work of time and labor, even to those who begin early, and whose natural talents are tolerably fitted for it. This is the last of the powers of the mind that unfolds itself ; and though many persons seem incapable of acquiring it in any considerable degree, it may be greatly improved by exercise. It is by the proper employment of this power that men become fitted to discover the laws by which their own thoughts are regulated, and to make advances in the science of intellectual philosophy.

2. When two persons are speaking to us at once, we can attend to either of them at pleasure, without being much disturbed by the

other. If we attempt to listen to both, we can understand neither. The fact seems to be, that when we attend constantly to one of the speakers, the words spoken by the other make no impression on the mind, in consequence of our not attending to them; and affect us as little as if they had not been uttered. This power, however, of the mind, to attend to either speaker at pleasure, supposes that it is, at one and the same time, conscious of the sensations which both produce. And the power of reflection, in like manner, turns the mind inward, to view and observe its own actions and operations; but art and pains are requisite to set it at a distance, as it were, from itself, and make it an object of its own scrutiny. Yet art and pains will daily diminish this difficulty, and thereby enable us to think with precision and accuracy on many important subjects, wherein others must blindly follow a leader.

CHAPTER VI.

OF THE DIFFICULTY OF ATTENDING TO THE OPERATIONS OF OUR OWN MINDS, INTERSPERSED WITH OBSERVATIONS WHICH MAY ASSIST US IN OVERCOMING THIS DIFFICULTY.

89. THE difficulty of attending to our mental operations ought to be well understood, and justly estimated, by those who would make any progress in the art of logic; that they may neither, on the one hand, expect success without labor and application of thought, nor, on the other, be discouraged, by conceiving that the obstacles which lie in the way are insuperable, and that there is no certainty to be attained in the science of intellectual philosophy.

Obs. The following development of the causes of this difficulty, and the effects which have arisen from it, will enable us to form a true judgment of these causes and effects.

90. The number and quick succession of the operations of the mind make it difficult to give due attention to them. It is well known, that if a number of objects be presented even to the eye (in quick succession) they are confounded in the mind and imagination. We retain a confused notion of the whole, and a more confused one of the several parts, especially if they are objects to which we have never before given particular attention. No succession can be more quick than that of thought. The mind is busy while we are awake, continually passing from one thought and one operation to another. The scene is constantly shifting. You

will be instantly sensible of this, if you try but for one minute to keep the same thought in your imagination without addition or variation.

Illus. Think, for illustration, on Daniel cast into the lions' den; and you will find it impossible to keep the scene of your imagination fixed. Other objects will intrude without being called: the machinations of his enemies to get a royal statute established, that whosoever should ask a petition of any god or man for thirty days, save of king Darius, should be cast into the den of lions—the immutability of the laws of the Medes and Persians—the king's command—the remarkable presentiment of Darius, that the God whom Daniel served would deliver him—the king's disquietude over night—his going early to the den on the following morning, and crying with a lamentable voice, O Daniel, servant of the living God, is thy God, whom thou servest continually, able to deliver thee from the lions?—the reply of Daniel, " My God hath sent his angel, and hath shut the lions' mouths, that they have not hurt me "—the reason of this, " forasmuch as before him innocence was found in me "—the appeal to Darius, " and also before thee, O king, have I done no hurt "—the punishment of the men who accused Daniel—of their wives and children—and, finally, the decree of the king, " that in every dominion of my kingdom men tremble and fear before the God of Daniel "—these, all these objects will intrude, without being called; and all you can do is to reject the intruders as quickly as possible, and return to the principal object, if you would picture to yourself only Daniel shut up in the lions' den.

91. We proceed in this examination, contrary to habits which have been early acquired, and confirmed by long, unvaried practice. From infancy we are accustomed to attend to objects of sense, and to them only; and, when sensible objects have acquired such strong hold of the attention by confirmed habit, it is not easy to dispossess them. When we grow up, a variety of external objects solicits our attention, excites our curiosity, engages our affections, or touches our passions; and the constant round of employment about external objects, draws off the mind from attending to itself.

Illus. Yet here much may be done by experience, and nothing will contribute so much to form this talent of reflection, as that study which has the operations of the mind for its object. By habituating us to reflect on the subjects of our consciousness, it enables us to retard, in a considerable degree, the current of thought; to arrest many of those ideas, which would otherwise escape our notice; and to render the arguments, which we would employ for the conviction of others, an exact transcript of those trains of inquiry and reasoning, which originally led us to form our opinions.

92. Mental operations, from their very nature, lead the mind to give its attention to some other object. Our sensa-

3

tions are natural signs, and turn our attention to the things signified by them. In perception, memory, judgment, imagination, and reasoning, there is an object distinct from the mind itself; and, while we are led by a strong impulse to attend to the object, the operation escapes our notice. Our passions, affections, and all our active powers, have, in like manner, their objects, which engross our attention, and divert it from the powers themselves.

93. When the mind is agitated by any passion, as soon as we turn our attention from the object of the passion to the passion itself, the passion subsides or vanishes, and by that means escapes our inquiry.

Illus. Thus, when a man is angry, he is conscious of his passion; yet he attends not to it, but to an external object; his attention is turned to the person who offended him, and the circumstances of the offence, while the passion of anger is not in the least the object of his attention. This, indeed, is common to almost every operation of the mind. When it is exerted, we are conscious of it; but then we do not attend to the operation, but to its object. When the mind is drawn off from the object, to attend to its own operation, that operation ceases, and escapes our notice.

94. In what relates to the operations of the mind, it is not enough that we be able to give attention to them; we must, by exercise and habit, acquire the ability of distinguishing accurately their minute differences, of resolving and analyzing complex operations into their simple ingredients, of unfolding the ambiguity of words, which in this science is greater than in any other, and of giving them the accuracy and precision of mathematical language. For, doubtless, the same precision in the use of words; the same cool attention to the minute differences of things; the same talent for abstraction and analyzing, which fit one for the study of mathematics, are no less necessary in the science of mind.

CHAPTER VII.

DIVISION OF THE POWERS OF THE MIND.

95. THE powers of the human mind, and the science of intellectual philosophy, furnish the proper basis upon which every other science rests, because the human faculties are

the instruments by which alone invention in all the sciences can be accomplished. But the powers of the human mind are so many and so various, and so connected and complicated, in almost all its operations, that the most general division, which is also the most common of them, into the powers of *understanding*, and those of the *will*, is perhaps the least liable to objection.

96. The UNDERSTANDING comprehends our contemplative powers, by which we perceive objects, by which we conceive or remember them, by which we analyze or compound them, and by which we judge and reason concerning them. Under the WILL we arrange our active powers, and all that lead to action, or influence the mind to act; such as appetites, passions, affections.

Illus. 1. Although this general division may be of use in order to our proceeding more methodically in our subject, we are not to understand that, in those operations which are ascribed to the understanding, there is no exertion of will, or activity, or that the understanding is not employed in the operations of the will; for we conceive that there is no operation of the understanding wherein the mind is not also active in some degree.

2. We have some command over our thoughts, and can attend to this or to that, of many objects which present themselves to our senses, to our memory, to our imagination. We can survey an object on this side or that, superficially or accurately, for a longer or a shorter time; so that our contemplative powers are under the guidance and direction of the active; and the former never pursue their object without being led and directed, urged or restrained, by the latter. And because the understanding is always more or less directed by the will, mankind have ascribed some degree of activity to the mind in its intellectual operations, as well as in those which belong to the will, and have expressed them by active verbs, such as *seeing, hearing, judging, reasoning,* and the like.

3. And as the mind exerts some degree of activity even in the operations of understanding, so it is certain, that there can be no act of will which is not accompanied with some act of understanding. The will must have an object, and that object must be apprehended or conceived in the understanding.

Corol. It is therefore to be remembered, that in most, if not all operations of the mind, both faculties concur; and we range the operation under that faculty which we conceive to have the largest share in it.

97. In conducting our analysis of the intellectual powers, it is proposed to adopt the following arrangement :—

I. To treat of CONSCIOUSNESS, or that faculty or mode of thinking, by which the various powers of our minds are made known to us.

II. SENSATION, or the faculty whereby we experience

pleasing or painful effects from various objects, through the medium of the senses.

III. PERCEPTION, or the faculty by which we are informed of the properties of external objects, in consequence of the impressions which they make on the organs of sense.

IV. ATTENTION, or the faculty which detains, for our examination, ideas or perceptions in the mind, and excludes other objects that solicit its notice.

V. CONCEPTION, or the faculty by which we represent to our minds the objects of any other of our faculties variously modified.

VI. ABSTRACTION, or the faculty by which we analyze objects of consciousness, sensation, perception, &c., and contemplate their various properties apart from each other.

VII. ASSOCIATION, or *combination* of ideas, the faculty by which we connect together these objects, according to various relations, essential or accidental, so that they are suggested to us, the one by the other.

VIII. MEMORY, or the faculty by which the mind has a knowledge of what it had formerly perceived, felt, or thought.

IX. IMAGINATION, or the faculty which makes a selection of qualities and circumstances from a variety of different objects, and by combining and disposing these, forms new creations of its own.

X. JUDGMENT, or the faculty by which the mind comes to determinations concerning the truth or falsehood of any thing that is affirmed or denied.

XI. REASON, or the faculty by which we are made acquainted with abstract or necessary truth; and enabled to discover the essential relations of things.

XII. MORAL PERCEPTION, or the faculty which determines the choice of a rational being, as to what is good for him upon the whole. and what appears to be duty.

BOOK II.

OF THE INTELLECTUAL POWERS

CHAPTER 1

OF CONSCIOUSNESS

98. Consciousness, being the faculty whereby the various powers of our own minds are made known to us, has been already noticed among the first principles which are common to all men. (*Art.* 48.) In an investigation of the principles of human thought, this faculty stands in the first rank.

Illus. The power of consciousness appears to be denied to the lower animals; nor does it show itself in man till he is advanced towards maturity. The wants and purposes of life require that we should form an intimate acquaintance with those objects of nature with which we are externally connected, and which are the chief sources of our pleasures and pains. Hence our senses, or perceptive powers, come first to maturity; and those which are purely intellectual, such as consciousness, are reserved for the more contemplative period of life.

99. To the exercise of consciousness, as we have already observed, all men are indebted for the conviction, or notion, of personal identity.

Illus. Every man holds himself to be absolutely certain, that whatever changes, his body may undergo in this life, his soul, or mind, always continues one and the same; not liable to that alteration and disunion of parts to which all corporeal beings appear to be subject. Along with consciousness, however, we must conjoin memory, in order to give a rational explanation of the origin of this conviction. For consciousness reaches only to the present, while memory alone gives a knowledge of past thoughts; and it is by comparing our past and present mental operations together, that we form a conviction of our personal, or, rather, intellectual identity.

Corol. 1. The *mind* or *soul* of man being indivisible, or not subject to a dissolution of parts, and annihilation being unknown in the order of nature, it follows, that *the soul is physically immortal.*

2. The properties of mind having no analogy to those of matter, the fact at death is, that the body ceases to be animated, or to give signs of the presence of mind; but the mind, being active, indivisible, and indissoluble, may exist apart.

3 *

3. Hence, every question relating to a future state must be solved from the nature of the soul, from the state of the fact at death, or from the principles of religion.

100. The operation of *consciousness* is accompanied with an irresistible belief of the real existence of those objects of which it gives us information.

Illus. The belief which we entertain in the existence of our own minds, and of their various faculties, rests upon this evidence alone; and it is by means of it, that we acquire our most accurate kn. wledge of the laws by which these faculties are regulated. Nor can the belief accompanying consciousness be resolved into any process of reasoning, or any other intellectual operation; for if we are asked, why we believe that we have a soul, and that that soul has faculties or active powers, which may all be exerted together, or in the least measurable portion of time, we shall be unable to give any better reason, than that we *feel* such to be the case; that is, in more accurate language, that we are conscious of it.

101. No man can divine the mysterious union of soul and body, but every man *feels* that his mind is present, in a particular manner, to whatever affects his senses; and, in other instances, that it is equally present to the most remote, as to the nearest object of thought.

Corol. Thus we may consider the evidence of consciousness as one of those intuitive truths most universally admitted.

CHAPTER II.

OF SENSATION.

102. SENSATION has been defined the faculty by which we experience pleasing or painful effects from various objects, through the medium of the senses.

Obs. The senses come to maturity even in infancy, when other powers have not yet sprung up. They are common to us with brute animals, and furnish us with the objects about which our other powers are most frequently employed. We find it easy to attend to their operations; and because they are familiar, the names which properly belong to them are applied to other powers that are thought to resemble them: for these reasons they claim our attention in an analysis of the faculty of sensation, which naturally demands to be first considered among the objects of our consciousness.

103. The media by which all sensation is communicated to the mind, are the five senses of *seeing smelling, tasting, hearing,* and *touch.*

104. Of these senses, *sight* is, without doubt, the noblest. The variety of information and of enjoyment that we receive by it, the rapidity with which this information and enjoy‧ment are conveyed to us ; and, above all, the intercourse which it enables us to maintain with the more distant parts of the universe, as, for example, with the planets and their satellites, cannot fail to give it, even in the apprehension of the most careless observer, a preëminence over all our oth‧er perceptive faculties.

105. The sense of *smelling* informs us of certain quali‧ties or virtues in bodies, which we call their smell ; and we shall therefore consider the term *smell* as signifying a sensa‧tion, a feeling, or an impression upon the mind ; and which can only be in a mind, or sentient being.

Illus. 1. The sensation produced by this sense can have no exist‧ence but when something that emits an odor is smelled. It there‧fore appears to be a simple and original affection or feeling of the mind, altogether inexplicable and unaccountable. It is indeed impos‧sible that it can be body ; nor can we ascribe to it figure, color, exten‧sion, or any other quality of a body : it is a sensation, and a sensation can only be in a sentient being.

2. The various *odors* have each their different degrees of strength and weakness. Most of them are agreeable or disagreeable ; and fre‧quently those that are agreeable when weak, are disagreeable when stronger. We can compare different smells together ; we can per‧ceive very few resemblances or contrarieties, or indeed relations of any kind between them. They are all simple in themselves, and so differ‧ent from each other, that it is hardly possible to divide them into *gen‧era* and *species*. Most of the names that we give them are particular ; as, the smell of a *jessamine*, of a *rose*, and the like. Yet there are some general names ; as, *sweet, stinking, musty, putrid, cadaverous, aromatic.* Some of them seem to refresh and animate the mind, others to deaden and depress it.

3. But the power, quality, or virtue, in the rose, or in the effluvia proceeding from it, hath a permanent existence, independent of the mind, and which, by the constitution of our nature, produces the sensation in us. By the original constitution of our nature, we are both led to believe, that there is a permanent cause of the sensa‧tion, and, prompted to seek after it, experience determines us to place it in the rose.

106. The relation which the sensation of smell bears to the memory and imagination of it, and to a mind or subject, is common to all our sensations, and indeed to all the opera‧tions of the mind : the relation it bears to the will, is common to it with all the powers of the understanding : and the relation it bears to that quality or virtue of bodies which it indicates, is common to it with the sensations of taste, hearing, color, heat, cold; so that what hath been said of this sense, may easily be applied to several of our senses, and other operations of the mind.

Obs. 1. But in what manner the organs of our corporeal frame con-tribute to excite the various sensations which we are capable of expe-riencing, or how the communication between material objects and our immaterial thinking principle, is carried on, are questions which have hitherto eluded the ingenuity of inquisitive men.

2. Anatomists have carefully analyzed the various organs of sense, as well as the structure of the nerves and brain ; and are able to show us that, in all the senses, the peculiar impressions seem to be communicated to the nerves ; and as all the nerves terminate in the brain, the impressions are, probably, conveyed thither finally. Here all our inquiries must terminate. (See *Illus. Art.* 67, and *Illus. Art.* 70.)

107. When sensation is excited in the mind, it is gen-erally in consequence of some impression first made upon the corporeal senses. But, in some instances, the cause ori-ginates in the mind (as is evident from the thrilling sensa-tion which accompanies certain affections of mind), and is thence communicated to the bodily organs, while apparently an effect is produced precisely similar to that of the more usual kind of sensation.

Illus. It is well known, that the mere thought of pain, in any par-ticular part of the body, is sufficient to excite the corresponding sen-sation in a certain degree. Thus, the idea of sore eyes produces a certain degree of pain in those organs; and the strong imagination of any particular taste or flavor, is accompanied with a slight sensation of that taste or flavor.

108. We have already noticed the difference between sensation and perception (*Art.* 42); and it is obvious, that to speak intelligibly and scientifically, we should say, "the sensation of hunger, of fear, of joy," and "the perception of extension, figure, magnitude," and the like.

109. Many affections of the mind are accompanied with strong sensations, either pleasant or painful.

Illus. 1. Anger, terror, envy, revenge, and all the malevolent pas-sions, have a very powerful effect upon the bodily frame, and excite sensations which are of a very disagreeable kind. Upon the other hand, joy, admiration, love, and all the amiable emotions, produce sen-sations which are decidedly pleasurable.

2. Such sensations are frequently, in common langauge, called feelings ; a name, however, which more properly belongs to the pleas-urable effect of our benevolent affections, and moral judgments, as well as to the pleasure accompanying our approbation in matters of taste. (*Obs. Art.* 42.)

110. These feelings appear to be almost purely of an intellectual nature; while the term sensation, as we wish to limit it, includes a distinct affection of the body, as well as of the mind.

Illus. Thus, the sensation produced by the smell of a rose is a certain affection or feeling of the mind. What is the *smell* of the rose? It is a quality or virtue of the rose, of something proceeding from it, which we perceive by the sense of smelling; and this is all we know of the matter. But what is *smelling?* It is an act of the mind, but is never imagined to be a quality of the mind. (*Illus. Art.* 39)

Corol. Therefore smell in the rose, and the sensation caused by it, are not conceived to be things of the same kind, although they have the same name.

111. According to the views now brought forward and illustrated, our sensations may be divided into those which arise from the operation of material objects upon the five senses; those which accompany our appetites, as hunger, thirst, and the like; and those which arise from the action of the passions, and stronger emotions.

Obs. These last are by far the most numerous of the three kinds; but so little attention is paid to them, that they have no names, and are immediately forgotten, as if they had never been; so that it requires a considerable degree of attention to the operations of our minds, to be convinced of their existence. (See *Illus. Art.* 93.)

112. The Author of Nature, in the distribution of agreeable and painful feelings, hath wisely and benevolently consulted the good of the human species, and hath even shown us, by the same means, what tenor of conduct we ought to hold.

Illus. For, *first,* the painful sensations of the animal kind, are admonitions to avoid what would hurt us; and the agreeable sensations of the same kind, invite us to those actions that are necessary to the preservation of the individual or of the species.

Secondly. By the same means nature invites us to moderate our bodily exercise, and admonishes us to avoid idleness and inactivity on the one hand, and excessive labor and fatigue on the other.

Thirdly. The moderate exercise of all our rational powers gives pleasure.

Fourthly. Every species of beauty is beheld with pleasure, and every species of deformity with disgust; and we shall find all that we call beautiful, to be something estimable or useful in itself, or a sign of something that is estimable or useful.

Fifthly. The benevolent affections are all accompanied with an agreeable feeling, the malevolent with the contrary.

And, *Sixthly.* The highest, the noblest, and most durable pleasure, is that of doing well, and acting the part that becomes us; and the most bitter and painful sensation the anguish and remorse of a guilty conscience.

Note. The faculty of sensation receives additional illustration in Chapter 1st, Book III., under the investigation of the "*primary and secondary qualities of bodies.*"

CHAPTER III.

OF PERCEPTION.

113. PERCEPTION we explained to be the faculty by which we are informed of the properties of external objects, in consequence of the impressions which they make on the organs of sense; and the distinction between it and conception, consciousness, remembrance and sensation, was sufficiently illustrated under Articles 22, 23, and 24.

Obs. The corporeal organs of sense are subservient to the operation of the faculty of perception, as well as of sensation, which generally accompanies it. Yet it is not unreasonable to suppose, that these organs rather limit and circumscribe this intellectual faculty, than that they are essential to its operation; and that beings of a superior order, uncircumscribed by bodily organs like ours, may enjoy perception in a much more perfect degree than we do. A person who had been all his life shut up in a chamber with a single window, would naturally conceive that window to be essential to his sight, instead of being the cause of his very limited view. (See *Obs.* 3. *Art.* 6.)

114. When we attend to that act of our mind which we call the perception of an external object, we shall find in it these three things:

First. Some conception or notion of the object perceived. (*Illus.* 1. *Art.* 22.)

Secondly. A strong and irresistible conviction and belief of its present existence. (*Illus.* 2. *Art.* 22.)

Thirdly. That this conviction and belief are immediate, and not the effect of reasoning. (*Illus.* 3. *Art.* 22.)

115. *First.* It is impossible to perceive an object without some notion or conception of that which we perceive. We may indeed conceive an object which we do not perceive; but when we perceive the object, we must, at the same time, have some conception of it; and we have commonly a more clear and steady notion of the object while we perceive it, than we have from memory or imagination, when it is not perceived. Yet, even in perception, the notion which our senses give of the object may be more or less clear, more or less distinct, in all possible degrees.

Illus. Thus, we see more distinctly an object at a small than at a great distance. The satellites of Jupiter are invisible to the naked eye, but we discern them by means of a telescope. An object at a great distance is seen more distinctly in a clear than in a foggy day. An object seen indistinctly with the naked eye, on account of its smallness, may be seen distinctly with a microscope. The objects in this room will be seen, by a person in the room, less and less distinctly as the light of the day fails;—they pass through all the various degrees of distinctness according to the degrees of the light, and at last, in total darkness, they are not seen at all. What has been said of the objects of sight, is so easily applied to the objects of the other senses, that the application may be left to the reader.

116. *Secondly.* In perception we not only have a notion more or less distinct of the object perceived, but also an irresistible conviction and belief of its existence. This is always the case when we are certain that we perceive it. There may be a perception so faint and indistinct, as to leave us in doubt of its reality.

Illus. 1. Thus, when a star begins to twinkle, as the light of the sun withdraws, one may, for a short time, think he sees it, without being certain, until the perception acquires some strength and steadiness. When a ship just begins to appear in the utmost verge of the horizon, we may at first be dubious whether we perceive it or not. But when the perception is in any degree clear and steady, there remains no doubt of its reality; and when the reality of the perception is ascertained, the existence of the object perceived can no longer be doubted.

2. By the laws of all nations, in the most solemn judicial trials, wherein men's fortunes and lives are at stake, the sentence passes according to the testimony of eye and ear witnesses of good credit. An upright judge will give a fair hearing to every objection that can be made to the integrity of a witness, and allow it to be possible that he may be corrupted; but no judge will ever suppose that witnesses may be imposed upon by trusting to their eyes and ears. And if a skeptical counsel should plead against the testimony of the witnesses, that they had no other evidence for what they declared but the testimony of their eyes and ears, and that the jury ought not to put so much faith in the witnesses' senses, as to deprive a man of life and fortune upon the testimony of the witnesses' eyes and ears, the judge would reject such a plea with disdain, and, by men of common sense, the counsel would be classed among lunatics and hypochondriacal persons. (*Obs.* 1 and 2. *Art.* 63.)

117. The whole conduct of mankind in the daily occurrences of life, as well as in the solemn procedure of judicatories in the trial of causes, civil and criminal, demonstrates that the evidence of sense is a kind of evidence which we may securely rest upon, and against which we ought not to admit any reasoning; for, being perfectly conclusive and unanswerable to reason either for or against it, is an insult

to common sense. (See *Obs.* and *Corol. Art.* 60; and *Obs.* and *Corol. Art.* 61.)

118. *Thirdly.* This conviction is not only irresistible, but it is immediate; that is, it is not by a train of reasoning and argumentation that we come to be convinced of the existence of what we perceive: we ask no argument for the existence of the object but that we perceive it :—perception commands our belief upon its own authority, and disdains to rest that authority upon any reasoning whatsoever.

119. The conviction of a truth may be irresistible, and yet not immediate.

Illus. 1. Thus, my conviction that the three angles of every plain triangle are equal to two right angles, is irresistible, but it is not immediate. I am convinced of it by demonstrative reasoning.
2. Our belief of the axioms in Euclid is not grounded upon argument; for these truths carry with them not only an irresistible, but an immediate conviction. Arguments are not grounded upon them, but their evidence is discerned immediately by the human understanding. (See *Art.* 44. and its *Illus.*)

120. It is, no doubt, one thing to have an immediate conviction of a self-evident axiom; it is another thing to have an immediate conviction of what we see; but the conviction is equally immediate and irresistible in both cases. (See *Illus.* 1 and 2. *Art.* 52.)

Illus. No man thinks of seeking a reason to believe what he sees; and before we are capable of reasoning, we put no less confidence in our senses than after. The rudest savage is as fully convinced of what he sees, and hears, and feels, as the most expert logician; both are alike incapable of giving any better reason for this belief, than the original constitution of their nature.
Corol. The constitution of our understanding determines us to hold the truth of a mathematical axiom as a first principle, from which other truths may be deduced, but it is deduced from none; and the constitution of our power of perception determines us to hold the existence of what we distinctly perceive as a first principle, from which other truths may be deduced, but it is deduced from none.

121. The account which we have given of the faculty of perception, amounts to this; that the mind is so formed, that certain impressions produced on our organs of sense by external objects, are followed by corresponding sensations; and that these sensations, which have no more resemblance to the qualities of matter, than the words of a language have to the things they denote, are followed by a perception of the existence and qualities of the bodies by which the impressions are made; that all the steps in this process

are equally incomprehensible; and that, for any thing we know to the contrary, the connection between the sensation and perception, as well as between the impression and the sensation, may be both arbitrary; that it is, therefore, by no means impossible, that our sensations may be merely the occasions on which perceptions are excited; and that, at any rate, the consideration of these sensations, which are attributes of mind, can throw no light on the manner in which we acquire our knowledge of the existence and qualities of bodies. (STEWART'S *Philosophy of the Human Mind.*)

Corol. From this view of the subject, it follows, that it is the external objects themselves, and not any species or images of these objects, that the mind perceives; and that, although, by the constitution of our nature, certain sensations are rendered the constant antecedents of our perceptions, yet it is just as difficult to explain how our perceptions are obtained by this means, as it would be upon the supposition that the mind were all at once inspired with them, without any concomitant sensations whatever. The information of the senses is as perfect, and gives as full conviction to the most ignorant, as to the most learned; and the conviction we have of their reality rests upon consciousness, a faculty that puts the poorest of mankind upon a level with the greatest. (See *Art* 69. *Obs.*)

CHAPTER IV.

OF ATTENTION.

122. ATTENTION is the faculty which detains, for our examination, ideas or perceptions in the mind, and excludes other objects that solicit its notice.

Illus. When we are deeply engaged in conversation, or occupied with any speculation that is interesting to the mind, the surrounding objects do not produce in us the perceptions they are fitted to excite; or those perceptions are instantly forgotten. Thus, a clock may strike in the same room with us, without our being able the next moment to recollect whether we heard it or not.

123. In these, and similar cases, it is commonly taken for granted, that we really do not perceive the external object. But analogous facts may serve to prove that this opinion is not well founded.

Illus. 1. Thus, a person who falls asleep at church, and is suddenly awaked, is unable to recollect the last words spoken by the

4

preacher, or even to recollect that he was speaking. And yet, that sleep does not suspend entirely the powers of perception, may be inferred from this, that, if the preacher were to make a sudden pause in his discourse, every person who was asleep in the congregation would instantly awake.

Corol. In this case, therefore, it appears, that a person may be conscious of a perception, without being able afterwards to recollect it.

Illus. 2. When we read a book, especially in a language that is not perfectly familiar to us, we must perceive successively every different letter, and must afterwards combine these letters into syllables and words, before we comprehend the meaning of a sentence. This process, however, passes through the mind without leaving any trace in the memory.

3. It has been proved by optical writers, that in perceiving the distances of visible objects from the eye, there is a judgment of the understanding antecedent to perception. In some cases this judgment is founded on a variety of circumstances combined together—the conformation of the organs necessary for distinct vision—the inclination of the optic axes—the distinctness or indistinctness of the minute parts of the object—the distances of the intervening objects from each other and from the eye—and, perhaps, on other circumstances besides these;—and yet, in consequence of our familiarity with such processes from our earliest infancy, the perception seems to be instantaneous.

4. As a further illustration, we shall produce another instance of a nature still more familiar. It is well known (says Mr. Stewart, to whom, for authority's sake, I attribute the materials of which this chapter is composed), that our thoughts do not succeed each other at random, but according to certain laws of association, which modern philosophers have been at pains to investigate. It frequently happens, particularly when the mind is animated by conversation, that it makes a sudden transition from one subject to another, which, at first view, appears to be very remote from it; and that it requires a considerable degree of reflection, to enable the person himself, by whom the transition was made, to ascertain what were the intermediate ideas. A curious instance of such sudden transition is mentioned by Hobbs, in his Leviathan : " In a company (says he), in which the conversation turned on the civil war, what could be conceived more impertinent, than for a person to ask abruptly, What was the value of a Roman denarius ? On a little reflection, however, I was easily able to trace the train of thought which suggested the question ; for the original subject of discourse naturally introduced the history of the king, and the treachery of those who surrendered his person to his enemies ; this again introduced the treachery of *Judas Iscariot,* and the sum of money which he received for his reward. And all this train of ideas passed through the mind of the speaker in a twinkling, in consequence of the velocity of thought." Upon this anecdote Mr. Stewart observes very justly, " It is by no means improbable, that if the speaker himself had been interrogated about the connection of ideas which led him aside from the original topic of discourse, he would have found himself, at first, at a loss for an answer."

Corol. The three last illustrations furnish us with proof that a perception or an idea, which passes through the mind, may yet serve to introduce other ideas connected with it by the laws of association.

124. When a perception or idea passes through the mind, without our being able to recollect it the next moment, persons the most illiterate ascribe their want of memory to a want of attention.

Illus. Thus, in the instance already mentioned of the clock, (*Illus. Art.* 122.) a person, upon observing that the minute-hand had just passed twelve, would naturally say, that he did not attend to the clock when it was striking.

Corol. There seems, therefore, to be a certain effort of mind upon which, even in the judgment of those who make no pretensions to philosophy, memory in some measure depends; and this effort they distinguish by the name of *attention.*

125. The memory depends much on the degree of attention which we give it; and it seems essential to memory, that the perception of the idea which we would wish to remember, should remain in the mind for a certain space of time, and should be contemplated by it exclusively of every thing else; and that attention consists partly (perhaps entirely) in the effort of the mind to detain the idea or perception, and to exclude the other objects that solicit its notice. And though there may be some difficulty of ascertaining in what this act of the mind consists, every person must be satisfied of its reality from his own consciousness, and of its essential connection with the power of memory.

Obs. The several instances which have already been mentioned, of ideas passing through the mind without our being able to recollect them the next moment, were produced merely to illustrate the meaning which we annex to the word *attention*, and to recall to the recollection of the student a few striking cases, in which the possibility of carrying on a process of thought, which we are unable to attend to at the time, or to remember afterwards, is acknowledged in the received systems of philosophy.

126. Among the phenomena which appear to be very similar to those we have introduced, illustrative of the faculty of attention, and which are explicable in the same manner, may be classed the wonderful effect of practice in the formation of habits—one of the most curious circumstances in the human constitution.

Illus. A mechanical operation, for example, which we at first performed with the utmost difficulty, comes, in time, to be so familiar to us, that we are able to perform it without the smallest danger of mistake ; even while the attention appears to be completely engaged with other subjects. The truth seems to be, that in consequence of the association of ideas, the different steps of the process present themselves successively to our thoughts, without any recollection on our part, and with a degree of rapidity proportioned to the length of our experience ; so as to save us entirely the trouble of hesitation and reflection, by giving us every moment a precise and steady notion of the effect to be produced.

127. In the case of some operations which are very familiar to us, we find ourselves unable to attend to the acts of the will by which they were preceded, or even to recollect those acts ; but the circumstance of our inability to recollect our volitions, does not authorize us to dispute their possibility, any more than our inability to attend to the process of the mind, in estimating the distance of an object from the eye, authorizes us to affirm that the perception is instantaneous.

128. Habit differs from instinct, not in its nature, but in its origin ; the last being natural, the first acquired. Both appear to operate without will or intention, without thought, and have therefore been called mechanical principles.

Illus. Thus, suppose a person who has a perfectly voluntary command over his fingers to begin to learn to play on the harpsichord The first step is to move his fingers from one key to another, with a slow motion, looking at the notes, and exerting an express act of volition in every motion. By degrees the motions cling to one another, and to the impressions of the notes, in the way of association, the acts of volition growing less and less express all the time, till at last they become evanescent and imperceptible. For an expert performer will play from notes, or notions of notes, laid up in the memory ; and at the same time carry on a train of thoughts in his mind quite different from the piece of music which he is playing, or even hold a conversation with another. Here, it appears, that those operations which have become habitual from long practice, preclude the possibility of recollecting every different volition of the mind ; yet it is not to be doubted that there is an act of the will preceding every motion of each finger, since the most rapid performer can, when he pleases, play so slowly, as to be able to attend to every separate act of his will in the various movements of his fingers, and even to recollect those volitions afterwards ; and he can gradually accelerate the rate of his execution, till he is unable to recollect these acts.

Corol. The operations in these two cases appear to be carried on precisely in the same manner, and differ only in the degree of rapidity ; and when this rapidity exceeds a certain rate, the acts of the will are too momentary to leave any impression on the memory.

129. The corollary just drawn from this second illustra-

tion, is supported by the analogy of many other facts in our constitution.

Illus. 1. Thus, an expert accountant can sum up, almost at a single glance of his eye, a long column of figures; nay, of farthings, pence, shillings, and pounds, at one and the same time;— he can tell the sum with unerring certainty, while, at the same time, he is unable to recollect any one of the figures of which that sum is composed; and yet nobody doubts that each of these figures has passed through his mind, or supposes that when the rapidity of the process becomes so great that he is unable to recollect the various steps of it, he obtains the result by a sort of inspiration.

2. It has been found, by actual trial, that it is possible to pronounce about two thousand letters in a minute, and though the inconceivable rapidity with which our intellectual operations proceed, render it impossible to discriminate the volitions of our mind, the articulation of every letter, in reading aloud, must be preceded by a separate volition. Here, then, we have evidence that the mind is so formed as to be able to carry on certain intellectual processes, in intervals of time too short to be estimated by our faculties; yet, were our powers of attention and memory more perfect than they are, so as to give us the same advantage in examining rapid events, which the microscope gives us for examining minute portions of extension, they would enlarge our views with respect to the intellectual world, no less than that instrument has with respect to the material.

130. As the great use of *attention* and *memory* is to enable us to treasure up the results of our experience and reflection for the future regulation of our conduct, it would have answered no purpose for the Author of our nature to have extended their province to those intervals of time, which we have no occasion to estimate in the common business of life. All the intellectual processes which have been mentioned, are subservient to some particular end, either of perception or of action; and it would have been perfectly superfluous, if, after this end were gained, the steps which are instrumental in bringing it about, were all treasured up in the memory: such a constitution of our nature would have had no other effect but to store the mind with a variety of useless particulars.

131. In confirmation of these reasonings on the faculty of attention, the following illustration affords a more palpable instance than any that we have yet mentioned, of the rapidity with which the thoughts may be trained up, by practice, to shift from one thing to another.

Illus. 1. When an equilibrist balances a rod upon his finger, not only the attention of his mind, but the observation of his eye, is con-

4 *

stantly requisite. It is evident that the part of his body which supports the object is never wholly at rest; otherwise the object would
no more stand upon it, than if placed in the same position upon a table. The equilibrist, therefore, must watch, in the very beginning,
every inclination of the object from the proper position, in order to
counteract this inclination by a contrary movement. In this manner
the object has never time to fall in any one direction, and is supported
in a way somewhat analogous to that in which a top is supported on
a pivot, by being made to spin upon an axis.

2. That a person should be able to do this in the case of a single
object, is curious; but that he should be able to balance, in the same
way, two, three, nay, half a dozen of objects, upon different parts of
his body, and at the same time balance himself on a small cord or
wire, is indeed wonderful. Nor is it possible to conceive, that in such
an instance, the mind, at one and the same moment, attends to these
equilibriums; for it is not merely the *attention* which is requisite, but
the eye. We must therefore conclude, that both the attention and the
eye are directed successively to the different equilibriums, but change
from one object to another with such velocity, that the effect, with
respect to the experiment, is the same as if they were directed to all
the objects constantly.

Corol. This last illustration affords direct evidence, as Mr. Stewart
observes, of the possibility of our exerting acts of the will, which
we are unable to recollect; for the movements of the equilibrist do
not succeed each other in regular order, like those of the harpsichord player, in performing a piece of music; but must, in every
instance, be regulated by accidents, which may vary in numberless
respects,—and which indeed *must* vary in numberless respects *every
time* he repeats the experiment; and, therefore, though, in the case
of the musician, we should suppose that the motions cling to one
another, and to the impressions of the notes, in the way of association, without any intervention in the state of mind called *will*, yet
in this instance of the equilibrist, even the possibility of such a sup
position is directly contradicted by the fact which has been established.

132. The faculty of attention is susceptible of much improvement, as may be established from the well-known fact,
that a person who accidentally loses his sight, never fails to
improve gradually in the sensibility of his touch.

Illus. Now there are only two ways of explaining this. The one
is, that, in consequence of the loss of the one sense, some change
takes place in the physical constitution of the body, so as to improve
a different organ of perception. The other is, that the mind gradually acquires a power of attending to and remembering those slighter
sensations of which it was formerly conscious, but which, from habits
of inattention, made no impression whatever on the memory. No
one, surely, can hesitate, for a moment, in pronouncing which of these
two suppositions is the more philosophical.

133. Hitherto we have treated only of those habits in
which both mind and body are concerned; but there are

phenomena purely intellectual, that are explicable on the same principles.

Illus. 1. Every person who has studied the elements of geometry, must have observed many cases in which the truth of a theorem struck him the moment he heard the enunciation ; yet he might not be able to state immediately to others upon what his conviction was founded ; but there can be no doubt but that, before he gave his assent to the theorem, a process of thought passed through the mind, but passed so quickly, that he could not, without difficulty, arrest his ideas in their rapid succession, and state them to others in their proper and logical order.

134. In politics, in morals, and in common life, many questions daily occur, in considering which, we almost instantaneously see where the truth lies, although we are not in a condition, all at once, to explain the grounds of our conviction. But even in those cases in which the truth of a proposition seems to strike us instantaneously, although we may not be able, at first, to discover the media of proof, we seldom fail in the discovery by perseverance. And nothing contributes so much to form this talent as that study which has the operations of the mind for its object ; for, by habituating us to reflect on the subjects of our consciousness, it enables us to retard, in a considerable degree, the current of thought ; to arrest many of those ideas which would otherwise escape our notice ; and to render the arguments which we employ for the conviction of others, an exact transcript of those trains of inquiry and reasoning, which originally led us to form our opinions.

135. Men of business, who are under the necessity of thinking and deciding on the spur of the occasion, are led to cultivate, as much as possible, a quickness in their mental operations ; and sometimes acquire it in so great a degree, that their judgments seem to be almost intuitive. A stock-jobber knows this.

Obs. And the greatest generals, in new and untried difficulties, in the midst of battle, have, with a quickness that astonished all around them, decided upon movements no less hazardous than successful. Now, long practice in the field might give them the power of carrying on certain intellectual processes concerning modes of attack and defence, but the reasonings by which their judgments were swayed, in those particular instances we have alluded to, consisted only of a few steps, which, as soon as the intellectual process was finished, vanished, perhaps forever, entirely from the memory.

136. On the other hand, men of speculation, who have not merely to form opinions for themselves, but to communicate them to others, find it necessary to retard the train

of thought as it passes in the mind, so as to be able afterwards to recollect every different step of the process ; a
habit which, in some cases, has such an influence on the
intellectual powers, that there are men who, even in their
private speculations, not only make use of words as an instrument of thought, but form these words into regular sentences.

137. When a train of thought leads to any interesting
conclusion, or excites any pleasant feeling, it becomes peculiarly difficult to arrest our fleeting ideas, because the mind
has little inclination to retrace the steps by which it arrived
at the pleasure which it now feels.

Obs. This is one great cause of the difficulty attending philosophical
criticism; and exquisite sensibility, so far from being useful in this
species of criticism, both gives a disrelish for the study and disqualifies for pursuing it legitimately.

138. There is a great variety of cases, in which the mind
apparently exerts different acts of attention at once ; but
from the illustrations which we have given of the astonishing
rapidity of thought, it is obvious, that those acts are not co-
existent ; or, in other words, that we do not attend, at one
and the same instant, to objects which we can attend to
separately.

Illus. 1. The case of the equilibrist and rope-dancer affords direct
evidence of the possibility of the mind's exerting different successive
acts in an interval of time so short, as to produce the same sensible
effect as if they had been exerted at one and the same moment. In
this case, every movement of the eyes precedes a thought of the
mind, every thought a volition, every volition a separate action of
muscular force, but so rapidly does each of these succeed the other,
that though they seem instantaneous, they cannot be mathematically
coëxistent.

2. In a concert of music, a good ear can attend to the different
parts of the music separately, or can attend to them all at once,
and feel the full effect of the harmony ; but the mind is constantly
varying its attention from one part of the music to the other, and its
operations are so rapid as to give us no perception of an interval of
time.

3. In viewing a picture, the mind at one and the same time
perceives every point in the outline of the object (provided the
whole be painted on the retina at one and the same instant), for
perception, like consciousness, is an involuntary operation; but as
no two points of the outline are in the same direction, every point,
by itself, constitutes just as distinct an object of attention to the
mind, as if it were separated by an interval of empty space from all
the rest. As, therefore, it is impossible for the mind to attend to
more than one of those points at once, and as the perception of the

figure of the object implies a knowledge of the relative situation of the different points with respect to each other, we must conclude that the perception of the figure by the eye, is the result of a number of different acts of attention. These acts of attention, however, are performed with such rapidity, that the effect, with respect to us, is the same as if the perception were instantaneous.

Corol. 1. If the perception of visible figure were an immediate consequence of the picture on the retina, we should have, at the first glance, as distinct an idea of a figure of a thousand sides, as of a triangle or a square; for when the figure is very simple, the process of the mind is so rapid, that the perception seems to be instantaneous; but when the sides are multiplied beyond a certain number, the interval of time necessary for these different acts of attention becomes perceptible.

2. If these reasonings be admitted, it will follow, that without the faculty of memory, we could have no perception of visible figure.

CHAPTER V.

OF CONCEPTION.

139. CONCEPTION is that faculty of the mind which enables us to form a notion of an absent object of perception; or of a sensation which it has formerly felt.

Illus. When a painter paints a picture of a friend who is absent or dead, he is commonly said to paint from memory; and the expression is sufficiently correct for common conversation. But, in an analysis of the powers of the mind, there is ground for a distinction between conception and the other powers, with some of which it is often confounded. The power of conception enables the painter to make the features of his friend an object of thought, so as to copy the resemblance; the power of memory recognizes these features as a former object of perception. Thus, conception is distinguished from memory. Every act of memory includes an idea of the past; conception implies no idea of time whatever.

Note Shakspeare calls this power *the mind's eye.*

  Hamlet. My father! Methinks I see my father.
  Horatio. Where, my lord?
  Hamlet. In *my mind's eye,* Horatio.
     HAMLET, Act 1. Scene 4.

140. Conception corresponds, according to the view we have taken of it, to what the schoolmen call *simple apprehension;* with this difference only, that they include, under this name, our apprehension of general propositions; whereas the word conception is, in this volume, limited to our sensations and the objects of our perceptions.

Illus. This distinction is warranted by the authority of philoso-phers in a case perfectly analogous. Thus, in ordinary language, we apply the same word *perception* to the knowledge which we have by our senses of external objects, and to our knowledge of a speculative truth. And between the conception of a truth, and the conception of an absent object of sense, there is obviously as wide a difference as between the perception of a tree and the perception of a mathe-matical theorem. Conception, therefore, is that faculty whose prov-ince it is to enable us to form a notion of our past sensations, or of the objects of sense that we have formerly perceived.

141. Conception is frequently used as synonymous with imagination, but imagination is distinguished from concep-tion as a part from a whole.

Illus. The business of conception is to present us with an exact transcript of what we have felt or perceived. But we have, more-over, a power of modifying our conceptions, by combining the parts of different conceptions together, so as to form new wholes of our own creation. This power, according to Mr. Stewart, is expressed by the word *imagination;* and he apprehends, that this is the proper sense of the word; if imagination be the power which gives birth to the productions of the poet and the painter. This is not a simple faculty of the mind, for it presupposes abstraction, to separate from each other qualities and circumstances which have been perceived in conjunction; and also judgment and taste to direct us, in forming the combinations.

Obs. People, in common discourse, often use the phrase *thinking upon an object,* to express what we have illustrated as the *concep-tion of it.* Shakspeare, whose talent for philosophizing was equal to his imaginative powers as a poet, uses, in the following passage, the former of these phrases in the same sense as we should use *conception,* and the words imagination and apprehension are synony-mous with each other.

> ———Who can hold a fire in his hand
> *By thinking* on the frosty Caucasus?
> Or cloy the hungry edge of appetite
> By bare *imagination* of a feast?
> Or wallow naked in December's snow,
> *By thinking* on fantastic summer's heat?
> Oh no! the *apprehension* of the good
> Gives but the greater feeling to the worse.
> K. RICHARD II. Act 1. Scene 6

142. We can conceive the objects of some senses much more easily than those of others. And, *first,* as to visible objects; we can conceive the structure of a building that is familiar to us much more easily than a particular sound, a particular taste, or a particular pain which we have former-ly felt.

Illus. The peculiarity in the case of visible objects seems to arise from this; that when we think of a sound or of a taste, the object of our conception is one single detached sensation; whereas every visible object is complex; and the conception that we form of it is aided by the association of ideas. We attend not, at one instant, to every point of the picture of an object on the retina (*Corol. 1. Art.* 138); nor at one instant, therefore, do we form a conception of the whole of any visible object; but . our conception of the object as a whole, is the result of many conceptions. The association of ideas connects the different parts together, and presents them to the mind in their proper arrangement; and the various relations which these parts bear to one another in point of situation, contribute greatly to strengthen the associations. This illustration is confirmed by the fact, that it is more easy to remember a succession of sounds, than any particular sound which we have heard detached and unconnected. The war-hoop of the American Indians, the yell of Cossacks, the shout of victory, or any cry that alarmed or encouraged us, may be considered a particular sound, but the conception of such a sound depends on the association of ideas.

143. The power of conceiving visible objects, like other powers that depend on the association of ideas, may be greatly improved by habit.

Il'us. A person accustomed to drawing, retains a much more perfect notion of a building, or of a landscape, which he has seen, than one who has never practised that art. A portrait painter traces the forms of the human body from memory. with as little exertion as he employs in writing the letters which compose his name.

144. *Secondly.* In the power of conceiving colors, too, there are striking differences among individuals; and probably, in the greater number of instances, the supposed defects of sight, in this respect, ought rather to be ascribed to a defect in the power of conception, than in the organ of the perception of color.

Illus. We often see two men who are perfectly sensible of the difference between two colors when they are presented to them, who cannot give names to these colors with confidence, when they see them apart; and are perhaps apt to confound the one with the other. They feel the sensation of color like other men, it should seem, when the object is present, but are incapable, probably in consequence of some early habit of inattention, to conceive the sensation distinctly when the object is removed. Without this power of conception, Mr. Stewart thinks, that it is evidently impossible for them, how lively soever their sensations may be, to give a name to any color; for the application of the name supposes not only a capacity of receiving the sensation, but a power of comparing it with one formerly felt. In some cases, perhaps, the sensation is not felt at all; and in others, the faintness of the sensation may be one cause of those habits of inattention, from which the incapacity of conception has arisen.

145. *Thirdly.* A talent for lively description, at least in the case of sensible objects, depends chiefly on the degree

in which the describer possesses the power of conception. Nor is it merely to the accuracy of our description, in common conversation, that this power is subservient; it contributes more than any thing else to render them striking and expressive to others, by guiding us to a selection of such circumstances as are most prominent and characteristical.

Obs. The best rule for descriptive composition, is, to attend to those rules which make the deepest impression on our own minds. Now, these particulars are in general the outline; and it is the province of conception to neglect a minute specification of particulars, and to select only such as struck us most at the moment the object we are describing from recollection was present to our view. A person may therefore write a happier description of an object from the conception than from the actual perception of that object.

146. The foregoing observations, with their respective illustrations, apply to conception, as distinguished from imagination. The two faculties, we observed, are very nearly allied; and are frequently so blended and compounded, that it is difficult to say, to which of the two some particular operations of the mind are to be referred. There are also general facts which hold equally with respect to both.

147. The exercise both of conception and imagination is always accompanied with a belief that their objects exist.

Illus. 1. Thus, when the imagination is very lively, as in dreaming and madness, a real existence is ascribed to its objects; and in the case, too, of those who, in spite of their own general belief of the absurdity of the vulgar stories of apparitions, dare not trust themselves alone with their own *imaginations* in the dark, we have all the evidence that the thing admits of, that imagination is attended with belief. Dr. Reid's friend, who could not sleep in a room alone, nor go alone into a room in the dark, felt and acted in the same manner as he would have done, if he had believed that the objects of his fear were real, which is the only proof that the philosophers produce, or can produce, of the belief which accompanies perception.

2. The painter, who conceives the face and figure of an absent friend, in order to draw his picture, believes, for the moment, that his friend is before him. The belief is only momentary, for it is extremely difficult, in our waking hours, to keep up a steady and undivided attention to any object we conceive or imagine; and as soon as the *conception* or imagination is over, the belief which attended it is at an end. We, in fact, consider them as creations of the mind, which have no separate and independent existence, from the facility with which we can recall or dismiss the objects of these powers at pleasure. But when the conceptions of the mind are rendered steady and permanent, by being strongly associated with any sensible impression, as when we gaze on a magnificent prospect, they command our belief no less that our actual perceptions; and, therefore, if it were possible for us, with our eyes shut, to keep up for a length

of time, the conception of the immense extent of the whole scene that had formerly engaged our eyes, we should, as long as this effort continued, believe that all the different parts of which it was composed, were present to our senses.

148. The knowledge we obtain by the eye, of the tangible qualities of bodies, is the result of a complex operation of the mind; comprehending, *first*, the perception of those qualities, which are the proper and original objects of sight; and, *secondly*, the conception of those tangible qualities, of which the original perceptions of sight are found from experience to be the signs.

Corol. The notions, therefore, we form by means of the eye, of the tangible qualities of bodies, and of the distances of these objects from the organ, are *mere conceptions;* strongly, and indeed indissolubly, associated, by early and constant habit, with the original perceptions of sight.

149. The effects which exhibitions of fictitious distress produce on the mind, may all be resolved into the conceptions we have, for the moment, that the whole is real.

Illus. 1. During the representation of a tragedy, we have a general conviction that the whole is a fiction ; but, I believe, no person ever witnessed Mrs. Siddons, Miss O'Neill, Mr. John Kemble, and Mr. Kean, in tragedy, who did not partake in the emotions which those artists created ; who did not entertain a momentary belief that the distresses, which were but fictitious, were actually real. But whence arose this belief? whence the conception ?—but from the contagion spread by the faithful expression of the passions.

2. The emotions produced by tragedy are, thence, analogous to the dread we feel when we look down from the battlements of a tower ;— or the horror which seizes a person, who, fleeing from a conflagration, escapes from the top of a house by a path, which, at another time, he would have considered as impracticable ;—or to the astonishment of soldiers, who, in mounting a breach, have found their way to the enemy, by a route which appeared inaccessible after their violent passions had subsided. We have a general conviction that there is no ground for the feelings which we experience during the representation of a tragedy, or when we look down from the battlements of a tower, any more than the person who has escaped from the fire has to feel horror at the recollection of the imminent danger he was in as he traversed the hazardous path, or than the soldier's wonder at himself in having scrambled by a route the bare contemplation of which suspends his curiosity to retrace his footsteps.

5

CHAPTER VI.

OF ABSTRACTION.

150. ABSTRACTION is the faculty by which we analyze the actual assemblages of nature into their constituent parts. It is this faculty which enables us to ascertain what qualities an object has peculiar to itself, and what are in common to it and other objects of a like nature, which will therefore be referred to the same class with it. In short, the whole process of the formation of general notions is due to the faculty of abstraction alone.

Obs. Had we possessed no such faculty as abstraction, all our knowledge would have been limited to an acquaintance with individual beings and individual facts. But the very essence of science consists in generalizing and reducing to a few classes, or general principles, the multitude of individual things which every branch of human knowledge embraces. Hence, without abstraction, science would have had no existence; and the knowledge of man would have been like that of the lower animals, in whom no traces of this faculty are discernible; circumscribed to an acquaintance with those objects and events in nature with which he was connected by a regard to his own knowledge and preservation.

151. It is in the discovery of general principles, that reason has its noblest exercise. It is generalization alone that makes it possible for us continually to go on in scientific improvement.

Obs. It is in consequence of this, that at the moment when a multitude of particular solutions and of insulated facts begin to distract the attention, and to overcharge the memory, the former gradually lose themselves in one general method, and the latter unite in one general law; and that these generalizations, continually succeeding one to another, like the successive multiplications of a number into itself, have no other limit than that infinity which the human faculties are unable to comprehend. Hence it appears, that abstraction is completely subservient to all the nobler exertions of reason, to those, in particular, by which man has attained the high distinction of being denominated a rational animal.

152. In proportion as a man familiarizes himself in the exercise of abstraction, and accustoms himself to consider what are the distinguishing characteristics of the various objects of his contemplation, and what they have in common with others, does he fit himself for scientific pursuits

Obs. But it has been supposed that the formation of general principles is not entirely suited to the direction of our conduct in the more ordinary occurrences of life ; and hence the origin of that max im which has been so industriously propagated by the dunces of every age—that a man of genius is unfit for business ! But when theoretical knowledge and practical skill are happily combined in the same person, the intellectual power of man appears in its full perfection, and fits him equally to conduct with a masterly hand the duties of ordinary business, and to contend successfully with the untried difficulties of new and hazardous situations.

I. *Of Abstract or General Terms.*

153. The words we use in language are either general words or proper names. Proper names belong to individuals, as George, London, Thames; common names, or general words, are not appropriated to signify any one individual thing, but are equally related to many ; as man, horse, star.

Obs. Under general words are comprehended not only those which the logicians call general terms : that is to say, such words as may make the subject or the predicate of a proposition, but likewise their auxiliaries or accessories, such as prepositions, conjunctions, articles, which are all general words, though they cannot properly be called general terms.

154. In every language, rude or polished, general words make the greatest part, and proper names the least. Grammarians have reduced all words to eight or nine classes, which are called parts of speech.

Illus. Proper names are found only among nouns. All verbs, participles, pronouns, conjunctions, interjections and articles, are general terms. Of nouns, all adjectives are general, and the greater part of substantives. Every substantive that has a plural number, is a general word ; for no proper name can have a plural number, because it signifies only one individual. Custom, however, hath made a few proper names plural, but the position we have laid down is not overthrown by an exception. In all the books of Euclid's Elements, there is not one word that is not general.

Obs. At the same time, we observe, that all the objects which we perceive are individuals. Every object of sense, of memory, or of consciousness, is an individual. All the good things we desire or enjoy, and all the evils we feel or fear, must come from individuals.

155. The reason why proper names make but a very small and inconsiderable part of a language, is, that these names are local, and having no names answering to them in other languages, are not accounted a part of the language, any more than the customs of a hamlet are accounted part of the law of the nation, much less of the whole human family.

For this reason there are but few proper names belonging to a language.

156. And the reason why general words make the greatest part of every language, may be easily accounted for by the following illustrations.

Illus. 1. Every individual that falls within our view has various attributes ; and it is by these that it becomes useful or hurtful to us. We know not the essence of any individual object. All the knowledge we can gain of it is the knowledge of its attributes, its quantity, its various relations to other things, its place, its situation, its motions. It is by such attributes of things only that we communicate our knowledge of them to others. By their attributes, our hopes and fears from them are regulated ; and it is only by attention to their attributes that we can make them subservient to our ends ; and therefore we give names to such attributes.

2. Now, all attributes must, from their nature, be expressed by general words, and are so expressed in all languages. Anciently, attributes were, in general, expressed by two names which express their nature. They were called *universals*, because they might belong equally to many individuals, and are not confined to one. They were also called *predicables*, because whatever is predicated, that is, affirmed or denied of one subject, may be affirmed or denied of more than one, and is, therefore, an universal, and expressed by a general word. A predicable, therefore, signifies the same thing as an attribute, with this difference only, that the first word is Latin, the last English. The attributes which we find either in the works of nature, or of human ingenuity, are common to many individuals. We either find them to be so, or presume them to be so, and give them the same name in every subject to which they belong.

3. There are not only attributes belonging to individual subjects, but there are likewise attributes of attributes, which may be called secondary attributes. Most attributes are capable of different degrees and different modifications, which must be expressed by general words.

Example. Thus, it is an attribute of many bodies to be moved, but motion may be in an endless variety of directions. It may be quick, or slow, rectilineal, or curvilineal ; it may be equable, accelerated, or retarded.

Corol. As all attributes, therefore, whether primary or secondary, are expressed by general words, it follows, that in every proposition which we express in language, what is affirmed or denied of the subject of the proposition, must be expressed by general words. And that the subject of the proposition may often be a general word, will appear from the next illustration.

Illus. 4. The same faculties by which we distinguish the different attributes belonging to the same subject, and give names to them, enable us likewise to observe, that many subjects agree in certain attributes, while they differ in others. By this means we are enabled to reduce individuals which are infinite, to a limited number of *classes*, which are all kinds or sorts, and, in the scholastic dialect, these are called *general species.*

157. Observing many individuals to agree in certain at-tributes, we refer them all to one class, and give a name to the class. This name comprehends in its signification, not one attribute only, but all the attributes which distinguish that class, and by affirming this name of any individual, we affirm it to have all the attributes which characterize the class.

Illus. Thus men, dogs, horses, elephants, are so many different classes of animals. In like manner we marshal other substances, vegetable and inanimate, into classes; as oaks, elms, firs; earths, minerals. We form also into classes, qualities, relations, actions, af-fections, and passions, and all other things.

158. When a class is very large, it is divided into sub-ordinate classes; the higher class being called a *genus* or kind; the lower a *species*, or sort of the higher. Sometimes a species is still subdivided into subordinate species; and this subdivision is carried on as far as is found convenient for the purpose of language, or for the improvement of knowledge.

Illus. In this distribution of things into *genera* and *species*, it is evident that the name of the species comprehends more attributes than the name of the genus. The species comprehends all that is in the genus, and those attributes likewise which distinguish that species from others belonging to the same genus; and the more such divisions we make, the names of the lower become still the more comprehensive in their signification, but the less extensive in their application to in-dividuals.

Corol. Hence it is an axiom in logic, that the more extensive any general term is, it is the less comprehensive; and on the contrary, the more comprehensive, the less extensive.

Example. In the following series of subordinate general terms, an-imal, man, Frenchman, Parisian, every subsequent term comprehends in its signification, all that is in the preceding, and something more; and every antecedent term extends to more individuals than the sub-sequent.

159. Every genus, and every species of things, may be either the subject or the predicate of a proposition, nay, of innumerable propositions; for every attribute common to the genus or species, may be affirmed of it; and the genus may be affirmed of every species, and both genus and species of every individual to which it extends.

Illus. 1. Thus, of man, it may be affirmed, that he is an animal made up of body and mind; that he is of few days and full of trouble; that he is capable of various improvements in arts, in knowledge, and in virtue. In a word, every thing common to the species may be af-firmed of man; and of all such propositions, which are innumerable man is the *subject*.

5 *

2. Again, of every nation and tribe, and of every individual of the human race that is, that was, or that shall be, it may be affirmed that they are men. In all such propositions, which are innumerable, *man is the predicate* of the proposition.

Obs. We have observed above an extension and comprehension of general terms; and that in any subdivision of things, the name of the lowest species is most comprehensive, and that of the highest genus most extensive; we shall now see that, by means of such general terms, there is also an extension and comprehension of propositions, which is one of the noblest powers of language, and fits it for expressing, with great ease and expédition, the highest attainments in knowledge of which the human understanding is capable.

160. When the predicate is a genus or a species, the proposition is more or less comprehensive, according as the predicate is so.

Illus. Thus, when I say, *that this seal is gold,* by this single proposition I affirm of it all the properties which that metal is known to have. When I say of any man, that *he is a mathematician,* this appellation comprehends all the attributes that belong to him as an animal, as a man, and as one who has studied mathematics. When I say, that *the orbit of the planet Mercury is an ellipse,* I thereby affirm of that orbit all the properties which Apollonius or other geometricians have discovered, or which may be discovered, of that species of figure.

161. Again, when the subject of a proposition is a genus or a species, the proposition is more or less extensive, according as the subject is.

Illus. Thus, when I am taught, that *the three angles of a plane triangle are equal to two right angles,* this proposition extends to every species of plane triangle, and to every individual plane triangle which has existed, which does exist, or which can exist.

Obs. Such extensive and comprehensive propositions condense human knowledge, and adapt it to the capacity of our minds with great addition to its beauty, and without any diminution to its distinctness and perspicuity.

II. *Of General Conceptions.*

162. Words could have no general signification, unless there had been conceptions in the minds of those who used them, of things that are general; and it is to such that we give the names of *general conceptions.* These conceptions take this denomination, not from the act of the mind in conceiving, which is an individual act, but from the object or thing conceived, which is general.

163. General conceptions are expressed by general terms, that is, by such general words as may be the subject or the predicate of a proposition; and these terms are ei-

ther attributes of things, or they signify *genera* or *species* of things.

164. We have a more distinct conception of the attributes of all the individuals with which we are acquainted, than of the subject to which those attributes belong.

Illus. 1. The conception that we form of any individual body we have access to know, is, that it has length, breadth, and thickness; such a figure, and such a color; that it is hard, or soft, or fluid; that it has such qualities, and is fit for such purposes. If it is a vegetable, we may know where it grows, what is the form of its leaves, and flower and seed; if an animal, what are its natural instincts, its manner of life, and of rearing its young. Of these attributes belonging to this individual, and numberless others, we may surely have a distinct conception; and we shall find words in language by which we can clearly and distinctly express them.

2. If we consider, in like manner, the conception that we form of any individual person of our acquaintance, we shall find it to be made up of various attributes, which we ascribe to him; such as, that he is the son of such a man, the brother of such another, that he has such an employment or office, such a fortune, that he is tall or short, well or ill made, comely or ill favored, young or old, married or unmarried; to this we may add his temper, his character, his abilities, and perhaps some anecdotes of his history. Such is the conception we form of individual persons of our acquaintance; by such attributes we describe them to those who know them not; and by such attributes historians give us a conception of the personages of former times; nor is it possible to describe them in any other way.

Corol. All the distinct knowledge we have or can have of any individual, is the knowledge of its attributes, for we know not the essence of any individual; and indeed this seems to be beyond the reach of the human faculties.

165. Now, every attribute is what the ancients called an *universal.* It is, or may be, common to various individuals; and, on this account, attributes are expressed by *general words.*

Obs. 1. It appears, likewise, from every man's experience, that he may have as clear and distinct a conception of such attributes as we have named, and of innumerable others, as he can have of any individual to which they belong.

2. Indeed, all that we distinctly conceive about individuals is about their attributes. It is true we conceive a subject to which they belong; but of this subject, whether it be body or mind, when its attributes are set aside, we have but an obscure and relative conception.

166. The other class of general terms are those that signify the *genera* and *species,* into which we divide and

subdivide things.   And if we be able to form distinct conceptions of attributes, it cannot surely be denied that we have
distinct conceptions of *genera* and *species;* because they are
only collections of attributes, which we conceive to exist in
a subject, and to which we give a general name.   If the attributes comprehended under that general name be distinctly
conceived, the thing meant by the name must be distinctly
conceived ; and the name may be justly attributed to every
individual that has those attributes.

Illus. Thus, we can conceive distinctly what it is to have wings,
to be covered with feathers, to lay eggs. Suppose, then, we give the
name of *bird* to every animal that has these three attributes. And if
this be admitted to be the definition of a bird, there is nothing that we
can conceive more distinctly ; for undoubtedly our conception of the
animal is as distinct as our notion of the attributes which are common to the species. If we had never seen a bird, and can but be
made to understand the definition, we can easily apply it, without
danger of mistake, to every individual of the species.

167. When things are divided and subdivided by men of
science, and names given to the *genera* and *species,* those
names are defined.

Illus. Thus, the genera and species of plants, and of other natural
bodies, are accurately defined by writers in the various branches of
natural history ; so that, to all future generations, the definition will
convey a distinct notion of the genus or species defined.

168. When we meet with words signifying genera and
species of things, which have a meaning somewhat vague
and indistinct, so that they who speak the same language
do not always use them in the same sense, we may rest
assured that there is no definition of them which has authority.

Illus. Thus, a man may know, that when he applies the name of
beast to a *lion* or a *tiger ;* and the name of *bird* to an *eagle* or a *turkey,*
he speaks properly ; but whether a *bat* be a bird or a beast, he may be
uncertain. If of a beast and of a bird there was any accurate definition, of sufficient authority, he could be at no loss. And, strange as
it may seem, legislators have seldom or never thought fit to give the
definition of a man.
Corol. A *genus* or *species,* being a *collection of attributes,* conceived
to exist in *one subject,* a definition is therefore the only way to prevent
any addition or diminution of its ingredients in the conception of
different persons ; and when there is no definition that can be appealed
to as a standard, the name will hardly retain precision in its sig
nification.

169. To conceive the meaning of a general word, and to conceive that which it signifies, is the *sam thing.*   We conceive

distinctly the meaning of general terms, therefore we conceive distinctly that which they signify. But such terms do not signify any individual, but what is common to *many* individuals; therefore we have a distinct conception of things common to many individuals;—that is, we have distinct *general conceptions*.

170. We must here beware of the ambiguity that is sometimes thrown around the word *conception* in popular language, which sometimes makes it signify *the act of the mind in conceiving*, sometimes the *thing conceived*, which is the object of that act. When the word is taken in the first sense, every act of the mind is an individual act: the *universality*, therefore, *is* not in the act of the mind, but *in the object*, or thing conceived. The thing conceived is an attribute common to many subjects, or it is a genus or a species common to many individuals.

Illus. Suppose we conceive a triangle; that is, a plane figure terminated by three right lines. He that understands this definition distinctly, has a distinct conception of a triangle. But a triangle is not an individual; it is a species. The act of my mind in conceiving it is an individual act, and has a real existence; but the thing conceived is general, and cannot exist without other attributes, which are not included in the definition. Every triangle that really exists must have a certain length of sides and measure of angles; it must besides have place and time; but the definition of a triangle includes neither existence, nor any of those attributes; and therefore they are not included in the conception of a triangle, which cannot be accurate if it comprehended more than the definition.

Corol. Thus it appears to be evident, that we have general conceptions that are clear and distinct, both of attributes of things and of genera and species of things.

III. *Of general Conceptions formed by analyzing Objects.*

171. The operations of the mind, by which we are enabled to form general conceptions, appear to be three:

First. The resolving or analyzing a subject into its known attributes, and giving a name to each attribute, which name shall signify that attribute, and nothing more.

Secondly. The observing of one attribute, or more attributes than one, to be common to many objects. The first is by philosophers called *abstraction;* the second may be called *generalizing;* but both are commonly included under the name of *abstraction.*

A *third* operation of the mind, by which we form abstract conceptions, is the combining into one whole a certain number of those attributes of which we have formed abstract no-

tions, and giving a name to that combination. It is thus
we form abstract notions of the genera and species of
things.

172. There is nothing with regard to abstraction, strictly
so called, that is either difficult to be understood or practised.

Illus. What can be more easy than to distinguish the different attributes which we know to belong to any subject? In a man, for instance, to distinguish his size, his complexion, his age, his fortune, his
birth, his profession, and twenty other things that belong to him. To
think and speak of those things with understanding, is surely within
the reach of every man endowed with human faculties.

173. There may be distinctions that require nice discernment, or an acquaintance with the subject that is not
common.

Illus. Thus, a critic in painting may discern the style of Raphael or
Titian, when another man could not. A lawyer may be acquainted
with many distinctions in crimes, and contracts, and actions, which
never entered the head of a man who has not studied law. One man
may excel another in the talent of distinguishing, as he may in memory or in reasoning; but there is a certain degree of this talent, without
which a man could have no title to be considered a reasonable creature.

174. We may in our conception, with perfect ease, distinguish and disjoin attributes, which cannot be actually
separated in the subject.

Illus. Thus, in a body, we can distinguish its solidity from its extension, and its weight from both. In extension, we can distinguish
length, breadth, and thickness, yet none of these can be separated
from the body, or from one another.

175. There may be attributes belonging to a subject, and
inseparable from it, of which we have no knowledge, and
consequently no conception; but this does not hinder us
from conceiving distinctly those of its attributes which we
do know.

Illus. Thus, all the properties of a circle are inseparable from the
nature of a circle, and may be demonstrated from its definition; yet a
man may have a perfectly distinct notion of a circle, who knows very
few of those properties belonging to it which mathematicians have
described; and a circle has, probably, many properties which mathematicians never dreamed of.

Corol. It is therefore certain, that attributes, which, in their nature,
are absolutely inseparable from their subject, and from one another,
may be disjoined in our conception; one cannot exist without the
other, but one can be conceived without the other

IV. *Of the Operation of Generalizing.*

176. We proceed now to consider the operation of generalizing, which is nothing but the observing of one attribute, or more attributes than one, to be common to many subjects.

Illus. There are many men above six feet high, and many below that height; many men are rich, many poor; many born in Britain, many born in France. But here, size, fortune, and country, are attributes. There are, therefore, innumerable attributes which are common to many individuals; and if this be what the schoolmen called *universale a parte rei*, we may affirm, with certainty, that there are such universals.

177. There are some attributes expressed by general words, and of these, this position may seem more doubtful; as, for instance, the qualities which are inherent in their several subjects. It may be said that every subject hath its own qualities, and that which is the quality of one subject cannot be the quality of another subject.

Illus. 1. Thus, the whiteness of the sheet of paper that I write upon cannot be the whiteness of another sheet, though both are called white. The weight of one guinea is not the weight of another guinea, though both are said to have the same weight.

2. To this we answer, that the whiteness of this sheet is *one thing*, whiteness is *another;* the *first* signifies an *individual quality really existing*, and is not a general conception, though it be an abstract one; the *second* signifies a *general conception*, which implies *no existence*, but which, in the same sense, may be predicated of every thing that is white.

3. On this account, if any one should say, that the whiteness of this sheet is the whiteness of another sheet, every one perceives this to be absurd; but when he says both sheets are white, this is true and perfectly understood. The conception of whiteness implies no existence; it would remain the same, though every thing in the universe that is white were annihilated.

Corol. 1. It appears, therefore, that the general names of qualities, as well as of other attributes, are applicable to many individuals in the same sense, which cannot be if there be not general conceptions signified by such names.

2. It appears further, that, since no individual can have a plural number (*Art.* 154. *Illus.*), as soon as a child can say with understanding, that he has two brothers or two sisters; as soon as he can use the plural number, *so* soon must he have general conceptions.

178. As there are not two individuals in nature that agree in every thing, so there are very few that do not agree in some things.

Illus. 1. We take pleasure, from our earliest years, in observing such agreements; and one branch of what we call *wit*, which, when innocent, gives pleasure to every good man consists in discovering unexpected agreements in things. Thus, the author of Hudibras could discern a property common to the *morning* and a *boiled lobster*, which both turn from *black* to *red*. And Swift could see something common to *wit* and an *old cheese*. (See *Art.* 213. *Illus.*)

2. Such agreements may show wit; but there are innumerable agreements of things which cannot escape the notice of the lowest understanding; such as agreements in color, magnitude, figure, features, time, place, age, and so forth. And these agreements are the foundation of so many common attributes, which are found in the rudest languages.

179. The ancient philosophers called those *universals*, or *predicables*, and endeavored to reduce them to five classes: namely, *genus*, *species*, *specific difference*, *properties*, and *accidents*.

180. The proneness of mankind to form general conceptions, is seen from the case of metaphor and of the other figures of speech, grounded on similitude.

Illus. Similitude is nothing else but an agreement of the objects compared in one or more attributes; and if there be no attribute common to both, there can be no similitude. (See *Book* IV. of my Grammar of Rhetoric for a complete illustration of this matter.)

181. Sometimes the name of an individual is given to a general conception, and thus the name of an individual, by being applied to his attributes, instead of his person, becomes generalized.

Illus. 1. Thus, Shylock, in the Merchant of Venice, says:

A Daniel come to judgment; yea, a Daniel!

In this speech *a Daniel* is an attribute, or an *universal*.

2. And when we say of any eminent mathematician or astronomer, that "he is *a Newton*," we generalize the name of the individual *Newton;* and it thus becomes an attribute or *universal*

3. In the first example, the character of Daniel, as a man of singular wisdom; and in the second, that of Newton, as an eminent mathematician or astronomer, is abstracted from his person, and considered as capable of being attributed to other persons.

182. Upon the whole, these two operations of abstracting and generalizing, appear to be common to all men that have understanding. The practice of them is, and must be, familiar to every man that uses language; but it is one thing to practise them, and another to explain how they are performed; as it is one thing to see, and another to explain how we do see.

Illus. Thus, when I consider a billiard ball, its *color* is *one attribute*, which I signify by calling it *white;* its *figure* is *another*, which is signified by calling it *spherical;* the firm *cohesion* of its parts is signified by calling it *hard;* its *recoiling*, when it strikes a hard body, is signified by its being called *elastic;* its *origin*, being part of the tooth of an *elephant*, is signified by calling it *ivory;* and its *use*, by calling it a billiard *ball*.

Corol. The words whereby each of those attributes is signified, have distinct meanings, and under these meanings they are applicable to many individuals. They signify not any individual thing, but attributes common to many individuals ; and it is within the capacity of a child to understand them perfectly, and to apply them properly to every individual in which they are found.

V. *General Conceptions formed by Combinations.*

183. As, by an intellectual analysis of objects, we form general conceptions of single attributes (which, of all conceptions that enter into the human mind, are the most simple), so, by combining several of these into one parcel, and giving a name to that combination, we form general conceptions that may be very complex, and at the same time very distinct.

Illus. 1. Thus, one who, by analyzing extended objects, has got the simple notions of a point, a line—straight or curved—an angle, a surface, a solid, can easily conceive a plane surface terminated by four equal straight lines, meeting in four points at right angles To this species of figure he gives the name of a *square.* In like manner, he can conceive a solid terminated by six equal squares, and give it the name of a *cube.* A square, a cube, and every name of mathematical figure, is a general term, expressing a complex general conception, made by a certain combination of the simple elements into which we analyze extended bodies. The definition contains the whole essence of the figure defined ; and every property that belongs to it may be deduced by demonstrative reasoning from the definition. It is not a thing that *exists*, for then it would be an individual ; but it is a thing that is *conceived* without regard to existence.

2. A farm, a manor, a parish, a county, a kingdom, are complex general conceptions, formed by various combinations and modifications of inhabited territory, under certain forms of government.

3. Different combinations of military men form the notions of a company, a regiment, a brigade, an army.

4. The several crimes which are the objects of criminal law, such as theft, murder, robbery, piracy, are only certain combinations of human actions defined in criminal law, and which it is found convenient to apprehend under one name, and consider as one thing.

184. When we observe that nature, in her animal, vegetable, and inanimate productions, has formed many individuals that agree in many of their qualities and attributes, we are led by natural instinct to expect their agreement in other qualities, which we have not had occasion to perceive.

Illus. Thus, a child, who has once burned his finger, by putting it in the flame of a candle, expects the same event to happen if he puts it

G

in the flame of another candle, or in any flame, and is thereby led to think that the quality of burning belongs to all flame.

Obs. This instinctive induction is not justified by the rules of logic, and it sometimes leads us into harmless mistakes, which experience may afterwards correct ; but it preserves us from innumerable dangers to which we are exposed.

185. We have noticed, in this place, this principle in human nature, because the distribution of the productions of nature into *genera* and *species* becomes, on account of this principle, more generally useful.

Illus. 1. The physician expects that the *rhubarb* which has never been tried will have the like medical virtues with that which he has prescribed on former occasions. Two parcels of rhubarb agree in certain sensible qualities, from which agreement they are both called by the same general name *rhubarb.* Therefore, it is expected that they will agree in their medical virtues. And as experience has discovered certain virtues in one parcel, or in many parcels, we presume, without experience, that the same virtues belong to all parcels of rhubarb that shall be used.

2. If a traveller meets a horse, an ox, or a sheep, which he never saw before, he is under no apprehension, believing these animals to be of a species that is tame ; but he dreads a lion, a bear, or a tiger, because they are of a fierce and ravenous species.

Corol. We have, therefore, a strong and rational inducement, both to distribute natural substances into classes, *genera* and *species*, under general names ; and, moreover, to do this with all the accuracy and distinctness with which we are capable ; for the more accurate our divisions are made, and the more distinctly the several species are defined, the more accurately we may rely, that the several qualities which we find in one individual, or in a few individuals, will be found in all the individuals of the same species.

186. Every *species* of natural substances, which has a name in language, is an *attribute* of many individuals, and is itself a combination of more simple attributes, which we observe to be common to those individuals. And almost all the words of every language signify combinations of more simple general conceptions, which men have found proper to bind up, as it were, in one parcel, by being designated by one name.

187. There are, however, some general conceptions, which may more properly be called *compositions*, or *works of mere combination*.

Illus. 1. Thus, one may conceive a machine which never existed. He may conceive an air in music, a poem, a plan of architecture, a constitution of government, a plan of conduct in private or in public life, a discourse, a tragedy, a comedy, a treatise on some science or art. Such compositions are things conceived in the mind of the

author, not individuals that really exist; and the same general conception which the author had, may be communicated to others by language. Thus, the OCEANA of *Harrington* was conceived in the mind
of its author. The materials of which it is composed, are things conceived, not things that existed. His senate, his popular assembly, his
magistrates, his elections, are all conceptions of his mind, and the
whole is one complex conception. And the same may be said of every
work of the human understanding.

2. The works of God, on the contrary, are works of creative power,
not of understanding only. They have a real existence. Our conceptions of them are, however, partial and imperfect. But of the
works of the human understanding our conception may be perfect and
complete. They are nothing but what the author conceived, and what
he can express by language, so as to convey his conception perfectly
to men like himself. But these works of the human understanding
are the objects of judgment and taste, rather than of bare conception
or simple apprehension.

188. To return, therefore, to those complex conceptions,
which are formed merely by combining others that are more
simple, let us observe, that nature has given us the power of
combining such simple attributes, and such a number of them,
as we find proper; and of giving one name to that combination, and considering it as one object of thought.

Illus. The simple attributes of things, which fall under our observation, are not so numerous, that they might not all have names in a
copious language; but to give names to all the combinations that
can be made of two, three, or more of those attributes, would be impossible. The most copious languages have names but for a very
small part of them.

Corol. We conclude, therefore, that there are either certain common
occurrences of human life, which dispose men, out of an infinite
number that might be found, to form certain combinations rather than
others. And nature, in a manner, points out those simple ideas which
are most proper to be united into a complex one, not solely by the
relations between simple ideas, of contiguity, causation, and resemblance, but rather by the fitness of the combinations we make, to aid
our own conceptions, and to convey them easily and agreeably to
others by written or spoken language.

189. The end and use of language lead men that have
common understanding to form such complex notions as
are proper for expressing their wants, their thoughts, their
desires; and in every language we shall find these to be the
complex notions that have names.

Illus. 1. In the rudest languages, men must have occasion to form
the general notions of man, woman, father, mother, son, daughter,
sister, brother, neighbor, friend, enemy, and many others, to express
the common relations of one person to another.

2. If they are employed n *hunting* and *fishing*, they must have

general terms to express the various operations of the chase, the stream, the lake, or the sea. Their houses and clothing will furnish another set of general terms, to express the materials, the workmanship, and the excellencies and defects of those fabrics.

3. The arts of *agricu'ture* and *pasturage* will give occasion to other general terms for communicating thoughts peculiar to those arts; and the invention of those terms, as far as the shepherd or the farmer finds them necessary, requires no other talent but that degree of understanding which is common to men.

4. With *commerce* have originated the notions of debtor and creditor, of profit and loss, of account, balance, stock on hand, and many other terms equally general.

5. To *navigation* are owing the notions of latitude, longitude, course, distance run, windward, leeward; as well as those notions which we have of ships, and their various parts, furniture, and operations.

6. The *anatomist* has his names for the various similar and dissimilar parts of the human body, and words to express their figure, position, structure, and use. The *physician* must have names also for the various diseases of the body, their causes, symptoms, and the means of cure.

7. The grammarian, the logician, the critic, the rhetorician, the moralist, the naturalist, the mechanic, and, in a word, every man that professes any art or science, must have general terms for expressing his sentiments in every branch of the knowledge he would communicate to others.

190. Discoveries in nature, art, and science, give rise to new combinations and new words, the invention of which is easy to those who have a distinct notion of the thing to be expressed; and such words are readily adopted, and receive the public sanction, because the most necessary and useful arts are common property—because the important parts of human knowledge are common property; and, among civilized nations, their several languages will be fitted to express these new complex notions and new names, which will spread as far as the invention or discovery becomes known.

191. What is peculiar to a nation in its customs, manners, or laws, will give occasion to complex notions and words peculiar to the language of that nation.

Illus. Hence it is easy to see why an *impeachment* and an *attainder* in the English language, and *ostracism* in the Greek language, have not names answering to them in other languages.

Corol. Whence it would appear, that utility, not the associating qualities of ideas (*Corol. Art.* 18.), most frequently lead men to form only certain combinations, and to give names to them in language, while they neglect an infinite number that might be formed.

192. The common occurrences of life, in the intercourse of men, and in their occupations, give occasion to many complex notions.

Illus. 1. Thus men have formed the complex notions of eating, drinking, dressing, sleeping, walking, riding, running, buying, selling, ploughing, sowing, a dance, a fair, a feast, a wedding, a burial, war, a battle, victory, triumph, peace; and other words without number.

2. Such things must frequently be the subject of conversation; and if we had not a more compendious way of expressing them than by a detail of all the simple notions which they comprehended, we should lose the benefit of speech; for who, for example, to communicate the complex notion which the word war gives civilized men, would ever go about gravely to tell us, " The consideration of safety leads to the invention of arms, and places of retreat. The earliest weapons were men's fists, then clubs, slings, and bows and arrows. To these succeeded, in process of time, the spear and the sword, joined to the buckler and the shield; fire-arms, called matchlocks, cannon, and then musketry and rockets. But the desire of retreats gave rise to fortification; and the art of war, in every age, must be accommodated to the species of arms, engines and methods of fortification in use."—Yet even this roundabout meaning of the complex notion we have of the general term war, hath not included companies, regiments, brigades, armies; magazines of provisions, commissaries; barracks, camps; army contractors, army agents, army accoutrement makers; a commander in chief, loans to government to carry on the war, and a thousand other terms, not one of which is simple, are all component parts of the complex notion which the experience of our own times gives us of that detestable word *war.*

3. The different talents, dispositions, and habits of men in society, have in every language general names; such as wise, foolish, knowing, ignorant, proud, vain.

4. In every operative art, the tools, instruments, materials, the work produced, and the various excellencies or defects of these, must have general names.

5. Technical terms in the sciences make another class of general names of complex notions; as in mathematics, axiom, definition, problem, theorem, corollary, scholium, lemma.

6. The various relations of persons and of things, which cannot escape the observation of men in society, lead them to many complex general notions; such as, father, brother, friend, enemy, master, servant, property, theft, rebellion.

7. In all the languages of mankind, not only the writings and discourses of the learned, but the conversation of the vulgar, is almost entirely made up of general words, which are the signs of general conceptions, either simple or complex. And in every language, we find the terms signifying complex notions to be such, and only such, as the use of language requires.

193. A very large class of complex terms are those by which we name the species, genera, and tribes of natural substances. Utility leads to the adoption of these general names, and nature directs us in combining the attributes which are included under any specific name; but in forming other combinations of mixed modes and relations, the

6 *

actions or thoughts of men, or the occurrences of life, bring
the ingredients t gether.

Illus. We form a general notion of those attributes wherein many
individuals agree. To this combination we give a specific name,
which is common to all substances, having those attributes, which
either do or may exist. The specific name comprehends neither more
nor fewer attributes than we find proper to put into its definition. It
comprehends not time, nor place, nor even existence, though there
can be no individual without these.

194. Without some general knowledge of the qualities of
natural substances, human life would not be preserved.
And there can be no general knowledge of this kind, without
reducing them to species under specific names.

Illus. For this reason, among the rudest nations, we find names for
fire, water, earth, air, mountains, fountains, rivers; for the kinds of
vegetables which those nations use; for the animals which they hunt
or tame, or which are found useful or hurtful. Each of those names
signifies, in general, a substance having a certain combination of attributes. The name must therefore be common to all substances in
which those attributes are found.

195. As the knowledge of nature advances, more species
of natural substances are observed, and their useful qualities
discovered. And in order that this important part of human
knowledge may be communicated, and handed down to future generations, it is not sufficient that the species have
names;—the fluctuating state of language does not permit
general names always to retain the same precise signification;—hence the necessity of definitions, in which men are
disposed to acquiesce.

Illus. 1. To give names and accurate definitions of all the known
species of substances is necessary, in order to form a distinct language
concerning them, and consequently to facilitate our knowledge respecting them, and to convey it to future generations.

2. Every species that is known to exist ought to have a name; and
that name ought to be defined by such attributes as serve best to distinguish the species from all others.

3. Nature invites to this work, by having formed things so as to
make it both easy and important.

For, *first,* We perceive numbers of individual substances so like
in their obvious qualities, that the most unimproved tribes of men consider them as of one species, and give them one common name.

Secondly. The more latent qualities of substances are generally the
same in all the individuals of a species; so that what, by observation
or experiment, is found in a few individuals of a species, is presumed,
and commonly found, to belong to the whole. By this we are enabled,
from particular facts, to draw general conclusions. This kind of induction is indeed the master-key to the knowledge of nature, without

which we could form no general conclusions in that branch of philosophy.

And, *thirdly,* By the very constitution of our nature, we are led, without reasoning, to ascribe to the whole species what we have found to belong to the individuals. It is thus we come to know that fire burns, and that water drowns; that bodies gravitate, and that bread nourishes.

196. The species of the animal and vegetable kingdoms seem to be fixed by nature, by the power which they have of producing their like. And in these, men, in all ages and nations, have accounted the parent and the progeny the same species.

Obs. 1. The differences observed by naturalists, with regard to the species of these two kingdoms, are termed varieties, and may be produced by soil, climate, and culture, and sometimes by monstrous productions, which are, however, comparatively rare.

2. In the inanimate kingdom things have been divided into species, though the limits of these species seem to be somewhat arbitrary; but, from the progress already made, there is ground to hope, that even in this kingdom, as the knowledge of it advances, the various species may be so well distinguished and defined, as to answer every valuable purpose.

197. When the species are so numerous as to burden the memory, it is greatly assisted by distributing them into *genera;* the genera into *tribes;* the tribes into *orders;* and the orders into *classes.* Such a regular distribution of natural substances, by divisions and subdivisions, has got the name of a *system.*

Illus. 1. It is not, however, a system of truths, but a system of general terms with their definitions; and it is not only a great help to the memory, but facilitates very much the definition of the terms. For the definition of the genus is common to all the species of that genus, and is so understood in the definition of each species, without the trouble of repetition. In like manner the definition of a tribe is understood in the definition of every genus, and every species of that tribe; and the same may be said of every superior division.

2. The effect of such a systematical distribution of the productions of nature, is seen in our systems of zoology, botany, and mineralogy; in which a species is accurately defined in a line or two, which, without this systematical arrangement, could hardly be defined in a page.

3. The talent of arranging properly affords the strongest proof of genius, and is entitled to a high degree of praise. There is an intrinsic beauty in arrangement; it captivates the mind and gives pleasure, even abstracting from its utility. The arrangement of an army drawn up for battle, is a grand spectacle; the same number of men crowded together in a fair has no such effect.

4. In order to remove all ambiguity in the names of diseases, and

to advance the healing art, very eminent medical men have now reduced into a systematical order the diseases of the human body, and
given distinct names, and accurate definitions, of the species, *genera,*
orders and classes, into which they distribute them.   And in Paris
there is now a professor of medicine, who, in lecturing to his students
on cutaneous diseases, arranges the patients according to the classes
or varieties of the disease, under trees when the weather will permit, on which a large placard is fixed to indicate the class or variety
of the disease; and when it is necessary for the professor to have a
patient beside him, to afford ocular demonstration of the illustrations
he is giving, in place of calling the patient by his Christian or surname,
the professor calls him by the name of the class to which his disease
belongs.   Such improvements, like the invention of printing, serve
to embalm a most important branch of human knowledge, and to preserve it from being corrupted or lost.

CHAPTER VII.

OF THE ASSOCIATION OF IDEAS, OR COMBINATION.

198. ASSOCIATION, or the combination of ideas, is the
faculty by which we connect objects together, according to
various relations, essential or accidental, so that they are
suggested to us, the one by the other.

Obs. It is matter of the most familiar observation, that we are apt
to connect together the various objects of our thoughts according to
some real or supposed relations which we observe among them; so
that they come afterwards to be suggested to the mind, the one by
the other.   By the faculty of *abstraction* we analyze individual
objects, so as to make their various qualities and attributes separate
subjects of our thoughts; by the faculty of *combination,* we form
these objects into various classes, or groups, according to some observed
resemblance among them, or we connect together certain individuals
which have no real relation to one another, merely on account of some
accidental circumstance which has occasioned them to be present to
our thoughts at the same moment.   Both faculties are eminently subservient to the advancement of our knowledge, and the progress of
scientific investigation; the object of which is, to ascertain those
general laws, or first principles, according to which the phenomena
of whole classes of beings are regulated.

199. Association, or the combination of ideas, naturally
divides itself into two parts; the first, as it relates to the
influence of association, in regulating the succession of our
thoughts; the second, as it relates to its influence on the
intellectual powers, and on the moral character, by the more

intimate and indissoluble combinations which it leads us to form in infancy and early youth.

200. The influence of association in regulating the *succession of our thoughts*, is a fact familiar to all men : that *one thought is often suggested to the mind by another ;* and that *the sight of an external object often recalls former occurrences*, and *revives former feelings*, are facts which have never been disputed by those who speculate least on the principles of their nature.

Illus. 1. Travelling along a road that we have formerly traversed with a friend, the particulars of the conversation in which we were then engaged are frequently suggested to us by the objects with which we meet. A field, a house, a plantation, a stream, will suggest the conversation, and the arguments which were discussed start like apparitions to our mind's eye, or recur spontaneously to the memory.

2. On the same general law of our nature, are obvious the connection formed in our mind between the different words of a language and the ideas they denote ; that between the different words of a discourse we have committed to memory ; and that between the notes of a piece of music in the mind of the musician.

201. The influence of perceptible objects, in reviving former thoughts and former feelings, is peculiarly remarkable.

Illus. " Whilst we were at dinner," says Captain King, " in this miserable hut, on the banks of the river Awatska, the guests of a people with whose existence we had before been scarce acquainted, and at the extremity of the habitable globe, a solitary, half-worn pewter spoon, whose shape was familiar to us, attracted our attention ; and, on examining it, we found it stamped on the back with the word *London.* I cannot pass over this circumstance in silence, out of gratitude for the many pleasant thoughts, the anxious hopes, and tender remembrances, it excited in us. Those who have experienced the effects that long absence and extreme distance from their native country, produce on the mind, will readily conceive the pleasure such a trifling incident gave us."

202. The relations in consequence of which association takes place, are either *essential* or *accidental.*

203. Among the *essential* relations, the most remarkable appear to be, 1. *Resemblance ;* 2. *Analogy ;* 3. *Contrariety ;* 4. *Mutual Dependence ;* as of cause and effect, premises and conclusion, means and end, and the like.

204. The *accidental* relations, or the *sources of association*, seem chiefly reducible to the circumstance of the two objects of thought having been presented to the mind together ; or from what the philosophers call the contiguity of time and place, in consequence of which we are led after-

wards to think of them at the same time, and to conceive some real connection between them.

I. *Essential Relations, Sources of Association.*

205. (I.) That RESEMBLANCE is a natural species of relation, and leads us to connect together the objects of our thoughts, is matter of the most familiar observation.

Illus. It is our proneness to trace out this kind of relation, that leads us to give generic names to certain classes of objects ; such as animals, trees, stones, and other things that engage our attention. This was fully illustrated in the last chapter ; and so powerfully are we prompted to this exercise of our faculties, that we are in much greater danger of supposing resemblances between objects which are essentially different, than of not discovering a resemblance where it really exists. The gratification, however, which nature has attached to the exercise of this act of the mind, is of the greatest advantage in promoting our knowledge ; for by continually seeking to discover new points of likeness in the objects of nature, we are led to reduce them to a few simple classes, and to discover the general laws by which their phenomena are regulated.

206. Many of the *pleasures of taste* may be ascribed to the gratification accompanying the discovery of resemblance.

Illus. Thus, in *comedy*, much of the pleasure of an audience arises from the resemblance they discover in the sentiment, the action, and the business of the piece, with what they have already heard, or seen, or engaged in themselves.

207. The merit of *wit* appears to be justly placed in tracing remote and unexpected resemblances among the objects of our thoughts, which, from their novelty and singularity, are calculated to excite admiration. (See *Art.* 178. *Illus.* 1 *and* 2.)

Illus. Sublimity elevates, beauty charms, wit diverts : the first enraptures and dilates the soul ; the second diffuses over it serene delight ; the third tickles the fancy, and throws the spirits into an agreeable vibration. And the limning of wit differs from rhetorical painting in two respects : one is, that the *latter* requires not only a resemblance in that particular on which the comparison is founded, but demands also a general similitude in the nature and quality of that which is the basis of the imagery, to that which is the theme of discourse ; whereas the *former*, though requiring an exact likeness in the first particular, demands, in the second, a contrariety rather, or remoteness. Rhetorical painting, in respect of dignity, or the impression it would make upon the mind, brings together things homogeneous ;—thus, whatever has magnificence, must be portrayed by whatever is magnificent ; objects of importance by objects of importance ; such as have grace by things graceful. The limning of wit, like an enchantress, exults in reconciling contradictions, and in hitting on that special light and attitude wherein you can discover an unexpected similarity in objects which, at first sight, appear the most dissimilar and heterogeneous : thus high and low are coupled, humble and superb, momentous and trivial, common and extraordinary. (*Ex. Art.* 222.)

Corol. Wit, therefore, implies a power of calling up at pleasure the ideas which it combines, and the entertainment it affords is founded on the surprise it creates ; for a *bon mot* pleases more in conversation than in print, and premeditated wit never fails to disgust ; and he who sports a *bon mot* at the game of *cross purposes* doth not fail to create amusement ; but, in such cases, our pleasure seems chiefly to arise from the surprise we feel at so extraordinary a coincidence between a question and an answer coming from persons who had no direct communication with each other.

208. The pleasing effect of simile, poetical allusion, metaphor, and allegory, also arises, in a great measure, from the same cause ; although, very generally, in all these cases, the principle of relation, or association, is rather reducible to analogy than to resemblance ; as there is more room for ingenuity and the exercise of fancy, in tracing a similarity of effects or general consequences, which constitutes an analogy, than in discovering a mere likeness, or precise identity.

Illus. In the case of poetical imagination, it is the association of ideas that supplies the materials out of which the combinations are formed ; and when such an imaginary combination is become familiar to the mind, it is the association of ideas that connects its different parts together, and unites them into one whole.

Corol. 1. The association of ideas, therefore, although perfectly distinct from the power of imagination, is immediately and essentially subservient to all its exertions.

2. A man whose habits of association present to him a number of resembling or analogous ideas, for illustrating or embellishing a subject, we call a man of *fancy* :—it is therefore the province of *fancy* to collect materials for the imagination ; and, consequently, the latter power presupposes the former, while the former does not necessarily suppose the latter :—but for an effort of imagination, other powers are necessary, as of taste and of judgment, without which nothing can be produced that will be a source of pleasure to others. The power of fancy supplies the poet with metaphorical language, and with all the analogies which are the foundation of his allusions ; but it is the power of imagination that creates the complex scenes he describes, and the fictitious characters he delineates. Hence, to fancy we apply the epithets of rich and luxuriant ; to imagination, those of beautiful and sublime.

209. Resemblance of sound is one pretty copious source of this kind of gratification. This resemblance is found in the structure of modern verse, which, in most European languages, has not only the accompaniment of rhythm, or a measured number of long and short, or emphatic and unem-

phatic syllables, but likewise that of rhyme, or a recurrence of resembling sounds at the termination of its lines.

Obs. This accompaniment of verse was rejected by the poets of Greece and Rome, which seems to have arisen from its being considered as of no value, on account of the great facility with which it might have been accomplished in the ancient languages. But rhyme, as I have sufficiently shown in my Grammar of Rhetoric, appears to have been adopted in the poetical compositions of our Gothic forefathers; and it is likewise found in the poetry of various Eastern nations, as well as of the Indian tribes; so that it is a source of gratification evidently founded in the natural constitution of man.

210. The alliteration which is so common in poetry and proverbial sayings, seems to arise, partly, at least, from associations of ideas founded on the accidental circumstance of two words which express them beginning with the same letter.

Example 1. But thousands die, without or this or that,
Die; and endow a college, or a cat.
POPE'S EPIST.
2. Ward tried on puppies and the poor his drop.
ID. IMIT. OF HORACE.
3. Puffs, powders, patches; bibles, billetdoux.
RAPE OF THE LOCK.

211. The pun, or *paronomasia*, which hath been so generally decried, and yet so universally practised, consists in nothing more than employing a word which is ambiguous either in sense or sound, and of which both the meanings are suggested at once, by the way in which it is used. It gratifies, therefore, as an example of a newly-discovered resemblance.

Example. The French call this figure *jeu de mots ;* and the following examples are puns from Milton: "Which tempted our attempt." PAR. LOST, B. I. "To begin at the Almighty's throne, beseeching or besieging." B. V.
Obs. The gravity of that man is not to be envied who believes the assertion of Lord Chesterfield, that "genuine wit never made any man laugh since the creation of the world ;"—for, banishing that noisy and convulsive agitation which is excited by the ludicrous, genuine wit (and there is none such without some mixture of humor) does unquestionably create a smile of surprise and wonder, appropriated to its flashes.

212. (II.) ANALOGY is a copious source of combination among our thoughts. It may be defined a similarity, or correspondence, not of the objects of thoughts themselves, but of their general effects or consequences. (See *Art.* 74. and *Illus.*)

Illus. Thus, the spring of the year, or the morning of the day, suggests to our thoughts the period of infancy, or youth; as winter, or evening, is naturally associated with old age. The mind is prone to trace out analogies, which are, after all, but resemblances of a particular kind; and, in many cases, it may fancy them to exist without any real foundation. Of this we have the most remarkable example in the so generally conceived analogy between the properties of body and those of mind (*Art.* 83); the erroneousness of which we have already had occasion to remark. (*Corol. Art.* 85.)

213. The relations observable in the effusions of wit, in. poetical allusion, simile, metaphor, and allegory, belong rather to the combinations of analogy, than to those of resemblance; and in tracing the former there is much more ingenuity than in tracing the latter.

Illus. Thus, the well-known similitude of Hudibras—

" And now, like lobster boil'd, the morn
From black to red began to turn"—

exhibits an analogy certainly very remote from common apprehension. (See *Art.* 178. *Illus.* 1.)

214. An allusion pleases by presenting a new and a beautiful image to the mind. The analogy or resemblance between this image and the principal subject, is agreeable of itself, and is indeed necessary to furnish an apology for the transition which the writer makes, but the pleasure is wonderfully heightened, when the new image thus presented is a beautiful one.

Illus. The following allusion, from one of Home's tragedies, seems to unite every excellence :

Hope and fear, alternate, sway'd his breast,
Like light and shade upon a waving field,
Coursing each other, when the flying clouds
Now hide, and now reveal, the sun.

Here the analogy is perfect; not only between *light* and *hope*, and between *darkness* and *fear*, but between the rapid succession of *light* and *shade*, and the momentary impulses of these opposite emotions; while, at the same time, the new image which is presented to us, recalls one of the most pleasing and impressive incidents in rural scenery ; namely,

Light and shade upon a waving field,
Coursing each other, when the flying clouds
Now hide, and now reveal, the sun.

215. The discovery of such analogies has the twofold merit of embellishing and illustrating a subject ; and they are, therefore, with propriety, introduced, not only into the amusing kinds of composition, but also into those of the grave and didactic form.

7

Illus. The following are happy instances of the effects of such well-chosen analogies, though the writings in which they occur are not professedly didactic

Example 1. To endeavor to work upon the vulgar with fine sense, is like attempting to cut blocks of marble with a razor.—POPE.

2. Did you ever observe one of your clerks cutting his paper with a blunt knife ? Did you ever know the knife to go the wrong way ? Whereas, if you had used a razor or a penknife, you had odds against you of spoiling the whole sheet.—SWIFT.

The dean very happily employs this allusion to illustrate the diversity between genius and ordinary useful abilities.

216. The pleasure we receive from analogy arises very much from the illustration which it affords of the author's ideas.

Illus. Thus, Cicero, and after him Locke, in illustrating the difficulty of attending to the subjects of our consciousness, have compared the *mind* to the eye, which sees every object around it, but is invisible to itself. To have compared the *eye*, in this respect, to the *mind*, would have been absurd.

Again, Pope's comparison of the progress of youthful curiosity, in the pursuits of science, to that of a traveller among the Alps, owes all its beauty to this—the Alps furnish only the *illustration* of the allusion, not the *original* subject.

217. Allusions from material objects, both to the intellectual and the moral worlds, are found chiefly in compositions written under the influence of some particular passion, or which are meant to express some peculiarity in the mind of the author.

Illus. Thus, a melancholy man, who has met with many misfortunes in life, will be apt to moralize on every physical event, and every appearance of nature; because his attention dwells more habitually on human life and conduct than on the material objects around him.

Example. This is the case with the banished duke, in Shakspeare's " As you like it," who, in the language of the poet,

> " Finds tongues in trees, books in the running brooks,
> Sermons in stones, and good in every thing."

But this is plainly a distempered state of mind; and the allusions please, not so much from the analogies they present, as by the picture they give of the character of the person to whom they have occurred.

218. An analogy of the most remote kind, consisting merely in the general effect produced upon the mind, is expressed in the following beautiful similitude of Ossian.

Example. The music of Carryl was like the memory of joys that are past: pleasant and mournful to the soul.

219. (III.) CONTRARIETY, or CONTRAST, is also a common source of combination among our ideas.

Illus. 1. Thus, the darkness of night induces us to think of the splendor of day; and winter's cold turns our thoughts to the heat of summer.

2. It was contrariety that associated in the mind of Xerxes the melancholy idea of mortality and dissolution, with the prospect of his millions in the pride of activity and military splendor, when he lamented that, in a short period of time, not one of them would be found upon the earth.

220. The associating principle of contrast is calculated to suggest the finest poetical transitions.

Illus. 1. Thus, in Goldsmith's Traveller, the transitions are managed with consummate skill; and yet how different from that logical method which would be suited to a philosophical discourse on the state of society in the different parts of Europe! Thus, after describing the effeminate and debased Romans, the poet proceeds to the Swiss :—

> My soul, turn from them—turn we to survey
> Where rougher climes a nobler race display.

And, after painting some defects in the manners of this gallant but unrefined people, his thoughts are led to those of the French :—

> To kinder skies, where gentler manners reign,
> I turn—and France displays her bright domain.

2. The transition which occurs in the following lines, seems to be suggested by the accidental mention of a word; and is certainly one of the happiest in our language :—

> Heavens ! how unlike their Belgic sires of old !
> Rough, poor, content, ungovernably bold !
> War in each breast, and freedom on each brow,
> How much unlike the sons of *Britain* now !—
> ——Fired at the sound, my genius spreads her wing,
> And flies where *Britain* courts the western spring.

221. This bias of the mind for contrast, in its association of ideas, is likewise eminently conducive to the advancement of our knowledge; for it leads us to inquire in what respects the various objects of nature differ from one another, as well as wherein they agree; and thus stimulates us to acquire an accurate knowledge of their properties.

Note. The student may refer back to the illustrations of *Articles* 164, 166, and 168, which, though illustrative of general conceptions, stimulate us to acquire an accurate knowledge of the properties or attributes of nature that differ from one another, or agree in general and characteristic particulars.

222. The relation of contrariety enters pretty largely into the allusions of wit, in conjunction with those of resemblance

or analogy; for this obvious reason, that the combinations
of wit must not be readily discoverable; in other words,
they must partake both of resemblance, or analogy, and of
contrariety.

Illus. That species of wit which constitutes the ludicrous, exhibits a due share of this mixture of resemblance and contrast; for,
according to the most legitimate analysis of the ludicrous, it consists in a mixture of relation and contrariety; or of incongruity in
the parts of an object, or assemblage of related objects. (*Illus.
Art.* 207.)

Example. In the following spirited similitude of Pope, the parent
of the celestials is contrasted by the daughter of night and chaos :
heaven by Grub-street; gods by dunces; and, besides, the parody
which it contains on a beautiful passage of Virgil, adds particular
lustre to this aggrandizement of little things, *or mock majestic.*

> As Berecynthia, while her offspring vie
> In homage to the mother of the sky,
> Surveys around her, in the blest abode,
> An hundred sons, and every son a god,*
> Not with less glory mighty Dulness crowned
> Shall take through Grub-street her triumphant round,
> And, her Parnassus glancing o'er at once,
> Behold an hundred sons, and each a dunce.

223. (IV.) MUTUAL DEPENDENCE is the fourth natura
source of connection among the objects of our thoughts
which we enumerated. If we find one occurrence or phenomenon constantly succeeded by another, it is extremely
natural that the one should be suggested by the other to
our minds. On the same principle, the notion of means
employed, suggests the end which they are designed to
accomplish.

Illus. 1. Thus, when we observe the labors of the husbandman,
we naturally think of the harvest that is to ensue; and the study of
an argument, or a piece of reasoning, leads to the consideration of the
conclusion or conviction which it tends to produce.

2. To this source of combination we, in a great measure, owe
our desire to discover the hidden causes of the phenomena of nature, or the established dependence which these have upon one
another. The philosopher accomplishes this by long and patient
study of nature herself; but the illiterate are sufficiently ready to
assign causes for whatever they see, though experience tells them

---

* The passage in Virgil is this :
> Felix prole virum, qualis Berecynthia mater
> Invehitur curru Phrygias turritu per urbes,
> Læta deûm partu, centum complexa nepotes,
> Omnes cœlicolas, omnes supera alta tenentes.
>   ÆNEIDOS.

that their want of knowledge is a copious source of error in this field of speculation. And to this ignorance of the real dependence of events upon each other, and a proneness to admit a connection where none really exists, must we ascribe the many superstitious observances which prevail among the vulgar, and still more among savage nations.

II. *Accidental Relations, or Sources of Association.*

224. We not only connect the objects of our thoughts together according to those essential and natural relations which we observe among them, but also in consequence of the mere *accidental* circumstances of their having been presented to the mind together. (*Art.* 204.)

Illus. " We agreed," says Cicero, in the introduction to the fifth book *de finibus,* " that we should take our afternoon's walk in the academy, as, at that time of the day, it was a place where there was no sort of company. Accordingly, at the hour appointed, we went to Piso's. We passed the time in conversing on different matters during our short walk from the double gate, till we came to the academy, that justly celebrated spot; which, as we wished, we found in perfect solitude. I know not, said Piso, whether it be a natural feeling, or an illusion of the imagination founded on habit, that we are more powerfully affected by the sight of those places which have been much frequented by illustrious men, than when we either listen to the recital, or read the detail, of their great actions. At this moment I feel that emotion which I speak of. I see before me the perfect form of Plato, who was wont to dispute in this very place; these *gardens* not only *recall him to my memory,* but present *his very person to my senses.* I fancy to myself that *here* stood Speusippus; *there* Xenocrates, and *here,* on *this bench,* sat his disciple Polemo. To me, our ancient *senatehouse seems peopled* with the like visionary forms; for, often, when I enter it, the *shades* of Scipio, of Cato, and of Lælius, and, in particular, of my venerable *grandfather,* rise to my imagination. In short, such is the effect of *local situation* in recalling associated ideas to the mind, that it is not without reason, some philosophers have founded on this principle a species of artificial memory "

Obs. The student will please to observe, that the foregoing illustration shows clearly the difference, also, between the effect of a perception and an idea, in awakening associated thoughts and feelings.

225. This law of association is manifestly of the greatest utility in promoting the exercise of memory; and, indeed, spontaneous or involuntary memory seems entirely to depend on those associations which the mind has previously formed, whether according to natural or accidental relations.

Illus. After time has in some degree reconciled us to the death of a friend, how wonderfully are we affected the first time we enter the house where he lived!—Every thing we see; the apartment where

7 *

he studied ; the chair upon which he sat, recall to us the happiness which we have enjoyed together ; and we should feel a sort of violation of that respect we owe to his memory, to engage in any light or indifferent discourse when such objects are before us.   " That man," says Dr. Johnson, " is little to be envied, whose patriotism would not gain force on the plain of Marathon, or whose piety would not grow warmer among the ruins of Iona."

226. On account of their unlimited range, the accidental or merely arbitrary combinations are extensively useful to the memory ; and what is called *mechanical artificial memory* is founded entirely upon these co ·binatio s.   (See *Illus. Art.* 224.)

Illus. It is, in general, a merely arbitrary relation that subsists between the sign and the thing signified ; as between the letters of the alphabet and the sounds of which they are expressive ; as well as between these sounds, or the various words of a language, and the thoughts which they are intended to denote.   Thus, the whole fabric of language, whether oral or written, rests upon that law of the human constitution, whereby things, which are *repeatedly* presented to the mind *together*, are afterwards suggested, *the one by the other*.   The same may be said of the symbols of the algebraist; the notes of the musician ; and various other like signs.

227. Associations, which are merely *arbitrary*, appear to operate upon the mind with fully as much power as those which are founded in nature.

Illus. The well-known effect of the *national air*, called " RANS DES VACHES," upon the Swiss regiments in foreign lands, in exciting what is emphatically called the *maladie du pays*, furnishes a very striking illustration of the peculiar power of a perception, or of an impression on the senses, to awaken associated thoughts and feelings. And I cannot here omit to mention an anecdote of my late venerable and worthy friend Adam Callendar, who in his younger days had served as an officer in India.   A Highland regiment had been ordered up the country, and on the parade, the bag-piper played the famous air of " *Lochaber no more*."   The effect was not anticipated even by the piper.   The sensibilities of his companions were awakened, and the very men who could rush upon death in all the forms of battle, refused to go, as they thought, further from home ; and the governor-general had too much good sense to call this *maladie du pays* by the ungracious name of mutiny.   In the Peninsula, during the late war, the piper of a Highland regiment was struck in the leg with a bullet, and could not stand; yet, regardless of his wound, did he seat himself on his knapsack, and cheer his comrades to the charge with the martial tune of " Up and War them a' Willie."   It would be an insult to this brave man's virtues to inquire, whether he had associated the idea of victory with his " spirit-stirring lay." (See *Illus. Art.* 142.)

228. The consequences of these arbitrary associations are sometimes exceedingly whimsical ; of which Locke records two remarkable instances.

Illus. 1. The first is, of a person perfectly cured of madness, by a very harsh and offensive operation. The gentleman, who was thus recovered, with great sense of gratitude and acknowledgment, owned the cure, all his life after, as the greatest obligation he could have received; but, whatever gratitude and reason suggested to him, he could never bear the sight of the operator. This has an illustrious parallel! to which it is sufficient to allude.

2. The second instance is of a young gentleman, who having learned to dance, and that to great perfection, but there happened to stand an old trunk in the room where he learned, and the idea of this remarkable piece of household stuff had so mixed itself with the turns and steps of his dances, that though in that chamber he could dance excellently well, yet it was only while the trunk was there; nor could he perform well in any other place, unless that, or some such other trunk, had its due position in the room.

229. The facility with which ideas are associated in the mind, is very different in different individuals; a circumstance this, which lays the foundation of remarkable varieties among men, both in respect of genius and character. In the female mind, ideas seem to be more easily associated together than in the minds of men.

Corol. Hence the liveliness of their fancy, and the superiority they possess in epistolary writing, and in those kinds of poetry, in which the principal recommendations are, ease of thought and ease of expression, delicacy of sentiment and acuteness of feeling. Hence, too, the facility with which they contract or lose habits, and accommodate their minds to new situations. Hence, too, the disposition they have to that species of superstition which is founded on accidental combinations and circumstances.

Example. " I remember," says Dr. Reid, " many years ago, a white ox was brought into the country, of so enormous a size, that people came many miles to see him. There happened, some months after, an uncommon fatality among women in child-bearing. Two such uncommon events following one another, gave a suspicion of their connection, and occasioned a common opinion, among the country people, that the white ox was the cause of this fatality."

Obs. How silly and ridiculous soever this opinion was, it sprung from the same root in human nature, on which all natural philosophy grows, namely, an eager desire to find out connections in things, and a natural, original, and unaccountable propensity to believe, that the connections which we have observed in time past, will continue in time to come.

230. To the law of our constitution, which induces us to form arbitrary connections among the objects of our thoughts, are due many of the errors and prejudices of the human mind in the judgments and decisions of the moral faculty.

Note. The importance of this subject is therefore sufficient to justify its separate illustration, which will form the subject of the next section.

III.   *Of the Influence of Association on our various Judgments.*

231. The influence of ARBITRARY *association* in giving a bias to our opinions and judgments, appears to divide itself into three heads :

First, As it affects the decisions of *Taste*.
Secondly, As it affects the *speculative Opinions* of mankind.
Thirdly, As it influences our *moral Judgments*.

First, as it affects the Decisions of Taste.

232. To the influence of association in regulating the decisions of taste, is to be ascribed the approbation which we bestow upon the dress, pronunciation, language, and manners of the great and the fashionable.

Illus. 1. It is not any intrinsic excellence in the mode itself that causes our approbation, because when it ceases to be the fashion, we cease to approve it, and bestow our approbation on some other mode that now comes to be sanctioned by the adoption of the great.

2. The pronunciation or language of the court may frequently be inferior, in real merit, to that of the provinces ; but the latter is held disreputable, because associated with the ideas of coarseness and vulgarity, while the former is considered reputable on account of the contrary association. (See my Grammar of Rhetoric, Book II., in which the nature and character of the use which gives law to language is fully examined.)

Corol. Thus, the cause of our approbation of whatever is called fashionable, is to be sought in the principle of association alone.

233. The effect of arbitrary association in matters of taste, is still more strongly evinced in the permanent character which it frequently gives to the taste of a nation.

Illus. 1. Thus, the Chinese love a foot, in their women, so small as to be scarcely of any use in walking, for no other reason than this—they have associated with a small foot the notion of delicacy and elegance ; while they despise a foot of the just proportions which nature gives it, because, in their minds, it is associated with mean and vulgar qualities.

2. The same principle serves to explain why, in Holland, France, and indeed in most parts of the world, a style of gardening prevails, which the *better taste* of Englishmen condemns as stiff and unnatural. In those countries, the efforts of skill, artifice, and labor, have become associated with a garden. In Holland, the more visible the exertion of these is rendered, the more admirable, the more beautiful, nay, perfect, is the work rendered. At Versailles, Frenchmen are delighted with the profusion of parterres, terraces, alleys, fountains, statues, formal shrubs, artificial cascades, and grottoes, trees whose foliage is clipped into many fantastic shapes, and hedges

dressed laterally and altitudinally, like to so many regiments of riflemen on parade.

234. The influence of arbitrary association is also manifested in the high value that we set upon the compositions with which we have been familiarized in early youth.

Illus. These are connected, in our minds, with a variety of pleasing occurrences which have happened at that period; and, therefore, acquire a value in our estimation, which they do not intrinsically possess. Thus Addison himself, though so acute a critic, under the bias of this natural prepossession, could find every beauty of Homer or Virgil in the ancient ballad of *Chevy Chase*, of which, undoubtedly, the principal merit is a native and unadorned simplicity. (See *Spectator*, Nos. 70 and 74.)

235. It is upon a similar principle, that the compositions of celebrated authors come to be considered as perfect models of imitation; and their very defects are exalted into beauties, on account of their being so closely combined with those parts of their works which are justly entitled to our admiration.

Illus. Few things have tended more to retard the progress of genuine taste, than this superstitious veneration for great names. In this way the dictates of nature have been made to yield to authority; and the practice of an eminent writer has passed into a law, which none violates with impunity. Hence the necessity that some literary men have conceived themselves under, of choosing models on which to form their style and sentiment, as much so as the architect, who would build a magnificent palace, follows the Grecian or Roman style of his art; or as a painter selects for his study the best masters of the Flemish, the Italian, or the French schools. Bossu, a celebrated French critic, can find no better foundation for the numerous rules which he has given, than the practice of Homer or Virgil, supported by the authority of Aristotle. " Strange," says Lord Kaimes, " that in so long a work, the concordance or disconcordance of these rules with human nature, should never once have entered his thoughts."

Corol. The decisions of the faculty of taste have their foundation in the original constitution of man ; and, as science diffuses her genial influence, the standard of true taste comes gradually to be ascertained; therefore, the cultivation of philosophical criticism must progressively dissipate the prejudices which are so apt to warp our decisions in matters of taste, and correct the influence of arbitrary association.

Secondly, as it affects the speculative Opinions of Mankind.

236. CASUAL *association* unduly influences many of our speculative opinions and conclusions of reasoning.

Illus. The association of ideas, says Mr. Stewart, has a tendency to warp our speculative opinions chiefly in the three following ways.

First, by blending together in our apprehensions things which are really distinct in their nature, so as to introduce perplexity and error into every process of reasoning in which they are involved.

Secondly, by misleading us in those anticipations of the future from the past, which our constitution disposes us to form, and which are the great foundation of our conduct in life.

Thirdly, by connecting in the mind erroneous opinions with truths which irresistibly command our assent, and which we feel to be of importance to human happiness.

237. *First.* The association of ideas has a tendency to warp our speculative opinions, by blending together in our apprehensions things which are really distinct in their nature, so as to introduce perplexity and error into every process of reasoning in which they are involved.

Illus. 1. This branch of the subject embraces our notions of *color* and *extension.* The former of these words expresses that which is the cause of a *sensation* in the mind; the latter denotes a *quality* of an external object; so that there is, in fact, no more connection between the two notions than between those of pain and solidity; and yet, in consequence of our always perceiving extension, at the same time at which the sensation of color is excited in the mind, as when we look upon an extended verdant plain, we find it impossible afterwards to think of that sensation, without conceiving extension along with it.

2. Another intimate association is formed in every mind between the ideas of *space* and time. When we think of an *interval of duration,* we always conceive it analogous to a *line,* and we apply the same language to both subjects. Hence the terms *long* and *short time,* as well as *long* and *short distance.* Now, this apprehended analogy is obviously founded on the association between the ideas of space and time, arising from our always measuring the one by the other.

Example. We measure time by motion, and motion by extension. In an hour, the hand of the clock moves over a certain space; in two hours, over double the space; and so on. Hence the ideas of space and time become intimately united, and we apply to the latter the words *long* and *short, before* and *after,* in the same manner as to the former.

Illus. 3. From an accidental association of ideas arises also the apprehended analogy between the relation which the different notes in the scale of music bear to each other; and from a similar apprehended analogy arises the relation of *superiority* and *inferiority,* in point of position, among material objects.

Corol. In the instances which have now been mentioned, our habits of combining the notions of two things become so strong, that we find it impossible to think of the one without thinking, at the same time, of the other. Hence we may easily conceive the manner in which the association of ideas has a tendency to mislead the judgment, except the mind be accustomed to those discriminations which science requires, and which will not suffer it to be imposed on by that confusion of ideas which warps the judgments of the multitude in moral, religious, and political inquiries.

238. *Secondly.* The association of ideas is a source of speculative error, by misleading us in those anticipations of the future from the past, which are the foundation of our conduct in life.

Illus. 1. The great object of philosophy is *to ascertain the laws* which regulate the succession of events both in the physical and in the moral worlds; in order that, when called upon to act in any particular combination of circumstances, we may be enabled to anticipate the probable course of nature from our past experience, and to regulate our conduct accordingly. Nature has not only given all men a strong disposition to remark, with attention and curiosity, those phenomena which have been observed to happen nearly at the same time, but has beautifully adapted, to the uniformity of her own operations, the laws of association in the human mind. By rendering *contiguity in time* one of our associating principles, she has conjoined together in our thoughts the same events which we have found conjoined in our experience, and has thus accommodated (without any effort on our part) the order of our ideas to that scene in which we are destined to act.

2. The laws of nature, which it is most material for us to know, are exposed to the immediate observation of our senses; and establish, by means of the principle of association, a corresponding order in our thoughts long before the dawn of reason or reflection.

3. This bias of the mind to associate events which have been presented to it nearly at the same time, is, nevertheless, with all its boasted advantages, attended with inconveniences; for among the various phenomena which are continually passing before us, there is a great proportion whose vicinity in time does not indicate a constancy of conjunction; and they who do not distinguish between these two classes of connections, will become a prey to that superstitious disposition which confounds together accidental and permanent connections. Hence the regard which is paid to unlucky days, to unlucky colors, and to the influence of the planets.

Example. An Indian once found himself relieved of a bodily indisposition by a draught of cold water. This man was a second time afflicted with the same disorder, and was desirous to repeat the same remedy. He applied to a philosopher to be informed whether the cure was owing to the water which he had drank, to the shell in which it was contained, to the fountain from which it was taken, to the particular time of the day, or to the particular age of the moon. The philosopher smiled at the Indian's simplicity. A juggler, who was by at the time, overhearing what passed, looked gravely at the sick man, and, with as much pomposity, bade him repeat the experiment. In order, therefore, to ensure the success of the remedy, the Indian very naturally and very wisely copied, as far as he could recollect, every circumstance which accompanied the first application of the water. He made use of the same kind of shell, he drew the water from the same fountain, he held his body in the same posture, and he turned his face to the same point of the horizon. He recovered a second time. At the time of the second experiment, and ever after, all the accidental circumstances in which the first experiment was made, were associated equally, with the effect produced, in the

Indian and in the juggler's mind. The fame of the cure was spread far and wide. The fountain from which the water was drawn was ever after considered as possessed of particular *virtues,* the shell from which it was drank was set apart from vulgar uses, the day on which the experiment was made received a new name, and was deemed lucky; the posture of the body, and the point of the horizon in which the face was held, were also accounted lucky, for the sake of those who might afterwards have occasion to apply the remedy.

Corol. 1. Here, then, is the source of one species of superstition due to the influence of association; and it sufficiently proves how mankind are misled in those anticipations of the future from the past, which are the foundation of their conduct in life.

2. The reasonings we have now used may be extended also to analogous prejudices which warp our opinions respecting the customs and manners of our country; the form and exercise of its government; the execution of its laws, and the administration of justice; our manner of life and course of education; but weakness and versatility of mind, and the same facility of association we have contemplated in the Indian, are sources of national prejudice and national bigotry, among enlightened Europeans.

239. *Thirdly.* We have now to consider the third class of our speculative errors, arising from the association of ideas connecting in the mind erroneous opinions, with truths which irresistibly command our assent, and which we feel to be of importance to our happiness.

Illus. We have seen how all the different circumstances which accompanied the first administration of a remedy, come to be considered as essential to its future success, and are blended together in the conceptions of the mind, without any discrimination of their relative importance; and we shall now show, that whatever tenets and religious ceremonies men have been taught to connect with the religious creed of their infancy, become almost a part of their constitution, by being indissolubly united with truths which are essential to their happiness, and which they are led to reverence and to love with all the best dispositions of the heart.

Example. A young English officer had saved the life of a Brahmin's daughter. The Brahmin grew old and fell sick. On his deathbed he exclaimed to the officer, " Is it possible that he to whose compassion I owe the preservation of my child, and who now soothes my last moments with the consolations of piety, should not believe in the god *Vistnou,* and his nine metamorphoses!"

Here we have all the evidence the thing admits of, that the astonishment of the learned and venerable Brahmin was of a piece with what the rudest of mankind feel when they see the rites of a religion different from their own The Brahmin seemed to question whether there could be any thing worthy in the mind which treated with indifference what awakened in his own breast all its best and sublimest emotions. The peasant views the rites of a religion different from that in which he was educated, with an astonishment as great as if he saw some flagrant breach of the moral duties, or some direct act of impiety to God.

Corol. What has now been said on the nature of religious superstition, may be applied to many other subjects; and in particular to those political prejudices which bias the judgment even of enlightened men in all countries of the world. And with this remark we may therefore conclude here, that as, in ancient Rome, it was regarded as the mark of a good citizen never to despair of the fortunes of the republic;—so the good citizen of the world, the philosopher, and the Christian, whatever may be the political, the scientific, and the religious aspect of their own times, will never despair of the fortunes of the human race; but will act upon the conviction that prejudice, slavery, and corruption—ignorance, error, and speculative mysticism—irreligion, vice, and impiety—must gradually give way to truth, liberty, and virtue; to knowledge, good sense, and happiness; to piety, charity, and benevolence.

Thirdly, of the Influence of arbitrary Associations, as it affects our moral Judgment.

240. Our moral judgments may be modified and even perverted to a certain degree, in consequence of the influence of arbitrary associations; for there is a fashion, not only in matters of taste and speculative inquiry, but even in morality and religion.

Illus. In the same manner in which a person who is regarded as a model of taste, may introduce, by his example, an absurd or fantastical dress, so a man of splendid virtues may attract some esteem also to his imperfections; and, if placed in a conspicuous situation, may render his vices and follies objects of general imitation among the multitude. What a libel on human reason! to be ever swayed by the mere influence of casual association, and the false shame of avowing ourselves habitually the friends of virtue, because knaves have nick-named such tergiversations marks of superior endowments, and proofs of a mind emancipated from vulgar prejudices. (See *Dr. Smith's Theory of Moral Sentiments, for the most luminous views of this part of our subject.*)

241. Again, if we examine the moral and religious opinions which have prevailed in different ages of the world, and among people of different climates and nations, we shall find a striking diversity in many important particulars.

Illus. 1. The ancient heathen and the modern savage enjoin us, while we do all the good we can to our friends, to be equally studious to injure our enemies. The milder precepts of Christianity, on the other hand, exhort us to an unlimited forgiveness of injuries. Among the Romans, suicide was a virtue; among Christians, it is a crime of the deepest dye. The South Sea Islanders, and the ancient Lacedemonians, practised theft without scruple; while, by the laws of Europe it is punished with imprisonment, banishment, and death

8

2. The heathen and the savage combine the ideas of valor and heroism with the revenge of injuries and the destruction of their enemies; and hence deem such conduct as praiseworthy, as gratitude for benefits received. But the more enlightened Christian discerns true magnanimity in the forgiveness of injuries; and justly accounts it a greater act of heroism to return good for evil, than to satisfy the impulse of his vengeance. The heathen looks upon suicide as an heroic act; the better instruction of the Christian leads him to consider it as a proof of timidity, as well as a highly culpable renunciation of the control of the supreme power. This diversity of opinion proves the extensive influence of the principle of association, which, however it may bias, can never totally subvert the power of the moral sense. (See *Chapter XII. of this Book.*)

3. With respect to the practice of theft, so prevalent among certain tribes, it may be remarked, that in those countries where it has prevailed, property has been considered as of little or no value. In the South Sea Islands, the spontaneous bounty of nature renders hoarding almost superfluous; and, in ancient Sparta, the accumulation of property was positively prohibited. In this latter country, too, it was merely the display of skill that sanctioned the theft; for detection was sure to cover the perpetrator with indelible disgrace.

Corol. Thus, it appears, that the diversities which are discovered in the moral sentiments of mankind, arise from known laws of the human constitution. The basis on which these moral sentiments are founded is immutable; but they may be variously modified, according to circumstances peculiar to the individual. It is thus that the language of different tribes assumes a particular character and idiom, according to the peculiar circumstances of their situation; but the fundamental principles of grammar continue radically the same in all dialects. (*Illus.* 1, 2. and *Corol. Art.* 62.)

Note. The power of association or combination, in regulating the succession of our ideas, and in directing the transition from one object of thought to another, will be examined when we come to treat of " IMAGINATION," and " THE TRAIN OF THOUGHT IN THE MIND."

CHAPTER VIII.

OF MEMORY.

I. *Things obvious with Regard to Memory.*

242. MEMORY is the faculty by which the *mind* has a knowledge of what it had formerly *perceived, felt* or *thought.* (See *Illus. Art.* 22. and the *Illus.* to *Art.* 139.)

Illus. 1. It is by memory that we have an immediate knowledge of things *past.* The senses give us information of things only as they

exist in the *present* moment; and this information, if it were not preserved by Memory, would vanish instantly, and leave us as ignorant
as if it had never been. (See *Art.* 124. *Illus.* and *Corol.*)

2. *Memory* must have an *object.* Every man who remembers, must
remember *something*, and *that* which he remembers, is called the *object*
of his remembrance. In this, Memory is allied to Perception, but differs from Sensation, which has no object but the *feeling* itself. (See
Art. 125. and its *Illus.*)

3. We can distinguish the thing remembered from the remembrance of it. We may remember any thing which we have seen, or
heard, or known, or done, or suffered; but the remembrance of it is
a particular *act* of the mind which *now exists*, and of which we are
conscious. (See *Illus. Art.* 99.)

Corol. The object of Memory being something that is past, and the
object of Perception and of Consciousness something which is present;
what now is, cannot be an object of Memory; neither can that which
is past and gone be an object of Perception or of Consciousness.

243. Memory is always accompanied with the BELIEF of
that which we remember, as Perception is accompanied
with the belief of that which we *perceive*, and Consciousness
with the belief of that whereof we are *conscious.* (See *Art.*
100. *Illus.*)

Illus. This *belief*, which we have from distinct Memory, we account
real knowledge, no less certain than if it was grounded on demonstration; no man in his wits calls it in question, nor will he hear any argument against it. But it cannot be resolved into the evidence of sense,
or of any process of Memory, but must be stated as a peculiar kind of
evidence, which we are so constituted as to admit of itself immediately,
and incontestably. The testimony of witnesses, in causes of life and
death, depends upon it, and all the knowledge mankind have of past
events is built upon this foundation. (See *Illus.* 2. *Art.* 116.)

Obs. There are cases in which our Memory is less distinct and de-
terminate, and where we must frequently allow that it may have failed
us; but this does not in the least weaken its credit where it is perfectly distinct.

244. To the exercise of Memory, we appear to be entirely indebted for the notion of *time* or *duration;* for a *being*,
destitute of that faculty, could never have possessed that
notion; and without Memory, he would have no idea of such
a thing as *motion*, for motion is a successive change of place,
and presupposes the notion of succession, or duration.

Illus. 1. Memory implies a *conception* and *belief* of past DURATION;
for it is impossible that we should remember any thing distinctly,
without believing some interval of duration, more or less, to have
passed between the time it happened, and the present moment; and,
if we had no Memory, we could acquire no notion of duration.

2. Things remembered must be things formerly perceived or known.
I remember the comet of 1811.   must, therefore, have perceived it

at the time it appeared, otherwise I could not remember it. (See *Illus*. 2. *Art.* 59.) Our first acquaintance with any object of thought cannot therefore be by remembrance; for Memory can only produce a *continuance* or *renewal* of a former acquaintance with the thing remembered.

3. The notion of limited duration which we distinctly remember, leads us, by a kind of necessity, to the admission of a duration which has no limits—which neither began nor will have an end. In like manner, the notions of limited extension and magnitude, which we acquire by the senses, leads to the belief of an unlimited extension, or of space which has no bounds.

4. Thus are acquired the notions of infinite space, and of infinite time or eternity. It cannot, however, be pretended, that our finite capacities are capable of forming adequate conceptions of that which is infinite and unbounded; it can only be said, that there is less difficulty in conceiving infinite space, than in conceiving the final boundaries of space, or the beginning or end of time.

245. The remembrance of a past event is necessarily accompanied with the *conviction of our own* EXISTENCE *at the time the event happened.*

Illus. I cannot call to my remembrance the death of the amiable and lamented Princess Charlotte, that happened a year ago, without a conviction as strong as memory can give, that I, the identical person who now remember that mournful event, *did then exist.* (See *Illus.* to *Art.* 52.)

Obs. These are principles obvious and certain, of which the reader must judge by what he feels; and they admit no other proof but an appeal to his own reflection.

II. *Of Memory as an original Faculty.*

246. Of our ORIGINAL FACULTIES, of which Memory is one, we can give no account, but that they were given us by the Author of our being. (See *Art.* 130.)

Illus. 1. The knowledge we have by Memory of things *past*, seems as unaccountable as an immediate knowledge would be of things to *come.* I find in my mind a distinct conception and a firm belief of a series of past events, as the battle of Trafalgar, the battle of Vittoria; but I know not how this is produced. I call it Memory, but this is only giving a *name* to it; it is not an account of its *cause.* I remember the building of Waterloo Bridge; I have seen hundreds of men employed on it, and thousands of blocks of granite used in its construction, and I most firmly believe these facts; but I am unable to give any *reason* of *this belief.* I conclude, therefore, that it is the inspiration of my Maker that gives me this understanding.

2. When I believe that I washed my hands and face this morning, there appears no necessity in the truth of this proposition : it might be, or it might not be. You may distinctly conceive it without believing it. But how do I come to believe it?—I remember it distinct

ly; and this is all I can say about it. But this *remembrance* is an *act* of my mind. Could this *act* of my mind have *existence* if the *event* had *not happened?* If you can show that it could not have existence, you will then have fairly accounted for that belief which we have of what we remember; but on the other hand, if you cannot show this, allow me still to think that this belief is unaccountable, and that we can say no more but that it is the result of our constitution.

Corol. We are so constituted as to have an *intuitive* knowledge of many things *past* (*Art.* 47.); but we have no intuitive knowledge of the *future.* The past was, but now is not; we only remember things past. The future will be, but is not; we can have no remembrance of the future, because we have no knowledge of it. We might perhaps have been so constituted as to have an intuitive knowledge of the future; but not of the past: nor would this constitution have been more unaccountable than the present, though, for any thing we know to the contrary, it might be much more inconvenient. Had this been the constitution of the human kind, they who doubt the prescience of the Deity, or his knowledge of things future, would be plunged into an opposite disbelief of admitting his knowledge of things that are past. How limited, then, are proud man's most comprehensive conceptions!

III. *Analysis of the Faculty of Memory.*

247. The faculty of Memory implies two things: *first,* a CAPACITY of retaining knowledge; and, *secondly,* a POWER of recalling that knowledge to our thoughts when we have occasion to make use of it.

Obs. The word Memory is sometimes employed to express the *capacity,* and sometimes the *power.* When we speak of a *retentive memory,* we use it in the *former* sense; when of a *ready Memory,* in the latter.

248. The various particulars which compose our stock of knowledge are, from time to time, recalled to our thoughts in *two* ways: sometimes they recur to us *spontaneously,* or at least without any interference on our part; in other cases, they are recalled in consequence of an *effort of will.*

Note. It would probably be as philosophical to say, Memory is either *casual* or *intentional*—CASUAL, when subjects or thoughts, by any connection of their own, recur to the mind—INTENTIONAL, when the mind, from design, recalls any subject or thought.

Illus. For the former operation of the mind, we have the appropriate name *Reminiscence,* or *Remembrance:* in our language, the latter, too, is often called by the name of *memory,* but is more properly distinguished by the word *recollection.* (*Art.* 254.)

249. The OPERATIONS of Memory relate either to *things* and their *relations,* or to *events.*

8*

Illus. In the former case, thoughts which have been formerly in the mind, may recur to us; but whether, at that time, we have the idea of the past suggested or not, there is, doubtless, a certain modification of time, because what we remember is past. In the latter case, it is more evident, that if we recall to mind former objects of its thoughts, we refer the event to a particular time; so that of every such act of Memory, the idea of the past is a necessary concomitant. (See *Illus.* 1. *Art.* 245.)

250. The evidence, or belief, of past existence, which always accompanies Memory, (*Art.* 243.) forms one important distinction between that faculty and Association.

Illus. 1. The suggestions which are made by the faculty of Association alone, impress us with no belief of their reality. In fact, the very materials upon which they are employed, if not supplied by the immediate perception of the moment, must be furnished by the memory, or that faculty which enables us to treasure up past knowledge.

Corol. Thus the power of Association, in its most useful exercise, presupposes the power of Memory; and when, during the *spontaneous* flow of the current of thought, we recognize a combination of which we had formerly been conscious, and distinguish it from one newly formed, this necessarily implies an exercise of a faculty which can distinguish *former* knowledge from *new;* which is not an attribute of the faculty of *Association*, but of the MEMORY alone.

Illus. 2. In the case of some old men, who retain pretty exactly the information which they receive, but are sometimes unable to recollect in what manner the particulars which they find connected together in their thoughts at first came into the mind, whether they occurred to them in a dream, or were communicated to them in conversation, we have an example of the power of Association operating without any aid from Memory. (See *Art.* 254. *Illus.* 2. and *Example.*) But in most cases, the suggestions of Memory are made by means of the combinations previously established among our thoughts.

3. This, however, is but one part of the province of Memory; for, as was observed above, (*Art.* 247.) this faculty implies two things; a *capacity* of retaining knowledge, and a *power* of recalling it to our thoughts when we have occasion to apply it to use. The first of these is entirely independent of the faculty of Combination; but this faculty is the principal, though not the sole instrument, by which the latter purpose is accomplished.

4. The advantages of this law are thus stated by Mr. Stewart. On the other hand, says he, it is evident that without the associating principle, the power of retaining our thoughts, and of recognizing them when they occur to us, would have been of little use; for the most important articles of our knowledge might have remained latent in the mind, even when those occasions presented themselves to which they are immediately applicable.

Corol. In consequence of this law of our nature, not only are all our various ideas made to pass from time to time in review before us, and to offer themselves to our choice as subjects of meditation, but, when an occasion occurs which calls for the aid of our past experience, the occasion itself recalls to us all the information upon the subject which that experience hath accumulated.

IV. *Varieties of Memory in different Individuals.*

251. Of all our faculties, Memory is that which nature nas bestowed in the most unequal degrees on different individuals; but the original disparities are by no means so immense as they seem to be at first view; and much of this diversity is to be ascribed to different habits of Attention, and to a difference of selection among the various objects and events presented to our curiosity.

Illus. As the great purpose to which this faculty is subservient, is, to enable us to collect and retain, for the future regulation of our conduct, the results of our past experience, it is evident that the degree of perfection which it attains in the case of different persons, must vary; *first*, with the *facility* of making the original acquisition; *secondly*, with the *permanence* of the acquisition; and, *thirdly*, with the *quickness* or readiness with which the individual is able, on particular occasions, to apply it to use.

Corol. The qualities, therefore, of a good Memory, are, in the first place, to be *susceptible*; secondly, to be *retentive*; and, thirdly, to be *ready*.

252. *Susceptibility* and *readiness* are both connected with a facility of associating ideas, according to their more *obvious relations; retentiveness* or *tenaciousness* of Memory, depends principally on what is seldom united with this facility—a *disposition* to *system* and *philosophical arrangement*.

Illus. 1. The more obvious relations which befriend susceptibility and readiness, are those of *resemblance* and of *analogy*, and the casual relations arising from the *contiguity* of *time* and *place;* the philosophical *arrangement* upon which retentiveness and tenaciousness of Memory depend, has for its basis the relations of *cause* and *effect*, or of *premises* and *conclusion*.

Obs. This difference in the modes of Association in different men, is the foundation of some very striking diversities between them in respect of intellectual character. But we have anticipated the further illustration of this position in Chapters IV., VI., and VII., to which we must therefore refer the reader.

Illus. 2. Again, our ideas are frequently associated in consequence of the associations which take place among their arbitrary signs. All the signs by which our thoughts are expressed, are addressed either to the eye or to the ear; and the impressions made on these organs at the time when we first receive an idea, contribute to give us a firmer hold of it. *Visible* objects are remembered more easily than those of any of our other senses (see *Art.* 142. *Illus.*); and hence it is, that the bulk of mankind are more aided in their recollection by the impressions made on the *eye*, than by those made on the ear.   But in the philosopher, whose habits of constantly employing words as an instrument of thought, coöperating with that inattention which he is apt to contract to things external, the original powers of recollection and conception with respect to *visible* objects are commonly greatly weakened; while the power of retaining propositions and reasonings expressed in language is greatly strengthened by his habits of *abstraction* and *generalization*.

3. A prejudice has obtained, that a great Memory is scarcely compatible with that acuteness of parts denominated *genius*; and the effect of this opinion is such, that no one blushes at acknowledging a shortness of Memory, while to be accused of a defect of judgment, or a want of penetration, is usually considered a high affront.   This prejudice, however, appears to be without foundation; and Memory, far from being incompatible with genius, seems even to be necessary, in its utmost perfection, for those happy exertions of intellect which confer immortality upon their authors.

Example. Robert Bloomfield, that completely self-taught genius and pleasing poet, composed the latter part of the *Autumn*, and the whole of the *Winter* of his FARMER's BOY, *mentally*, without ever putting pen to paper.   Nor was this all; for he even thoroughly corrected and revised this extensive portion of his poem, before he ever wrote a word of it; and this, too, while at work with his fellow journeymen, in a garret; and then, as he himself expressed it, *he had nothing to do but to write it down!*

Illus. 4. The following example, on the contrary, justifies the foregoing prejudice; for none who have perused the writings of the amusing author of whom we are now to speak, can doubt that he possessed genius.

Example. MONTAIGNE frequently complains, in his writings, of his want of Memory; and he indeed gives many very extraordinary instances of his ignorance on some of the most ordinary topics of information.   But it is obvious, as Mr. Stewart justly remarks, that this ignorance did not proceed from an original defect of memory, but from the singular and whimsical direction which his curiosity had taken at an early period of life.   "I can do nothing," says Montaigne, "without my memorandum-book; and, so great is my difficulty in remembering proper names, that I am forced to call my domestic servants by their offices.   I am ignorant of the greater part of our coins in use; of the difference of one grain from another, both in the earth and in the granary; what use leaven is in making bread, and why wine must stand some time in the vat before it ferments.   When I have an oration to speak, of any considerable length, I am reduced to the miserable necessity of getting it, word for word, by heart."—Malebranche doubted the veracity of Montaigne on these matters; Mr. Stewart acquits him of affectation; but whoever has seen the statue of Montaigne in the vestibule of the " *Institute of France*," will not question the credibility of his assertions, provided the sculptor hath fairly chiselled a likeness of the most inanimate-looking mortal, in whom a spark of genius ever shone.

V. *Of the Decay of Memory in old People.*

253. The decay of Memory in old people is a matter of familiar observation, as well as that peculiarity with which it is usually accompanied;—namely, that a complete, and even minute recollection, usually remains of the events of an older date, and the occurrences of early life.

Illus. 1. The failure of Memory, in regard to recent occurrences, is owing to the decay of *Attention.* From this decay, these occurrences do not make a sufficient impression on the mind to be afterwards recollected ; but the associating principle remaining in full vigor, and the train of thought continuing to perform its office, circumstances which have been already familiarized to the mind are still suggested with the wonted accuracy.

2. The foregoing illustration may be reckoned satisfactory, if we understand, by the decay of Memory, not the diminished energy of some one particular faculty of the mind, but the relaxed vigor of all, or most of the mental faculties, which, like the bodily functions, being impaired by the approach of old age, are incapable of contemplating their respective objects with that degree of force which is requisite to their being distinctly remembered afterwards. The decay of *sensibility* and the extinction of *passion*, which are the consequences of old age, likewise powerfully coöperate in producing this effect, by diminishing the interest which the common occurrences of life are calculated to produce.

254. That kind of Memory which old people possess, generally in a state of vigor, and by which circumstances are presented spontaneously to the mind, without any voluntary effort, has been called REMINISCENCE or REMEMBRANCE ; while that which requires a more vigorous effort, and is more dependent upon the will of the individual, has been distinguished by the name of *Recollection.* (*Art.* 248. *Note and Illus.*)

Illus. 1. The former, as mentioned above, (*Art.* 250. *Illus.* 2.) is chiefly dependent upon the faculty of Association ; while the latter will not be found but where the mind possesses the active exertion of the faculty called *Attention.* The distinction is as old as the days of Aristotle,* who remarks, that the brutes possess the first kind of Memory, but exhibit no traces of the last, which is therefore a valuable characteristic of man.

2. This Reminiscence of ideas formerly impressed on the mind, and forgetfulness of recent ones, is no unusual circumstance attending a paralysis, though our physiology is not yet sufficiently advanced to account for it.

Example. Both the foregoing illustrations are corroborated by the authority of the late learned Dr. Watson, Bishop of Llandaff: " My father," says he in his Memoirs, " had been afflicted with a palsy for several years before his death. I have heard him ask twenty times in

* DE MEMOR. ET REMINISC.

a day, ' What is the name of the lad that is at college?' (my elder brother); and yet he was able to repeat, without a blunder, hundreds of lines out of classic authors.''

VI. *Of the Improvement of Memory.*

255. The cultivation of so noble a faculty as the Memory, is a matter of the highest importance; at the same time we must not expect that any cultivation, how assiduous so ever, will altogether make up for natural deficiencies of Memory, any more than those of *judgment, taste,* or any other faculty.

Illus. 1. Of a human Memory improved to no extraordinary pitch, how vast is the comprehension! With what an endless multitude of thought is it supplied, by reflection, by reading, by conversation, and by a diversified experience! Things *natural;* as animals, vegetables, minerals, fossils; mountains, valleys; land and water; earth and heaven; the sun, moon, and stars, with their several appearances, motions, and periods; the atmosphere and meteors, with all the vicissitudes of the weather;—things *artificial,* as towns, streets, houses, roads, bridges, and machines, with their various appendages;—*abstract* notions with regard to truth and falsehood, beauty and deformity, virtue and vice;—*proportions* in quantity and number;—*religion,* commerce, and policy, whereof the brutes know nothing, and which are the chief materials of human conversation.

2. These are some of the general heads under which may be arranged the manifold treasures of human memory; and under each of these heads, what an infinity of individual things are comprehended! How numerous, for example, are the words of one language! He who is master of *four,* must be supposed to retain at least two hundred thousand words; with all the different ways of applying them, according to rule, and innumerable passages in books to illustrate their meaning. And that four languages do not exceed the capacity of an ordinary man, will not be denied by those who are acquainted with the writings of Sir William Jones; much less if they believe, with Pliny and Quinctilian, that Mithridates understood two and twenty!

256. The utmost that can be expected from any exertion of our own, is, to direct the Memory to its proper objects, and in that order and succession which will most facilitate its operation; to remove as much as possible those obstructions which are likely to retard the proper action of the faculty; and, by a repeated and industrious exertion, to bring it to that state of maturity and that degree of energy, which, in every human attainment, are so highly promoted by exercise.

Illus. 1. In order successfully to cultivate the Memory, we must cultivate the powers of Attention and Association, on which it mainly depends. And nothing will contribute more to the recollection of things at any future period, than clear and distinct conceptions of them at the present; that is to say, when they first become objects of our attention, for vaguely formed and indefinite notions will leave no permanent traces on the mind.

2. When we read, therefore, let us labor to understand clearly and precisely our author's meaning; let us compare what goes before with what follows in his work; let us search for the characteristic features of his system, and compare his opinions with those of other authors who have treated of the same subject. By this means, not only the faculties of *Conception* and *Attention*, but the *Reasoning* powers, will be usefully exercised; and the best provision will be made for a distinct recollection.

257. It has been much disputed whether it be an useful exercise to write down those things which we are desirous to remember; but there can be little doubt that, in some cases, this may be exceedingly proper; in others, not so.

Illus. To write a great deal cannot be highly useful to the Memory; for the attention is but too apt to be diverted from the matter itself to the mere manual operation; but it is surely useful to transcribe certain short passages, which we select on account of the importance or curiosity of the matters they contain, and to which we, by this means, can afterwards conveniently refer. It would likewise, no doubt, be very useful to write a short abridgment and character of any important book we have read; or, at least, to state the leading tenets of the work, and our opinion of its merits, in a few short paragraphs. We should thus come, in time, to think for ourselves—we should form a sort of register of our studies, to which we might afterwards refer with the greatest advantage—and we would thus improve the faculties of Association and Attention. For, without comparing together the different parts of an author's work, so as to form out of it one consistent whole, and comparing it also with the writings of others on the same subject, so as to digest the whole into a system, Association will not be promoted, Attention will not be increased, and all our reading will furnish nothing but a desultory collection of ideas, scarcely applicable to any useful purpose. Professor Porson, who could at will recite any passage from the Greek poets, thus speaks: "I never remember any thing but what I transcribe three times, or read over six times, at the least; and if you will do the same, you will have as good a memory;" and his memory was most excellent.

258. With respect to the mechanical expedients which have been proposed for aiding the Memory, it does not appear that much real advantage is to be expected from them. The *loci* of the ancients, and the *memorial lines* of the moderns, are the chief, of each of which we shall give a brief illustration.

Illus. 1. The intention of the celebrated *loci*, or Topical Memory, of the ancient rhetoricians, was to facilitate the recollection of the various heads of an oration, by associating them in the mind with the different apartments of a house, or the various houses in a street, the precise succession of which had been previously rendered familiar to the mind. The subordinate parts of the discourse were to be associated with the furniture of the rooms, or the subdivisions of the houses; and thus the whole oration was to be suggested to the Memory, with very little effort. The writings of Cicero and Quinctilian contain a full account of this mechanical contrivance, which, without doubt, is founded on nature; but Quinctilian candidly acknowledges that he never received any benefit from this artificial kind of Memory. The case was otherwise with Cicero. It has for ages fallen into disuse; but, in allusion to it, the heads of a discourse are still called *topics*, and we continue to say—*in the first place, in the second place,* &c

Example. Mr. Stewart gives an instance of Topical Memory. It is this:—A young woman, in a very low rank of life, contrived a method of committing to memory the sermons she was accustomed to hear, by fixing her attention, during the different heads of the discourse, on different compartments of the roof of a church, in such a manner as that, when she afterwards saw the roof, or recollected the order in which its compartments were disposed, she recollected the method which the preacher had observed in treating his subject.

Illus. 2. The memorial lines, or verses, are more useful than the method of *loci*, since, by the substitution of the letters of the alphabet for the numeral characters, we can easily commit to Memory certain dates, measures, computations, and other things. Gray's *Memoria Technica*, a small volume on this artificial help, contains an ample collection of such memorial verses. There is also a small volume by Mr. Jackson, on " A New and Improved System of Mnemonics, or the Art of Memory, applied to Figures, Chronology, Geography, Statistics, History, and Poetry, illustrated with many Plates." This is an ingenious little book, founded on Watts's Improvement of the Mind; and its brevity and perspicuity entitle it to notice in every work on intellectual philosophy. M. Feinagle, too, has published a new Art of Memory, adapted to the meanest capacity, and its application is rather a source of amusement than labor. It possesses all the advantages of the methods which preceded its development, and, as a whole, is perhaps superior to any book on this art that has yet appeared. But this important object, it would seem, can be accomplished only by cultivating those exertions of the mind on which the faculty of Memory depends, namely, Attention and the Association of Ideas.

CHAPTER IX.

OF IMAGINATION.

259. IMAGINATION is the faculty which makes a selection of qualities and circumstances from a variety of different

objects, and by combining and disposing these, forms new creations of its own. (See *Art.* 97. *No.* IX.)

Obs. 1. Thus, Imagination is distinguished from Abstraction, in which we endeavor to generalize. Imagination invests objects with all their qualities, real or fictitious: it exerts itself in matters which we know to be real, as well as in matters which we invent, or believe to be fictitious. (See *Chapter* VI. *on Abstraction, Sections* II. and III.)

2. The distinction between *Imagination* and *Conception* was fully drawn in ARTICLE 141. and its *Illustration* and *Note*, to which, therefore, to avoid the tediousness of repetition, the reader is referred.

I. *Analysis of the Operations of Imagination.*

260. The operations of the faculty of Imagination are general, extending to the representation of notions or combinations of thought, as well as of sensible impressions originally made on the external organs; and, if we establish this, we shall have proved that the province of Imagination is not barely limited to objects of sight.

Illus. 1. Although the greater part of the materials which Imagination combines, be supplied by the sense of sight, it is nevertheless indisputable, that our other perceptive faculties also contribute their share. How many pleasing images, says Mr. Stewart, have been borrowed from the fragrance of the fields and the melody of the groves; not to mention that sister art, whose magical influence over the human frame, it has been, in all ages, the highest boast of poetry to celebrate! In the following passage, even the more gross sensations of taste form the subject of an ideal repast, on which it is impossible not to dwell with some complacency; particularly after the perusal of the preceding lines, in which the poet describes " the wonders of the torrid zone."

> Bear me, Pomona! to thy citron groves;
> To where the lemon and the piercing lime,
> With the deep orange, glowing through the green,
> Their lighter glories blend. Lay me reclined
> Beneath the spreading tamarind, that shakes,
> Fanned by the breeze, its fever-cooling fruit;
> Or, stretched amid these orchards of the sun,
> O let me drain the cocoa's milky bowl,
> More bounteous far than all the frantic juice
> Which Bacchus pours! Nor on its slender twigs,
> Low bending, be the pomegranate scorned;
> Nor, creeping through the woods, the gelid race
> Of berries: oft in humble station dwells
> Unboastful worth, above fastidious pomp,
> Witness thou best Anana, thou the pride
> Of vegetable life, beyond whate'er
> The poets imaged in the golden age:

9

Quick let me strip thee of thy spicy coat.
Spread thy ambrosial stores, and feast with Jove.

THOMSON'S SUMMER.

Corol. This quotation shows how inadequate a notion of the prov ince of Imagination (considered even in its reference to the sensible world) we must entertain, if we would limit its operations to objects of sight merely.

261. But the sensible world, in its widest range, is not the only field in which Imagination exerts her powers. All the objects of human knowledge supply materials to her forming hand ; diversifying infinitely the works she produces, while the mode of her operation remains essentially uniform.

Illus. 1. Thus the Imagination becomes a bond of association for those intellectual processes which are constantly going on in the mind, and acts a principal part in those creations of Fancy, which, derived from an union of Abstraction, Generalization, and Taste, constitutes works of genius in the fine arts. The Imagination does not abstract nor generalize, but it reproduces and supplies materials for these several processes, according to the laws of association, which regulate the procedure of the mind, in its recollections and combinations.

2. As it is the same power of reasoning which enables us to carry on our investigations with respect to individual objects, and with respect to classes and genera, so it was by the same processes of analysis and combination, that the genius of Milton produced the *Garden of Eden* (*Illus.* 2. *Art.* 264.), that of Harrington, the Commonwealth of Oceana (*Art.* 187. *Illus.* 1.), and that of Shakspeare, the characters of Hamlet and Sir John Falstaff.

Corol. The difference between these several efforts of invention consists only in the manner in which the original materials were acquired ; as far as the power of Imagination is concerned, the processes appear, to my mind, to be perfectly analogous.

262. The mind, however, has a greater facility, and, of consequence, a greater delight in recalling the perceptions of the sense of sight, than those of any of the other senses, while, at the same time, the variety of the qualities perceived by it is incomparably greater.

Illus. It is this sense, accordingly, which supplies the painter and the statuary with *all* the subjects on which their genius is exercised. It is this sense, too, which furnishes to the descriptive poet the largest and the most valuable portion of the materials which he combines. It is observed by Mr. Stewart, that in that absurd species of prose composition, also, which borders upon poetry, nothing is more remarkable than the predominance of *phrases* that recall to the memory, *glaring colors*, and those *splendid appearances* of nature, which make a strong impression on the *eye*. Thus, in the Oriental style, the greater part of the metaphors are taken from the celestial luminaries; and the works of the Persians, as is observed by Voltaire, are like the titles of their kings, in which we are perpetually dazzled with the *sun*, and the *moon*, and the *stars*. The juvenile productions of every author, possessed of a warm Imagination, partake of this characteristic; and the compositions of every people, among whom a cultivated and philosophical taste has not established a sufficiently marked distinction between the appropriate styles of poetry and prose, partake sufficiently of the infantine reveries of poetic genius, to show why the word *Imagination*, in its most ordinary acceptation, should be applied to cases where our conceptions are derived from the *sense of sight;* although the province of this power be, in fact, as unlimited as the sphere of human enjoyment and of human thought. But in these illustrations we may clearly trace the origin of the word Imagination; the *etymology* of which implies manifestly a reference to *visible objects.*

263. The mind forms combinations out of the materials supplied by the power of *Conception;* and these combinations recommend themselves strongly to our constitution, both by their simplicity, and by the interesting nature of the discussions to which they lead.

Obs. The arts of poetry and painting furnish the most pleasing and instructive illustrations of the operations and intellectual processes of Imagination. In those analogous exemplifications of this faculty, which fall under the observation of the moralist, the mind deviates from the models presented to it by experience, and forms to itself new and untried objects of pursuit. And how little soever such processes may be attended to, they are habitually passing in the thoughts of all men; and it is in consequence of these processes that human affairs exhibit so busy and so various a scene; tending in one case to improvement, and, in another, to decline; according as our notions of excellence and happiness are just or erroneous.

264. But besides Conception, or simple Apprehension, which enables us to form a notion of those former objects of perception or of knowledge, out of which we are to make a selection, Imagination includes Abstraction, which separates the selected materials from the qualities and circumstances which are connected with them in nature; and Judgment, or Taste, too, which selects the materials and directs their combination. Nor does this complex power include only those powers we have just enumerated, and to which, under Conception and Abstraction, we have shown their alliance; but that particular habit of association also, to which we gave the name of *Fancy*, when illustrating the pleasing effect of simile, poetical allusion, and allegory. (See *Article* 208.)

Illus. 1 FANCY collects materials for the Imagination (*Corol.* 2

Art. 208.) ; and though her principal stores are commonly supposed to be borrowed from the material world, as the metaphorical language of the poet, and his analogies, which are the foundation of his allusions, but too forcibly prove ; yet the favorite excursions of Fancy are from intellectual and moral subjects to the appearances with which our senses are conversant. (*Art.* 261. *Illus.* 1.) In a word, wherever her stores may be treasured up, in what direction soever her flights may be taken, it is Fancy which presents to our choice all the different materials which are subservient to the efforts of Imagination, and which may therefore be considered as forming the groundwork of poetical genius.

2. This illustration is confirmed by an analysis of the steps by which Milton must have proceeded in creating his imaginary *Garden of Eden.* (*Illus.* 2. *Art.* 261.) When he first proposed to himself that subject of description, it is reasonable to suppose that his Fancy crowded into his mind a variety of the most striking scenes which he had seen. The *Association of ideas* would suggest those scenes ; the *combinations of Fancy* would link such as might be real or imaginative, and fit objects of description ; the *power of conception* would place each of them before him with all its beauties and imperfections. For in every natural scene, which we may destine for a particular purpose, there are defects and redundancies, which art may sometimes, but cannot always, correct. And as objects may be imagined separately or jointly—as the power of Imagination is unlimited—as, in the separate images of things, she can consider their real or possible qualities and circumstances—as, in their joint images, she can consider their similitude, analogy and opposition—as she can create and annihilate ; Milton, accordingly, would not copy his EDEN from any one scene, but would select from each the features which were most eminently beautiful. The power of Abstraction enabled him to make the separation, and Taste directed him in the selection. Thus was Milton furnished with his materials, by a skilful combination of which he has created a landscape, more perfect, probably, in all its parts, than was ever seen by any writer who has attempted to describe nature.

Corol. 1. Since, then, Imagination is not a simple power of the mind, but a combination of various faculties, it must appear under very different forms in the case of different individuals. And since the variety of the materials out of which the combinations of the poet or the painter are formed, will depend much on the tendency of external situation, to store the mind with a multiplicity of conceptions, and the beauty of those combinations will depend entirely on the success with which the power of Taste has been cultivated ; it is further evident, that its component parts are liable to be greatly influenced by habit and other accidental circumstances. (*Art.* 128. *Illus.*)

2. The illustrations which have been offered of the power of Imagination, according to the reasoning of Mr. Stewart, lead to the conclusion that this *power* is not the gift of nature, but the result of acquired habits, aided by favorable circumstances ; that it is not an original endowment of the mind, but an accomplishment formed by experience and situation ; and which, in its different gradations, fills up all the interval between the first efforts of untutored genius

and the sublime creations of Raphael or of Milton. (See *Art.* 275. and *Illus.*)

265. That men differ from each other greatly in the force of their Imagination, or in the power of forming or conceiving new creations and combinations, is matter of the most familiar observation. And, as far as the term *genius* has yet been distinctly limited, it appears to denote a facility in forming such combinations. This, in fact, is the proper province of invention, which is the peculiar prerogative of genius; for this can have no farther range than an analysis, and new disposition, of the various objects which nature presents to us; and never can extend to a new creation of its own, in the strict and proper sense of the word.

Illus. Thus, a blind man, let his invention be ever so lively, could never discover a new property of light. And, according to this view of the subject, a man of genius is no more than a man of active Imagination; and though both terms are more usually appropriated to literary eminence, yet, if we take them in this sense, the inventor in mechanics, in mathematics, in agriculture, or in any of the useful arts, or pursuits of life, is as much entitled to the appellation of a man of Genius and Imagination, as the poet, the painter, and the orator.

266. A *passive* Imagination is that which is limited to a ready conception of new combinations, when suggested to it, but it does not extend to the original formation of such combinations. And that there does exist such a species of Imagination, we think is evident, from the proof contained in the following illustration.

Illus. This kind of Imagination does not go so far as to constitute a man of genius, yet it seems to furnish the proper qualification for the man of taste, since it enables him to relish and appreciate the productions of genius, although not to rival and excel in them. Of the two qualifications, it may be doubted whether the latter does not most contribute to real enjoyment. The pleasures which the man of fine taste derives from contemplating the productions of genius, is scarcely inferior to the high relish which the exercise of invention itself imparts; and the inventive Imagination of the man of genius is but too apt to conjure up phantoms for his own torment; and to burn with jealousies, which his fancy knows but too well how to feed. The histories of Rousseau, Chatterton, Swift, Johnson, and other geniuses of *heated,* or of *gloomy* Imaginations, afford ample confirmation of the truth of this fact.

267. That *belief* may be attached to certain operations of the Imagination, which are then mistaken for realities, and produce as remarkable effects upon the individual, as

9 *

if they were the very things they are mistaken for, is a fact none will dispute, who have attended to the inexplicable phenomena of the human mind, in the case of those unfortunate persons who are in the state of hypochondriacs, or imaginary invalids.

Illus. 1. The wildest suggestions of the Imagination impress upon these unfortunate persons the full conviction of reality ; and all the reasoning of their friends, or physicians, is insufficient to convince them that they are formed like other men, and have not some part of their bodies either unnaturally distorted, or fashioned of different materials from flesh, and blood, and bones.   When hypochondriasis arrives at this height, it makes a near approach to certain stages of madness ; and if the physician should deny that the bodily disease exists of which his patient complains, he must yet allow that there is a real disease of the mind. The Imagination of the hypochondriac is not so much bewildered as it is lost in absurdities.   And when the actions, the looks, and the language of any person whom we respect, or with whom we have had an acquaintance, show that his mind has been soured by cruel vicissitudes in life—his hopes of domestic happiness blasted by keen disappointment—his affections withered by the loss of some being who had just begun to cherish them—or his brain set on fire by treachery and ingratitude, in those from whom he had a right to expect fidelity and kindness—or his faculties deluged by a chaos of business, which he had neither the ingenuity to arrange, nor the resolution to abandon, for his own peace and ease—or beclouded by the reaction of a distempered conscience,—when, in one word, a congregation of unlooked-for, and, as the individual is almost always sure to imagine, unmerited calamities, give such a view of human affairs, as to represent life *a scene of mere illusions ;* then is that mortal forlorn indeed ; but still he is less an object of pity than those unfeeling brutes who can sport with so sublime a picture of mysterious, wretched man ;—and it is ten to one, the spirit of the being we have sketched, like a lonely sentinel guarding the ashes of his general, in moody solitude, yet loves to keep house with its friendless subject, now more to be compassioned and wooed to reason and sprightliness, than spurned and shunned for his imbecility and dulness.

2. This is no overcharged picture—I have had very much intercourse with its original, and from communion with the operation of the faculty now under consideration, I am willing it should be recorded.   But the following is a striking case of hypochondriasis within, perhaps, the precincts of madness. Monsieur Pinel is the physician of an hospital of lunatics in Paris, and, from his amiable manners and gentle treatment of his patients, receives no other name, from the most ferocious, than " papa ; " and from the females of that

" Gay, sprightly land of mirth and social ease,"

the courtesy of their sex—the compliment of a salutation. This is **treating** mad folks as they ought to be treated, and forms a brilliant contrast to the brutal system of cudgelling, adopted in the treatment of the illustrious, or the man of genius, by some of our own physicians. A patient was brought to Monsieur Pinel, accusing himself of having denounced many persons to the revolutionary tribunals during the *reign of terror.* M. Pinel heard from the lips of this patient his own tale of wo; and adopted the following method of treatment, or cure. As the lunatic wanted to be brought to justice, for having brought many virtuous and good citizens to the block, M. Pinel had his patient brought to trial. The court consisted of M. Pinel and other physicians, in the capacity of judges. Some of the medical students bore the characters and assumed the offices of counsel against and for the accused. On an appointed day, the poor lunatic was carried from his cell to the tribunal of justice, or, in other words, to a saloon of the hospital, where every thing bore the appearance of a criminal court. He was placed at its bar; the charges were preferred against him, as himself had developed his imaginary crimes to M. Pinel; these charges were substantiated by pretended eye and ear witnesses. But, on the other hand, the lunatic, as he had revealed to M. Pinel, had to value himself on many good deeds which he had rendered to his fellow-citizens during the phrensy of the Revolution. The counsel for the accused, in their defence, brought witnesses to support these services, and urged their weight against the charges of the *Attorney-General.* M. Pinel, who acted as chief judge, summed up the evidence. The crimes of the prisoner amounted to *so many;* his essential good deeds to *so many more* than the former. This preponderance the jury were charged to well consider, in giving their verdict. They did so—they found the prisoner guilty of such and such things, but he had done so much good to the nation, that he was still an object of mercy; and, therefore, they recommended him to mercy. The sentence of the court was, that the accused should be kept in confinement for three months, and then set at liberty. Before the trial was ended, the unfortunate man was nearly as free from hypochondriasis as his judges, and, long before the period of his sentence had expired, M. Pinel restored him to his friends quite well. But, unhappily, one of the students chanced, some time after, to mention in a company the case we have now described; and its subject happened to be one of the company. The effect was like a shock of electricity upon him. His Imagination instantly lost its equipoise, and he relapsed into his former unfortunate state of hypochondriasis; and he was not again to be cheated into sanity by M. Pinel. I relate this case from memory, on the authority of two gentlemen, who attended as students the hospital which M. Pinel governs.

268. But even when the intellects are in a comparatively sound state, the visions of the Imagination may be made to produce, in certain persons, all the effects of reality. The success of certain empirical impositions, among which we may particularize the *Animal Magnetism* of *Mesmer*, and the *Tractors* of *Perkins*, sufficiently establish this fact.

Illus. 1 The reign of *animal magnetism* is now over; but its fame was rapidly circulated, and its wonders detailed and swallowed with avidity.   The most incredulous could not deny the reality of its effects ; as convulsions were produced, and strong bodily agitations excited, in persons who could not be suspected of lending their aid to the imposture.   But the examination of the Academy of Sciences at Paris dispelled the illusion, and satisfactorily established that, as far as the effects were real, they were to be ascribed merely to the influence of the Imagination.

2. The more modern quackery of the *metallic tractors* seems fairly reducible, says Mr. Scott, to the same class.   If these ever produced a real cure, the effect is to be ascribed to the influence of the Imagination, and not to the virtue of the metal.   This seems, indeed, to be completely established by Dr. Haygarth, who found that his patients thought themselves equally benefited, whether he employed the tractors of Perkins, or tractors of his own manufacture, or even *tractors of wood*, colored so as to resemble those of metal.   (See his " Treatise on the Imagination, as a Cause and Cure of Disease.")

Corol. This influence of the Imagination on the corporeal frame, forms one feature of the mysterious union between the body and mind, in consequence of which, the one cannot be affected without some corresponding change in the other ; a union so difficult to be comprehended, although of its reality we have the testimony of our daily experience.

II. *Of Imagination in its Relation to some of the Fine Arts.*

269. Among the arts which are connected with the faculty of Imagination, some not only take their rise from it, but produce objects which are directly addressed to this power. Others result from Imagination, but produce objects which are addressed to the power of perception.

Illus. 1. GARDENING, or the *art of creating landscape*, belongs to the latter of those two classes.   For, here, Nature limits the designer in his creations ; and his utmost efforts are to correct, to improve, and to adorn.   In some arts, the designer, to observe the effect of his plans, can repeat his experiments ; but the *landscape gardener* cannot do this, and must, therefore, conjure up, in his Imagination, the entire scene he intends to produce.   His taste and judgment must beforehand be applied to this imaginary scene, that he may have a lively conception of the effect which it will actually produce when exhibited to the senses of others.

Corol. The landscape thus produced is, therefore, a copy of the picture which the artist's Imagination, by the " prophetic eye of taste," had seen, long before all its beauties were born ; and the scene which he exhibits, in a finished state, being addressed to the senses, may produce its full effect on the minds of others, without any effort on their part either of Imagination or of Conception.

Obs. The foregoing illustration directs itself merely to the natural effects produced by a landscape, and the reader is left to supply

in his own Imagination, the pleasure which may result from the acci·
dental association of ideas with a particular scene.

Illus. 2. The painter who paints a faithful copy of an individual
object, whether it be a portrait or a landscape, or some particular
scene for the stage, is not permitted to indulge in Imagination.
But when he conceives some subject for a painting, for which he
has no copy, the original idea must be formed in the Imagination;
and, that the picture may produce the effect on the mind of the
spectator which the artist has in view, the exercise of Imagination
must concur with perception.

Corol. Painting, therefore, has something in common with those
arts which not only take their rise from the power of Imagination,
but produce objects which are addressed to it, and with those arts
also which take their rise from Imagination, but produce objects
which are addressed to the power of perception.

Illus. 3. In poetry, and in every species of descriptive composition, the power of the Imagination is requisite both to the author
and the reader; to the former, to present to the mind of another
the objects of his own Imagination; and to the latter, to form in
his mind a distinct picture of what is described. But no two persons possess Imagination in the same degree, or those other powers,
abstraction, conception, and association, on the proper exercise of
which the full display of Imagination depends; and, therefore,
though both may be pleased, the agreeable impressions that each
may feel, may be widely different from those of the other, according
as the pictures by which those impressions are produced, may be
more or less happily imagined.

4. In landscape gardening, the designs of Kent, of Brown, and of
Loudon, evince, in their authors, a degree of Imagination analogous
to that of the descriptive poet; and whatever they have designed
meets the eye of *every* spectator, bating always the beauties and
pleasures resulting to some individuals from association. But in
poetry, the reader must actually possess some degree of the author's
genius, and a mind furnished, by previous habits, with the means of
interpreting his language, to be able, by his own Imagination, to
coöperate with the efforts of the author.

5. In article 195, it was observed, that "the fluctuating state of
language does not permit general names always to retain the same
precise signification;" and we may here add, that general words,
which express complex ideas, seldom convey precisely the same
meaning to different individuals; hence arises the ambiguity of language, in respect to sensible objects. For who, for example, in a descriptive composition, attaches the same precise idea to the words
river, grove, mountain? The youth, the man of lively Imagination,
has a very different conception of those words from another youth
or another man of a blunt Imagination. The former thinks of some
particular river, grove, mountain, that has made an impression on his
mind; the latter, destitute of any such impression, and perhaps a
native of London, would think of the Thames, Hornsey Wood, and
the Surrey Hills. The youth who has been educated at Eton, at
Winchester, or at Harrow, would be in the same predicament
with him who had received the rudiments of his education at West-
minster. For myself, I ever think with delight of the little Island

of Bute, where I was born, and partly educated; its wood-crowned hills, its lakes, its rocky coast, its ancient castle, whence the Prince of Wales derives the title of Duke of Rothsay; my ancient and venerable masters Macartney and Mackinlay; the recollection of early friendships and all those agreeable ideas associated with the scenes of childhood and of youth, rush spontaneously on my mind, and would afford many pleasing descriptions were they thrown together in some boyish tale. Every man feels the same; every youth will assent to this; and it sufficiently establishes the position we have in hand, provided always common sense be our guide. But, to fill up any descriptive picture, both Imagination and Conception are requisite; hence, those who have seen Loch Catherine will be able to judge correctly of Walter Scott's description of that charming scene; and those who have visited Florence, Athens, and Rome, as they now are, can judge of Lord Byron's pictures of those places, and of their inhabitants. And the foregoing reasoning leads to the inference, that in descriptive composition, much is left to be supplied by the Imagination of the reader, on whose mind the effect will be in the direct ratio of his own invention and taste to that of the author's, or that with which the picture is finished.

Corol. 1. It is therefore possible, on the one hand, as is remarked by Mr. Stewart, that the happiest efforts of poetical genius may be perused with perfect indifference by a man of sound judgment, and not destitute of natural sensibility, and on the other hand, that a cold and common-place description may be the means of awakening, in a rich and glowing Imagination, a degree of enthusiasm unknown to the author.

2. The primary object in these arts which we have mentioned, is *to please;* and this circumstance distinguishes poetry from philosophical compositions, which usually have for their object *to inform* and *enlighten* mankind; and also from oratory, whose object is to acquire an ascendant over the will of others, by bending to the speaker's purposes their judgments, their imaginations, and their passions.

III. *The Relation of Imagination and of Taste to Genius.*

270. Persons accustomed to analyze and combine their conceptions, may acquire ideas of beauty far above any which they have seen realized. A habit of forming such mental combinations, and of remarking their effect on our own minds, must, therefore, contribute to exalt the Taste to a degree which it never can attain in those people who study to improve it by the observation and comparison only of external objects. (STEWART.)

Illus. 1. Genius in the fine arts is nothing more than a cultivated Taste combined with a creative Imagination. Without Taste,. Imagination could only produce a random analysis and combination of our conceptions; and without Imagination, Taste would be destitute of the faculty of invention. These two ingredients of genius may be mixed together in all possible proportions; and when either is possessed in a degree remarkably exceeding what falls to the ordinary share of mankind, it may compensate, in some measure, for a deficiency in the other. An uncommonly correct Taste, with little Imagination, if it does not produce works which excite admiration, produces, at least, nothing that can offend. An uncommon fertility of Imagination, even when it offends, excites our wonder by its creative powers, and shows what it could have performed, had its exertions been guided by a more perfect model. (STEWART.)

2. In the infancy of the arts, an union of these two powers in the same mind is necessary for the production of every work of genius. At that period there are no monuments of ancient genius on which Taste can be formed. It must therefore be from the result of experiments, which nothing but the Imagination of every individual can enable him to make, that Taste can be formed. At that period, therefore, Taste, without Imagination, is impossible. But, as experience becomes extended, Taste will be acquired, and, as it becomes perfect, Imagination will produce more chaste, more beautiful, and more finished pictures, or descriptions, or scenes.

Coro'. Hence, as the productions of genius accumulate, Taste may be formed by a careful perusal of the works of others ; and, as formerly Imagination served as a necessary foundation for Taste, so Taste now begins to invade the province of Imagination. The multiplicity and variety of the combinations, which, for a long succession of ages, Imagination has formed, present ample materials for a judicious selection. A high standard of excellence is now continually present to the artist's thoughts. He may, therefore, by industry, assisted by the most moderate degree of Imagination, produce, in time, performances not only more free from faults, but incomparably more powerful in their effects, than the most original efforts of untutored genius, which, guided by an uncultivated taste, copies after an inferior model of perfection.

IV. *Of the Influence of Imagination on Human Character and Happiness.*

271. The power of Imagination has been hitherto considered chiefly as it is related to the arts of poetry, painting, sculpture, and the creation of landscape ; but its powerful influence on human character and happiness recommend it eminently to the attention of youth

Illus. The lower animals, says Mr. Stewart, as far as we are able to judge, are entirely occupied with the objects of their present perceptions ; and the case is nearly the same with the inferior orders of our own species. One of the principal effects which a liberal education produces on the mind, is to accustom us to withdraw our attention from the objects of sense, and to direct it, at pleasure, to those intellectual combinations which delight the Imagination. And, among men of cultivated understandings, this faculty is possessed in very unequal degrees by different individuals ; and these differences.

whether resulting from original constitution, or from early education, lay the foundation of some striking varieties in human character.

272. That *sensibility* depends, in a great measure, on the power of Imagination, will appear evident from the following illustration.

Illus. Point out to two men any object of compassion ; a man, for example, reduced by misfortune from easy circumstances to indigence. The one feels merely in proportion to what he perceives by his senses. The other follows, in Imagination, the unfortunate man to his dwelling, and partakes with him and his family in their domestic distresses. He listens to their conversation, while they recall to remembrance the flattering prospects they once indulged ; the circle of friends they had been forced to leave ; the liberal plans of education which were begun and interrupted ; and pictures to himself all the various resources which delicacy and pride suggest to conceal poverty from the world. As he proceeds in the painting, his sensibility increases, and he weeps, not for what he sees, but for what he imagines. Granted that his sensibility originally roused his Imagination, the warmth of his Imagination increased and prolonged his sensibility. Let any of my young friends take up the " Sentimental Journey " of Sterne, and he will find this position verified in numerous instances. The *reflections on the state prisons of France,* suggested by the accidental sight of a *starling confined in a cage,* is a case in point. And I have myself, without a shadow of vanity in what I say, had several illustrations of this remark during a residence of ten years in the metropolis ; as well among the aged and infirm who had seen better days, as among those of my own age, who have had the cup of bliss dashed from their lips when they were about to sip its nectar.

273. On some persons, who discover no sensibility to the distresses of real life, the exhibitions of fictitious scenes of distress produce effects analogous to those we have illustrated.

Illus. In a novel or a tragedy, the picture is completely finished in all its parts ; and we are made acquainted (as in " THE VICAR OF WAKEFIELD," for example, or " KING LEAR") not only with every circumstance on which the distress turns, but with the sentiments and feelings of every character, with respect to the situation of that character. In real life we see, in general, only detached scenes of the tragedy, and the impression is slight, unless Imagination finishes the characters, and supplies the incidents which are wanting to make them complete.

274. Imagination, however, does not only increase our sensibility to scenes of distress ; it gives us a double share of enjoyment in the prosperity of others, and fits us to participate, with a more lively interest, in every fortunate incident that falls to the lot either of individuals or of communities.

Obs. 1. Even from the productions of the earth, and the vicissitudes of the year, Imagination carries forward our thoughts to the enjoyments they bring to the sensitive creation, and by interesting our benevolent affections in the scenes we behold, lends a new charm to the beauties of nature. In confirmation of this observation, I recommend to the student's perusal, Thomson's "Seasons," or Bloomfield's "Farmer's Boy."

2. As to those callous beings who feel wholly for themselves, and have no emotions for the fate of others ; who, in fact, evince no feeling for the distresses to which humanity is so much a prey ; their coldness and selfishness may be traced to a want of attention, and a want of Imagination ; and I shall not, therefore, insult the mind of generous youth, by portraying principles that bar the heart against the eloquent and pathetic language of beggary, famine, disease, and all the distress which exists in the world.

V. *On the Culture of the Imagination.*

275. It may be asserted, without fear of contradiction, that, with regard to the faculty of Imagination, as with regard to all the other endowments of the mind, certain degrees of improvement are within the reach of every individual who earnestly endeavors to attain it.

Illus. In truth, says Professor Jardine, the simple consideration that this faculty, like most others, is in a constant state of action, necessarily implies the notion of culture and improvement. In very young persons, too, its efforts are weak, and its combinations unsteady ; but, as the range of knowledge enlarges, and the number of ideas is increased, its growing power makes itself manifest in the vivid reproductions which it places before the mind, and in the boldness of its varied creations.

Example 1. When Philip planned the conquest of Greece, or when Scipio and Polybius anticipated the destruction of Carthage, their Imaginations must have been strong and steady enough to present, before the eye of their minds, extensive combinations of distant events respecting the relative state and condition of these nations, and the various probabilities which fell within their view. Their Imaginations could not have performed for them this office when they first began to study politics.

2. When Sir Isaac Newton first began to study astronomy, he would probably find it extremely difficult to combine the revolutions of the Earth and Moon in their orbits round the Sun ; but, in process of time, his Imagination would, with the utmost ease and steadiness, place before him the whole solar system, in the order of the relative distances, magnitudes, and dependencies of the several planets of which it is composed.

3. When the celebrated Edmund Burke, too, at the very time when the greatest part of the learned men of Europe were rejoicing at the *pleasing prospect* opened by the French Revolution. foresaw the confusion, anarchy, and bloodshed, that followed so hard upon it, his Imagination must have held up t him a long train of events,

10

linked together as cause and effect, and must have manifested a degree of energy to which, in the early periods of his life, it would have been totally inadequate.

Corol. These examples make it very obvious that there is a gradual progress in the development of this faculty, and, consequently, that there is a fair field spread out for the application of culture.

276. It is well known, from experience, that the activity and consequent improvement of the Imagination, depend not a little upon the character of the objects with which it is first occupied.

Illus. The great, the sublime, the beautiful, the new, and the uncommon, in external nature, are not only striking and agreeable in themselves, but, by association, these qualities powerfully awaken the sensibilities of the heart, and kindle the fires of youthful Imagination. On the other hand, there are certain objects so mean, so tame, and pursuits so ignoble, amidst which the early years of life are sometimes doomed to be spent, as neither to have produced one impression, nor excited one train of thought, which could ever afterwards enter into the conceptions, or aid the fancy, of the painter or the poet. (JARDINE.)

Corol. If, therefore, the student shall permit objects which are mean, low, or sensual, to usurp possession of his mind; if the books which he reads, and the studies that he pursues, are contaminated with gross ideas, he has no right to expect that this omnipotent faculty shall ever draw from the polluted treasures of his memory any thing noble, useful, or praiseworthy; or that his name shall ever be enrolled among those who have delighted, instructed, and honored their native land and the world at large :—" Out of the fulness of the heart, the mouth speaketh."

277. But the Imagination is not only improvable in point of vigor and activity; it likewise admits of culture in respect of regularity and chasteness. (*Corol. Art.* 270.)

Illus. No faculty is naturally more irregular and rambling in its motions, or demands more loudly the control of a governing power. Whilst we are awake, indeed, and in a sound state of mind, it is kept within some bounds by the presence of external objects, and by the impression derived from them through the medium of the senses; but in a dream, those sentinels being off their guard, we have sufficient experience of its eccentric flights, and its fantastic combinations. The first efforts, too, of men of genius, may be compared to the curvetings of an unbridled colt, which scampers over the fields, spurning all constraint, till its strength is exhausted; nor is it until experience, with its usual accompaniments of improved knowledge and enlightened taste, has tamed the impetuosity of youthful feeling, that this faculty becomes subjected to those regular movements of reason, sensibility, and passion, to which we owe the many fine specimens of poetry, eloquence, statuary, and painting, that adorn the brighter eras of civilized society. (JARDINE.)

Corol. 1. From the foregoing illustrations in this *section*, it naturally occurs, as a rational inquiry, whether there might not be constructed such a scheme of discipline and instruction, as would invigorate and call forth, in regular and systematic exercises, the latent powers of Imagination? The enlightened tutor of a well-adjusted plan of education, will find many of the first steps within his reach, and the virtuous student will find, in the end, that the company he has kept, the conversation he has maintained, and the books he has used, are of some avail in influencing his general taste, and in determining the bias of fancy, and improving or deteriorating the powers of Imagination.

2. From certain varieties, which no doubt subsist in the original constitution of the intellectual powers, from early habits and particular associations, the Imagination of some youths may be more early directed to sensible or to visible imagery than to other trains of thought; but, in all cases, the Imagination, the active instrument of reproduction, is within the reach of culture, when applied properly, and at a proper season. Great poets, and illustrious painters, are, it is true, distinguished by original differences of activity and strength of Imagination; nor is it less true, on the other hand, that no degree of labor or of industry can raise a weak and feeble Imagination to the highest degree of poetical or of limning genius; still, it may be maintained (see *Corol. Art.* 270. *Section* III. of this chapter), that, by reasonable culture, this power can be made capable of greater efforts, and invested with higher qualities, than could arise from the mere natural and unimproved endowments.

This is the opinion of Professor Jardine, and it is supported by the authority of Dugald Stewart. See the " Outlines of a Philosophical Education," by the former, and the " Elements of the Philosophy of the Human Mind," ch. vii. vol. 1. by the latter.

CHAPTER X.

OF JUDGMENT.

I. *Analysis of this Faculty in general.*

278. JUDGMENT has been defined the faculty by which the mind comes to determinations concerning the truth or falsehood of any thing that is affirmed or denied. (*Art.* 97. *No.* X. p. 44.)

Obs. As it is impossible, by a definition, to give a notion of color to a man who never saw colors, so it is impossible, by any definition, to give a distinct notion of *Judgment*, to a person who has not often judged, and who is not capable of *reflecting* attentively upon this act of the mind. The best use of a definition, is to prompt the reader to that reflection; and without it the best definition will be apt to mislead him. The definition we have given is confirmed by the following illustrations

Illus. 1. True it is, that by affirmation or denial, we express our judgments; but there may be judgments which are *not* expressed. Judgment is a solitary act of the mind, and the expression of it, by affirmation or denial, is not at all essential to it. It may be tacit, and not expressed. Nay, it is well known, that men may judge contrary to what they affirm or deny; the definition must, therefore, be understood of mental affirmation or denial, which indeed is only another name for Judgment. (See *Illus. Art.* 28.)

2. The affirming or denying a thing, is very often the expression of *testimony*, which is a direct act of the mind, and ought to be distinguished from Judgment.

Example. A judge asks a witness what he knows of such a matter, to which he was an eye or an ear witness. The witness answers by affirming or denying something. But his answer does not express his Judgment; it is his *testimony*. Again, you ask a man his opinion in a matter of science, or of criticism. His answer is not testimony; it is the expression of his *judgment*. Thus, *testimony* is distinguished from *judgment*. (See *Illus.* 2. *Art.* 116.)

Illus. 3. Testimony is a social act, and it is essential to this act that it be expressed by words or signs. A tacit testimony is a contradiction; but there is no contradiction in a tacit Judgment: it is complete, without being expressed. In testimony, a man pledges his veracity for what he affirms; so that a *false testimony* is a *lie;* but a *wrong judgment* is *not a lie;* it is only an *error.* In the structure of all languages, says Dr. Reid, testimony and judgment are expressed by the same form of speech. A proposition, *affirmative* or *negative*, with a verb in what is called the indicative mood, expresses both. (See *Art.* 25.)

4. Although men must have judged in many cases before tribunals of justice were erected, yet it is very probable that there were tribunals before men began to speculate about Judgment, and that the word may be borrowed from the practice of tribunals. As a judge, *after* taking the proper evidence, passes sentence, in a cause, and that SENTENCE is called his *judgment*, so the *mind*, with regard to whatever is true or false, *passes sentence*, or determines according to the evidence that is before it. Some kinds of evidence leave no room for doubt, and sentence is passed immediately, without seeking or hearing any contrary evidence, because the thing is certain and notorious. In other cases, there is room for weighing evidence, on both sides, before sentence is passed.

Corol. The analogy between a tribunal of justice and this inward tribunal of the mind, is too obvious to escape the notice of any man who ever appeared before a judge; and we may thence infer, that the word *Judgment*, as well as *many other words* which we use in speaking of this operation of the mind, are grounded on this analogy. (See Chapter IV. Book I.)

279. In Article 140, we pointed out the distinction between *conception*, as used in Chapter V. of this book, and *simple apprehension*, which, in the language of the schoolmen, includes our apprehension of general propositions. *Judgment* is an act of the mind specifically different from

simple apprehension, or the bare conception of a thing. (See *Illus. Art.* 25.)

Illus. Although there can be no Judgment without a conception of the things about which we judge, yet conception may be without any Judgment. Judgment can be expressed by a proposition only, and a proposition is a complete sentence ; but simple apprehension may be expressed by a word, or words, which make no complete sentence. When simple apprehension is employed about a proposition, every man knows that it is one thing to apprehend a proposition, that is, to conceive what it means ; but it is quite another thing to judge it to be true or false. (*Illus. Art.* 28.)

280. Every Judgment must be either true or false, but simple apprehension can neither be true nor false. (See *Corol. Art.* 52.)

Illus. One Judgment may be contradictory to another ; and it is impossible for a man to have, at the same time, two Judgments, which he perceives to be contradictory. But contradictory propositions may be conceived at the same time without any difficulty. That the Sun is greater than the Earth, and that the Sun is not greater than the Earth, are contradictory propositions. He that apprehends the meaning of the one apprehends the meaning of both. But it is impossible for him to judge both to be true at the same time. He knows that if one is true, the other is false.

Corol. For these reasons, we hold it to be certain, that Judgment and simple apprehension are acts of the mind specifically different. (See *Art.* 279.)

281. There are notions, or ideas, that ought to be referred to the faculty of Judgment as their source ; because, if we had not this faculty, they could not enter into our minds ; and to all those that have this faculty, and are capable of reflecting upon its operations, they are obvious and familiar. ●

Illus. Among these we may reckon the notion of Judgment itself ; the notions of a proposition, of its subject, of its predicate, and of its copula ;—of affirmation and negation, of true and false, of knowledge, belief, disbelief, opinion, assent, evidence. From no source could we acquire these notions, but from reflecting upon our judgments. Relations of things make one great class of our notions, or ideas ; and we cannot have the idea of any relation, without some exercise of Judgment.

282. In persons come to years of understanding, Judgment necessarily accompanies all sensation, perception by the senses, consciousness, and memory.

Obs. Infants and idiots are of course excluded in the consideration of this position.

Illus. 1. In persons having the exercise of Judgment, it is evident, that the man who feels pain, judges and believes that he is really

10 *

pained. (See *Illus. Art.* 39.) The man who perceives an object believes that it exists, and that it is what he distinctly perceives it to be ;
nor is it in his power to avoid such a Judgment. And the same may
be affirmed of Memory, and of Consciousness.

2. Whether Judgment ought to be called a necessary concomitant
of these operations, or rather a part or ingredient of them, enters not
into the illustration before us ; but it is certain, that all of them are
accompanied with a determination and a consequent belief that something is true or false. If this determination be not Judgment, it is an
operation that has received no name by philosophers ; for it is not
simple apprehension, neither is it reasoning ; it is a mental affirmation
or negation ; it may be expressed by a proposition affirmative or negative, and it is accompanied with the firmest belief. These are the
characteristics of Judgment.

283. The judgments which we form are either of things
necessary, or of things *contingent.*

Illus. 1. That three times three are *nine ;* that the whole is greater than its part ;—are judgments about things *necessary.* Our assent to such necessary propositions is not grounded upon any operation of sense, of memory, or of consciousness, nor does it require their
concurrence ; it is unaccompanied by any other operation but that
of conception, which must accompany all Judgment. (See *Art.* 147.
Illus. 1.)

2. Our Judgment of things *contingent* must always rest upon some
other operation of the mind, such as sense, or memory, or consciousness, or credit in testimony, which is itself grounded upon sense.
That 1 now write upon a desk covered with green baize, is a contingent event, which I judge to be most undoubtedly true. My Judgment is grounded upon my perception (*Art.* 23.), and is a necessary
concomitant, or ingredient, of my perception. That I yesterday dined
with such a person, 1 judge to be true, because I remember it, and my
Judgment necessarily goes along with this remembrance, or makes a
part of it. (See *Art.* 49.)

284. There are many forms of speech in common language which show that the *senses, memory*, and *consciousness*,
are considered as *judging faculties.*

Illus. We say that a man judges of *colors* by his *eye*, of *sounds* by
his *ear.* We speak of the evidence of sense (*Corol. Art.* 121), the
evidence of memory (*Art.* 243. *Illus.*), and the evidence of consciousness (*Corol. Art.* 101). Evidence is the basis of Judgment ; and when
we see evidence, it is impossible not to judge.

Corol. 1. Hence, when we speak of seeing or remembering any
thing, we hardly ever add that *we judge it to be true ;* because such
an addition would be a superfluity of speech. And, for the same reason, in speaking of what is self-evident, or strictly demonstrated, we
do not say that we judge it to be true. Hence the grammarians
say, that *to see with the eyes*, is a tautology ; and they are perfectly
correct.

2. There is, therefore, good reason why, in *speaking* or *writing*,
Judgment should not b·expressly mentioned, when all men know

it to be necessarily implied ; that is to say, when there can be no doubt. The bare mention of the *evidence* is all that men require ; but when the *evidence* mentioned *leaves room for doubt*, then, without any superfluity, or tautology, we say we judge the thing to be so, because this is not implied in what was said before.

285. The judgments grounded upon the evidence of sense, of memory, and of consciousness, are called *judgments of nature*, because she has subjected us to them, whether we will or not,—because she has thus put all men upon a level (*Art.* 121. *Corol.*), and thus deprived the philosopher of any prerogative above the illiterate, or even above the savage. Belief in our senses, and in our memory, is not learned by *culture*. It is necessary to all men for their being and preservation, and therefore is unconditionally given to all men by the Author of Nature.

II. *Of the Exercise of Judgment in the Formation of abstract and general Conceptions.*

286. That some exercise of Judgment is necessary in the formation of all abstract and general conceptions, whether more simple or more complex in *dividing*, in *defining*, and, in general, in forming all clear and distinct conceptions of things, which are the only fit materials of all reasoning, we shall now proceed to illustrate.

Obs. These operations are allied to each other, and have, therefore, been brought under one article ; but they are more allied to our *rational* nature than those considered in the last section, and are therefore to be considered by themselves. And, that the illustrations we are to offer may not be mistaken for what they really are not, we take leave to premise, that it is not meant to be affirmed that abstract notions, or other accurate notions of things, *after they have been formed*, cannot be barely conceived without any exercise of Judgment about them. All that is meant by the position laid down in the article now in hand, is, that, in the formation, at first, of those " abstract and general conceptions " of the mind, *there must be some exercise of Judgment.*

Illus. 1. It is impossible to distinguish the different attributes belonging to the same subject, without judging that they are really different and distinguishable, and that they have that relation to the subject which logicians express by saying that they may be *predicated* of it. We cannot generalize, without judging that the same attribute does, or may, belong to many individuals. (*Art.* 188.) Our simplest general notions are formed by distinguishing and generalizing ; hence we may infer that Judgment is exercised in forming the simplest general notions.

2. In those that are more complex, and which have been shown to be formed by combining the more simple, there is another act of the

Judgment required; for such combinations are not made at random, but for an end, and Judgment is employed in fitting them to that end. We form complex general notions for the conveniency of arranging our thoughts in discourse and reasoning ; and therefore, of an infinite number of combinations that might be formed, we choose only those that are useful and necessary.

287. That Judgment must be employed in dividing, as well as in distinguishing, appears evident. It is one thing to divide a subject properly, another to cut it to pieces. *Hoc non est dividere, sed frangere rem,* said Cicero, when he censured the improper division of Epicurus.

Illus Reason, as we shall see by and bye, has discovered rules of division, which have been known to logicians for more than two thousand years. There are rules, likewise, of definition, of no less antiquity and authority. A man may, no doubt, divide or define properly without attending to these rules, or even without knowing them ; but this can only be when he has Judgment to perceive *that to be right in a particular case,* which *the rule determines* to be right in *all cases.*

Corol. What has now been advanced, leads to the inference that, without some degree of Judgment, we can form no accurate and distinct notions of things ; so that one province of Judgment is to aid us in forming clear and distinct conceptions of things, which are the only fit materials for reasoning.

288. The necessity of some degree of Judgment, to have clear and distinct conceptions of things, may thus be illustrated, even to the philosophers, who have always considered the formation of ideas of every kind as belonging to simple apprehension, and that the sole province of Judgment is to put them together in affirmative or negative propositions.

Illus. An artist (suppose a carpenter) cannot work in his art without tools, and these tools must be made by art. The exercise of the art, therefore, is necessary to make the tools, and the tools are necessary to the exercise of the art ; and this is illustrative of the necessity of some degree of Judgment in order to form clear and distinct conceptions of things. These are the tools which we must use in judging and reasoning, and without them our work must be very bungling indeed ; yet these tools cannot be made without some exercise of Judgment.

289. The necessity of some degree of Judgment, in forming accurate and distinct notions of things, will further appear, if we consider attentively what notions we can form, without any aid of Judgment, of the *objects* of sense, of the *operations* of our own minds, or of the *relations* of things.

(1.) *To begin with the* OBJECTS OF SENSE.

290. It is acknowledged, on all hands, that the first no-tions we have of sensible objects are acquired by the external senses only, and probably before Judgment is brought forth ; but these first notions are neither simple, nor are they accurate and distinct. They are gross and indistinct, and, like a chaos, an indigested heap of rude materials. Before we can have any distinct notion of this mass, it must be analyzed ; the heterogeneous parts must be separated in our conception, and the simple elements, which before lay hid in the common mass, must first be distinguished, and then put together into one whole.

Illus. In this way it is that we form distinct notions even of the objects of sense ; but this analysis and composition become so easy by habit, and can be thence performed so readily, that we are apt to overlook it, and to impute the distinct notion we have formed of the object, to the senses alone ; and this we are the more prone to do, because, when once we have distinguished the sensible qualities of the object from one another, the *sense* gives *testimony* to each of them.

Example. Suppose a cube of brass to be presented at the same time to a child of a year old and to a man. The regularity of the figure will attract the attention of both. Both have the sensations of sight and of touch in equal perfection ; and, therefore. if any thing be discovered in this object by the man, which cannot be discovered by the child, it must be owing, not to the senses, but to some other faculty, which the child has not yet attained.

Illus. 1. *First*, then, the man can easily distinguish the body from the surface that terminates it : this the child cannot do. *Secondly*, the man can perceive, that this surface is made up of six planes of the same figure and magnitude ; the child cannot discover this. *Thirdly*, the man perceives that each of these planes has four equal sides, and four angles ; and that the opposite sides of each plane, and the opposite planes, are parallel. (See *Illus.* 1. *Art.* 183.)

2. It will surely be allowed, that a man of ordinary Judgment may observe all this in a cube which he makes an object of contemplation, and takes time to consider ; that he may give the name of a *square* to a plane terminated by four equal sides and four equal angles ; and the name of a *cube*, to a solid terminated by six equal squares ; all this, then, is nothing else but analyzing the figure of the object presented to his senses into its simplest elements, and again compounding it of those elements.

3. By this analysis and composition *two effects* are produced. *First*, from the one complex object which his senses presented to his mind, though one of the most simple the senses can present, he educes many simple and distinct notions of right lines, angles, plane surface, solid, equality, parallelism ; notions which the child has not yet faculties to attain. *Secondly*, when the man considers the cube as compounded of these elements, put together in a certain order,

he has then, and not before, a distinct and scientific notion of a cube. The child neither conceives those elements, nor in what order they must be put together, so as to make a cube ; and therefore of a cube he has no accurate notion which can make it a subject of reasoning.

Corol. Whence we may conclude, that the notions which we have from the senses alone, even of the simplest object of sense, are indistinct, and incapable of being either described or reasoned upon, until the object is analyzed into its simple elements, and considered as compounded of those elements. (See *Illus.* and *Corol. Art.* 188.)

Illus. 4. And if we should apply this reasoning to more complex objects of sense, the conclusion is still more evident.

Example. A dog may be taught to turn a jack, but he can never be taught to have a distinct notion of a jack. He sees every part of it as well as a man ; but the *relation* of the parts to one another, and to the whole, he has not Judgment to comprehend. (See *Illus.* 6. *Art.* 192.)

Illus. 5. A distinct notion of an object, even of sense, is never got in an instant ; but the sense performs its office in an instant. Time is not required *to see* it better, but *to analyze it,* to *distinguish* the different parts, and their *relation* to one another, and to the whole.

Corol. Hence it is, that when any vehement passion or emotion hinders the cool application of Judgment, we get no distinct notion of an object, even though the sense be long directed to it.

Examp'e. A man who is put into a panic, by thinking he sees a ghost, may stare very long, without having any distinct notion of what he fancies he beholds ; it is his *understanding,* and not *his sense,* that is *disturbed* by his *horror.* If he can lay that aside, Judgment immediately enters upon its office, and examines the length and breadth, the color and figure, and distance of the object. Of these, while his panic lasted, he had no distinct notion, though his eyes were open all the time.

Illus. 6. When the visual organ is open, but the Judgment disturbed by a panic, or any violent emotion that engrosses the mind, we see things confusedly, and probably much in the same manner that brutes and perfect idiots do, and infants also before the use of Judgment.

Corol. There are, therefore, notions of the objects of sense, which are gross and indistinct, and there are others which are distinct and scientific. The former may be acquired from the senses alone ; but the latter cannot be obtained without some degree of Judgment.

291. (II.) Having said so much on the notions which we acquire of the objects of sense from the senses alone, let us next consider what notions we can have of the *operations* of our minds, from *consciousness* alone.

Illus. Consciousness is an internal sense, (*Art.* 24.) that gives the like immediate knowledge of things in the mind, that is, of our own thoughts and feelings (*Illus. Art.* 10C , as the senses give us of things external. (*Art.* 103.) There is this difference, however, that an external object may be at rest, and the sense may be employed about it for some time. (*Illus. Art.* 115.) But the objects of consciousness are never at rest; the stream of thought flows like a river, without stopping for one moment; the whole train of thought passes in succession under the eye of consciousness, which is always employed about the present. But is it consciousness that analyzes complex operations, distinguishes their different ingredients, and combines them in distinct parcels, under general names?—No.—(*Art.* 24. and *Illus. Art.* 48.)—This is not the work of consciousness, nor can it be performed without reflection (*Art.* 51.), recollecting and judging of what we were conscious, and what we distinctly remember. This reflection does not appear in children, and, of all the powers of the mind, it comes latest to maturity, whereas consciousness is coeval with the earliest. (*Obs. Art.* 102. and *Illus. Art.* 129.) But this subject has been so sufficiently handled in the fifth Chapter of Book I. that further proofs in this place are unnecessary.

292. (III.) We proposed, in the *third place*, to consider our notions of the *relations* of things; and here it appears, that *without Judgment we cannot have any notion of relations.*

Illus. 1. There are two ways in which we acquire the notion of *relations.* The *first* is, by comparing the related objects, of which we have before had the conception. By this comparison we perceive the relation, either immediately, or by a process of reasoning.

Examples. That the fifth finger of my hand is shorter than the middle finger, I perceive immediately; as well as that three is the half of six. This instantaneous perception is immediate and intuitive Judgment. (See *Art.* 114. and 118.) The angles at the base of an isosceles triangle are equal, I perceive by a process of reasoning, in which it will be acknowledged that there is Judgment. (See *Illus. Art.* 119.)

Illus. 2. Another way in which we get the notions of *relations* is, when, by attention to one of the related objects, we perceive, or judge, that it must, from its nature, have a certain relation to something else, which before perhaps we never thought of; and thus our attention to one of the related objects produces the notion of a correlate, and of a certain relation between them.

Example. Thus, when you attend to color, figure, weight, you cannot help judging these to be qualities which cannot exist without a subject (*Illus. Art.* 18.); that is, something which is colored, figured, heavy. (See *Illus. Art.* 182.) If you had not perceived such things to be qualities, you would never have had any notion of their subject, or of their relation to it. (See the *Illustrations to Article* 195.)

Illus. 3. By attending to the operations of thinking, memory, reasoning, we perceive, or judge, that there must be something which thinks, remembers, and reasons; and this something we call the mind. (*Art.* 5.) When we attend to any change that happens in nature, Judgment informs us, that there must be a cause of this change, which had power to produce it; and thus we get the notions of cause and effect, and of the relation between them. (See *Art.* 13 *Illus.* 1, 2, 3.) When we attend to body, we perceive that it cannot exist without space; hence we get the notion of space, which is neither an object of sense nor of consciousness, and of the relation which bodies have to a certain portion of unlimited space, as their place. (See *Art.* 244. *Illus.* 3 and 4.)

Corol. All our notions, therefore, of relations, may more properly be ascribed to Judgment, as their source, and origin, than to any other power of the mind. For we must first perceive relations by our Judgment, before we can conceive them without judging of them; as we must first perceive colors by sight, before we can conceive them without seeing them.

Illus. 4. The relations of unity and number are so abstract, that it is impossible they should enter into the mind until it has some degree of Judgment. We see with what difficulty, and how slowly, children learn to use, with understanding, the names even of small numbers, and how they exult in this acquisition whenever they have attained it. Every number is conceived by the relation which it bears to unity, or to known combinations of units; and, upon that account, as well as on account of its abstract nature, all distinct notions of it require some degree of Judgment.

Corol. In Chapter IX. of this Book, it was clearly shown how much Judgment enters, as an ingredient, into all determinations of Taste; and in Chapter XII. we shall have occasion to show, that, in all moral determinations, and in many of our passions and affections, Judgment is a necessary concomitant; so that this faculty, after we come to those years in which reason exercises its powers, mingles with most of the operations of our minds, and, in analyzing them, cannot be overlooked without confusion and error.

CHAPTER XI.

OF REASON.

I. *Definition and Analysis of this Faculty.*

293. REASON is the faculty by which we are made acquainted with abstract or necessary truth, and enabled to discover the essential relations of things.

Obs. The power of Reasoning is very nearly allied to that of judging; and, in the common affairs of life, the same term is applied to both. We include both under the name of Reason.

Illus. The distinction that has been made between Judgment and Reasoning, is not, perhaps, founded so much in any natural diversity of the nature or the objects of the faculties, as in the various manner in which the same faculty is occasionally applied. This, then seems to be the foundation of the distinction. When the truth which is asserted, or the falsity which is denied, is perfectly obvious, and requires little or no examination, the faculty is then commonly called *Judgment* (*Art.* 278. *Illus.* 1.); but, when the truth which is asserted, or the falsity which is denied, is more remote from common apprehension, and requires a careful examination, the faculty has then been dignified with the name of *Reasoning.*

Corol. 1. *Reasoning* being, then, the process by which we pass from one judgment to another, which is a consequence of the preceding, our judgments are distinguished into INTUITIVE, which are not grounded upon any preceding judgment, and DISCURSIVE, which are deduced from some preceding judgment by Reasoning.

2. In all Reasoning, therefore, there must be a proposition inferred, and one or more from which it is inferred; and this power of inferring, or drawing a conclusion, is only another name for Reasoning, the proposition inferred being called the *conclusion,* and the proposition or propositions from which that conclusion has been inferred being called the *premises.*

294. Reasoning may consist of many steps, the first conclusion being a premise to the second, the second to a third, and so on, till we come to the last·conclusion. A process, consisting of many steps of this kind, is so easily distinguished from Judgment, that it is never called by that name; but when there is only a single step to the conclusion, the distinction is less obvious, and the process is, as we have shown above, sometimes ·called *Judgment,* sometimes *Reasoning.*

Obs. The Logicians themselves, as well as the illiterate, sometimes confound judgment with Reasoning, though their definition of both be, in general terms, what we have now (*Art.* 294.) expressed. So various, indeed, are the *modes* of speech, that what, in one mode, is expressed by two or three propositions, may, in another, be expressed by one.

Example. Thus, I may say, *God is good; therefore all good men shall be happy.* This species of Reasoning the Logicians call an *Enthymeme,* as it consists of an antecedent proposition, and a conclusion drawn from it. But this reasoning may be expressed by one proposition, thus: *Because God is good, good men shall be happy.* This other species of Reasoning they call a *casual proposition,* which, therefore, expresses judgment; yet the Enthymeme, which is Reasoning, expresses no more.

295. Reasoning, as well as Judgment, must be true or false (*Art.* 45.); both are founded upon evidence, which may be PROBABLE or DEMONSTRATIVE (*Art.* 302.), and both are accompanied with ASSENT or BELIEF. (*Illus. Art.* 48.)

Obs. What Reasoning is, can be understood only by a man who has reasoned, and who is capable of reflecting upon the operations

11

of his own mind. We can define it only by synonymous words, or phrases, such as *inferring*, *drawing a conclusion*, and such like.

Corol. The very notion, therefore, of Reasoning, can enter into the mind by no other channel than that of reflecting upon the operation of Reasoning in our own minds; and the notions of *Premises* and *Conclusions*, of a *Syllogism* and all its constituent parts, of an *Enthymeme*, of *Sorites*, *Demonstration*, *Paralogism*, and many other technical terms of logic, have the same origin.

296. The faculty of Reasoning is undoubtedly *the gift of Nature;* and in vain shall we attempt to supply the want of this gift where it is not, by art or education. In *different individuals* this faculty will be found in *different degrees;* yet the power of Reasoning seems to be acquired by habit, as much as the power of walking, running, or swimming.

Illus. We *are not ab'e* to recollect its *first exertions* in ourselves, nor clearly to discern them in others, because they are then feeble, and need to be *led by example*, and *supported by authority;* but, by degrees, the faculty acquires strength, chiefly by means of imitation and exercise.

297. The exercise of Reasoning on various subjects, not only strengthens the faculty, but furnishes the mind with stores of materials.

Illus. 1. Every train of Reasoning, which is familiar, becomes a beaten track, or pathway of many others; it removes many obstacles which lie in our way, and smooths many roads which we may have occasion to travel, in future disquisitions.

2. When men of equal parts apply their reasoning powers to any subject, the man who has reasoned much on the same, or on similar subjects, has a like advantage over him who has not, as the mechanic who has all the tools of his art, has over him who has his tools to make, or even to invent.

298. In a train of Reasoning, *the evidence of every step*, where nothing is left to be supplied by the reader or the hearer, *must be immediately discernible* to every man of ripe understanding, who has a distinct comprehension of the premises and conclusions, and who compares them together.

Obs. To be able to comprehend, in one view, a combination of steps of this kind, is more difficult, and seems to require a superior natural ability; yet, in all of us, it may be much improved by habit.

299. But the highest talent in reasoning is the *Invention of proofs*, by which truths remote from the premises are brought to light.

Obs. In all works of understanding, *Invention* has the highest praise (*Art.* 26. *Illus.*); it requires an extensive view of what relates to the subject, and a quickness in discerning those affinities and relations which may be subservient to the purpose. (See *Art.* 264. *Illus.* 1 and 2. and *Corol.* 1 and 2.)

300. In all Invention there must be some end in view; and *Sagacity* in finding out the road that leads to that end, is, properly speaking, what we call *Invention.*

Obs. In this chiefly, and in clear and distinct conceptions, consists that superiority of understanding which we have called *Genius.* (See *Art.* 265. *Illus.*)

301. In every chain of Reasoning, the evidence of the last conclusion can be no greater than that of the *weakest link* of the chain, whatever may be the strength of the rest. (See *Art.* 294. *Obs.* and *Example.*)

302. Reasonings are either PROBABLE or DEMONSTRATIVE. (See *Art.* 295. *Illus.*)

I. In every step of *Demonstrative* Reasoning, the inference *is necessary*, and we perceive it to be *impossible* that the *conclusion* should not follow from the premises.

II. In *Probable* Reasoning, the connection between the premises and the conclusion *is not necessary*, nor do we perceive it to be *impossible* that the *first should be true* while the *last is false.*

Corol. Hence Demonstrative Reasoning has no degrees, nor can one demonstration be stronger than another, though, in relation to our faculties, one may be more easily comprehended than another. Every demonstration gives equal strength to the conclusion, and leaves no possibility of its being false.

II. *Analysis of Demonstrative Reasoning.*

303. DEMONSTRATIVE Reasoning can be applied only to *truths that are necessary*, and not to those that are contingent.

Obs. Of all created things, the existence, the attributes, and, consequently, the relations resulting from those attributes, are contingent. They depend on the power and will of him who made them. These are matters of fact, and admit not of demonstration.

Corol. The field of Demonstrative Reasoning, therefore, is the various relations of things *abstract;* that is to say, of things which we conceive, without regard to their existence. We have a clear and adequate comprehension of these, as they are conceived by the mind, and are nothing but what they are conceived to be. Their relations and attributes are immutable.

Obs. 1. They are the things to which the Pythagoreans and Platonists gave the name of ideas; and, if we take leave to borrow this meaning of the word *idea* from those ancient philosophers, we must then agree with them that *ideas are the only objects about which we can reason demonstratively.*

2. There are many even of our ideas about which we can carry on no considerable train of reasoning; let them be ever so well defined, ever so perfectly comprehended, their agreements and disagreements are few, and these are discernible at once. A step of

two brings us to the conclusion, and there we are stopped. (*Example* 294.) There are others, about which we may, by a long train of Demonstrative Reasoning, arrive at conclusions very remote and unexpected

304. *Demonstrative Reasonings* are reducible to two classes :

I. They are either METAPHYSICAL,

II. Or they are MATHEMATICAL.

Illus. 1. In *Metaphysical Reasoning*, the process is always short. The conclusion is but a step or two, seldom more, from the first principle, or axiom, on which it is grounded, and the different conclusions depend one upon another.

2. In *Mathematical Reasoning*, on the contrary, the field has no limits. One proposition leads on to a second, that to a third, and so on, without end. And the reason why Demonstrative Reasoning has such extensive limits in the Mathematics is owing chiefly to the *nature of quantity*, which is the object of Mathematical Reasoning.

Example 1. Every *quantity*, as it has *magnitude*, and is *divisible* into *parts* without end; so, in respect of its magnitude, it has a certain *ratio* to every quantity of that kind. The ratios of quantities are innumerable ; such as a half, a third, a fourth, a tenth, double, triple, quadruple, centuple, and so on. All the powers of number are insufficient to express the varieties of ratios. For there are innumerable ratios which cannot be expressed perfectly by numbers ; such as, the ratio of the side to the diagonal of a square, of the circumference of a circle to its diameter. And, of this infinite variety of ratios, every ratio may be clearly conceived, and distinctly expressed, so that it shall not be mistaken for any other.

2. Extended quantities, such as lines, surfaces, solids, besides the variety of relations they have in respect of *magnitude*, have no less variety in respect of *figure* ; and every Mathematical figure may be accurately defined, so as to be distinguished from every other figure.

Illus. 3. There is nothing of this kind in other objects of *Abstract* Reasoning. Some of them have various degrees ; but these are not capable of measure, nor can they be said to have an assignable ratio to others of the kind. They are either simple, or compounded of a few indivisible parts ; and, therefore, if we may be allowed the expression, touch only in a few points. But Mathematical quantities, being made up of parts without number, can touch in innumerable points, and be compared in innumerable different ways.

305. Some Demonstrations are called *Direct*, others *Indirect.*

Illus. 1. Every youth acquainted with the elements of Euclid, knows that *Direct Demonstration* leads straight forward to the conclusion to be drawn, while the *Indirect* arrives at the proof by a proposition contradictory to that which is to be proved. The inference drawn from demonstration *ad absurdum*, is grounded on an axiom in logic, " That of two contradictory propositions, if one be false, the other must be true."

2. Another kind of *Indirect* Demonstration proceeds by enumerating all the suppositions that can possibly be made concerning the proposition to be proved, and then demonstrating, that, except that which is to be proved, all of them are false ; whence it follows, that *the excepted proposition is true.*

Example. Thus one line is proved to be equal to another, by proving *first* that it cannot be greater ; and *then* that it cannot be less ; for it must be either greater, or less, or equal ; and two of these suppositions being demonstrated to be false, the *third must be true.*

III. *Analysis of Probable Reasoning.*

306. The field of Demonstration, as has been shown, is necessary truth ; the field of PROBABLE REASONING is *contingent truth*, not what necessarily must be at all times, but what *is*, or *was*, or *shall be*.

307. No *contingent* truth is capable of strict Demonstration ; but *necessary* truths may sometimes have probable evidence.

Illus. 1. Dr. Wallis discovered many important truths, by that kind of *induction* which draws a *general conclusion* from *particular premises.* This is not strict Demonstration, but in some cases, it gives as full conviction as Demonstration itself ; and a man may be certain, that a truth is demonstrable before it ever has been demonstrated. (*Art.* 133. *Illus.*) In other cases, a Mathematical proposition may have such probable evidence from induction or analogy, as encourages the mathematician to investigate its Demonstration. (*Illus.* 2. *Art.* 304.) But still the Reasoning proper to Mathematical and other necessary truths, is *Demonstration ;* and that which is proper to *contingent truths*, is *Probable Reasoning.*

2. These two kinds of Reasoning differ in other respects. *First.* In Demonstrative Reasoning, one argument is as good as a thousand. One Demonstration may be more elegant than another ; it may be more easily comprehended, or it may be more subservient to some purpose beyond the present. On any of these accounts it may deserve a preference. But, then, it is sufficient by itself ; it needs no aid from another ; it can receive none. To add more Demonstrations of the same conclusion, would be a kind of tautology in Reasoning ; because one Demonstration, clearly comprehended, gives all the *Evidence* we are capable of receiving.

Secondly. The strength of *Probable Reasoning*, for the most part, depends not upon any one argument, but upon many, which unite their force, and lead to the same conclusion. Any one of them by itself would be insufficient to convince ; but the whole taken together may have a force that is irresistible, so that to desire more *Evidence* would be absurd. Who, for example, would seek new arguments to prove that there were such persons as Maria Antoinette and Queen Charlotte ; or Charles the First and Oliver Cromwell ?

Corol. Such *Evidence* of Probable Reasoning may be compared

11*

to a rope made up of many slender filaments twisted together.——
The rope has strength more than sufficient to bear the stress laid
upon it, though no one of the filaments of which it is composed
would be sufficient of itself for that purpose.

308. It is unreasonable to require Demonstration for
things which do not admit of it; nor is it less unreasonable
to require Reasoning of any kind for things which are known
without Reasoning. All Reasoning must be grounded upon
truths which are known without Reasoning.

Illus. In every branch of real knowledge, there must be *first
principles*, the truth of which is known intuitively, without Reasoning, either Probable or Demonstrative. (*Art.* 45.) They are not
grounded on Reasoning, but all Reasoning is grounded on them.
There are *first principles* of *necessary truths* (*Illus.* 1. and 2. *Art.* 52.)
and first principles of *contingent truths.* (*Obs.* and *Corol. Art.* 60.)
Demonstrative Reasoning is grounded upon the *former*, and *Probable
Reasoning* upon the *latter*.

309. *Probable Evidence* has a popular meaning, which
we must not confound with the philosophical meaning above
explained.

Illus. 1. In common language, *Probable Evidence* is considered
as an inferior degree of Evidence, and is opposed to certainty; so
that *what is only probable is not certain.* Philosophers consider *Probable Evidence*, not as a degree, but as a *species* of Evidence which
is opposed, *not to certainty*, but to another species of Evidence, called
Demonstration.
2. *Demonstrative Evidence* has no degrees; but Probable Evidence,
taken in the philosophical sense, has all degrees, from the very least
to the greatest, which we call certainty.
Example. That there is such a city as Edinburgh, I am as certain
as of any proposition in my Euclid; but the Evidence is not demonstrative, but of that kind which philosophers call *probable.* Yet,
in common language, it would sound oddly in me to say to Mr.
Gilbert, my printer, that, " It is probable there is such a city as
Edinburgh," because it would imply some degree of doubt or uncertainty.
Corol. Taking *Probable Evidence*, therefore, in the philosophical
sense, as it is opposed to demonstrative, it may have any degree of
Evidence, from the least to the greatest.

310. In most cases, we measure the *degrees* of Evidence
by the *effect* they have upon a sound understanding, when
comprehended clearly, and without prejudice.

Illus. Every degree of Evidence perceived by the mind, produces a *proportional degree of assent*, or belief. The judgment may
be in perfect suspense between two contradictory opinions, when
there is no Evidence for either, or equal Evidence for both. The
least preponderancy on one side inclines the judgment in proportion. Belief is mixed with doubt, more or less, until we come to

the highest degree of Evidence, when all doubt vanishes, and the belief is firm and immovable. This degree of Evidence, the highest the human faculties can attain, we call *certainty.*

IV. *Division of Probable Evidence into different Kinds.*

311. Probable Evidence not only *differs in kind* from demonstrative, but *is itself of different kinds.*

Obs. Without pretending to make the enumeration complete, we select, from Dr. Reid, the following kinds of Probable Evidence.

I. The Evidence of human testimony, upon which the greater part of knowledge is built.

II. The authority of those who are good judges of the point in question.

III. That whereby we recognize the identity of things, and persons of our acquaintance.

IV. That which we have of men's future actions and conduct, from the general principles of action in man, or from our knowledge of the individuals.

V. That by which we collect men's characters and designs from their actions, speech, and other external signs.

VI. That which mathematicians call the Probability of Chances.

VII. That by which the known laws of Nature have been discovered, and the effects which have been produced by them, in former ages, or which may be expected in time to come. Now, to illustrate these different kinds of *Probable Evidence.*

312. (I.) The Probable Evidence of HUMAN TESTIMONY is that upon which the greatest part of human knowledge is built.

Illus. 1. The faith of history is built upon it, as well as the judgment of solemn tribunals with regard to men's acquired rights, and with regard to their guilt or innocence, when they are charged with crimes. A great part of the business of the judge, of the counsel at the bar, of the historian, of the critic, and of the antiquarian, is, to canvass and weigh this kind of Evidence ; and no man can act with common prudence in the ordinary occurrences of life, who has not some competent judgment of it. (See *Art.* 64. *Illus.* 1, 2, 3. and *Corol.*)

2. The belief which, in many cases, we give to testimony, is not solely grounded upon the veracity of the testifier. In a single testimony, we consider the motives which a witness might have to falsify. If there be no appearance of any such motive, much more, if there be motives on the other side, his testimony has weight independent of his moral character. If the testimony be *circumstantial*, we consider how far the circumstances agree together, and with things that are known. It is so very difficult to fabricate a story, which cannot be detected by a judicious examination of the circumstances, that circumstantial testimony always acquires evidence by being able to bear such a trial. There is an art in judicial proceedings, in detecting false evidence, well known to able judges and barristers, so

that we daily hear of witnesses leaving behind them at the bar a suspicion of perjury.

Corol. Where there is an agreement of many witnesses, in a great variety of circumstances, without the possibility of a previous concert, the Evidence may be equal to that of Demonstration.

313. (II.) A second kind of Probable Evidence is, the AUTHORITY of those who are GOOD JUDGES of the point in question.

Illus. The supreme court of judicature of the British nation, (the PARLIAMENT,) is often determined by the opinion of lawyers, in a point of law ; of physicians, in a point of medicine ; and of other artists in what relates to their several professions. And, in the common affairs of life, we frequently rely upon the judgment of others in points of which we are not proper judges ourselves.

314. (III.) A third kind of Probable Evidence is, that by which we recognize the IDENTITY of *things*, and *persons* of our acquaintance.

Illus. That two swords, two horses, two men, may be so perfectly alike, as not to be distinguishable by those to whom they are best known, cannot be shown to be impossible. Who that has not, from this identity, mistaken, in the street, an entire stranger for a friend ? But we learn, either from nature, or from experience, that it never happens, or so very rarely, that a person, or thing, well known to us, is immediately recognized without any doubt, when we perceive the marks or signs by which we were wont to distinguish him or it from all other individuals of the kind.

Corol. This Evidence we rely upon in the most important affairs of life ; and, by this Evidence, the identity both of things and of persons, is determined in courts of judicature. (See *Art.* 116. *Illus.* 2.)

315. (IV.) A fourth kind of Probable Evidence is, that which we have of *men's future actions and conduct*, from the GENERAL PRINCIPLES of action in man, or from our knowledge of the individuals. (See *Art.* 87. *Illus.* 1 and 2.)

Illus. 1. In spite of all the folly and vice that we behold among our species, there is a certain degree of prudence and probity upon which we rely, in every man that is not an inhabitant of a mad-house. The pupil may find, in his own experience, a thousand examples to confirm this illustration. Men are not so much disposed to hurt as to do good to each other ; to lie as to speak truth ; else would the race soon perish : there is, therefore, notwithstanding the absurd dogmas of some fanatics, a greater share of good than of evil, and of truth than of falsehood, in the world.

2. We expect that men will take some care of themselves, of their family, their friends, and reputation ; that they will not injure others without some temptation ; that they will have some gratitude for good offices, and some resentment of injuries.

Corol. Such maxims, with regard to human conduct, are the foundation of all political reasoning, and of common prudence in the conduct of life.

316. (v.) Another kind of Probable Evidence, the counterpart of the last, is that by which we collect *men's* CHARACTERS *and designs from their actions, speech, and other external signs.* (See *Illus.* 1 and 2. *Art.* 87.)

Illus. We see not the hearts of men, nor are the principles by which they are actuated labelled on their forehead; but there are external signs of their principles and dispositions, which, though not certain, may sometimes be more trusted than their professions; and it is from *external* signs that we must draw *all the knowledge* which we can attain of men's *characters.*

317. (vi.) The next kind of Probable Evidence we mentioned, is, that which mathematicians call the PROBABILITY *of Chances.*

Illus. Chance is not commonly understood, either in philosophy or in vulgar language, to imply the *exclusion* of a cause, but our *ignorance* of the cause. When the term is employed to denote bare possibility of an event, when nothing is known either to produce or hinder it; in this meaning it can never be made the subject of calculation. In the former sense are understood all the chances about which my friend Mr. G. Davies, or any other mathematician, reasons, in the calculations of assurances, annuities, reversions, &c.

Example. In throwing a die upon a table, we say there is an equal chance which of the six sides shall be turned up; because neither the person who throws, nor the bystanders, can know the precise measure of force and direction necessary to turn up one side rather than another. There are here, therefore, *six events,* one of which *must* happen; and as all are supposed to have *equal* probability, the probability of any one side being turned up, the *ace,* for instance, is as *one* to the remaining number *five.* The probability of turning up *two* aces with *two dice,* is as *one* to *thirty-five;* because here there are thirty-six events, each of which has equal probability.

Corol. 1. Upon such principles as these, the doctrine of chances has furnished a field of Demonstrative Reasoning of great extent, although the events about which this Reasoning is employed, be *not necessary,* but *contingent;* and be *not certain,* but *probable.*

2. This may seem to contradict a principle before advanced, that contingent truths are not capable of demonstration (*Art* 307. *Illus.* 1.); but it does not:—For, in the Mathematical Reasonings about *chance,* the conclusion demonstrated is not, that *such* an event shall happen, but that the *probability* of its happening bears *such a ratio* to the probability of its failing; and this conclusion is necessary upon the suppositions on which it is grounded.

318. (vii.) The last kind of Probable Evidence we enumerated, is, that by which the *known laws of Nature* have been discovered, and the *effects* which have been *produced* by them in former ages, or which may be *expected* in time to come. (See *Illus. Art.* 45.)

Illus. 1. The laws of Nature are the rules by which the Supreme

Being governs the world. We deduce them only from facts which fall within our own observation, or are properly attested by those who have observed them. (See *Art.* 74. *Illus.*)

2. The knowledge of some of these laws is necessary to all men, and all men soon discover them. Who does not know that fire burns, that water drowns, that bodies gravitate towards the earth; that day and night, spring and autumn, regularly succeed each other? As far back as our experience and information reach, we know that these have happened; and, upon this ground, we are led, by the constitution of human nature, to expect that they will happen in time to come, in like circumstances. (*Illus. Art.* 75.)

3. The knowledge which the philosopher attains of the laws of Nature, differs from that of the vulgar, not in the first principles on which it is grounded, but in its extent and accuracy. He collects with care the phenomena that lead to the same conclusion, and compares them with those that seem to contradict or to limit it. He observes the circumstances on which every phenomenon depends, and distinguishes them carefully from those that are accidentally conjoined with it. He puts natural bodies in various situations, and applies them to one another in various ways, on purpose to observe the effect; and thus acquires from his senses a more extensive knowledge of the course of nature, in a short time, than could be collected by casual observation in many ages.

4. The result of his laborious researches is then barely this:—as far as he has been able to observe, such things have always happened, in such circumstances, and such bodies have always been found to have such properties. These are matters of fact, attested by sense, and memory, and testimony, just as the few facts which the vulgar know are attested to them.

5. And the conclusions which the philosopher draws from the facts which he has collected, are barely these:—that like events have happened in former times, in like circumstances, and will happen in time to come; and these conclusions are built on the very ground on which the simple rustic concludes that the sun will rise to-morrow. (See *Art.* 76. *Corol.*)

6. Facts reduced to general rules, and the consequences of those general rules, are all that we really know of the material world. And the Evidence that such general rules have no exceptions, as well as the Evidence that they will be the same in time to come as they have been in time past, can never be demonstrative. It is only that species of Evidence which philosophers call probable. General rules may have exceptions, or limitations, which no man ever had occasion to observe. The laws of Nature may be changed by Him who established them. But we are led, by our constitution, to rely upon their continuance with as little doubt as if it were demonstrable.

Note. The foregoing classification of Probable Evidence makes it incumbent on me that I enumerate also a few of the *first principles,* or *intuitive truths,* which other philosophers have laid down as the bases of Evidence; and the more so as the sophistry of all knaves is founded on the perversion, or the setting aside, of such first principles.

319. FATHER BUFFIER, a name entitled to the highest

encomium, finds two great sources from which he derives his first principles, viz.

I. *The consciousness we have of our own thoughts.*

II. *Common sense ;*—a phraseology which he employs in the common acceptation of language, as denoting the *faculty* by which men form judgments on the ordinary objects of their experience, which are not proper subjects of consciousness.

320. The following, though not, perhaps, a complete enumeration, are the examples of this good man's principles of common sense.*

I. There are other beings, and other men, in the world besides myself.

II. There is in them something that is called truth, wisdom, prudence ; and this something is not merely arbitrary. (See *Art.* 58. *Corol.*)

III. There is in me something that I call intelligence, or mind, and something which is not that intelligence, or mind, and which is named *body ;* so that each possesses properties different from the other. (See *Art.* 52. and 54.)

IV. What is generally said and taught by men, in all ages and countries of the world, is true. (*Art.* 60.)

V. All men have not combined to deceive and impose upon me.

VI. What is not intelligence, or mind, cannot produce all the effects of intelligence, or mind ; neither can a fortuitous jumble of particles of matter form a work of such order, and so regular motion, as a watch. (*Corol. Art.* 73.)

321. This original thinker mentions three qualities, or tests, by which first truths, or maxims of common sense, may be distinguished from all others.

I. They are so clear that they cannot be proved by any thing clearer.

II. They have been admitted in all countries, and at all times, with exceedingly few exceptions.

III. They are so strongly imprinted in our minds that we regulate our conduct by them, in spite of all the speculative refinements of that philosophy which denies them.

Obs. This illustrious genius lived in the beginning of the last century. Buffier considers the testimony of the senses as, at best, affording but Probable Evidence, and by no means entitled to be ranked on the footing of certain and intuitive truth ; and he places the evidence of Memory on the same level as the evidence of sense. As far as I have been able to ascertain, he was the FIRST who successfully taught the important science of *first truths,* in opposition to the career of skepticism, that then stalked over Europe. To M. Buffier's writings may be traced some of the finest thoughts, which sparkle like diamonds, in the productions of Drs. Reid, Beattie, Campbell, and Paley

---

* See his " Traité des Premiers Vérités et de la Source des nos Judgmens "

322. Dr. Beattie, in his " Essay on the Immutability of Truth," makes many observations on the nature of *Evidence*, the grounds of rational *Belief*, and the different kinds of *Truth*. In this work, the author proposes the following enumeration of the various kinds of evidence and sources of belief :—

I. *Mathematical* Evidence.
II. The evidence of *External Sense.*
III. The evidence of *Consciousness.*
IV. The evidence of *Memory.*
V. That evidence which we have, when, from *effects, we infer causes.*
VI. *Probable Evidence.*
VII. The evidence of *Testimony.*

Obs. 1. The first *five* he states to be *certain* and intuitive truths, or maxims of common sense ; the remaining *two* he likewise considers intuitive truths, or maxims of sense, but which Dr. Reid holds to be only probable, and not certain ; and he divides the sixth class into two species.

1st. The evidence by which we judge of future events by our past experience from similar events ; and,

2dly. The evidence of analogy.

Obs. 2. In Dr. Campbell's " Philosophy of Rhetoric " (which proceeded from the same school, at the head of which is Father Buffier, and which gave birth to the writings of Reid and Beattie), are ably handled, with the greatest similarity of sentiments to Dr. Reid, the two kinds of evidence, *Intuitive* and *Deductive.*

323. According to Dr. Campbell, INTUITIVE evidence is that which is admitted immediately, on a bare attention to the ideas under review, and DEDUCTIVE, which is admitted mediately, by a comparison of these with other ideas.

Illus. 1. *Intuitive* evidence the Doctor arranges under three heads.

I. MATHEMATICAL AXIOMS, which he states to be the result of pure *Intellection.*
II. CONSCIOUSNESS ; and,
III. COMMON SENSE ; under which last he comprehends both the evidence of Sense and Memory.

2. *Deductive evidence* is founded upon the Intuitive, and Dr. Campbell considers it as of two kinds :—*First*, that which is founded upon the axioms of pure intellection ; and, *Secondly*, that which is founded upon the dictates of consciousness and common sense, which he calls Moral or Probable Evidence, and divides into—

I. The knowledge we derive from experience.
II. That from analogy.
III. That from testimony ; and,
IV. The calculation of chances ; which last he considers as a mixed kind of evidence, partly certain, and partly probable only.

Note. Truth is one, in which we have all a common property ;

and the greatest pleasure I have in closing this Chapter, is, to refer my readers to the writings of those celebrated men whose names I have mentioned, and to the " Elements of the Philosophy of the Human Mind," by Mr. Stewart. These productions are so many altars of truth : the live coal on which is common sense—its vestal, *Reason.*

CHAPTER XII.

OF MORAL PERCEPTION.

324. MORAL PERCEPTION is the faculty which determines the choice of a rational being, as to what is *good for him upon the whole,* and what appears *to be duty.*

Obs. 1. That there is such a faculty as *Moral Perception* in man, I take for granted, on two grounds ; *first,* because he is endowed with Consciousness, Memory, and Judgment ; *Secondly,* because this faculty can have no existence but in a being endowed with Reason and all the other faculties, upon which, as principles or auxiliaries, it displays its exertions, in the various acts of Intention, of Will, and of Judgment.

2. This faculty spreads before our view a wide and variegated field of discursive inquiry and illustration, and we shall therefore arrange it under several sections.

I. *The Rational Principles of Action in Man.*

325. There can be no exercise of reason without judgment ; nor, on the other hand, any judgment of things abstract and general, without some degree of reason.

Corol. If, therefore, there be in the human constitution any principles of action, which, in their nature, necessarily imply such judgment, they are the principles which we may call *rational,* to distinguish them from *animal* principles, which imply desire and will, but not judgment.

326. Every deliberate action must be done either as the *means,* or as an *end ;* as the means to *some* end to which it is subservient, or as an end for its *own* sake, and without regard to any thing beyond itself ; and that it is a part of the office of reason to determine what are the proper means to any end which we desire, no man ever denied. The philosophers, who assign to Taste, or Feeling, the office which we assign to Reason, cease to consider Reason a principle of action.

Obs · We shall, therefore, endeavor to show, that, among the

12

various ends of human actions, there are some, of which, *without* Reason, we could not even form a conception ; and that, as soon as they are perceived, a regard to them is, by our constitution, not only a *principle* of action, but a *leading* and *governing* principle, to which all our animal principles are subservient, and to which they *ought* to be subject.

Corol. These we call *rational* principles, because they can only exist in beings endowed with Reason ; and because, to act from those principles, is what has always been meant by acting according to Reason.

327. The ends of human actions which we have here in view, are two.

First. What is good for us upon the whole.

Secondly. And what appears to be duty.

II. *Of Regard to our Good on the Whole.*

328. It will not be denied, that as soon as we come to years of understanding, we are led, by our rational powers, to form the conception of what is good for us upon the whole.

Obs. The general notion of *good,* which enters the mind at an early age, is one of the most general and abstract notions we form.

329. WHATEVER makes a man more happy, or more perfect, is GOOD, and is an object of desire as soon as he is capable of forming the conception of it. The contrary is ILL, and is an object of aversion. In other words, the *neglect* of *good* is, in moral actions, matter of indignation or blame.

Corol. Hence MORAL LAWS may be considered under different aspects, and distinguished by different titles.

I. Considered in respect to their source, they may be distinguished as *original,* or *natural,* or *adventitious,* or *conventional.*

II. Considered in respect to their subjects, they may be distinguished by denominations taken from those subjects ; as, *laws of religion,* or of *society,*—as, *laws of peace,* or of *war ;*—as, *laws political, civil,* or *criminal.*

III. Considered in respect to the persons to whom they are applicable, they are *laws of nations,* or the *laws of particular states.*

330. *Moral philosophy* is, thence, the knowledge of *Moral* laws, respecting their sources and their applications.

Obs. The obligation of every law, whether original or adventitious, general or partial, may be resolved into an *obligation* of the *law of nature.* And the *first,* or *fundamental,* law of nature to mankind, is, an expression of the greatest good competent to man's nature. All subsequent laws are branches or applications of this.

331. That which, taken with all its discoverable connections and consequences, brings *more good* than *ill,* we call GOOD UPON the WHOLE.

Illus. There is no reason to believe that brute animals have any conception of this. Nor do we ourselves have any conception of what is good for us on the whole, till reason be so far advanced, that we can seriously reflect upon the past, and take a prospect of the future part of our existence.

Corol. It appears, therefore, that the very conception of what is good or ill for us upon the whole, is the offspring of reason, and can only be in beings endowed with reason. And if this conception give rise to any principle of action in man, which he had not before, that principle may very properly be called *a rational principle of action.* (*See the first Book of Cicero's Offices.*)

332. As soon as we have the conception of what is good or ill for us upon the whole, we are led, by our constitution, to seek the good and avoid the ill; and this becomes not only a principle of action, but a leading or governing principle, to which all our animal principles ought to be subordinate.

Illus. 1. In intelligent beings, the *desire* of what is *good,* and the *aversion* of what is *ill,* is necessarily connected with the intelligent nature; and it is a contradiction to suppose such a being to have the *notion of good* without the *desire* of it, or the *notion of ill* without an *aversion* to it.

2. To prefer a greater good, though distant, to a less good that is present—to choose a present evil, in order to avoid a greater evil, or to obtain a greater good,—is, in the judgment of all men, wise and reasonable conduct; and when a man acts the contrary part, all men will acknowledge that he acts foolishly and unreasonably.

3. No man was ever drawn one way by his *animal principles,* leading him to vicious indulgence, without at the same time experiencing the reflection, that a regard to what is good on the whole, pulled, though feebly, in the contrary direction.

4. That in every conflict of this kind, the rational principle ought to prevail, and the animal to be subordinate, is too evident to need proof.

Corol. Thus, it appears, that to pursue what is good upon the whole, and to avoid what is ill upon the whole, is a rational principle of action, grounded upon our constitution as reasonable creatures.

333. It appears, that it is not without just cause, that this principle of action has, in all ages, been called REASON, in opposition to our animal principles, which, though alike the gift of the Author of our existence, are, in common language, called by the general name of *Passions.**

Illus. The *first* not only operates in a calm and cool manner, like reason, but implies real judgment in all its operations. The *second,* to wit, the passions, are blind desires of some particular object, without any judgment or consideration whether it be *good* or *ill for us* upon the whole.

---

* See Cogan's Philosophical and Ethical Treatises on the Passions.

334. It appears, also, that the fundamental maxim of prudence, and of all good morals—*That the passions ought, in all cases, to be under the dominion of reason*—is not only self-evident, when rightly understood, but is expressed according to the common use and propriety of language.

Obs. To judge of what is true or false in speculative points, is the office of *speculative reason;* and to judge of what is good or ill for us upon the whole, is the office of *practical reason.* Of *true* and *false* there are *no degrees;* but of *good* and *ill* there are *many degrees,* and *many kinds;* and we are very apt to form erroneous opinions concerning them; misled by our passions, by the authority of others (*Art.* 240. *Illus.*), and by other causes. (See the Influence of Arbitrary Associations, as it affects our Moral Judgments, p. 101 and 102.)

335. Wise men, in all ages, have reckoned it a chief point of wisdom to make a right estimate of the good and evils of life. They have labored to discover the errors of the multitude on this important point, and to warn others against those errors.

Illus. 1. The same station or condition of life, which makes one man happy, makes another miserable, and to·a third it is perfectly indifferent. We see some men miserable through life, from vain fears, and anxious desires, grounded solely upon wrong opinions. We see others wear themselves out with toilsome days and sleepless nights, in pursuit of some object which they never attain; or which, when attained, gives little satisfaction, perhaps real disgust.

2. The evils of life have very different effects upon different men; what sinks one into despair and absolute misery, rouses the virtue and magnanimity of another, who bears it as the lot of humanity, and as the discipline of a wise and merciful Father in heaven. He rises superior to adversity, and is made wiser and better by it, and consequently happier.

Corol. It is, therefore, of the last importance, in the conduct of life, to have just notions with respect to good and evil; and surely it is the province of reason to correct wrong opinions, and to lead us into those that are just and true.

336. He who feels the bad effects of following his passions and appetites, and imputes them to himself, would be stung with remorse for his folly, though he had no account to make to a superior Being. His reason convinces him that he has sinned against himself: in his self-condemnation, he feels that he has brought upon his own head the punishment which his folly deserved.

Corol. From this, we may see that this rational principle of a regard to our own good upon the whole, gives us the conception of a *right* and a *wrong* in human conduct, at least of a *wise* and a *foolish.* It produces a kind of self-approbation, when the passions and appetites are kept in their due subjection to this rational principle of a regard to our own good upon the whole, and a kind of remorse and compunction when it yields to them.

Obs. In these respects, this principle is so similar to the *moral principle* or *conscience*, and so interwoven with it, that, to make the distinction apparent, we shall make *conscience* the subject of the next section.

III. *Analysis of Conscience, or the Moral Principle.*

337. CONSCIENCE, or the faculty of distinguishing right conduct from wrong, like all our other faculties, comes to maturity by degrees, or is tutored by the experience we have of our own conduct, and by the examples of good and ill which are furnished us by others.

Illus. The seeds of moral discernment are, if I may use a figure, planted in our mind by Him that made us. They grow up in their proper season ; they are at first tender and delicate, and easily warped ; hence their progress depends very much upon their being duly cultivated and properly exercised. All the arguments applied to prove the cultivation of our other faculties, attention, abstraction, memory, association, judgment, and reasoning, bear with united force in proof of the fact that *moral discernment*, or *conscience*, is susceptible of a high degree of improvement.

Corol. Since, then, the natural power of discerning between right and wrong needs the aid of instruction, education, exercise, and habit, as well as our other natural powers, and, by these means of improvement, may be informed of its duty, of the good its subject ought to pursue, and the evils that he ought to shun, that man must indeed be a stranger to his own heart, and to the state of human nature, who does not see that he has need of all the aid which his situation affords him, in order to know how he ought to act in any given case, in which accident or circumstances may place him.

338. *Conscience* is peculiar to man, and is one of those prerogatives by which he is raised above brute animals, in which not a vestige of *Moral Perception* can be traced.

Corol. 1. Man alone, of the animals that inhabit this earth, is a moral agent. The dog that runs away with a piece of meat is not so ; therefore this action is no crime in the dog, though, by an abuse of language, we say of that quadruped, that "He is a great thief." Brute animals are neither immoral nor virtuous ; and when we say of a horse, that "He is vicious," our meaning is that he has such qualities, or has acquired, by ill treatment or otherwise, such habits as lead to such actions.

2. These things. and others, which the ingenuity of the reader can easily supply, show that there is just reason why we should consider the brute creation destitute of the noblest faculties with which God hath endowed man, and particularly of that faculty which makes us *moral* and *accountable beings.*.

12 *

339 *Conscience* is evidently intended by nature to be the immediate *guide* and *director* of our conduct, after we arrive at the years of understanding.

Illus. 1. The bones, muscles, arteries, blood, and variously-complicated parts of our frame, show intuitively the end for which they were made and put together with such exquisite skill and nicety of adaptation and action.

2. That we may discern those qualities of bodies which may be useful or hurtful to us, we are endowed with five senses, the media of all *sensation ;* that we may retain the knowledge which we have acquired, we have the faculty of *memory* given us; that we may distinguish what is true from what is false, we have the faculties of *judgment* and *reasoning*, as original powers of the mind.

3. The appetites and passions of our nature all point out their end ; else what are the natural appetites of hunger and thirst, the natural affections of parents to their offspring, and of relations to each other, the natural docility and credulity of children, the affections of pity and sympathy with the distressed, the attachment we feel to neighbors, to acquaintance, and the esteem and love we feel towards individuals? What is our obedience to the laws and the constitution of Britain? What are these, I ask, but parts of our constitution, which plainly point out their end? And he must be intellectually blind, or a wretched knave, who will not allow, who does not perceive, that the intention for which both the intellectual and the active powers were given him, is written in legible and in golden characters upon the face of each of them.

340. Nor is this the case with any of them more evidently than with Conscience, the intention of which is manifestly implied in its office—to show us what is good, what bad, and what indifferent, in human conduct.

Illus. 1. " He hath showed thee, O man ! what is good," saith the Prophet Micah. Conscience judges of every action before it is done ; for we can rarely act so precipitately, but we have the consciousness that what we are about to do is right, or wrong, or indifferent. Like the bodily eye, it naturally looks forward, though its attention may occasionally be turned back to the past.

2. Conscience, if I may be so bold as to make the assertion, plunges into the future, when it prescribes measures to every appetite, affection, and passion, and says of every other principle of action, " Hitherto thou shalt go, but no farther." Whoever yet transgressed its dictates with innocence, or even with impunity? At any rate, I am not that man ; and, with my peccability, I have no ambition to be stripped of this sacred monitor. It is an honest, an amiable counsel, whose opinions are without expense and without delay.

3. Probably some of our other principles of action have more strength, but none of them can boast its authority. Set any other principle in opposition to it we please, its sentence makes us guilty to ourselves, and guilty in the eyes of our Maker.

Corol. 1. It is evident, therefore, that this principle has, from its nature, an authority to direct and determine, with regard to our conduct—to judge, to acquit, or to condemn, and even to punish—an authority that belongs to no other principle of the human mind. Other principles may urge, this only authorizes. Other principles ought to be controlled by this; this may be, but never ought to be, controlled by any other, and never can be with innocence to our bosoms.

2. The authority of conscience over the other principles of the mind is self-evident; for it implies no more than this—That in all cases a man ought to do his duty. He only, who does in all cases what he ought to do, is the perfect man.

Obs. To this all-powerful principle, then, rather than to any other, did Nelson appeal at the battle of Trafalgar, when that noble sentiment ran through his fleet—

" ENGLAND EXPECTS THAT EVERY MAN THIS DAY WILL DO HIS DUTY."

341. The *Moral Faculty*, or Conscience, is both an *active* and an *intellectual* power of the mind. It is an *active power*, as every truly virtuous action must be more or less influenced by it; and it is an *intellectual power*, because by it solely we have the original conceptions, or ideas of right and wrong in human conduct.

Illus. 1. *Of its being an active power.* Other principles may concur with it, and lead the same way; but no action can be called morally good, in which regard to what is right has not some influence

Example 1. There is no *virtue*, but there is *justice*, in paying just debts. When the moral *principle* wages war and overcomes the animal principles, there is certainly some activity shown. In some cases, a regard to what is right may be the sole motive, without the concurrence or opposition of any other principle of action; as when a judge, or an arbiter, determines a plea between two indifferent persons, solely from a regard to justice.

Corol. 1. Thus we see, that conscience, as an active principle, sometimes concurs with other principles, sometimes opposes them, and is sometimes the sole principle of action.

Illus. 2. *Of its being an intellectual power.* By *conscience*, solely as an *intellectual power*, we have the original conceptions, or ideas, of right and wrong in human conduct; and of right and wrong there are not only many different degrees, but many different species. Justice and injustice, benevolence and malice, prudence and folly, magnanimity and meanness, decency and indecency, are various moral forms, all comprehended under the general notion of right and wrong in conduct,—all of them objects of moral approbation or disapprobation, in a greater or less degree.

Again, the conception of these, as *moral qualities*, we have by our *moral faculty;* and by the same faculty, when we compare them together, we perceive various relations among them.

Example 2. Thus we perceive, that *justice* is entitled to a small degree of *praise*, but *injustice* to a high degree of *blame;* and the same may be said of gratitude and its contrary. When justice and gratitude interfere, gratitude must give place to justice, and unmerited beneficence to both.

Corol. 2. As this faculty, therefore, furnishes the human mind
with many of its original conceptions, or ideas, as well as with the
first principles of many important branches of human knowledge, it
may justly be accounted an *intellectual* as well as an *active power* of
the mind.

IV. *Analysis of Duty, Rectitude, and Moral Obligation.*

342. The subject of law must have the conception of a
general rule of conduct, and a sufficient inducement to
obey the law, even when his strongest animal desires draw
him the contrary way.

Illus. Without some degree of reason he cannot have this conception. Man is endowed with some degree of reason. We shall thence
pronounce him the subject of law, having the conception of a general
rule of conduct. The subject of law must likewise have a sufficient
inducement to obey the law, even when his strongest animal desires
draw him the contrary way. The possession of good is a sufficient
inducement to obey the law. Man, of all the animals of creation, desires the possession of good. We shall, therefore, consider man as
having a sufficient inducement to obey the law, even when his strongest animal desires draw him the contrary way.

343. This inducement may be a *sense of interest*, or a
sense of duty, or *both* concurring.

Obs. These are the only two principles, which, in Dr. Reid's opinion, can reasonably induce a man to regulate all his actions according
to a general rule or law.

Corol. They may, therefore, be justly called the *rational principles*
of action, since they can have no place but in a being endowed with
reason, and since it is by them only that man is capable either of political or of moral government.

344. Our notion, or conception of duty, is too simple to
admit a logical definition ; and when we say, that *it is
what we ought to do—what is fair and honest—what is
approvable—what every man professes to be the rule of his
conduct—what all men praise—and what is in itself laudable, though no man should praise it,*—we define it only by
synonymous words, or phrases, or by its properties and
necessary concomitants.

345. The notion of duty cannot be resolved into that of
interest, or what is most for our happiness.

Illus. 1. Every man may be satisfied of this, who attends to his
own conceptions, and the language of mankind shows it ;—for,
when I say, "This is my interest," I mean one thing ; and when I
say, "This is my duty," I mean another thing. And though the
same course of action, when rightly understood, may be both my
duty and my interest, the conceptions I have of each are very different. Both are reasonable motives to action, but quite distinct in
their nature

2. In every man of real worth, there is a principle of honor, a regard to what is honorable, or dishonorable, very distinct from a regard to his interest. It is folly in any man to disregard his interest, but to do what is dishonorable is baseness. The first may move our pity, or, in some cases, our contempt; but the last provokes our indignation.

Corol. 1. As these two principles are different in their nature, and not resolvable into one, so the principle of honor is evidently superior in dignity to that of interest.

2. No man would allow *him* to be a man of honor, who should plead his interest to justify what he acknowledged to be dishonorable; but to sacrifice interest to honor never costs a blush.

346. This principle is not to be resolved into a regard to our reputation among men, else the man of honor would not deserve to be trusted in the dark. He would have no aversion to lie, to cheat, to play the coward, when he had no dread of being discovered.

Corol. Every man of honor, therefore, feels an abhorrence of certain actions, because they are in themselves base, and feels an obligation to certain other actions, because they are in themselves what honor requires, and this independently of any consideration of interest or reputation.

347. This is an immediate *moral obligation;* and this principle of honor, which is acknowledged by all men who pretend to character, is only another name for what we call a regard to duty, to rectitude, to propriety of conduct. It is a moral obligation, which obliges a man to do certain things because they are right, and not to do other things because they are wrong.

Corol. There is, therefore, a principle in man, call it by what name you please, which, when he acts according to it, gives him a consciousness of worth, and when he acts contrary to it, a sense of demerit. Men of rank call it *honor;* the vulgar hind calls it *honesty, probity, virtue, conscience;* philosophers have given it the name of *the moral sense, the moral faculty, rectitude.*

348. The universality of this principle—the words that express it—the names of the virtues which it commands, and of the vices which it forbids—the *ought* and *ought not,* which express its dictates—make it evidently an essential part of language.

Illus 1. The natural affections—of respect to worthy people—of resentment of injuries—of gratitude for favors—of indignation against the worthless—are parts of the human constitution which suppose a right and a wrong in conduct.

2. Many transactions that are found in the rudest societies, go upon the same supposition. In all testimony—in all promises—in all contracts—there is necessarily implied a *moral obligation* on one party, and a *trust* in the other, *grounded upon this obligation.*

349. The leading principle of all our active powers is *Reason*, and it comprehends both a regard to what is right and honorable, and a regard to our happiness upon the whole. All the principles of action—whether they be *notions of duty, rectitude,* or *moral obligation*—when rightly understood, lead to the same course of life; they are fountains whose streams unite and run in the same channel.

Obs. When we say a man ought to do such a thing, *the ought,* which expresses the *moral obligation,* has a respect, on the one hand to the person who ought, and, on the other, to the action which he ought to do. Those two correlates are essential to every moral obligation; take away either, and the obligation ceases to exist.

350. The circumstances, both in the action and in the agent, necessary to constitute a *moral obligation,* are these :—

I. With regard to the action, it must be a *voluntary* action, or præstation of the person obliged, and not of another.

II. The *opinion* of the agent in doing the action gives it its moral obligation.

Obs. With respect to the person obliged, to things only which come within the sphere of his natural power can he be under a moral obligation. As respects the agent, if he does a materially good action, without any belief of its being good, but from some other principle, it is *no good action in him.* And if he does it with the belief of its being ill, it *is ill in him.*

Corol. These qualifications of the action, and of the agent, in moral obligation, are superevident; and the agreement of all men in them, shows that all men have the same notion, and a distinct notion, of moral obligation.

V. *Analysis of the Sense of Duty.*

351. We are next to consider how we learn to judge and determine that *this* is right, and *that* is wrong.

Obs. The abstract notion of moral good and ill would be of no use to direct our life, if we had not the power of applying it to particular actions, and determining what is morally good, and what is morally ill.

352. By the external senses, we have not only the original conceptions of the various qualities of bodies, but the original judgments that *this* body has such a quality, *that* such another : so by our moral faculty, we have both the original conceptions of right and wrong, of merit and demerit, in ourselves and others; and also the original judgments that *this* conduct is right, *that* is wrong; that *this* character has worth, *that* demerit.

Illus. 1. The testimony of our moral faculty, like that of the external senses, is the testimony of nature, and we have the same reason to rely upon it.

2. The truths immediately testified by the external senses, are the first principles from which we reason, with regard to the material world, and from which all our knowledge of it is deduced.

3. The truths immediately testified by our moral faculty, are the first principles of all *moral reasoning,* from which all our knowledge of our duty must be deduced.

353. *Moral reasoning* is all reasoning that is brought to prove that *such* conduct is right and deserving of moral approbation, or that it is wrong, or that it is indifferent, and, in itself, neither morally good nor ill.

Corol. 1. All that we can properly call *moral judgments,* are reducible to one or other of these, because all human actions, considered in a moral point of view, are either good, or bad, or indifferent.

2. Let it be understood, therefore, that in the reasoning which we call *moral,* the conclusion always is—That something in the conduct of moral agents is good or bad, in a greater or a less degree, or indifferent.

354. All moral reasonings rest upon one or more first principles of morals, whose truth is immediately perceived, without reasoning, by all men come to years of understanding.

Illus. This is common to every branch of human knowledge that deserves the name of science; and these first principles are the dictates of our natural faculties.

Example 1. In astronomy and in optics, the first principles are phenomena attested by the human eye; and with him who disbelieves the testimony of that little organ, the whole of those two noble fabrics of science falls to pieces like the visions of the night.

2. The principles of *music* all depend upon the testimony of the ear; those of *natural philosophy,* upon the facts attested by the senses; those of *mathematics,* upon the necessary relations of quantities considered abstractedly. (*Art.* 44. *Illus.*) The science of *politics* borrows its principles from what we know by experience of the character and conduct of man. The first principles of morals are the immediate dictates of the *moral faculty.*

3. He that will judge of the color of an object, must consult his eyes in a good light, when there is no medium, or contiguous object, that may give it a false tinge. In like manner, he that will judge of the first principles of morals, must consult his *conscience,* or moral faculty; when he is *calm* and *dispassionate, unbiased* by interest, affection, or fashion.

Corol. The sum of the reasonings that we have made, or that we might make, on this *analysis of the sense of duty,* is—that, by an original power of the mind, which we call *conscience,* or the *moral faculty,* we have the conception of right and wrong in human conduct, of merit and demerit, of duty and moral obligation, and our other moral conceptions; and that, by the same faculty, we perceive some things in human conduct to be right, and others to be wrong; that the first principles of morals are the dictates of this faculty; and that we have the same reason to rely upon those dictates, as upon the determinations of our senses, or of our other natural faculties.

VI. *Of Moral Approbation and Disapprobation.*

355. The judgments we form in speculative matters are dry and unaffecting ;—our *moral judgments*, from their nature, are necessarily accompanied with AFFECTIONS and FEELINGS, which we are now to consider.

Illus. We approve of good actions and disapprove of bad ones; and this approbation and disapprobation, when we analyze it, appears to include not only a moral judgment of the action, but some *affection*, favorable or unfavorable, towards the agent, and some *feeling* in ourselves.

356. Moral worth, even in a stranger, with whom we have not the least connection, never fails to produce some degree of *esteem*, mixed with good-will. The *esteem* which we have for a man on account of his moral worth, is different from that which is grounded upon his intellectual accomplishments, his birth, fortune, and connection with us.

Illus. Moral worth, when it is not set off by eminent abilities and external advantages, is like a diamond in the mine, which is rough and unpolished, and perhaps crusted over with some other baser material that takes away its lustre. But, when it is attended with these advantages, it is like a diamond cut and polished, and set round with pearls, in a massy crown. Its lustre then attracts every eye; and yet these things, which add so much to its appearance, add but little to its real value.

Corol. There is no judgment of the heart more clear, or more irresistible than this—That esteem and regard are really due to good conduct, and the contrary to base and unworthy conduct. Nor can we conceive a greater depravity in the heart of man, than it would be to see and acknowledge worth without feeling any respect to it; or to see and acknowledge the *highest* worthlessness without any degree of dislike and indignation.

357. The *object* of moral approbation is, then, either *some disposition* of the mind, or some *external action*.

Illus. Probity is the most approved disposition; and the external expressions of probity the most approved actions. These constitute the whole, or the most essential part of virtue. Other subjects may be admired or contemned, but these alone are the subjects of moral approbation, of esteem and love.

358. PARTIALITY, which makes us blind to the faults of our friends, and the merits of those to whom, from prejudice or passion, we are ill affected, is the foundation of our wrong

judgment with regard to the character of others, and of self-deceit with regard to our own.

359. *Moral approbation* or *disapprobation* is accompanied with *agreeable* or *uneasy feelings*, in the breast of the spectator or judge.

Illus. The benevolent affections give pleasure, the malevolent desires give pain, in one degree or another. And when we contemplate a noble character, though but in ancient story, or even in a novel, a comedy, or a tragedy, like a beautiful object, it gives a lively and pleasant emotion to the spirits; it warms the heart, and invigorates the frame; like the beams of a meridian sun, it enlivens the face of nature, and diffuses heat, light, and joy, all around.

Example. We feel a sympathy with the noble Caractacus, and are afflicted in his distress; and *Alfred the Great* compels us to rejoice in his prosperity; we even catch some sparks of that celestial fire that animated the conduct of the latter; and it is impossible to accompany the former to Rome, without feeling the glow of his virtue and magnanimity.

Corol. This sympathy is the necessary effect of our judgment of the conduct of those men, and of our approbation and esteem due to that conduct; for real sympathy is always the effect of some benevolent affection, such as esteem, love, pity, or humanity.

360. Sympathy gathers strength from the social tie, and bids us claim some property in the worth of a father, or a mother, a brother, or a sister, a relation, or an acquaintance, and chiefly so in that friend whom we value above all her sex; but the highest pleasure of our soul is, when we are conscious of good conduct in ourselves.

Obs. On the other hand, the view of a vicious character, especially if that character be connected with us, like that of an ugly and deformed object, is disagreeable, and our *sympathy* is very painful indeed; for we blush for those faults by which we feel ourselves dishonored.

Corol. If bad conduct, in those in whom we are interested, be uneasy and painful, it is much more so when we are conscious of it in ourselves. This uneasy feeling has a name in all languages; we call it *remorse.* In *repentance, contrition* and *remorse,* self-reproach, and even *indignation,* are largely intermixed with the *affection of sorrow.*

Note. We shall here close our division of "The Intellectual Powers," recommending to the more advanced reader the study of Reid and Stewart's writings on the same subject. What we have said is sufficient in an elementary treatise

13

BOOK III.

SUBJECTS OF COLLATERAL INQUIRY, WITH THE INTELLECTUAL POWERS.

CHAPTER I.

OF THE PRIMARY AND SECONDARY QUALITIES OF BODIES.

361. WE have observed in Chapter II. of Book II. that sensation is generally conjoined with perception ; but these terms denote two separate and distinct acts of the mind, and we have no appropriate name to designate the conjunction of sensation with perception. Both are generally confounded together under one term, which comes to be more strictly appropriated either to the sensation or the perception, according as the one or the other more strongly occupies the attention of the mind.

Illus. 1. If it be asked what I mean by the smell of a rose, it is evident that, in the general acceptation of the phrase, this denotes a sensation of the mind, as appears from the epithets *fragrant, agreeable,* &c., which are applicable to it, and which have meaning when referred to a sentient being. (*Art.* 105. *Illus.* 1, 2, and 3.) Along, however, with this sensation of an agreeable odor, there is conjoined a perception, by which we form a certain notion of that quality in the rose, which is the cause of its odor; but this perception is totally distinct from the sensation (*Art* 42 and 108.) ; for the perception cannot be said to be agreeable or otherwise, and it has an external object, the existence of which depends not upon the act of the mind, as doth the sensation. (See *Art.* 106. and *Illus. Art.* 110) Yet we have no name by which to distinguish the object of this perception, unless it be that which more properly belongs to the accompanying sensation, to wit, the *smell* of the rose ; a defect of language which is, no doubt, the source of much ambiguity.

2. Again, if it be asked, What is the effect produced by applying the hand upon any solid and compact substance? it will be answer

ed, that We *feel* the body to be *hard.* And, in like manner, when the parts of a body are easily displaced, or its figure changed by applying the hand to it, we call it *soft;* we feel it soft. These are the notions which all mankind have of hardness and softness. They are neither sensations, nor like any sensation; they were real qualities before they were perceived by touch, and continue to be so when they are not perceived; for if any man will affirm, that diamonds were not hard till they were handled, who would reason with him?

3. The sensation of hardness may be easily had, by pressing one's hand against the table, and attending to the feeling that ensues, setting aside, as much as possible, all thought of the table and its qualities, or of any external thing. But it is one thing to have the sensation, and another to attend to it, and make it a distinct object of reflection. The first is easy; the last, in most cases, extremely difficult.

4. The sensation of touch, and the hardness of bodies, have not the least similitude; yet the hardness of bodies is a thing that we conceive as distinctly, and believe as firmly, as any thing in nature; and no rules of reasoning are required to convince me of the consciousness I have of this sensation when I press my hand against the table. I see nothing left, but to conclude, that, by an original principle in my constitution, a certain sensation of touch both suggests to the mind the conception of hardness, and creates the belief of it; or, in other words, that this sensation is the natural sign of hardness.

362. This sensation may be increased in strength at pleasure, merely by increasing the pressure of the hand; and it may be increased to such a degree as to be very disagreeable. It then arrests the attention forcibly enough, and we give it the name of *Pain,* which is, however, no appropriate term, but the common appellation of all sensations that are disagreeable. If I hit my toe against a stone with violence, the sensation I experience is the same in kind, but different in degree, with what I feel when I gently press the table with my hand.

363. We have now shown, that language affords, in general, but a single term whereby to distinguish both the sensation and its accompanying perception; and that this term is chiefly appropriated either to the sensation or the perception, according as the attention is most engrossed by the one or the other. Upon this circumstance appears to be founded a distinction of the qualities of body into two kinds, called *primary* and *secondary*.

Illus. The reality of the distinction appears to be placed in this; that the *primary qualities* are those of which we have a distinct perception, and but a slight sensation; while, of the *secondary*, our perception is but obscure, and we have a strong sensation, which chiefly arrests our attention. Hence, the names of the primary qualities of body more usually refer to the perception by which they are made known to us; while those of the secondary qualities have more properly a reference to the accompanying sensation.

364. The three senses of taste, smell, and hearing, appear to give us information of the secondary qualities of body alone; the other two senses, of sight and touch, inform us both of primary and secondary qualities. Heat and cold are secondary qualities, discernible by touch; and color is a secondary quality, discernible by sight.

Iltus. The disposition of bodies to reflect a particular kind of light, or the fitness of certain particles of external bodies to reflect some only of the rays of light, occasions the sensation of color; and in this acceptation, it really exists in the sentient being, although early prejudice induces us to refer it to the external body alone; and the term is usually applied only to the external cause of the sensation, and not to the sensation itself, which is not the case with the other secondary qualities. All the primary qualities of body may be discovered by the sense of touch alone; and it is this sense, as diffused over our whole corporeal frame, which imparts the most accurate notions concerning those qualities. For the notions of extention and figure, as conveyed by the eye, require the correction of the touch; and even motion, which might be supposed to be the peculiar province of sight, can only certainly be ascertained by the touch, because the eye often judges motion to be real, when it is but apparent; as when, sailing along the shore in a vessel, we fancy the land moves.

365. There appears, upon the whole, to be a real distinction between the primary and secondary qualities of body: our senses give us a direct and distinct notion of extension, divisibility, figure, motion, solidity, hardness, softness, and fluidity, which are all *primary qualities;* but of the *secondary qualities,* sound, color, taste, smell, and heat or cold, our senses give us only a relative and obscure notion.

Obs. A relative notion of a thing is, strictly speaking, no notion of the thing at all, but only of some relation which it bears to something else. Thus, of the word gravity, I can have a distinct and accurate notion, when it signifies the tendency of bodies towards the earth; but when it signifies the cause of that tendency, I have no conception of what the thing is, though I may think of it as an unknown cause of a known effect. This is a *relative* notion; and there are many objects of thought and discourse, of which our faculties can give no better than a relative notion.

•

CHAPTER II.

OF NATURAL LANGUAGE AND SIGNS.

366. In *Illus.* 4. *Art.* 361. sensations were called NATU-RAL SIGNS. Mankind reciprocally communicate their thoughts and intentions, their purposes and desires, by language or signs.

Illus. These signs are of two kinds : first, such as have no meaning, but what is affixed to them by compact or agreement among those who use them; these are artificial signs. 2dly. Such as, previous to all compact and agreement, have a meaning which every man understands by the principles of his nature.

Corol. Language, therefore, so far as it consists of artificial signs, may be called *artificial ;* so far as it consists of natural signs, we call it *natural.*

367. If mankind had not had a natural language, they could never have invented an artificial one by their reason and ingenuity. For all artificial language supposes some compacts or agreements before the use of artificial signs ; but there can be no compact or agreement without signs, nor without language ; and, therefore, there must be a natural language, before an artificial language can be invented.

368. The elements of the natural language of mankind, or the signs that are naturally expressive of our thoughts, consist in modulations of the voice, gestures, and features.

Illus. By means of these, two savages, who have no common artificial language, can converse together; can communicate their thoughts in some tolerable manner; can ask and refuse, affirm and deny, threaten and supplicate; can traffic, enter into covenants, and plight their faith ! Historical facts of undoubted credit are the bases of this illustration.

369. Mankind having thus, by nature, a common language, though a scanty one, adapted only to the necessities of nature, their ingenuity improved it by the addition of artificial signs, to supply the deficiency of the natural.

Illus. These artificial signs multiply with the arts of life, and the improvements of knowledge. The articulations of the voice seem to be, of all signs, the most proper for artificial language ; and as mankind have universally used them for that purpose, we may reasonably judge that nature intended them for it   But nature does not intend that we should lay aside the use of the natural signs : it is enough that we supply their defects by artificial ones. Dumb people retain much more of the natural language than others, because necessity obliges

13 *

them to use it. And, for the same reason, savages have much more of it than civilized nations. •

370. It is by natural signs chiefly, that we give force and energy to language; and the less language has of them, it is the less expressive and persuasive.

Illus. Thus, writing is less expressive than reading, and reading less expressive than speaking without book. Speaking without the proper and natural modulations, force, and variations of the voice, is a frigid and dead language, compared with that which is attended with them : it is still more expressive, when we add the language of the eyes and features ; and is then only in its perfect and natural state, and attended with its proper energy, when to all these we superadd the force of action.

371. Where speech is natural, it will oe an exercise, not of the voice and lungs only, but of all the muscles of the body ; like that of dumb people and savages, whose language, as it has more of nature, is more expressive, and is more easily learned.

372. Artificial signs signify, they do not express ; they speak to the understanding, as algebraical characters may do, but the passions, the affections, and the will, hear them not ; these continue dormant and inactive, till we speak to them in the language of nature, to which they are all attention and obedience.

Corol. As men, therefore, are led by nature and necessity to converse together. they will use every means in their power to make themselves understood ; and where they cannot do this by artificial signs, they will do it, as far as possible, by natural ones ; and he that understands perfectly the use of natural signs, must be the best judge in all the expressive arts, such as music, painting, acting, and public speaking.

373. As in artificial signs there is often neither similitude between the sign and thing signified, nor any connection that arises necessarily from the nature of the things, so it is also in the natural signs.

Illus. 1. The word *gold* has no similitude to the substance signified by it ; nor is it in its own nature more fit to signify this, than any other substance ; yet, by habit and custom, it suggests this, and no other.

2. In like manner, a sensation of touch suggests hardness, although it hath neither similitude to hardness, nor, as far as we can perceive, any necessary connection with it. (*Art.* 361.) The difference between these two signs, lies on.y in this; that, in the first, the suggestion is the effect of habit and custom; in the second, it is not the effect of habit, but of the original constitution of our minds. (*Art.* 365.)

374. There are different orders of natural signs, and dif-

ferent classes into which they may be distinguished, whence we may more distinctly conceive the relation between our sensations and the things they suggest, and what we mean by calling sensations signs of external things. (*Art.* 366. *Corol.*)

Illus. 1. The first class of natural signs comprehends those whose connection with the thing signified is established by nature, but discovered only by experience. The use of genuine philosophy consists in discovering such connections, and reducing them to general rules. What we commonly call natural *causes*, might, with more propriety, be called natural *signs;* and what we call *effects*, the *things signified*. According to this illustration, we should no longer use the popular definitions of *causes*, which are of two kinds; 1st. The *efficient cause*, which is the energy or power producing an effect. 2dly. The *final cause*, which is the end or purpose for which an effect is produced.

2. A second class of natural signs is that wherein the connection between the sign and the thing signified is not only established by nature, but discovered to us by a natural principle, without reasoning or experience. Of this kind are the natural signs of human thoughts, purposes, and desires, which have been already mentioned as the natural language of mankind. Thus, an infant may be put into a fright by an angry countenance, and soothed again by smiles and blandishments. And a child that has a good musical ear, may be put to sleep or to dance, and may be made merry or sorrowful, by the modulation of musical sounds. The principles of all the fine arts, and of what we call *a fine taste*, may be resolved into connections of this kind.

3. A third class of natural signs comprehends those which, though we never before had any notion or conception of the thing signified, do suggest it, or conjure it up, as it were, by a natural kind of magic, and at once give us a conception and create a belief of it. Thus, our sensations suggest to us a sentient being or mind to which they belong; but the conception of mind is neither an idea of sensation nor of reflection; for it is neither like any of our sensations, nor like any thing of which we are conscious. The first conception of it, as well as the belief of it, and the common relation which it bears to all that we are conscious of, or remember, is suggested to every thinking being, we do not know how. The notion of hardness in bodies, as well as the belief of it, are got in a similar manner; being, by an original principle of our nature, annexed to that sensation which we have when we feel a hard body. (*Art.* 373. *Illus.* 2.)

Corol. 1. As the first class of natural signs is the foundation of true philosophy, and the second, the foundation of the fine arts, or of taste, so the last is the foundation of common sense.

2. And by all rules of just reasoning, we must conclude, that since sensations are invariably connected with the conception and belief of external existences, this connection is the effect of our constitution, and ought to be considered as an original principle of human nature, till we find some more general principle into which it may be resolved.

CHAPTER III.

OF MATTER AND SPACE.

375. OF MATTER.   We give the names of *matter, materi-al, substance, body,* to the subject of sensible qualities or properties.

Illus. I perceive in a billiard ball, figure, color, and motion; but the ball is not figure, nor is it color, nor motion, nor all these taken together ; it is something that has figure, and color, and motion. (*Illus. Art.* 182.)   This is a dictate of nature, and the belief of all mankind.   The essence of body is unknown to us; but we have the information of nature for the existence of those properties in matter which our senses discover.

376. The belief that figure, motion, and color, are qualities, and require a subject, must either be a judgment of nature, or it must be discovered by reason, or it must be a prejudice that has no just foundation.

Corol. 1. But extension must be in something extended, motion in something moved, color in something colored ; and in the structure of all languages, we find adjective nouns used to express sensible qualities; but it is well known that every adjective in language must belong to some substantive, expressed or understood ; that is, every quality must belong to some subject : therefore, our opinion, or belief, that the things immediately perceived by our senses, are qualities which must belong to a subject, is an immediate judgment of nature, not discoverable by reason, nor instilled as a prejudice that has no just foundation; and all the information our senses give us about this subject, is, that it is that to which such qualities belong.
2. From this it is evident, that our notion of body or matter, as distinguished from its qualities, is a relative notion.   (*Art.* 365. *Obs*)
Obs. The relation which sensible qualities bear to their subject, that is, to body, may be distinguished from all other relations.   Thus, you can distinguish it from the relation of an effect to its cause (*Art.* 14.) ; of a means to its end (*Art.* 337. *Corol.*) ; or of a sign to the thing signified (*Art.* 374).

377. Some of the determinations, however, which we form concerning matter, cannot be deduced solely from the testimony of sense, but must be referred to some other source.

Illus. There seems to be nothing more evident, than that bodies must consist of parts, and that *every part* of a body *is a body*, and a distinct *something* which may exist without the other parts ; and yet I apprehend this conclusion is not deducible solely from the testimony of sense.   For, besides that it is a necessary truth, and therefore no object of sense, there is a limit beyond which we cannot perceive any

division of a body   The parts become too small to be perceived by
our senses; but we cannot believe that it becomes then incapable
of being further divided, or that such division would make it not to
be a body.

378. We carry on the division and subdivision in our
thoughts, far beyond the reach of our senses, and we can
find no limit to it; nay, we plainly discern that there can be
no limit beyond which the division cannot be carried.

Illus. For, if there be any limit to this division, one of two things
must necessarily happen; either we shall come by division to a body
which is extended, but has no parts, and is absolutely indivisible; or
this body is divisible, but as soon as it is divided, it becomes no body.

Both of these positions seem to be absurd, and one, or the other
is the necessary consequence of supposing a limit to the divisibility
of matter.

379. On the other hand, if it is admitted, that the divisibility of matter has no limit, it will follow, that no body can
be called an individual substance; you may as well call it
two, or twenty, or two hundred.

Corol. For where it is divided into parts, every part is a body or
substance, distinct from all the other parts, and was so even before
the division.   Any one part, therefore, may continue to exist, though
all the other parts were annihilated.

380. There are other determinations concerning matter,
which, we apprehend, are not solely founded upon the testimony of sense.

Illus. These determinations are, that it is impossible that two
bodies should occupy the same place at the same time ; that the same
body should be in different places at the same time ; that a body can
be moved from one place to another without passing through the intermediate places either in a straight course, or by some circuit.

Corol. These appear to be necessary truths, and therefore cannot
be conclusions of our senses; for our senses testify only what is, not
what must necessarily be.

381. OF SPACE.   Though space be not perceived by any
of our senses, when all matter is removed; yet, when we
perceive any of the primary qualities, space presents itself
as a necessary concomitant; for there can neither be extension, nor motion, nor figure, nor divisibility, nor cohesion of
parts, without space.

382. There are only two of our senses, *touch* and *sight*,
by which the notion of space enters into the mind.

Illus. A man without either of these senses can have no conception
of *space.*   And supposing him to have both, until he sees or feels
other objects, he can have no notion of space ; for it has neither col-
or nor figure to make it an object of sight; and it is no tangible

quality, to make it an object of touch. But other objects of sight and touch carry the notion of space along with them, and not the notion only, but the belief of it; for a body could not exist, if there was no space to contain it; nor could it move, if there was no space; and its situation, its distance, and every relation which it has to other bodies, supposes space.

383. But though the notion of space seems not to enter at first into the mind, until it is introduced by the proper objects of sense, yet being once introduced, it remains in our conception and belief, though the objects which introduced it be removed.

Illus. We see no absurdity in supposing a body to be annihilated, but the space that contained it remains; and to suppose *that* annihilated, seems to be absurd. It is so much allied to *nothing*, or *emptiness*, that it seems incapable of annihilation or of creation.

384. *Space* not only retains a firm hold of our belief, even when we suppose all the objects that introduced it to be annihilated, but it swells to immensity. We can set no limits, either of extent or duration, to its profundity and immutability.

Corol. Hence we call it immense, eternal, immovable, and indestructible. But it is only an immense, eternal, immovable, and indestructible void or emptiness.

Obs. The student will here observe, that this language, though popular, is sufficiently definite, as is also our reference to the *aeriform elastic fluid*, that fills all space.

385. When we consider parts of space that have measure and figure, there is nothing we understand better, nothing about which we can reason so clearly and to so great an extent.

Illus. Extension and figure are circumscribed parts of space, and are the objects of Geometry, a science in which human reason has the most ample field, and can go deeper, and with more certainty, than in any other. But when we attempt to comprehend the whole of space, and to trace it to its origin, we lose ourselves in the search.

386. The philosophers tell us, that our sight, unaided by touch, gives a very partial notion of space, but yet a distinct one. This partial notion they call *visible space.* The sense of touch, say they, too, gives a much more complete notion of space; and when it is considered according to this notion, they call it *tangible space.*

Obs. Visible figure, *extension*, and *space*, may be made the subjects of mathematical speculation, as well as the tangible. In the visible, we find *two dimensions* only; in the tangible, *three;* in the one, magnitude is measured by angles; in the other, by lines.

Corol. Every part of *visible* space bears *some* proportion to the *whole ;* but *tangible* space being *immense,* any part of it bears *no* proportion to the whole. (*See Dr. Reid's Essays on the Powers of the Mind, Essay II. Chap. XIX.*)

CHAPTER IV.

OF DURATION, EXTENSION, AND NUMBER.

387. In the Illustration of Article 244, it was shown that *Memory* implies a *conception* and *belief* of past DURATION ; for it is impossible that we should remember any thing distinctly, without believing some interval of Duration, more or less, to have passed between the time that it happened and the present moment ; and, if we had no Memory, we could acquire no notion of *Duration.*

388. *Duration, extension,* and *number,* are the measures of all things subject to mensuration. When we apply them to finite things, which are measured by them, they seem of all things to be the most distinctly conceived, and most within the reach of the human understanding.

Illus. 1. *Extension,* having three dimensions, has an endless variety of modifications, capable of being accurately defined ; and their various relations furnish the human mind with its most ample field of demonstrative reasoning.

2. *Duration,* having only one dimension, has fewer modifications , but these are clearly understood ; and their relations admit of measure, proportion, and demonstrative reasoning.

3. *Number* is called *decrete quantity,* because it is compounded of units, which are all equal and similar, and it can only be divided into units.

4. *Duration* and *extension* are not decrete, but *continued* quantity. They consist of parts perfectly similar, but divisible without end. (See *Art.* 237. *Illus.* 1.)

389. In order to assist our conception of the magnitude and proportions of the various intervals of Duration, we find it necessary to give a name to some known portion of it, such as an *hour,* a *day,* a *year.*

Illus. These intervals we consider as units ; and, by the number of them continued in a larger interval, we form a distinct conception of its magnitude. A similar expedient we find necessary, to give us a distinct conception of the magnitudes and proportions of things extended. Thus, *number* is found necessary as a *common measure* of *extension* and *duration.*

390. Some parts of Duration have, to other parts of it, the relations of *prior* and *posterior ;* and to the present, they have the relations of *past* and *future.*

Illus. 1. The notion of *past* is immediately suggested by Memory, as has been shown above (*Art.* 387.) ; and when we have apprehended the notions of present and past, and of prior and posterior, we can, from these, frame a notion of the future ; for *the future* is that which is *posterior* to the present. Hence, we say of the past, *former,* that is, *prior* time ; and as we cannot give the name of *posterior* to the present, we must assign that term to the *future.* (*See Art.* 237. *Illus.* 2. *and Example* 1.)

2. *Nearness* and *distance* are relations equally applicable to *time* and *place.* But distance in time,· and distance in place, are things so different in their nature, and so like in their relation, that it is difficult to determine, whether the name of distance is applied to both in the same sense, or in an analogical sense. (*See Illus.* 3. *and Corol. Art.* 237.)

391. The *Extension* of bodies, which we perceive by our senses, leads us necessarily to the conception and belief of a *space,* which remains immovable when the body is removed. And the *Duration* of events which we remember, leads us necessarily to the conception and belief of a Duration, which would have gone on uniformly, though the event had never happened. (*See Art.* 243. *Illus.*)

Obs. Thus, this present month of November (1818) would have passed away, though no remarkable event had happened in it ; but the death of the QUEEN will make it to be long remembered.

392. Without space there can be nothing that is *extended ;* and without time, there can be nothing that hath Duration. This is undeniable ; and yet we find that Extension and Duration are not more clear and intelligible, than space and time are dark and difficult objects of contemplation.

Corol. As there must be space wherever any thing extended does exist or can exist ; and *time,* when there is or can be any thing that has Duration ; we can set no bounds to either, even in our Imagination. They bid stern defiance to all limitation. Pursue them in conception, you plunge with the one into immensity, and with the other, into eternity !

393. An eternity *past* is an object which we cannot comprehend ; but a *beginning* of time, unless we take it in a figurative sense, is a contradiction.

Illus. By a common figure of speech, we give the name of time to those motions and revolutions, by which we measure it ; such as, days and years. (*Art.* 389.) We can conceive a beginning of these sensible measures of time, and say that *there was* a time when they *were not—* a time undistinguished by any motion or change ; but to say that *there was a time before all* time, is a contradiction.

394. All *limited* Duration is *comprehended* in Time, and all *limited* Extension, in Space. These, in their capacious womb, contain *all finite existences*, but are *contained by none.*

Illus. Created things have their particular places *in space*, and their particular places *in time;* but time is *every where*, and space at *all times;* therefore you, and I, and all of us, who, in the language of *Trim*, "are here to-day and gone to-morrow," have our *particular places* in space, and our *particular places* in time. Time and space embrace each the other, and have that mysterious union which the schoolmen conceived between soul and body—the *whole* of each is in *every part* of the other.

~~~~~~~~~~~~~~

CHAPTER V.

OF IDENTITY.

395. In treating of Memory, one of our positions runs thus : " The remembrance of a *past event* is necessarily accompanied with the conception of our own EXISTENCE at the time the event happened." (*Art.* 245.)

Obs. The *conviction* which each of us has of his own *Identity*, as far back as his memory reaches, needs no aid of philosophy to give it strength; nor can it be weakened by any philosophy, without first producing some degree of insanity.

396. This *conviction* is indispensably necessary to all exercise of reason. The operations of reason, whether in action or in speculation, are made up of successive parts. The antecedent operations are the foundation of the consequent (*Art.* 132. *Illus.* and *Art.* 133.); and without the conviction that the antecedent have been seen or done by me, I could have no reason to proceed to the consequent, in any speculation, or in any active project whatever.

Obs. That we may form as distinct a notion as we are able of this phenomenon of the human mind, it is proper to consider, *first*, What is meant by Identity in general ; *Secondly*, What by our own personal Identity ; and how we are led to that invincible belief and conviction, which every man has of his own personal Identity, to any period in which his memory is present.

I. *What is meant by Identity in General.*

397. Dr. Reid takes *Identity in general* to be a relation between a thing which is known to exist at one time, and a thing which is known to have existed at another. If you ask,

14

" Whether they are one and the same, or two different things," every man of common sense understands perfectly the meaning of your question.

Corol. Whence we may infer with certainty, that every man of common sense has a clear and distinct notion of *Identity.* (See *Art.* 5.)

Obs. The term Identity conveys a notion too simple for a logical definition. It conveys an idea of *relation*, which none confound with other relations.

398. Identity supposes an *uninterrupted continuance* of existence. (See *Art.* 52. *Illus.* 1 and 2.)

Illus. That which hath ceased to exist, cannot be the same with that which afterwards begins to exist ; for this would be to suppose a being to exist after it had ceased to exist, and to have had existence before it was produced, which are manifest contradictions. Continued and uninterrupted existence is, therefore, necessarily implied in Identity.

Corol. Hence we may infer, that Identity cannot, in its proper sense, be applied to our pains, our pleasures, our thoughts, or any operations of our minds. The headache I feel this day is not the same individual headache which I felt yesterday ; though, as far as I can judge, they are similar in kind and intensity of pain, and probably have the same cause. The same may be said of every feeling, and of every operation of mind ; they are all successive in their nature, like time itself, no two moments of which can be the *same* moment. It is otherwise with the parts of space : they always are, they always were, and they always will be the same.

Note. The ground does not appear any further clear, in fixing the notion of *Identity in general.*

II. *Of Personal Identity.*

399. It is, perhaps, more difficult to fix with precision the meaning of *personality ;* but it is not necessary in the present subject. It is sufficient for our purpose to observe, that all mankind place their personality in something that cannot be divided, or that cannot consist of parts. A part of you or of me, is a manifest absurdity.

Illus. When a man loses his estate, his health, his strength, he is still the same person, and has lost nothing of his personality. The Marquis of Anglesea lost a leg at the battle of Waterloo, but he is the same person he was before. A person is something indivisible, and is what LEIBNITZ calls a *monad.*

400. Any personal identity, therefore, implies the continued existence of that indivisible thing, which I call *myself.* (*Art.* 52.)

Illus. Whatever this *self* may be, it is something which thinks, and deliberates, and resolves, and acts, and suffers. I am not thought, nor action, nor feeling; yet am I something that thinks, and acts, and suffers. My thoughts, and actions, and feelings, change every moment; they have no continued, but a successive existence; but that *self*, or *I*, to which they belong, am permanent, and have the same relation to all the succeeding thoughts, actions, and feelings, which I call mine.

401. Such are the notions that I have of my *personal Identity.* But perhaps it may be said, this is all fancy, without reality; and the skeptic may demand, How do you know, what evidence have you, that there is such a *permanent self*, which has a claim to all the thoughts, actions, and feelings, which you call yours?

Illus. To this I answer, that the proper evidence which I have of all this, is *remembrance.* (See *Art.* 246. and its *Illustrations.*) I remember, that, in the year 1814, I published "A Treatise on the Construction of Maps." I remember several things that happened while that work was printing; and among these, that my friend, Peter Nicholson, very obligingly read over the proof sheets of that work for me. My memory testifies, not only that the book in question was printed, but that it was printed from a manuscript, which I, who now remember, wrote or compiled. Supposing that no copy of this work were now extant; still, if it was done by me, I must have existed at that time, and continued to exist, in one place or another, from that time to the present. If the identical person, whom I call myself, did not write that book, my memory is fallacious; it gives a distinct and positive testimony of what is not true. But every man in his senses believes what he distinctly remembers; and every thing he remembers, convinces him, that he existed at the time remembered.

402 When we pass judgment on the Identity of other persons besides ourselves, we proceed upon other grounds, and determine from a variety of circumstances, which sometimes produce the firmest assurance, and sometimes leave room for doubt.

Obs. The Identity of persons has often furnished matter of serious litigation, before tribunals of justice.

Illus. The *Identity* of a person is a perfect identity; wherever it is real, it admits of no degrees; and it is impossible that a person should be in part the same, and in part different; because a person is a *monad*, and is not divisible into parts. The evidence of Identity in other persons besides ourselves, does indeed admit of all degrees, from what we account certainty, to the least degree of probability. But still it is true, that the same person is perfectly the same, and cannot be so in part, or in some degree only. The honest Hibernian who accosted a stranger in London, saying, "I thought it was you, but I see now it is your brother;" though the author of a sad *bull*, affords a happy illustration of the judgment we pass on other persons besides ourselves

403. Our judgments of the Identity of objects of sense seem to be formed much upon the same grounds as our judgments of the Identity of other persons besides the self-identity which we have of ourselves.

Illus. 1. Wherever there is great similarity, we are apt to presume Identity, if no reason appears to the contrary : when two objects, ever so like, are perceived at the same time, they cannot be the same. But if they are presented to our senses at different times, we are apt to think them the same, merely from their similarity.

2. Whether this is a natural prejudice, or from what cause soever it proceeds, it certainly appears in children from infancy ; and when they grow up, it is confirmed, in most instances, by experience ; for, of the same species, men rarely find two individuals that are not distinguishable by obvious differences.

Example. A man challenges a thief whom he finds in possession of his horse or his watch, only on similarity. When the watchmaker swears, that he sold this watch to such a person, his testimony is grounded on similarity. The testimony of witnesses to the identity of a person, is commonly grounded on no better evidence.

Corol. Thus it appears, that the evidence we have of our own Identity, as far back as we remember, is totally of a different kind from the evidence we have of the Identity of other persons, or of objects of sense. The first is grounded on memory, and gives undoubted certainty : the last is grounded on similarity, and on other circumstances, which, in many cases, are not so decisive as to leave no room for doubt.

404. The Identity of objects of sense is never perfect, because, as they consist of parts, which, from a variety of causes, are subject to continual changes, the substances of which they are made up, are insensibly changing, increasing, or diminishing.

Illus. Thus we say of an old regiment, the 42d, for example, that it scaled the heights of Abraham at Quebec, though there *now* is not a man alive that belonged to it *then.* Also a ship of war, which has successively changed her anchors, her tackle, her sails, her masts, her planks, and her timbers, while she keeps the same name, is still the same.

Corol. 1. The Identity, therefore, which we ascribe to bodies, whether natural or artificial, is not perfect Identity ; it is rather something, which, for the conveniency of speech, we call Identity. It admits of great change of the subject, providing the change be gradual, sometimes even of a total change ; as that of my countryman's pistol, which, with a *new* stock, a *new* lock, and a *new* barrel, was still his *old* pistol.

2. And the changes, which, in common language, are made consistently with Identity, differ from those that are thought to destroy it, not in kind, but in number and degree. It has no fixed nature when applied to bodies; and questions about the Identity of a body are very often questions about words. But Identity, when applied to persons, has no ambiguity, and admits not of degrees, or of more

or less. It is the foundation of all rights and obligations, and of all accountableness; and the notion of it is fixed and precise

CHAPTER VI.

OF THE TRAIN OF THOUGHT IN THE MIND.

405. EVERY man is conscious of a *Succession of Thoughts* which pass in his mind while he is awake, even when they are not excited by external objects.

Obs. The mind on this account has been compared to liquor in the state of fermentation. When it is not in this state, being once at rest, it remains at rest, until it is moved by some external impulse or internal prompter. But, in the state of fermentation, it has some cause of motion in itself, which, even when there is no impulse from without, suffers it not to be at rest a moment, but produces a constant motion and ebullition, while it continues to ferment.

406. There is surely no similitude between motion and Thought; but there is an analogy, so obvious to all men, that the same words are often applied to both; and many modifications of Thought have no name but such as is borrowed from the modifications of motion. (See *Art.* 223 and 238. *Illus.* 1 and 2.)

Obs. 1. Many Thoughts are excited by the senses. The causes or occasions of these may be considered as external; but, when such external causes do not operate upon us, we continue to think from some internal cause. From the constitution of the mind itself there is a constant ebullition of Thought, a constant intestine motion; not only of Thoughts barely speculative, but of sentiments, passions, and affections, which attend them. (See *Art.* 224. *Illus.*)

2. This continued succession of thought has, by some philosophers, been called the *imagination*. It was formerly called the *fancy*, or the *phantasy*. If the old name be laid aside, it were to be wished that a name were given to it less ambiguous than that of Imagination,—a name which has two or three meanings besides. (*Art.* 259. *Obs.* 1 and 2, and *Art.* 141.)

3. It is often called the *train of ideas.* This may lead one to think, that it is a train of bare conceptions; but this would surely be a mistake. It is made up of many other operations of mind, as well as of conceptions, or ideas. (*Art.* 200.)

Example. Memory, judgment, reasoning, passions, affections, and purposes; in a word, every operation of the mind (excepting those of sense) is exerted occasionally in this Train of Thought, and has its share as an ingredient; so that we must take the word *idea* in a

14 *

very extensive sense, if we make the Train of our Thoughts to be only a Train of Ideas. (See *Art.* 36. *Illus.* 1, 2, *and* 3.)

407. To pass from the name, and consider the thing, we may observe, that the TRAINS OF THOUGHT in the mind are of two kinds :

First, they are either such as flow spontaneously, like water from a fountain, without any exertion of a governing principle to arrange them. (*Art.* 202.)

Or, secondly, they are regulated and directed by an active effort of the mind, with some view and intention. (*Art.* 203 and 224.)

Obs. Before we consider these in their order, it is proper to premise, that these two kinds, how distinct soever in their nature, are for the most part mixed, in persons awake and come to years of understanding. (See *Art.* 199.)

Illus. 1. On the one hand, we are rarely so vacant of all project and design, as to let our Thoughts take their own course without the least check or direction ; or if at any time we should be in this state, some object will present itself, which is too interesting not to engage the attention, and rouse the active or contemplative powers that were at rest. (*Art.* 201.)

2. On the other hand, when a man is giving the most intense application to any speculation, or to any scheme of conduct, when he wishes to exclude every thought that is foreign to his present purpose ; such Thoughts will often impertinently intrude upon him, in spite of his endeavors to the contrary, and occupy, by a kind of violence, some part of the time destined to another purpose. One man may have the command of his Thoughts more than another man, and the same man, more at one time than at another ; but I apprehend, that in the best trained mind, the Thoughts will sometimes be restive, sometimes capricious and self-willed, even when it is wished to have them most under command.

408. We must ascribe to Him who made us, and not to the mind, the *power* of calling up any Thought at pleasure, because such a call or volition supposes that Thought to be already in the mind ; for otherwise, how should it be the object of volition ? As this must be granted on the one hand, so it is no less certain on the other, that a man has a considerable power in regulating and disposing his own Thoughts. Of this every man is conscious, and I can no more doubt of it, than I can doubt whether I think now, as I was obliged to think when I wrote the Illustration to Article 90.

Illus. 1. We seem to treat the Thoughts that present themselves to the Fancy in crowds, as a great man treats the persons who attend his levee. They are all ambitious of his attention ; he goes round the circle, bestowing a *bow* upon one, a *smile* upon another ; asks a *short question* of a third ; while a fourth is honored with a *particular conference ;* and the greater part have no particular mark of attention, but go as they came. It is true, he can give no mark of his attention to those who were not there, but he has a sufficient number for making a choice and distinction.

2. In like manner, a number of Thoughts present themselves to the Fancy spontaneously ; but if we pay no attention to them, if we hold no conference with them, they pass with the crowd, and are immediately forgotten, as if they had never appeared. But those to which we think proper to pay attention, may be stopped, examined, and arranged, for any particular purpose which we have in view. (See *Chap. VI. Book I.*)

409. It may likewise be observed, that a Train of Thought, which was at first composed by application and judgment, when it has been often repeated, and becomes familiar, will present itself spontaneously. Thus, when a man has composed an air in music, so as to please his own ear—after he has played or sung it often—the notes will arrange themselves in just order ; and it requires no effort to regulate their succession. (See *Art.* 136, and *Art.* 128. *Illus.*)

Illus. Thus we see, that the Fancy is made up of Trains of Thinking ; some of which are spontaneous, others studied and regulated ; and the greater part are mixed of both kinds, and take their denomination from that which is most prevalent ; and that a Train of Thought, which at first was studied and composed, may by habit present itself spontaneously. (See *Art.* 130.)

I. *Of Spontaneous Trains of Thought.*

410. When the work of the day is over, and a man lies down to relax his body and mind, he cannot cease from Thinking, though he desire it. Something occurs to his Fancy, that is followed by another thing ; and so his Thoughts are carried on from one object to another, until sleep closes the scene.

Illus. In this operation of the mind, it is not one faculty only that is employed ; there are many that join together in its production. Sometimes the transactions of the day are brought upon the stage, and acted over again, as it were, upon this theatre of the Imagination. In this case, Memory surely acts the most considerable part, since the scenes exhibited are not fictions, but realities, which are remembered ; yet in this case the Memory does not act alone— other powers are employed, and attend upon their proper objects. The transactions remembered will be more or less interesting ; and we cannot then review our own conduct, nor that of others, without passing some judgment upon it. This we approve, that we disapprove. (*Art.* 355.) This elevates, that humbles and depresses us. (*Art.* 359.) Persons that are not absolutely indifferent to us can hardly appear, even to the Imagination, without some friendly or unfriendly emotion. (*Art.* 360.) We judge and reason about things as well as persons in such reveries. We remember what a man said and did; from this we pass to his designs, and to his general character, and frame some hypothesis to make the whole consistent. Such Trains of Thought we may call *Historical*. (See *Example, Art*. 359.)

411. There are others which we may call *romantic*, in which the plot is formed by the creative power of Fancy, without any regard to what did or what will happen. In these, also, the powers of judgment, taste, moral sentiment, as well as the passions and affections, come in and take a share in the execution. (See *Art*. 264. *Illus*. 1 and 2.)

Illus. 1. In these scenes, the man himself commonly acts a very distinguished part, and seldom does any thing that he does not approve. Here the miser will be generous, the coward brave, and the knave honest. Mr. Addison, in the *Spectator*, calls this play of the Fancy, *castle-building*.

2. A castle-builder, in his fictitious scenes, will figure, not according to his real character, but according to the highest opinion he has been able to form of himself, and perhaps far beyond that opinion. For in those imaginary conflicts the passions easily yield to reason, and a man exerts the noblest efforts of virtue and magnanimity, with the same ease as, in his dreams, he flies through the air, or plunges to the bottom of the ocean

412. The Romantic scenes of Fancy are most commonly the occupation of young minds, not yet so deeply engaged in life as to have their Thoughts taken up by its real cares and business. (See *Art*. 275 and 269.)

Illus. 1. Those active powers of the mind, which are most luxuriant by constitution, or have been most cherished by education, impatient to exert themselves, hurry the Thought into scenes that give them play ; and the boy commences in Imagination, according to the bent of his mind, a general or a statesman, a poet or an orator. (See *Art*. 276.)

2. When the *Fair Ones* become castle-builders, they use different materials ; and while the young soldier is carried into the field of Mars, where he pierces the thickest squadrons of the enemy, despising death in all its forms ; the gay and lovely nymph, whose heart has never felt the tender passion, is transported into a brilliant assembly, where she draws the attention of every eye, and makes an impression on the noblest heart.

3. But no sooner has Cupid's arrow found its way into her heart, than the whole scenery of her Imagination is changed. Balls and assemblies have now no charms. Woods and groves, the flowery bank and the crystal fountain, are the scenes she frequents in Imagination. She becomes an Arcadian shepherdess, feeding her bleating flock beside that of her Strephon, and wishes for nothing more to complete her present happiness.

4. In a few years the love-sick maid is transformed into the solicitous mother. Her smiling offspring play around her. She views

them with a parent's eye. Her Imagination immediately raises them to manhood, and brings them forth upon the stage of life. One son makes a figure in the army, another shines at the bar; her daughters are happily disposed of in marriage, and bring new alliances to the family. Her "children's children" rise up before her, and venerate her gray hairs.

Corol. Thus, the spontaneous sallies of Fancy are as various as the cares and fears, the desires and hopes, of man.

Illus. 5. These fill up the scenes of Fancy, as well as the page of the satirist. Whatever possesses the heart, makes occasional excursions into the Imagination, and acts such scenes upon that theatre as are agreeable to the prevailing passion. The man of traffic, who has committed a rich cargo to the inconstant ocean, follows it in his thought; and, according as his hopes or his fears prevail, he is haunted with storms, and rocks, and shipwreck; or he makes a happy and a lucrative voyage, and before his vessel has lost sight of land, he has disposed of the profit which she is to bring at her return.

6. The poet is carried into the Elysian fields, where he converses with the ghosts of Homer and Orpheus. The philosopher makes a tour through the planetary system, or goes down to the centre of the earth, and examines its various strata. In the devout man, likewise, the great objects that possess his heart often play in his Imagination; sometimes he is transported to the regions of the blessed, from whence he looks down with pity upon the folly and the pageantry of human life; or he prostrates himself, with devout veneration, before the throne of the Most High; or he converses with celestial spirits about the natural and moral kingdom of God, which he now sees only by a faint light, but hopes hereafter to view with a steadier and a clearer eye.

413. In persons arrived at maturity, there is, even in these spontaneous sallies of Fancy, some arrangement of Thought; and I conceive that it will be readily allowed, that, in those who have the greatest stock of knowledge, and the best natural parts, even the spontaneous movements of Fancy will be the most regular and connected. They have an order, connection, and unity, by which they are no less distinguished from the dreams of one asleep, or the ravings of one delirious, on the one hand, than from the finished productions of art on the other.

Corol. 1. It is, therefore, in itself highly probable, to say no more of the matter, that whatsoever is regular and rational in a Train of Thought, which, without any study, presents itself spontaneously to a man's Fancy, is a copy of what had been before composed by his own rational powers, or those of some other person. (*Illus.* 2. *Art.* 264.)

Example. We certainly judge so in similar cases. Thus, in a book I find a Train of Thinking, which has the marks of knowledge and judgment. I ask how it was produced. It is printed in a book. This does not satisfy me, because the book has neither knowledge nor reason. I am told that a printer printed it, and a compositor set the types. Neither does this satisfy me. These causes, perhaps, knew very little of the subject. There must be a prior cause of the composition. It was printed from a manuscript. True ; but the manuscript is as ignorant as the printed book. The manuscript was written or dictated by a man of knowledge and judgment. Such a Train of Thinking could not originally be produced by any cause that neither reasons nor thinks. •

Corol. 2. Whether such a Train of Thinking be printed in a book, or printed, so to speak, in his mind, and issue spontaneously from his Fancy, it must have been composed with judgment by himself, or by some other rational being.

II. *Of a regular Train of Thought.*

414. By a regular Train of Thought, we mean that which has a beginning, a middle, and an end, and an arrangement of its parts, according to some rule, or with some intention. Thus the conception of a design, and of the means of executing it ; the conception of a whole, and the number and order of the parts—are instances of the most simple Trains of Thought that can be called regular.

Illus. Man has, undoubtedly, a power (whether we call it taste or judgment, is not of any consequence in the present argument) where by he distinguishes between a composition and a heap of materials ; between a house, for instance, and a heap of stones ; between a sentence and a heap of words ; between a picture and a heap of colors. Children have no regular Trains of Thought until judgment begins to operate. Those who are born such idiots as never to show any signs of judgment, show as few signs of regularity of Thought. It seems, therefore, that judgment is connected with all regular Trains of Thought, and may be the cause of them.

415. Such Trains of Thought discover themselves in children about two years of age. They can then give attention to the operations of older children in making their little houses and ships, and other such things, in imitation of the works of men.

Illus. 1. They are then capable of understanding a little of language, which shows both a regular Train of Thinking, and some degree of abstraction. I think we may perceive a distinction between the faculties of children of two or three years of age and those of the most sagacious brutes. They can then perceive design and regularity in the works of others, especially of older children ; their little minds are fired with the discovery ; they are eager to imitate it, and never at rest till they can exhibit something of the same kind.

2. When a child first learns by imitation to do something that requires design, how does he exult ! Pythagoras was not more happy in the discovery of his famous theorem. He seems then first to reflect upon himself, and to swell with self-esteem. His eyes sparkle

He is impatient to show his performance to all about him, and thinks himself entitled to their applause. He is applauded by all, and feels the same kind of emotion from this applause, as a Roman consul did from a triumph. He has now a consciousness of some worth in himself. He assumes a superiority over those who are not so wise; and pays respect to those who are wiser than himself. He attempts something else, and is every day reaping new laurels.

416. As children grow up, they are delighted with tales, with childish games, with designs and stratagems : every thing of this kind stores the Fancy with a new regular Train of Thought, which becomes familiar by repetition, so that one part draws the whole after it in the Imagination. (*Art.* 422.)

Obs. 1. The imagination of a child, like the hand of a painter, is long employed in copying the works of others, before it attempts any invention of its own.

2. The power of Invention is not yet brought forth, but it is coming forward, and, like the bud of a tree, is ready to burst its integuments, when some accident aids its eruption.

417. There is no power of the understanding that gives so much pleasure to the owner as that of Invention ; whether it be employed in mechanics, in science, in the conduct of life, in poetry, in wit, or in the fine arts.

Illus. One who is conscious of it, acquires thereby a worth and importance in his own eye which he had not before. He looks upon himself as one who formerly lived upon the bounty and gratuity of others, but who has now acquired some property of his own. (See *Ilus.* 6 and 7. *Art.* 427.) When this power begins to be felt in the young mind, it has the grace of novelty added to its other charms, and, like the youngest child of the family, is caressed beyond all the rest.

Corol. We may be sure, therefore, that as soon as children are conscious of this power, they will exercise it in such ways as are suited to their age, and to the objects about which they are employed. This gives rise to innumerable new associations, and regular Trains of Thought, which make the deeper impression upon the mind, as they are its exclusive property.

418. Thus we conceive, that the minds of children, as soon as they have judgment to distinguish what is regular, orderly, and connected, from a mere medley of Thought, are, by these means, furnished with regular Trains of Thinking.

Illus. 1. First and chiefly, by copying what they see in the works and in the discourse of others. Man is the most imitative of all animals ; he not only imitates intentionally what he thinks has any grace or beauty, but even without intention, he is led by a kind of instinct (which it is difficult to resist) into the modes of speaking, thinking, and acting, which he has been accustomed to see and hear in his early years. The more children see of what is regular and beautiful in what is presented to them, the more they are led to observe and to imitate it.

Corol. This is the chief part of their stock, and descends to them by a kind of tradition from those who came before them ; and we shall find, that the Fancy of most men is furnished from those with whom they have conversed, as well as from their religion, language, and manners.

Illus. 2. Secondly, By the additions or innovations that are proper·ly their own, their Trains of Thinking will be greater or less, in proportion to their study and invention ; but in the bulk of mankind, study and invention are not very considerable. Hence the barrenness of their mind.

Obs. Every profession, and every rank in life, has a manner of Thinking, and a turn of Fancy, that are peculiarly its own ; and by which it is characterized in plays and works of humor. The bulk of men of the same nation, of the same rank, and of the same occupation, are cast as it were in the same mould. This mould itself changes gradually, but slowly, by new inventions, by intercourse with strangers, or by other accidents.

419. The several imaginations even of men of good parts, never serve them readily, except in things wherein they have been much exercised. A minister of state holds a conference with a foreign ambassador, with no greater emotion than a professor in a college prelects to his pupils. The Imagination of each presents to him what the occasion requires to be said, and how it should be delivered. Let them change places, and either would find himself at a loss. (See *Art.* 421.)

Illus. The habits which the human mind is capable of acquiring by exercise, are in many instances wonderful ; in none more wonderful, than in that versatility of Imagination, which a well-bred man acquires, by being much exercised in the various scenes of life. In the morning he visits a friend in affliction. Here his Imagination brings forth from its store every topic of consolation ; every thing that is agreeable to the laws of friendship and sympathy, and nothing that is not so. From thence he drives to the minister's levee, where Imagination readily suggests what is proper to be said or replied to every man, and in what manner, according to the degree of acquaintance or familiarity, of rank or dependence, of opposition or concurrence of interests, of confidence or distrust, that is between them. Nor does all this employment hinder him from carrying on some design with much artifice, and endeavoring to penetrate into the views of others through the closest disguises. From the levee he goes to the House of Commons, and speaks upon the affairs of the nation ; from thence to a ball or assembly, and entertains the ladies. His Imagination puts on the friend, the courtier, the patriot, the fine gentleman, with more ease than we put off one suit and put on another.

Corol. This is the effect of training and exercise. For a man of equal parts and knowledge, but unaccustomed to those scenes of public life, is quite disconcerted when first brought into them. His thoughts are put to flight, and he cannot rally them.

420. Feats of Imagination may be learned by application and practice, as wonderful and as useless as the feats of balancers and rope-dancers. (*Art.* 131.)

Illus. 1. When a man can make a hundred verses standing on one foot, or play three or four games at chess at the same time, without seeing the board, it is probable he hath spent his life in acquiring such a feat. However, such unusual phenomena show what habits of Imagination may be acquired.

2. When such habits are acquired and perfected, they are exercised without any laborious effort; like the habit of playing upon an instrument of music. There are innumerable motions of the fingers upon the stops or keys, which must be directed in one particular train or succession. There is only one arrangement of those motions that is right, while there are ten thousand that are wrong, and would spoil the music. The musician thinks not in the least of the arrangement of those motions; he has a distinct idea of the tune, and wills to play it. The motions of the fingers arrange themselves, so as to answer his intention. (*Illus.* 2. *Art.* 138.)

3. In like manner, when a man speaks upon a subject with which he is acquainted, there is a certain arrangement of his Thoughts and words necessary to make his discourse sensible, pertinent, and grammatical. In every sentence, there are more rules of grammar, logic, and rhetoric, that may be transgressed, than there are words and letters in the sentence. He speaks without thinking of any of those rules, and yet observes them all, as if they were all in his eye.

4. This is a habit so similar to that of a player on an instrument, that both seem to be acquired in the same way, that is, by much practice, and the power of habit. (*Art.* 126.)

5. When a man speaks well and methodically upon a subject without study, and with perfect ease, I believe we may take it for granted that his Thoughts run in a beaten track. There is a mould in his mind, which has been formed by much practice, or by study, for this very subject, or for some other so similar and so analogous, that his discourse falls with ease into this mould, and takes its form from it.

III. *Of the Means of improving a Train of Thought.*

421. We have now considered the operations of Fancy that are either spontaneous or regular; and have endeavored to account for their regularity and arrangement. The natural powers of Judgment and Invention, the pleasure that always attends the exercise of those powers, the means we have of improving them by our imitation of others, and the effect of practice and habit, sufficiently account for this phenomenon, *this Train of Thought*, without supposing any

15

unaccountable attractions by which our Ideas arrange themselves.   (See *Art.* 127 and 128.)

Illus. 1. But we are able to direct our thoughts in a certain course,
so as to perform a destined task.

2. Every work of art has its model framed in the Imagination.
Here the Iliad of Homer, the Republic of Plato, the Principia of
Newton, were fabricated. Shall we believe, that those works took
the form in which they now appear of themselves? That the sentiments, the manners, and the passions, arranged themselves at once
in the mind of Homer, so as to form the Iliad? Was there no more
effort in the composition, than there is in telling a well-known tale,
or singing a favorite song? This cannot be believed. (*Example,
Art.* 413.)

3. Granting that some happy Thought first suggested the design
of singing the wrath of Achilles, yet, surely, it was a matter of
Judgment and choice *where* the narration should begin, and *where*
it should end.

4. Granting that the fertility of the poet's Imagination suggested
a variety of rich materials; was not Judgment necessary to select
what was proper, to reject what was improper, to arrange the materials into a just composition, and to adapt them to each other, and
to the design of the whole? (*Art.* 244.)

5. No man can believe that Homer's ideas, merely by certain
sympathies and antipathies, by certain attractions and repulsions inherent in their natures, arranged themselves according to the most
perfect rules of epic poetry; and Newton's according to the rules of
Mathematical composition. (See *Art.* 275. *Example* 2.)

Corol. The Train of Thinking, therefore, is capable of being
guided and directed, much in the same manner as the horse we ride.
The horse has his strength, his agility, and his mettle, in himself;
he has been taught certain movements, and many useful habits that
make him more subservient to our purposes, and obedient to our will;
but to accomplish a journey, he must be directed by the rider.

422. In like manner, Fancy has its original powers, which
are very different in different persons; it has, likewise, more
regular motions, to which it has been trained by a long
course of discipline and exercise; and by which it may,
ex tempore, and without much effort, produce things that
have a considerable degree of beauty, regularity and design.
(*Art.* 264.)

Illus. But the most perfect works of design are never extempo-
rary. Our first Thoughts are reviewed; we place them at a proper
distance; examine every part, and take a complex view of the
whole: by our critical faculties, we perceive this part to be redun-
dant, that deficient; here is a want of nerves, there a want of delicacy; this is obscure, that too diffuse: things are marshalled anew,
according to a second and more deliberate judgment; what was
deficient is supplied; what was dislocated is put in joint; redun-

dancies are lopped off, and the whole polished. (See *Art.* 270. and *Ilus.*)

2. Though poets, of all artists, make the highest claim to inspiration, yet, if we believe Horace, a competent judge, no production in that art can have merit, which has not cost such labor as this in the birth. (See *Art.* 277. and *Illus.*)

Corol. The conclusion we would draw from all that has been said upon this subject is, That every thing that is regular in that Train of Thought, which we call Fancy or Imagination, from the little designs and reveries of children, to the grandest productions of human genius, was originally the offspring of imitation, judgment, and taste, applied with some effort, greater or less. (*Corol.* 1. and 2. *Art.* 264.) What one person composed with art and judgment, is imitated by another with great ease. What a man himself at first composed with pains, becomes by habit so familiar, as to offer itself spontaneously to his Fancy afterwards; but nothing of merit that is regular, was ever conceived without design, nor executed without attention and care. (See the *Illus.* and *Examples* to *Art.* 275.)

CHAPTER VII.

OF PREJUDICES.

423. THE perfection of *judgment* is, to compare our ideas fairly and candidly, either by juxtaposition, as in the case of intuitive propositions, or by the intervention of intermediate ideas, when proof is requisite, and to pass a decision on that comparison, according to truth and justice, unbiased by partiality or prejudice, unseduced by fallacious appearances in things, by ambiguities in words, or by a disposition to deceive, or to be deceived. (See *Art.* 278. and 358.)

Illus. As, then, the purpose of all our inquiries is, to discover truth and knowledge, and as the completion of this discovery consists in discerning the agreement or disagreement of our ideas, it is plain that we cannot proceed one step without having constant recourse to the operation of judgment. We exert it immediately in cases of intuition; we exert it at the conclusion of every process of reasoning, in determining whether two principal ideas agree or disagree; and we exert it in every step of that process, in deciding concerning the agreement or disagreement of each couple of intermediate ideas. (*Illus. Art.* 279.) The candid inquirer, therefore, should study to preserve his mind in a state fitted to perform this operation in a proper manner, and to divest it of all obstructions or encumbrances which may interfere with its success. Without this precaution, it is vain to pretend to discover truth, because we shall only perplex and discompose our minds, spend our time in irksomeness to ourselves, in disturbance to others, and sink deeper in falsehood and in error. After all the candor and patience we can exercise. the investigation- of knowledge is a painful and laborious task ; but our labor and time are totally thrown away, without a legitimate exertion of judgment. (See *Art.* 285.)

Corol. It is, therefore, a matter of the highest importance, in searching for truth, to know those impediments which obstruct the rectitude of our judgments, and to learn the rules we must observe, in order to conduct them with justice and expedition. This is a subject deserving most serious attention, and must not be omitted in a system of logic.

424. ERRONEOUS JUDGMENTS are denominated *prejudices,* or rash judgments, that is to say, judgments passed before we have duly examined all the circumstances of the case on which we intend to decide. *Prejudices* generally relate to *opinions ; prepossessions* to *attachments ;* the *former* refer chiefly to *things,* the *latter* to *persons.* (See *Art.* 358.)

Obs. The term Prejudices, as here used, comprehends all the impediments which interfere with our forming judgments of every sort, whether of things or of persons. (*Corol.* 2. *p.* 100.)

425. Prejudices are arranged by Lord Bacon under four heads, which he calls, in the language of the schools, 1. IDOLA TRIBUS, the Prejudices of the species ; 2. IDOLA SPECUS, the Prejudices of the individual ; 3. IDOLA FORI, the Prejudices of language ; and, 4. IDOLA THEATRI, the Prejudices of authority.

Obs. These terms, though scholastic, are extremely significant. It is seldom we find the language of the schoolmen so replete with meaning. Prejudices are not improperly distinguished by the title of Idola ; because they occupy the place of truth in the mind, in the same manner as the idol attracts, in the grove or the temple, the devotion which belongs to the Author of nature.

I. *Prejudices of the first Class, or Idola Tribus.*

426. The first class, the *idola tribus,* are such Prejudices as beset the whole human species ; so that every man is in danger from them. They arise, says Dr. Reid, from principles of the human constitution, which are highly useful and necessary in our present state ; but, by their excess or defect, or wrong direction, may lead us into error. (See *Art.* 237. and *Illus.*)

Obs. As the active principles of the human frame are wisely contrived, by the Author of our being, for the direction of our actions, and yet, without proper regulation and restraint, are apt to lead us wrong ; so it is also with regard to those parts of our constitution that have influence upon our opinions. Of this we may take the following instances :—

427. (I.) *First,* Men are prone to be led too much by authority in their opinions. (See *Art.* 235. and *Illus.*)

Illus. 1. In the first part of life, we have no other guide ; and without a disposition to receive implicitly what we are taught, we should be incapable of instruction, and incapable of improvement. (See *Illus. Art.* 234.)

2. When judgment is ripe, there are many things in which we are incompetent judges. In such matters, it is most reasonable to rely upon the judgment of those whom we believe to be competent and disinterested. The highest court of judicature in the nation relies upon the authority of lawyers and physicians in matters belonging to their respective professions. (See *Art.* 313. *Illus.*)

3. Even in matters to the knowledge of which we have access, authority always will have, and ought to have, more or less weight, in proportion to the evidence on which our own judgment rests, and the opinion we have of the judgment and candor of those who differ from us, or agree with us. The modest man, conscious of his own fallibility in judging, is in danger of giving too much to authority ; the arrogant, of giving too little.

4. In all matters belonging to his cognizance, every man must be determined by his own final judgment, otherwise he does not act the part of a rational being. Authority may add weight to one scale ; but the man holds the balance, and judges what weight he should allow to authority.

Corol. As, therefore, our regard to authority may be either too great or too small, the bias of human nature seems to lean to the first of these extremes ; and it is perhaps good for men in general that it does so.

Illus. 5. When this bias concurs with an indifference about truth, its operation will be the more powerful. The love of truth is natural to man, and strong in every well-disposed mind. But it may be overborne by party-zeal, by vanity, by the desire of victory, or even by laziness. When it is superior to these, it is a manly virtue, resulting from the exercise of industry, fortitude, self-denial, candor, and openness to conviction.

6. As there are persons in the world of so mean and abject a spirit, that they rather choose to owe their subsistence to the charity of others, than by industry to acquire some property of their own, so there are many more who may be called mere beggars with regard to their opinions. Through laziness and indifference about truth, they leave to others the drudgery of digging for this commodity ; they can have enough at second hand to serve their occasions. Their concern is not to know what is true, but what is said and thought on such subjects ; and their understanding, like their clothes, is cut according to the fashion. (*Illus.* 1 and 2. *Art.* 87.)

7. This distemper of the understanding has taken such deep root in a great part of mankind, that it can hardly be said that they use their own judgment in things that do not concern their temporal interest ; nor is it peculiar to the ignorant ; it infects all ranks. We

15 *

may guess their opinions when we know where they were born, of what parents, how educated, and what company they have kept. These circumstances determine their opinions in religion, in politics, and in philosophy. (See *Art.* 233, and *Illus.* 1 and 2.)

428. (II. A *second* general prejudice arises from a disposition to measure things less known, and less familiar, by those that are better known and more familiar. (See *Art.* 74.)

Illus. 1. This is the foundation of analogical reasoning, to which we have a great proneness by nature ; and to it indeed we owe a great part of our knowledge. It would be absurd to lay aside this kind of reasoning altogether, and it is difficult to judge how far we may venture upon it The bias of human nature is to judge from too slight analogies. (See *Chapter IV. Book I.*)

2. The mistakes in common life, which are owing to this Prejudice, are innumerable, and are evident to the slightest observation. Men judge of other men by themselves, or by the small circle of their acquaintance. The selfish man thinks all pretences to benevolence and public spirit to be mere hypocrisy or self-deceit. The generous and open-hearted believe fair pretences too easily, and are apt to think men better than they really are. The abandoned and profligate can hardly be persuaded that there is any such thing as real virtue in the world. The rustic forms his notions of the manners and characters of men from those of his country village, and is easily duped when he comes into a great city. (See *Example* 2. *Art.* 239.)

3. It is commonly taken for granted, that this narrow way of judging of men is to be cured only by an extensive intercourse with men of different ranks, professions, and nations ; and that the man whose acquaintance has been confined within a narrow circle, must have many Prejudices and narrow notions, which a more extensive intercourse would have cured. (See *Corol. Art.* 239.)   •

429. (III.) Men are often led into error by the love of simplicity, which disposes them to reduce things to few principles, and to conceive a greater simplicity in nature than really exists.

Illus. To love simplicity, and to be pleased with it wherever we find it, is no imperfection. On the contrary, it is the result of good taste. We cannot but be pleased to observe, that all the changes of motion produced by the collision of bodies, hard, soft, or elastic, are reducible to three simple laws of motion, which the industry of philosophers has discovered.

Example. When we consider what a prodigious variety of effects depend upon the law of gravitation ; how many phenomena in the earth, sea, and air, which, in all preceding ages, had tortured the wits of philosophers, and occasioned a thousand vain theories, are shown to be the necessary consequences of this one law ; how the whole system of sun, moon, planets primary and secondary, and comets, are kept in order by it, and their seeming irregularities accounted for and reduced to accurate measures ; the simplicity of the cause, and the beauty and variety of the effects, must give pleasure to every contemplative mind. By this noble discovery, we are taken, as it were, behind the scene in this great drama of nature, and made to behold some part of the art of the divine Author of this system, which, before this discovery, eye had not seen nor ear heard, nor had it entered into the heart of man to conceive.

Corol. There is, without doubt, in every work of nature, all the beautiful simplicity that is consistent with the end for which it was made. But if we hope to discover how nature brings about its ends, merely from this principle, that it operates in the simplest and best way, we deceive ourselves, and forget that the wisdom of nature is more above the wisdom of man, than man's wisdom is above that of a child. (See *Art.* 69.)

Illus. 2. It was believed, for many ages, that all the variety of concrete bodies we find on this globe is reducible to four elements, of which they are compounded, and into which they may be resolved. It was the simplicity of this theory, and not any evidence from fact, that made it to be so generally received; for the more it is examined, we find the less ground to believe it.

Example. The Pythagoreans and Platonists were carried farther by the same love of simplicity. Pythagoras, by his skill in mathematics, discovered, that there can be no more than five regular solid figures, terminated by plain surfaces which are all similar and equal; to wit, the tetrahedron, the cube, the octahedron, the dodecahedron, and the eicosihedron. As nature works in the most simple and regular way, he thought that all the elementary bodies must have one or other of those regular figures; and that the discovery of the properties and relations of the regular solids would be a key to open the mysteries of nature.

Obs. 1. This notion of the Pythagoreans and Platonists has undoubtedly great beauty and simplicity. Accordingly it prevailed, at least to the time of Euclid. He was a Platonic philosopher, and is said to have written all the books of his Elements, in order to discover the properties and relations of the five regular solids. This ancient tradition of the intention of Euclid in writing his Elements, is countenanced by the work itself. For the last books of the Elements treat of the regular solids, and all the preceding are subservient to the last.

2. So that this most ancient mathematical work, which, for its admirable composition, has served as a model to all succeeding writers in mathematics, seems, like the two first books of Newton's *Principia*, to have been intended by its author to exhibit the mathematical principles of natural philosophy.

Illus. 3. It was long believed, that all the qualities of bodies, and all their medical virtues, were reducible to four; moisture and dryness, heat and cold; and that there are only four temperaments of the human body; the sanguine, the melancholy, the bilious, and the phlegmatic. The chemical system of reducing all bodies to salt, sulphur and mercury, was of the same kind. For ages men divided all the objects of thought into ten categories, and all that can be affirmed or denied of any thing, into five universals or **predi cables** (*Illus.* 2. *Art.* 156.)

430. (IV.) One of the most copious sources of error in *philosophy* is the misapplication of INVENTION (which Dr. Reid calls our noblest intellectual power) to purposes for which it is incompetent.

Illus. 1. Of all the intellectual faculties, that of *invention* bears the highest price. It resembles most the power of creation, and is honored with that name. Yet this power, so highly valuable in itself, and so useful in the conduct of life, may be misapplied; and men of genius, in all ages, have been prone to apply it to purposes for which it is altogether incompetent.

2. The works of men and the works of nature are not of the same order. The force of genius may enable a man perfectly to comprehend the former, and to see them to the bottom. What is contrived and executed by one man may be perfectly understood by another man. With great probability, he may from a part conjecture the whole, or from the effects may conjecture the causes; because they are effects of a wisdom not superior to his own.

3. But the works of nature are contrived and executed by a wisdom and power infinitely superior to that of man; and when men attempt, by the force of genius, to discover the causes of the phenomena of nature, they have only the chance of going wrong more ingeniously. Their conjectures may appear very probable to beings no wiser than themselves; but they have no chance to hit the truth. They are like the conjectures of a child, as to how a ship of war is built, and how it is managed at sea. (*Illus.* 1. *Art.* 71.)

4. The slow and patient method of induction, the only way to attain any knowledge of nature's work, leaves little room for the favorite talent of invention. In the humble method of information from the great volume of Nature we must receive all our knowledge of herself. To a man of genius, self-denial is a difficult lesson in philosophy as well as in religion. To bring his fine imaginations and most ingenious conjectures to the fiery trial of experiment and induction, by which the greater part, if not the whole, will be found to be dross, is a humiliating task. This is to condemn him to dig in a mine, when he would fly with the wings of an eagle.

5. In all the fine arts, whose end is to please, genius is deservedly supreme. In the conduct of human affairs, it often does wonders; but in all inquiries into the constitution of nature, it must act a subordinate part, ill-suited to the superiority it boasts. It may combine, but it must not fabricate. It may collect evidence, but must not supply the want of it by conjecture. It may display its powers by putting nature to the question in well-contrived experiments, but it must add nothing to her answers.

431. (V.) In avoiding one extreme, men are very apt to rush into the opposite.

Illus. 1. Thus, in rude ages, men accustomed to search for natural causes, ascribe every uncommon appearance to the immediate interposition of invisible beings; but when philosophy has discovered natural causes of many events, which, in the days of ignorance, were ascribed to the immediate operation of gods or demons, they

are apt to think, that all the phenomena of nature may be accounted for in the same way. and that there is no need of an invisible
Maker and Governor of the world.

2. Rude men are at first disposed to ascribe intelligence and
active power to every thing they see move or undergo any change.
Whenever savages see motion which they cannot account for, *there*
they suppose a soul. When they come to be convinced of the folly
of this extreme, they are apt to run into the opposite, and to think
that every thing moves only as it is moved, and acts as it is acted upon.

Corol. Thus, from the extreme of superstition, the transition is
easy to that of atheism ; and from the extreme of ascribing activity
to every part of nature, to that of excluding it altogether, and
making even the determinations of intelligent beings the links of
one fatal chain, or the wheels of one great machine.

432. (VI.) Men's judgments are often perverted by their
affections and passions. This is so commonly observed,
and so universally acknowledged, that it needs neither
proof nor illustration.

II. *Prejudices of the second Class, or Idola Specus.*

433. The Prejudices of the second class, or the *idola
specus*, have their origin in something peculiar to the individual.

Obs. As in a cave objects vary in their appearance according to
the form of the cave, and the manner in which it receives the light,
Lord Bacon conceives the mind of every man to resemble a cave,
which has its particular form, and its particular manner of being
enlightened ; and, from these circumstances, often gives false colors
and a delusive appearance to objects seen in it.

Illus. 1. For this reason, he gives the name of *idola specus* to those
prejudices which arise from the particular way in which a man has
been trained, from his being addicted to some particular profession,
or from something particular in the turn of his mind.

2. A man whose thoughts have been confined to a certain track
by his profession or manner of life, is very apt to judge wrong when
he ventures out of that track. He is apt to draw every thing within the sphere of his profession, and by its maxims to judge of things
that have no relation to it.

Example 1. The mere mathematician is apt to apply measure and
calculation to things which do not admit of it. Direct and inverse
ratios have been applied by an ingenious author to measure human
affections, and the moral worth of actions. An eminent mathematician, says Dr. Reid, attempted to ascertain, by calculation, the
ratio in which the evidence of facts must decrease in the course of
time, and fixed the period when the evidence of the facts on which
Christianity is founded shall become evanescent, and when, in consequence, no faith shall be found on the earth. And the same
ingenious author adds : " I have seen a philosophical dissertation,
published by a very good mathematician, wherein, in opposition to

the ancient division of things into ten categories, he maintains that there are no more, and can be no more, than two categories, to wit, *data* and *quæsita*."

2. The ancient chemists were wont to explain all the mysteries of nature, and even of religion, by salt, sulphur, and mercury.

3. Mr. Locke mentions an eminent musician, who believed that God created the world in six days, and rested the seventh, because there are but seven notes in music. Dr. Reid knew one of that profession, who thought that there could be only three parts in harmony, to wit, bass, tenor, and treble; because there are but three persons in the Trinity.

4. The learned and ingenious Dr. Henry More, having very elaborately and methodically compiled his *Enchiridium Metaphysicum*, and *Enchiridium Ethicum*, found all the divisions and subdivisions of both to be allegorically taught in the first chapter of Genesis.

Corol. Thus, even very ingenious men are apt to make a ridiculous figure, by drawing into the track, in which their thoughts have long run, things altogether foreign to it.

Illus. 3. Different persons, either from temper or from education, have different tendencies of understanding, which, by their excess, are unfavorable to sound judgment.

Example 5. Some have an undue admiration of antiquity and contempt of whatever is modern; others go as far into the contrary extreme. It may be judged, that the former are persons who value themselves upon their acquaintance with ancient authors, and the latter such as have little knowledge of this kind.

6. Some are afraid to venture a step out of the beaten track, and think it safest to go with the multitude; others are fond of singularities, and of every thing that has the air of paradox.

7. Some are desultory and changeable in their opinions; others unduly tenacious. Most men have a predilection for the tenets of their sect or party, and still more for their own inventions.

III. *Prejudices of the third Class, or Idola Fori.*

434. The *idola fori* are the fallacies arising from the imperfections and the abuse of language, which is an instrument of thought as well as of the communication of our thoughts.

Illus. 1. Whether it be the effect of constitution or of habit, it is perhaps difficult to determine; but, from one or both of these causes, it happens, that no man can pursue a train of thought or reasoning without the use of language. (*Art.* 90.) Words are the signs of our thoughts; and the sign is so associated with the thing signified, that the last can hardly present itself to the imagination, without drawing the other along with it.

Example. A man who would compose in any language, must think in that language. If he thinks in one language what he would express in another, he thereby doubles his labor, and, after all, his expressions will have more the air of a translation than of original composition.

Corol. 1. This shows, that our thoughts take their color, in some degree, from the language we use ; and that, although language ought always to be subservient to thought, yet thought must be sometimes, and in some degree. subservient to language.

Illus. 2. As a servant, that is extremely useful and necessary to his master, by degrees acquires an authority over him, so that the master must often yield to the servant, such is the case with regard to language. Its intention is to be a servant to the understanding ; but it is so useful and so necessary, that we cannot avoid being sometimes led by it when it ought to follow. We cannot shake off this impediment ; we must drag it along with us ; and therefore must direct our course, and regulate our pace, as it permits.

3. Language must have many imperfections when applied to philosophy, because it was not made for that use. In the early periods of society, rude and ignorant men use certain forms of speech, to express their wants, their desires, and their transactions with one another. Their language can reach no farther than their speculations and notions ; and if their notions be vague and ill defined, the words by which they express them must be so likewise.

Corol. 2. There is reason to hope, that the languages used by philosophers may be gradually improved in copiousness and in distinctness ; and that improvements in knowledge and in language may go hand in hand, and facilitate each other. But I fear the imperfections of language can never be perfectly remedied while our knowledge is imperfect.

3. However this may be, it is evident that the imperfections of language, and much more the abuse of it, are the occasion of many errors ; and that in many disputes which have engaged learned men, the difference has been partly, and in some wholly, about the meaning of words.

Obs. Mr. Locke found it necessary to employ a fourth part of his Essay on Human Understanding about words ; their various kinds ; their imperfection and abuse, and the remedies of both ; and has made many observations upon these subjects, well worthy of the student's attentive perusal.

435. Barron observes, most justly, that infinite almost is the variety of the external appearance of the human race, and no less various, perhaps, are the constitutions of the minds of men. For this reason, unanimity is not to be looked for, even concerning business, and the common intercourse of life, far less concerning speculative tenets of difficult conception, probably in some cases of exceptionable evidence.

Illus. 1. If judgments are formed by candid men on such topics, they will be different, according to the different aspects in which the objects appear to their respective apprehensions. No inconvenience ensues from these different judgments, either in affairs, or in speculation, if men are animated by charity, and proper respect for the opinions of their neighbors, as well as for their own. They add variety to conversation and to action, correspondent to the difference which nature has established in the individuals of the species. They inspire patience and toleration, which afford exercise for several of the most amiable and social virtues.

Corol. 1.   If any nation, then, or large society of men, pretend to be unanimous about tenets, speculative in their nature, and remote from vulgar comprehension, those of religion itself not excepted, the whole almost of the judgments from which that unanimity springs, will be indigested, if not inadequate; that is, they will be the judgments of teachers or leaders, adopted without examination. The greater part of the followers are incapable of forming opinions for themselves, on account either of the imbecility of their faculties, or the abstract nature of the topics; and of course their assent, founded on pretended judgment, is no better than acquiescence in the judgments of those they revere, concerning subjects which they do not fully understand.

Illus. 2.   But though systems of established tenets, whether political, philosophical or religious, are certain sources of many imperfect judgments, and should be embraced with caution, yet in some cases, particularly those of religion, they are perhaps necessary, if not altogether harmless. They are at least negatively good; and if they do not keep men right, they often prevent their going farther wrong. The body of the people are unqualified to judge concerning the theoretical part of religion, and must be led by the opinions of men they account wiser than themselves. If they are not guided by wise and good men, interested and designing men will take the direction of them. If decency and sobriety are not honored with the superintendence of their sentiments, extravagance, and violence, and enthusiasm, will assume that command. Nobody can doubt of the propriety of giving the preference to the former guides; nobody can hesitate that the peace and happiness of society require this preference to be maintained by every reasonable expedient.

Corol. 2.   An established system of religious faith, then, is certainly the combined opinion of the men best qualified to judge, held forth in opposition to the private opinions of all weak, or wild, or wicked men, with the laudable view of keeping the people as near the truth as possible, and of preventing controversies, which are often more pernicious than even heresies, to the comfort, to the improvement, and to the virtue of society.

436. Education, the professed purpose of which is to lead us to the temple of truth by the easiest and shortest road, will not readily be supposed to retard or embarrass our progress in that course in which it pretends to be a guide. It is, however, certain, that no station which we can occupy, no discipline that we can undergo, is more frequently prolific of partial judgments.

Obs. 1.   In all periods of society, the greater part of teachers have been more concerned to inculcate the philosophy of their sect, or the religion of their church, than the pure doctrines of truth; and the inexperience of youth, with the respect they naturally entertain for advanced years and superior wisdom, cannot often fail to render such education a hot-bed of errors and prejudices. History and experience teem with examples of the fertility of this soil, and teach, in the strongest language, the necessity of the most assiduous attention, to prevent or eradicate the plentiful crop of noxious plants with which it is in hazard of being overrun.

2. The fundamental error, perhaps, of education, has consisted in addressing truth, whether prudential, moral, or philosophical, to the memory rather than to the understanding. It is commonly supposed, if a great deal of information be lodged in the mind, and committed to the custody of faithful recollection, that it will prove a plentiful and useful magazine, from which the pupil may draw with facility and advantage every supply he may need in the conduct of life. But it is unfortunately forgotten, that accumulation of truth is only half the business of instruction, and is not even the more important half. The more important part is, to acquire the habit of employing to some good purpose the acquisitions of memory, by the exercise of the understanding about them ; and, till this habit be acquired, these acquisitions will not be found of very great use.

Illus. 1. With regard to prudential truth, or the conduct of a pupil respecting his instructors, his parents, his friends, his equals, his attachments and amusements, the great fundamental rule seems to be, that good behavior is both his duty and his interest, and that upon his observation of it, his treatment and gratifications will depend. If the uniform and discreet conduct of the teacher, or the parent, makes him consider what this behavior is, and forces him to reason about the practice of it, he will be happy and satisfied, he will be attentive and civil to others, and he will be prepared to judge for himself in the conduct of life, when he shall be obliged to think and act without the direction of his early guides. But if he have no rule of conduct, but the dictates of every sudden whim which may arise in his own fantastic imagination, or which the occasional indulgence or severity of an indiscreet superintendent may suggest, his conduct will be the result of foolish attachments or aversions, of caprice, or of passion. His wants will be multiplied beyond the bounds of nature, and the circumstances of his situation ; he will be miserable to himself, and disgusting to others. Advice and instruction will have with him no useful influence. His subjection to authority will be his utter aversion, because it interferes with his gratifications. His application to study will be disagreeable, because he has no conception of the utility of knowledge. From such a train of unfortunate prejudices, what other conduct can ensue, than that which we often survey ?—namely, a. headlong career of the most unlimited gratification, as soon as he is emancipated from that mortifying restraint from which he has so long and so ardently wished to disengage himself; and an insurmountable aversion to every path of inquiry and truth, into which it had been the purpose of education to lead him.

2. The history of Great Britain presents two striking examples of the pernicious effects of the prejudices of education, one political, and the other religious. Charles the First lost his life and his crown by the arbitrary maxims of government he had received from his ancestors. James the Second lost his crown by the Popish edu-

16

cation he had received in France. Though Charles the First is commonly called a martyr to the doctrine and worship of the Church of England, and is accounted by the vulgar to have sacrificed his life in defending her against the bigotry and violence of sectaries, whose hatred to her and him was insatiable, yet it is well known, that his attachment to that church was neither the first nor the chief cause of the discontents which generated and prolonged the civil war. Religious jealousies and fears were then employed, as they have often been, to rouse, and irritate, and alienate the people. But the encroachments on property contrary to law, and the levying of money without consent of Parliament, alarmed all wise men, and excited that tremendous spirit of resistance, which terminated in the lamentable fate of the king, and the destruction of the constitution,— evils that seem to have exceeded in magnitude every wish or conception of the patriots who first opposed the arbitrary measures of the crown.   That Charles knew the constitution reprobated the levying of money by his own authority, we have no reason to doubt; but he had been fatally educated in principles which suggested, that cases of necessity, or the wants of princes, were superior to the constitution or the laws; and that if Parliament refused to grant what supplies he thought necessary, a case of necessity took place, and he was at liberty to exert his sovereign power to provide for the salvation of the state.

3. The education of James the Second in France, and his attachment to the Church of Rome, were the springs of the Revolution, and of the ejection of the family of Stuart from the throne of their ancestors.   Nothing perhaps but the bigotry of that prince could have saved the liberties of this country from extinction.   Could he have relinquished his attachment to the Romish Church, could he have suspended or moderated that attachment, he might have reigned without a parliament, and trampled on the laws and religion of his subjects.   His finances, by economy and good management, were in perfect order, and nearly adequate to the annual expenses of government.   The calamities and disasters of the late civil wars were fresh in the memories of men, and all ranks were reluctant to renew them.   The enthusiastic spirit which had inflamed the body of the nation against his father, had now nearly spent its force, and nothing seemed wanting to success, but to allow the minds of men to cool, and to habituate them to the slavery that was preparing for them.   The blind zeal, however, of the king, and his intemperate attachment to his religion, for the happiness of this land of liberty, hastened every event to a crisis.   They so completely disgusted friends and enemies, that the people, with the most unprecedented unanimity, pushed from a throne, without violence or convulsion, a monarch and a family who would have sacrificed the happiness and peace of a great nation to particular religious tenets.

IV. *The Prejudices of the fourth Class, or Idola Theatri.*

437. The fourth class of Prejudices are the *idola theatri*, by which are meant Prejudices arising from the systems of

sects in which we have been trained, or which we have adopted.

Illus. 1. A false system once fixed in the mind, becomes, as it were, the medium through which we see objects: they receive a tincture from it, and appear in another color than when seen by a pure light.

Example 1. Upon the same subject, a Platonist, a Peripatetic, and an Epicurean, will think differently, not only in matters connected with his peculiar tenets, but even in things remote from them.

Illus. 2. As there are certain temperaments of the body that dispose a man more to one class of diseases than to another; and, on the other hand, diseases of that kind, when they happen by accident, are apt to induce the temperament that is suited to them; there is something analogous to this in the diseases of the understanding.

Example 2. A certain complexion of understanding may dispose a man to one system of opinions more than to another; and, on the other hand, a system of opinions, fixed in the mind by education or otherwise, gives that complexion to the understanding which is suited to them.

Illus. 3. Party spirit induces us to think, that all our friends are men of discernment, of integrity, of generosity, of liberal minds, of impartial views, and of great virtues. The case of our antagonists, their motives, qualities, and conduct, are directly the reverse. Their designs are the result of imprudence, folly, or iniquity. Weakness, wickedness, or selfishness, mark all their plans, and disfigure all their operations. They inherit no spark of discretion, enterprise, or public spirit. Truth is thus suppressed or misrepresented; and in all the subjects of contest, there will not be found, on either side, a single sound or impartial judgment.

4. Religious party-spirit, in former ages, chiefly misled and agitated the minds of men. Happily for the honor and peace of the present age, the influence of this most malignant disposition is now nearly extinguished. The progress of truth and knowledge has not been a little extended and accelerated by this fortunate event.

5. Political party-spirit, however, still keeps strong hold of the minds of men; and the misrepresentations and falsehoods with which it corrupts their hearts, and misleads their judgments, are sufficiently discernible. Did not attachment to party blind the understanding, and obliterate the feelings of modesty and candor, men would be ashamed of the contempt or neglect with which they receive the plainest truths. On some occasions, indeed, this spirit appears to prompt such partiality, as not only despises the dictates of truth and reason, but disregards even the most important interests of society; provided it may accomplish its favorite objects of ambition. It is this species of prejudice, against which, in this island, it is particularly necessary to fortify the mind, because the temptations to indulge it are very strong, while its effects are most detrimental to public prosperity and peace.

6. The prejudices of fashion seduce and pervert all mankind. Every thing experiences the influence of fashion. All ranks are subjected to its power. Manners, arts, language, dress, amusements, studies, science, even laws and religion, are not exempted from its

sway. Fashion is, on many occasions, the opinion of the majority of society, or of the more illustrious part of it; and so ductile are the minds of many men, that they consider its dictates as of superior authority to those of reason itself. (See *Illus. Art.* 240.) Of all our prejudices, however, those supported by fashion are, perhaps, the most justifiable; at least they are often the most difficult to surmount. In all matters of indifference, it would seem, we should submit to fashion; and as we would not choose to follow any authority, in judging of right and wrong, so it appears unreasonable to be singular in cases where neither is concerned.

Corol. The prejudices of fashion are nearly allied to those of authority. They differ only in the extent of the source from which they are derived. Under the former, we are guided by the practice or opinion of the great body of the people; under the latter, we follow the opinions and example of eminent individuals. Authority is most detrimental to all inquiries after truth, and has perhaps obstructed more the progress of knowledge, than all other causes conjoined. It has infested and corrupted the investigations of philosophy in all ages. Even the enlightened spirit of the present age, is not altogether delivered from its dominion.

V. *Rules to prevent Prejudices, and direct our Judgments.*

438. *Rule* 1. Beware of precipitation, and never decide concerning the truth or falsehood of any proposition, till you have ascertained, 1*st.* Whether the words accurately express the ideas, which the proposition would convey to your mind; 2*dly.* Whether you have distinct conceptions of those ideas; 3*dly.* Whether your mind is divested of prejudices; and, 4*thly.* Whether you have fully canvassed the evidence.

Obs. All this precaution may not be necessary to prevent mistake in every judgment we form. For in all sciences, arts, and affairs, we pass many judgments without much attention or premeditation, because the agreement or disagreement of the ideas compared is obvious on the slightest inspection. But when the pursuit of truth solicits us into new, and perhaps obscure, paths of inquiry; when we reach judgments which lead to inferences extraordinary and alarming; or when our decisions differ from those of men eminent for capacity and discernment, or are likely to involve us in controversy; we should reiterate, with patient attention, every precaution.

Illus. 1. Such a practice is suitable to, and is demanded by, the character of a candid inquirer. It may, perhaps, retard our progress, but it will cause us to march on surer ground. It will habituate our minds to accuracy, and will give us confidence in their operations. It will save the irksome sensation which results from the detection of precipitation and mistake; and it may prevent much trouble, by excluding errors from theories, which, if carelessly or rashly overlooked in their principles, may lay in ruins the labors of many painful hours

Example. The most patient investigators have always been the most successful inquirers, and the most prudent and fortunate men have generally been most remarkable for the candor and the coolness of their understandings. Two of the greatest philosophers the world ever saw, Lord Bacon and Sir Isaac Newton, are in nothing so much superior to all other philosophers, as in the deliberation and patience with which they proceeded in their researches. No confidence, no presumption, no vain censure of the precipitancy of former inquirers, no zeal for party, no partiality to system or authority, ever mislead their minds, or disgrace their investigations. They seek truth alone, and they search for her with the caution of men conscious of her importance, and of the difficulty of finding her. They embrace her with cordiality, wherever they meet her, but they will not adopt speculation for fact, nor be satisfied with the semblance in place of the reality.

Illus. 2. Prudent judgment in business chiefly distinguishes the wise man from the fool. The fool frequently possesses sensibility, vivacity, recollection, and information. He is often in these articles superior to the man of wisdom and discretion; but he cannot, or will not, make a proper use of the materials he has provided. He fancies ideas to agree, which do not agree. He judges precipitately and erroneously. His conduct is directed by his judgments. His opinions, accordingly, expose him to ridicule and contempt, and his actions to reproach and misfortune.

3. The essence of wisdom, on the other hand, consists in the passing of just judgments on the men, and the things, about which, in the affairs of life, we are called to decide. It is the offspring or companion of discernment, and discernment is nothing more than that prudent examination, previous to judgment, which leads us to decide according to truth. The wise man, it is said, sees farther into futurity than other men, or excels in the faculty of anticipation; but this superiority is an evidence only of the accuracy of his judgment relative to things past. He supposes that future events, in similar circumstances, will resemble the past. His conceptions of the past are accurate, and he can scarcely err in his opinions of the future.

439. *Rule* 2. If, after employing every precaution, you still find information incomplete, or ideas not sufficiently clear, suspend judgment till farther investigation or greater experience shall qualify you to decide.

Obs. This rule may be supposed to be comprehended under the preceding; because, if we never judge with precipitation, we must, eventually, suspend that operation, whenever the evidence is not satisfactory. But the prudent and rational conduct which this rule inculcates, is so momentous, both in science and in business, that it appeared to merit a separate enunciation and illustration.

Illus. 1. A degree of indecision, which presupposes a doubt of the truth of every proposition we have not examined, is requisite to every candid inquirer. But hesitation and suspense are uneasy feelings to many minds, that are impatient to reach a determination In many instances, if we proceed with propriety, we must observe

16*

the necessity o suspense of judgment, because our inquiries terminate in subjects beyond our comprehension. Barron considers the cases to which this rule especially applics, to be those in which judgment comes within our comprehension; but we hesitate, either because ideas are not sufficiently distinct, or because we have not discovered the intermediate steps which show their relation. In such cases, a candid inquirer must suspend judgment, because he can do nothing else. Should he go on, it is perfect accident if he reach a just determination.

2. When the mind is embarrassed and perplexed, it is often proper to relinquish the subject of inquiry for some time; and to resume it, after an interval of other employment. Its faculties return to the examination with new vigor, more experience, quicker discernment, and frequently with success. But the more common method is, to pore upon the topic which engages attention; and instead of seeking for intermediate ideas, if it be a subject of argument, or farther information, if it be a matter of fact, the inquirer retires to his closet, and forms theories which have no foundation either in reason or in truth. This spirit is fortunately banished, in a great measure, from the regions of philosophy, but it still remains in politics and in business.

Example. Men who cannot conduct their own private affairs, are usually expert theoretical politicians. The empiric who cannot find a panacea for his own disease, sets about curing the maladies of the state. A theoretical politician is exceedingly wise in conversation, but his speculations are rarely verified by experience. He proceeds on fallacious principles. He reasons on the supposition, that the motives and conduct of men are what they should be; or that men will act from steady principles of justice or interest. But the far greater part of their actions are the result of unaccountable attachment or passion, of fancy, feeling, whim, caprice. These can make no part of any theory, because they transcend all rules of calculation, and falsify every conclusion founded on reason and common sense.

Corol. 1. A man, therefore, who wishes to gain real influence in the world, will never rest resolutions on speculation. He will mix with mankind, and accommodate his opinions to characters and circumstances; and if these lead not to decision, he will patiently suspend judgment, and remain inactive; or he will act so ambiguously, that he may avail himself of better information when it shall occur.

2. Suspense of judgment, at least suspense in uttering judgments, if they contain any thing harsh, disagreeable, unpleasant, or even unpolite, is particularly necessary in all good company, and among all men of knowledge. Without this exercise of civility, we cannot expect to be favored with the communications of superior information. We cannot render ourselves acceptable to those from whom we may derive the most essential benefits. We shall discompose and embarrass delicate society; we shall be exposed to critical reprehension, or involved in controversy, the bane of all good intercourse, and insuperable impediments in the acquisition of truth.

Illus. 3. Modesty in judgment is peculiarly graceful and promising in young inquirers. It is always interpreted in the most favorable sense; as a mark of ingenuousness, and a consciousness of the difficulty of attaining useful knowledge; dispositions which powerfully solicit liberal and enlightened minds to impart important aid. On the other hand, petulance, forwardness, and presumption, subject young inquirers to every disadvantage, and to many mortifications. They alarm men of superior parts and improvement, and render them averse to intimacy with persons from whom nothing is to be expected but irritation or disgust. They bring into suspicion the soundness of their understandings; so that these can hardly obtain the reputation of just judgment even when it is deserved.

440. *Rule* 3. Always remain satisfied with the evidence which the nature of a proposition admits; because, To decide without evidence, is weakness and absurdity—To be satisfied with no evidence, is skepticism—To demand the same kind or degree of evidence for every proposition, is unnatural and unreasonable.

Illus. 1. The propositions of science, of arts, and of business, are supported by different kinds of evidence. No candid reasoner will demand the same species of evidence for them all. He is entitled to no other than the nature of each affords. Few subjects admit that complete conviction which excludes the possibility of doubt. The far greater part present only higher or lower degrees of probability. Though, in the sciences of quantity, the mind proceeds on the firm ground of demonstration, it would be absurd to expect equal satisfaction in morals, politics, or natural history, because these sciences are incapable of such evidence.

2. Moral and political propositions are supported by evidence deduced from the human constitution, the order of nature, the happiness of individuals, and of communities, which is far from being so conclusive and direct, as to exclude hesitation, or even difference of opinion: yet these propositions involve truths very important to mankind. The rewards or punishments, assigned by their own minds, by the opinion of their fellow-creatures, and by the laws of society, depend upon them.

Example. In natural history, which furnishes an account of animals, vegetables, and minerals; in geography, which supplies instruction concerning the surface of the earth, what parts are covered with land or water, where hills, valleys, capes, cities, are situated, where currents run, and particular winds blow; in civil history, which recounts the transactions, opinions, and manners of nations in former times; in the administration of justice and civil government, which applies the laws of the community to the actions of individuals, in order to protect the lives and property of the innocent, and to punish the guilty; in the relations we daily receive from foreign countries concerning the public events of nations, or the industry, customs, and sentiments of individuals;—in all these cases, we must depend upon the evidence of testimony; and if the information be not in its nature incredible, and we have no reason to question the veracity of the relater, we ought to be satisfied with that evidence.

Illus. 3. Testimony is perhaps among the least satisfactory channels by which truth is conveyed to the mind. It is less satisfactory than those of intuition and reasoning, at least in the sciences of quantity. It is also inferior to those of consciousness and sensation; but it is, notwithstanding, of high importance to the comfort, peace, and happiness of society. No inconvenience results from following it with discretion. Were it rejected, every disorder and danger would ensue. Man is made to be satisfied with it. His situation often admits nothing more convincing.

Obs. It was chiefly to vindicate the credibility of this species of evidence, to which inquirers sometimes will not allow the influence it deserves, that we advanced the rule under consideration; and it may not be improper to sketch the limits within which this evidence appears to be unexceptionable.

441. The first thing to be considered, then, is the nature of the relation which solicits our belief; because, if it be incredible, we need not go farther; we may reject the testimony without examination, because we are more certain that what is incredible cannot be true, than we can be certain of the truth of any testimony.

Illus. A relation is incredible two ways,—either by containing an action in itself impracticable, or by containing circumstances contradictory to one another.

I. If, for instance, we were told, that an ordinary man bore a mountain on his back from Italy to France; or that there are men in the world who believe two and three make six; we would reject such relations as unworthy of the least credit, because they contain actions and opinions which contradict all our conceptions and experience of human powers and faculties.

II. If, again, a relation represent the performer of an action in different places at the same time, we refuse credit, because it involves a contradiction, and supposes the coëxistence of things which we know to be impossible. But if the action be practicable, if the agent be adequate to the performance, and if the account be intelligible and consistent, the next step is to examine the nature of the testimony; and if that also be unexceptionable, the mind is prepared to believe, and it will be impatient if not permitted to bestow assent.

442. The circumstances of inquiry relative to the credibility of the testimony, are, 1*st*. Whether the relater was fully informed of the nature and particulars of the action; and, 2*dly*. Whether he could be seduced by any temptation to misrepresent them.

Illus. 1. The article of full information may be subdivided into several other inquiries; whether the action was an object of the senses of the relater; whether he had full time to examine it, and possessed the perfect use of his faculties at the time of examination; whether he examined the same action, or similar actions, at different times, and always formed similar judgments; and, finally, whether his account is supported, at least not contradicted, by other accounts of credit.

2. With regard to the character of the relater, we have reason to

rely on his veracity, if we have no cause to doubt it; and if, at the
same time, marks of sincerity, attention, or discernment appear, we
cannot demand better foundation for assent. If an historian be exposed to no temptation to falsify or misrepresent, we suppose that
he relates the truth; because it is much more easy to relate truth
than to relate falsehood. Truth requires no anxious caution to preserve consistency, no struggle to repress the remonstrances of conscience, which even the most abandoned men cannot altogether
silence. It follows the natural and consistent train of causes and
effects. It presents a credibility and authority which command conviction.

3. But if, besides a general attachment to truth, we discover in
an historian other symptoms of integrity, such as relating truth
when it was his interest to conceal or misrepresent it; when it might
hurt friends, gratify enemies, or expose himself to danger from the
resentment of those whom it might offend; we have the best reason to credit his testimony; because he discovers not only great
attachment to truth, but the strongest aversion to falsehood, and
evinces, that the temptations which induce men of little virtue to
disguise truth, and those of no virtue to suppress it, do not affect
him. He is at least sincere, and his testimony must be believed,
unless it can be proved that he was misinformed or had been mistaken.

4. If a relation be consistent, the only ground for charging its
author with mistake or misinformation, is its contradiction of other
accounts of credit, or its containing transactions of which we can
explain neither the motives nor the manner. If two historians contradict one another, which seldom happens, unless in cases of the most
violent prevalence of party-spirit, the evidence of both will be destroyed, or the small portion of credit that remains will operate in favor of the more respectable author. If one author omit what is related by another, the omission may excite suspicion, but forms no direct
argument against the credibility; because many circumstances, unknown to us, might occasion the oversight of which we complain.

5. Neither is the containing of transactions of which we cannot
explain the motives or the manner, a good argument against the authenticity of a narrative; because the deficiency may be chargeable
on the hearer or the reader, not on the relater. Men of all ages
measure the motives, opinions, and actions of others, however different from themselves in constitution, or dissimilar in situation, by
their own; and we need not be told, that nothing can be more fallacious than such a standard. A remarkable passage of history may
be produced to illustrate this observation.

Example. Herodotus, in travelling to collect materials for his history of Greece, received intelligence that some Phœnician seamen
had embarked on the Red Sea, sailed round the south coast of Africa,
and returned home by the Columns of Hercules, or the Straits of
Gibraltar; in which voyage, they must have circumnavigated the
Cape of Good Hope, commonly accounted one of the most brilliant
discoveries of modern enterprise. The historian subjoins his own
opinion; that the incident was incredible, because the voyagers re-
ported, that in some part of their navigations, they had beheld the
ecliptic, or the line of motion of the sun, situated to the north of
the zenith of their course. The historian, however, judged· by a

false standard; he condemned as incredible what he did not understand; because it was unknown, perhaps, in his time, that the appearance specified actually takes place, in the navigation he had related.
He reprobates the account for a circumstance which is the most
plausible characteristic of its authenticity; for it could hardly be supposed to have been conjectured unless it had been seen.

Conclusion. We have now offered every rule and observation,
which appeared of importance to be attended to in forming our judgments in science, arts, and business—we have unfolded the sources
of those prejudices which obstruct the rectitude of our judgments—
we have inculcated patience and attention in forming them when
we have full information—we have enjoined suspense of judgment
when information is wanting or deficient—we have recommended,
finally, satisfaction with the best evidence that can be procured, and
the propriety of judging and acting on that evidence :—we know
nothing more that can be done to render our judgments sound and
logical, but that we carefully habituate ourselves to the practice of
these rules.

REMARK.

Having thus far conducted the pupil through a popular
course of INTELLECTUAL PHILOSOPHY, agreeably to the doctrines of the most respectable and most authentic authors, I
take leave to offer him a word of advice previously to his
entrance upon the remaining portion of the volume. Logic
is neither a frivolous, an ostentatious, nor an unnecessary
branch of your studies; but she pretends not to make mechanical reasoners; she pretends only to lend you her aid
to find out truth, and to guide the exertions of your own
faculties in the pursuit of knowledge. Her pretensions are
at least commendable, and her efforts are entitled to the
most patient reflection and candid examination. If, then,
you will travel in the road that leads to the temple of truth,
if you will employ your faculties to discriminate that celestial
object when you have reached her sacred mansion, her hand-
maid, Logic, offers to conduct you thither : you have your
choice, then, whether you shall remain a stranger to her power,
and be always the companion of those whom Prejudice con-
signs to ignorance and insignificance; or press on with those
who become her candidates, who are grateful for her favors,
and who improve them for their advantage. Strive, then,
my friend, to obtain the flattering distinction claimed by superior judgment, and by which you can avoid the disgrace
attached to ignorance and stupidity.

BOOK IV.

CHAPTER I.

OF IDEAS.

443. That the young logician may proceed with perspicuity, we begin with examining IDEAS as existing separately, or detached from one another. Ideas, as the impressions made on the mind either by external objects, through the medium of the senses, or by the consciousness which it has of its own internal operations, have been defined in Articles **34 and 36.**

Illus. 1. When an external object presents itself to any of the five senses, sight, hearing, taste, touch, smell, some picture, or notion, or conception, of it is formed in the mind; but this picture, or notion, or conception, is totally different from the object, and is called the Idea of it; whereas, the object is called the *Archetype* of the Idea. (*Art.* 38. *Illus.* 1, 2, 3.)

2. By *sight*, we receive the greatest number, and the most lively of all our Ideas; as, for example, those of all the visible objects in nature, animated and inanimated, with which we are already acquainted, or can become acquainted. By *hearing*, we get Ideas of natural and artificial sounds, particularly of the sounds of language, and the important information which they convey. The Ideas of the other three senses, *taste, smell, touch*, are not nearly so numerous, and they relate mostly to the preservation or the comfortable subsistence of the individual. By *taste* and *smell*, we are directed to those aliments which are necessary and salutary, and are diverted from those which are hurtful or destructive. By the *touch*, we examine the surfaces of bodies, and receive all those Ideas which that operation is qualified to suggest. All the Ideas we acquire through the medium of the external senses, are said to be derived from sensation. (*Art.* 41.) The only other source of Ideas is our own consciousness of the feelings and operations, which pass within our own minds, and is called Reflection. (*Art.* 50. and 51.)

3. You will understand what is meant by Reflection, as a source

of Ideas, by the following examples. Every feeling or operation of the mind prompts an Idea of that feeling or operation : thus the Ideas suggested by the feelings of fear, joy, hope, or by the operations of perceiving, arranging, comparing, separating and compounding our Ideas, communicate as distinct and as palpable impressions, as any that we receive through the medium of the external senses. But, as these feelings and operations are all attended with consciousness or consideration passing within the mind, they are therefore called *Ideas of Reflection.* (*Art.* 88. *Illus.* 1, 2.)

444. After the mind has been replenished with IDEAS in the manner now explained, it begins to prepare them for the purposes of *Logic,* or the discovery of truth and knowledge. It arranges them into CLASSES, and assigns them different names, according as they are SIMPLE or COMPLEX, DISTINCT or CONFUSED, ADEQUATE or INADEQUATE, PARTICULAR or ABSTRACT.

I. *Of simple and complex Ideas.*

445. A SIMPLE IDEA, as its name imports, can be contemplated only in one view. It cannot be divided or taken to pieces, because it does not consist of parts, being naturally indivisible.

Illus. Most of our Ideas of the qualities of bodies are of this class, as hard, soft, round, smooth, white, black, cold, hot: all Ideas, perhaps, of tastes, smells, sounds, as bitter, sweet, low, loud, and many of our Ideas of the feelings and operations of the mind, as of desire, aversion, hunger, pain, thinking, willing, discerning, reasoning, are also of this class. We cannot divide them, even in imagination; they are perfectly uniform, and void of parts.

446. A COMPLEX IDEA contains two or more simple or subordinate Ideas, into which it may be divided; and these subordinate Ideas, when divided, may be considered separately.

Illus. All our Ideas of substances are complex, as of animals, vegetables, and the inanimate parts of nature. The Idea of a tree, for instance, includes a great variety of subordinate Ideas, as those of wood, stock, roots, branches, vegetable life, shape, leaves, bark, blossoms, fruit; several of which subordinate Ideas may be subdivided into other Ideas. All Ideas of figures, as of circles, squares, triangles, cubes, cylinders, pyramids; most of the Ideas of virtues and vices, as of justice, fortitude, veracity, theft, ingratitude, falsehood, deceit.

II. *Of distinct and confused Ideas.*

447. The second division of Ideas was, into *distinct* and *confused,* or, which is much the same thing, into *clear* and

obscure. Distinct or clear Ideas are those of which we have
a full and perfect comprehension, and which we can readily
separate or distinguish from all other Ideas. Confused or
obscure Ideas are those of which we have not a full and perfect comprehension, and which we cannot easily separate or
distinguish from all other Ideas.

Illus. Distinct and clear Ideas are perceived with a perspicuity and
energy similar to that by which the mind contemplates figures in
mathematics, or numbers in arithmetic; all their boundaries and their
differences are completely discernible. Confused or obscure Ideas are
like the colors of a rainbow; they run into one another, and the mind
neither perceives fully their nature nor their limits.

448. The acquisition of clear and distinct Ideas is of the
utmost consequence in the investigation of knowledge ; for
the degree of conviction with which it is presented to the
mind, is always in proportion to the degree of clearness and
distinctness which we have introduced among our Ideas.

Illus. 1. Were all our *Ideas clear*, all our knowledge would be *demonstrative*—a quality which belongs only to our scientific knowledge.
Obscurity, more or less, adheres to all our other Ideas, and leaves us
only greater or less degrees of Probable Evidence, corresponding to the
less or greater obscurity of our Ideas.
2. In the Mathematical sciences, and in Arithmetic, the evidence is
demonstrative, because our Ideas of all the figures and numbers about
which we reason are perfectly clear and distinct, and because, in comparing them, we perceive accurately whether they agree or disagree ;
and if they disagree, how great the excess of one is above another, so
that we can affirm, either that they are equal, or that the one exceeds
the other by a certain quantity.
3. In Morals, in Politics, in Arts, and in Business, almost all our
Ideas are more or less obscure : hence, in comparing them, we cannot
precisely pronounce whether they agree or disagree ; and though we
were sure that they disagree, yet we cannot accurately ascertain the
difference.
Corol. The necessary consequence is, that in all these branches of
knowledge, we can obtain no Demonstrative Evidence for truth. We
must be satisfied with Probable Evidence (*Art.* 309. and 311.), and we
should be attentive to procure Ideas as clear and distinct as possible,
that we may reach the highest degree of probability. (See *Art.* 440,
441, and 442, with all their *Illustrations.*)

III. *Of adequate and inadequate Ideas.*

449. The third division of *Ideas* is into those which are
ADEQUATE or INADEQUATE. An *Adequate* Idea is a perfect
picture of its *archetype*, or contains a representation of all
the parts of which the archetype consists.

Illus. 1. It is different from a distinct Idea, because an Idea may

17

be distinct and not adequate ; that is, we may have a clear perception of all the parts of an Idea, as far as these parts extend, though these parts may not constitute a complete collection of those of the archetype.

Example 1. We may have a distinct Idea of a triangle, and yet not possess an *Adequate Idea* of a right-angled triangle, an isosceles, or scalene ; which, besides the general Ideas of three sides and three angles, require that the sides and angles should be of a particular species.

Illus. 2. An *Inadequate Idea* is not a perfect picture of its archetype ; that is to say, it does not contain a complete representation of the parts of which the archetype consists.

Example 2. Almost all simple Ideas are adequate, as those of colors, tastes, or qualities ; all ideas of mathematical figures, and of numbers, as triangles, squares, cubes, cylinders, fifty, a hundred, a thousand, ten thousand.

Illus. 3. But although, when we examine Archetypes with attention, Ideas will be as *adequate* as we can make them ; and when knowledge is either demonstrative, or even highly probable, Ideas must really, or very nearly, be *adequate ;* yet, if we compare Ideas, not only with what we know of their Archetypes, but with what may be known of them, few of our Ideas, except those of mathematics and arithmetic, will be found to be adequate. There is hardly any other thing in nature, of which our knowledge is complete.

Example 3. We are acquainted with a few only of the properties of animals, vegetables, and inanimate matter : what substance is, whether of matter or spirit, is totally beyond our comprehension. (*Corol. Art.* 164.)

4. The whole system of the transmutation, or the assimilation of nature, by which the nutriment of animals is converted into the different parts of which their bodies consist, bones, flesh, sinews, blood, hair, horn, &c., and by which inanimate nature is converted into the numerous parts of vegetables and metals, seemingly so different from one another, as trees, shrubs, leaves, bark, blossoms, fruit, gold, silver, mercury, &c., is to us altogether unintelligible. (See *Art.* 164. *Illus.* 1, 2.)

Corol. In all these cases, and in many others which might be adduced as examples, our Ideas are unavoidably *inadequate.* Our Ideas are less adequate than they might be, chiefly from two causes ; first, *Carelessness* in the examination of Archetypes, which overlooks some of their properties or parts ; and, secondly, *Inattention* in ascertaining the meaning of the words employed to denote them, which words often do not express the same parts, or all the parts, in our minds, which they do in the minds of others. In both cases, our knowledge cannot be so complete as that of a person who has taken care to prevent these errors or defects ; and in every discourse or controversy with that person, we must misunderstand him when these words occur. (*Art.* 86. *Illus.* 1 and 2.)

IV. *Of particular or abstract Ideas.*

450. The last distinction of Ideas considers them as PAR-TICULAR or ABSTRACT. This is the most important distinc-

tion, because it enters deep into the constitution both of language and knowledge. All things exist in nature as individuals or particulars.

Example 1. Every *substance* is the substance of some particular animal, vegetable, mineral, or inanimate piece of matter.

2. Every quality of *matter*, as hard, soft, black, white, belongs to some substance or body, without which the quality cannot exist.

3. Every *virtue* or *vice* has always relation to some agent, and though we may speak, speculate, or reason concerning them, separated from this agent, yet we must admit, that, independent of him, they have no actual existence, nor any existence except in Idea.

451. PARTICULAR and ABSTRACT IDEAS have been so fully examined in Chapter VI. Book II. under the subject of Abstraction, that we here refer the student to that part of the Grammar, to save repetition.

Obs. We have now explained the nature of Ideas, and the divisions of them which appeared to be of consequence sufficient to merit attention ; but as this Grammar is not an introduction to the idle syllogism of the schools, but to sound reasoning in the sciences, in arts, and in business, and as Ideas are the materials of all reasoning, before we relinquish this subject, we shall point out the most frequent causes of their imperfections, and endeavor to suggest the best means of preventing or removing these imperfections. When we know the causes of error, the road to truth is to avoid it. When the Imperfections of Ideas are removed, they of course become clear and distinct.

V. *Rules for the Acquisition and Examination of Ideas and Words.*

452. *Rule* I. Furnish *yourself with a rich variety of Ideas* ; acquaint yourself with things ancient and modern ; things natural, civil, and religious ; things domestic and national ; things of your native land, and of foreign countries ; things present, past, and future ; and, above all, recollect, that " The proper study of mankind is man." Such a general acquaintance with things will be of very great advantage.

Illus. 1. The *first benefit* of it is this : it will assist the use of *reason* in all its following operations ; it will teach you to *judge* of things *aright*, to *argue justly*, and to *methodize* your thoughts with *accuracy*. When you shall find several things akin to each other, and several dissimilar, but agreeing in some part of the idea you form of them, and disagreeing in other parts, you will range your ideas in better order, you will be more easily led into a distinct knowledge of those things, and will obtain a rich store of proper thoughts and arguments upon all occasions.

2. Another *benefit* of it is this : such a large and general acquaint-

ance with things will secure you from perpetual *admirations* and *surprises*, and guard you against that weakness so peculiar to ignorant persons, who have never seen any thing beyond the confines of their own dwelling, and who therefore wonder at almost every thing they see ; every thing beyond the smoke of their own chimney, and the reach of their own windows, being new and strange to them.

3. A *third benefit* of such an universal acquaintance with things, is this ; it will keep you from being too *positive* and *dogmatical*, from an excess of *credulity* and *unbelief*, that is to say, from a readiness to believe, or to deny every thing, at first hearing ; when you shall have often seen, that strange and uncommon things, which often seemed incredible, are found to be true ; and things very commonly received as true, have been found false.

Corol. The *way of attaining such an extensive treasure of Ideas*, is, with diligence to apply yourself to read the best books ; converse with the most knowing and the wisest of men ; and endeavor to improve by every person in whose company you are ; suffer no hour to pass away in idleness, in impertinent chattering, or useless trifles ; visit other cities and countries when you have seen your own, under the care of one who can teach you to profit by travelling, and to make wise observations ; indulge a just curiosity in seeing the wonders of art and nature ; search into things yourselves, as well as learn them from others ; be acquainted with men as well as books ; learn all things as much as you can at first hand ; and let as many of your Ideas as possible be the representations of things, and not merely the representations of other men's Ideas : thus your soul, like some noble building, shall be richly furnished with original paintings, and not with mere copies.

453. *Rule* II. *Use the most proper methods to retain that treasure of Ideas which you have acquired;* for the mind is ready to let many of them slip, unless some pains and labor be taken to fix them upon the memory.

Direction. And more especially let those Ideas be laid up and preserved with the greatest care, which are most directly suited, either to your *eternal welfare,* as a *Christian,* or to your particular *station* and *profession* in this life ; for though the former rule recommends an universal acquaintance with things, yet it is but a more general and superficial knowledge that is required or expected of any man, in things which are utterly foreign to his own business ; but it is necessary you should have a more particular and accurate acquaintance with those things that refer to your peculiar province and duty in this life, or your happiness in another.

Obs. There are some persons who never arrive at any deep, solid, or valuable knowledge in any science, or any business in life, because they are perpetually fluttering over the surface of things, in a curious and wandering search of infinite variety ; ever hearing, reading, or asking after something new, but impatient of any labor to lay up and preserve the Ideas they have gained : their souls may be compared to a looking-glass, that wheresoever you turn it, it receives the images of all objects, but retains none.

454. In order to preserve your treasure of Ideas, and the knowledge you have gained, **Dr.** Watts advises you to pursue the following advices, especially in your younger years.

Advice 1. *Recollect every day the things you have seen, or heard, or read,* which may have made an addition to your knowledge: read the writings of God and men with diligence and perpetual reviews: be not fond of hastening to a new book, or a new chapter, till you have well fixed and established in your mind what was useful in the last: make use of your memory in this manner, and you will sensibly experience a gradual improvement of it, while you take care not to load it to excess.

2. *Talk over the things which you have seen, heard, or learned, with some proper acquaintance.* This will make a fresh impression upon your memory; and if you have no fellow-student at hand, none of equal rank with yourself, tell it over to any of your acquaintance, where you can do it with propriety and decency; and whether he learn any thing by it or no, your own repetition of it will be an improvement to yourself; and this practice also will furnish you with a *variety* of *words,* and copious language to express your thoughts upon all occasions.

3. Commit to writing some of the most considerable improvements which you daily make, at least such hints as may recall them again to your mind, when perhaps they are vanished and lost. And here I think Mr. *Locke's* method of *adversaria* or *common places,* which are described in the end of the first volume of his *posthumous works,* is the best; using no learned method at all, setting down things as they occur, leaving a distinct page for each subject, and making an index to the pages.

455. At the end of every week, or month, or year, you may review your remarks for these reasons : *first, to judge of your own improvement;* when you shall find that many of your younger collections are either weak and trifling; or if they are just and proper, yet they are grown now so familiar to you, that you will thereby see your own advancement in knowledge. And in the next place, what remarks you find there worthy of your riper observation, you may *note them with a marginal star,* instead of transcribing them, as being worthy of your second year's review, when the others are neglected.

Obs. To shorten something of this labor, if the books which you read are your own, mark with a pen or pencil the most considerable things in them which you desire to remember. Thus you may read that book the second time with half the trouble, by glancing over the paragraphs which your pencil has noted. It is but a very weak objection against this practice to say, *I shall spoil my book,* for I persuade myself, that you did not buy it, as a *bookseller,* to sell t again, but as a *scholar,* to improve your mind by it; and if the

17*

mind be improved, your advantage is abundant, though your book yields less money to your executors.*

456. *Rule* III. *As you proceed both in learning and in life, make a wise observation what are the Ideas, what the discourses and the parts of knowledge that have been more or less useful to yourself or others.*

Obs. In your younger years, while you are furnishing your mind with a treasure of Ideas, your experience is but small, and your judgment weak. It is therefore impossible, at that age, to determine aright concerning the real *advantage* and *usefulness* of many things you learn. But when age and experience shall have matured your judgment, then you will gradually drop the more *useless part* of your younger *furniture*, and be more solicitous to retain that which is most necessary for your welfare in this life, or a better. Hereby you will come to make the same complaint that almost every learned man has done after long experience in study, and in the affairs of human life and religion: *Alas! how many hours, and days, and months, have I lost in pursuing some parts of learning, and in reading some authors, which have turned to no other account, but to inform me that they were not worthy my labor and pursuit!* Happy the youth who has a wise tutor to conduct him through all the sciences in the first years of his study; and who has a prudent friend always at hand to point out to him, from experience, how much of every science is worth his pursuit! Happy the student that is so wise as to follow such advice!

457. *Rule* IV. In endeavoring to attain accurate Ideas by the information which you receive, two operations are required; first, *to compare Ideas with their Archetypes;* secondly, *to compare them with the established meaning of the words by which they are denoted.*

Obs. We need not employ much time to evince the necessity and utility of this rule. Unless accuracy be obtained, all our labor and search are in a great measure thrown away. If the foundation be not properly prepared and secured, the superstructure can never be finished with beauty and strength. Inaccurate Ideas are little better than no Ideas; they are sometimes worse. In respect of every deduction resulting from them, they are not preferable to ignorance, because such deduction cannot be legitimate. But this is not their only inconvenience; they lead us to suppose ourselves well informed when we are not so, and, of course, expose us to all

---

* *Note.* This advice of *writing, marking, and reviewing* your remarks, refers chiefly to those *occasional notions* you meet with either in reading or in conversation; but when you are *directly* and *professedly* pursuing any subject of knowledge in a good system in your younger years, the *system* itself is your *common-place book,* and must be entirely reviewed. The same may be said concerning any *treatise* which closely, succinctly, and accurately handles any particular theme.

the mortification which attends the detection of error, and to all those irksome contentions which arise from controversies about the mean ing of words.

Illus. 1. In comparing Ideas with their Archetypes, nothing more is requisite than *patience* and *attention;* for, by the exercise of these qualities, we shall render our Ideas as *adequate* and *accurate* as it is in our power to make them. We should, for this purpose, carefully and repeatedly make comparison, particularly of Ideas which lead, to con- sequences of importance, or which relate to topics of ambiguity or difficulty.

2. Of the three kingdoms of nature, as the writers on natural his- tory express themselves, *animals, vegetables,* and *inanimate* matter, the objects generally remain under our examination as long as we please, and we have sufficient time to attend to every particular necessary to be known. In the demonstrative sciences, also, Math- ematics and Arithmetic, our Ideas of principles at least will be ac- curate ; and it is seldom that our conceptions, even of proofs and conclusions, are liable to ambiguity. The precise and defined nature of the subjects of these sciences, the simple and perspicuous lan- guage in which most writers have agreed to communicate them, render it almost impossible for a reader endowed with ordinary at- tention not to comprehend distinctly the sense intended to be com- municated.

3. It is, then, in the sciences, susceptible only of probable proof, in morals, in politics, in metaphysics, in writings which convey miscel- laneous truth, as history, criticism ; but particularly in controversial writings, and in conversation, that the hazard of *inaccurate Ideas* is very considerable, and the probability of avoiding them altogether is exceedingly small. One great source of ambiguity, in all these cases, is the *indefinite nature* of the subjects, and the *different aspects* under which they appear to *different inquirers ;* but the greatest source is the unavoidable *ambiguity of language,* and the difficulty of ascertaining exactly the *meaning of words.* This double indis- tinctness, both of the subjects and of the means of communication, cannot fail to produce important consequences in all our opinions and reasonings.

VI. *Of the Ambiguity of Words.*

458. Simple Ideas are not very numerous, and they are called simple, *partly* because they admit *no divisions into parts,* but *chiefly* because, *in receiving them, the mind is perfectly passive,* and cannot acquire them without an actual survey of the external objects which suggest them, or an actual feeling of the mental operations which produce them.

Example 1 The chief simple Ideas are those of the QUALITIES of external objects, *light, colors, tastes, smells, sounds ;* those of the OPERATIONS of the mind, *perception, judgment, reasoning, will- ing ;* and those of *pleasure* and *pain, power, extension, unity, exist- ence,* which are derived partly from the SENSES, and partly from RE- FLECTION

Illus. There is no method of conveying any knowledge of these Ideas, but by presenting their *archetypes* to the *external* or *internal percipients ;* and if a person be deprived of any of the senses which should convey the knowledge of them, no words, no signs, no known mode of communication, can supply that defect : he must forever remain in ignorance.

Example 2. If a person be deprived of *sight,* for example, he must be destitute of all conceptions of *light* and *colors.* If he require an account of *thinking* or *willing,* of *pleasure* or *pain,* we can only refer him to *experience.*

Corol. About these *Ideas,* then, no controversy can exist ; because, as all men must receive them from their *archetypes,* all men must, of course, receive either the same impressions, and must have these impressions constantly suggested by the words allotted to denote them ; or, even if they receive impressions in a manner in some respects different, they must speak and reason about them as if they were the same ; for every person can speak and reason only about the *simple* Ideas in his own mind.

Example 3. It is reasonable to believe, that the Idea of the color denoted by the word *green,* is the same in the minds of all men ; but, though there were some difference of Idea in different men, yet it could not perhaps be detected, for every person must speak and reason concerning that color from the Idea of it which he possesses.

459. The next class of IDEAS, about which, and the words that denote them, little difference or ambiguity can take place, consists of those *complex Ideas,* which result from *collections* of *simple Ideas* of the *same kind.* These are removed the first step from *simple* Ideas ; and as *simple* Ideas are *clear* and *intelligible,* the *compositions* made out of them *partake* of the nature of their *constituent parts,* and are likewise *clear* and *intelligible.*

Illus. The two sciences susceptible of demonstration present collections of such Ideas, and, on this account, among others, they are capable of the highest species of evidence. All the operations in Arithmetic, how complex soever, exhibit at no time any collections of Ideas, which result not from different modifications or fractions of the *simple* Idea of *unity.* All the enunciations and demonstrations of Mathematics, how compounded and refined soever, contain no Ideas which are not formed from modifications of the *simple* Idea of *extension.* All the triangles, circles, squares, and parallelograms, about which the mathematician is conversant, exhibit only different views and modifications of the same *simple* Idea of *quantity.* About *simple* Ideas, of course, and those sciences which involve combinations of them, men have differed very little, either in the conceptions of them, or in the language by which they are denoted. (See my *Grammar of Rhetoric, Book III.*)

460. Thus far our path is luminous and patent ; here, however, the field of perfect light terminates, and in taking another step, we find ourselves in some degree of darkness

and obscurity. For, when we enter the confines of the other sciences, *morals, politics, criticism*—when we contemplate the subjects of miscellaneous knowledge, *oratory, poetry, history, essays*—or attend to the *business of arts and common life*—we immediately encounter COMPLEX IDEAS, comprehending large groups of *subordinate* Ideas, and these groups composed not of modifications of the same *simple* Idea, but of *combinations of different Ideas*, partly *simple* and partly *complex*, and we find it almost impossible to avoid mistakes.

Example 1. When we examine the IDEAS denoted by the word *beauty*, a word in every body's mouth, when speaking of *truth, arts*, and *animals*, we are amazed at the multiplicity which it includes, and the combinations which it exhibits. When applied to TRUTH, it denotes some important proposition, established by a clear, but a refined train of proof; as when we speak of a *beautiful theorem*, or a *beautiful discovery*. When applied to ANIMALS, it includes the Ideas of *shape, color, utility, sensibility*, acquired *bodily* and *mental* accomplishments, *youth, health, gracefulness;* as when we speak of a *beautiful woman:* when applied to ARTS, it includes *uniformity, variety, high polish, convenience, utility;* as when we speak of a *beautiful picture.*

Example 2. TASTE is another word in frequent use among men of genius, and lovers of the fine arts, and it also will serve to illustrate to what ambiguity communication is in many cases unavoidably exposed. *Taste* signifies that sensibility to the beauties of nature, of genius, and of art, which results from a sound state of the imagination, and thorough exercise of the understanding, which leads us to distinguish, and properly to prize, these beauties. (*Art.* 270. *Illus.* 1, 2.)

Illus. 1. It is plain, that much ground of difference is laid in the nature of the objects of this *internal* sense, because every man must judge from the state of his own faculties, and the cultivation of the faculties of no two men, perhaps, is entirely equal. Their Ideas of the objects of *taste* must share a similar difference, and must correspond to the state of their respective faculties. It were easy to multiply examples; but it will appear from those already adduced, that a double source of ambiguity prevails with respect to the *Ideas* and the *words* which we have mentioned, and many more similar *Ideas* and *words*, which every day occur in books and in the business of life.

2. The Ideas which compose a COMPLEX IDEA may really be different in different men's minds, according to the improvement of their faculties, or their powers of perception; but the greatest hazard of error results from the inattention with which the *complex Idea* may be formed.

Example 3. Thus, one man may omit some of the Ideas which compose the *complex ones* of *beauty* and *taste;* others may add to them more Ideas than they naturally and justly contain.

Illus. 3. Another great source of ambiguity in every inquiry where *body* or *spirit* is concerned, is the nature of substances, whether *corporeal* or *spiritual*. What substance is, we are utterly ignorant. (*Art.* 349. *Example* 3.) All we can conceive of it is, that it supports qualities, and, of course, all our Ideas of substances are nothing more than collections of the qualities which we have found to belong to them respectively. Now, if other persons form not the same conception with us of any of these qualities, or if they either add to their number, or diminish from it, it is plain that their *complex Idea* of the substance can never agree with ours, and that in all communication concerning it, we and they must misunderstand one another. (See *Chap. IV. Book III. Gram. of Rhetoric.*)

Corol. From these Illustrations, the following important practical rule will be allowed to result, as a good preservative against ambiguity.

461. *Rule* 1. In all cases, when COMPLEX IDEAS come under our consideration, we should employ every precaution to render our collection of the *constituent Ideas* as *complete* and *accurate* as possible; and whenever we discover that our reasonings and conclusions disagree with the reasonings and conclusions of those with whom we converse, or whose books we read, we should stop and reëxamine both the *constituent Ideas* and the expression of them, because it is possible, that in the reëxamination, we shall discover the cause of the difference.

Illus. 1. The propriety and utility of every part of this rule appear so obvious, as hardly to need any illustration. Happy had it been for the peace of society, fortunate had it been for the progress of knowledge, if it had always been punctually practised. All those irritating and frivolous disputes which pester conversation, almost all those controversies which have disturbed and distracted the world, would have been prevented. Consult the controversies which have involved, not individuals only, but classes and periods of learned men, and you will find that they have originated chiefly from misapprehensions of the *Ideas* and *terms* which furnish the ground of the difference, and that, if the parties had exercised any patience and pains to understand one another, before they began to dispute, they might have prevented much trouble and vexation to themselves, and much contention and disturbance to society. (See *Chap. III. Book III. Gram. of Logic.*)

2. The famous controversy concerning the superior merit of ancient or modern learning, which interested and divided almost all the learned men of Europe in the end of the Seventeenth and the beginning of the Eighteenth century, and which still interests, and sometimes divides, learned men, appears a pertinent illustration. It is a *controversy about the meaning of words*, and affords very little ground of difference of opinion, when the terms are fully ascertained. The parties have never considered, that no comparison of authors can exist, except in circumstances perfectly similar. If the state of ancient society gave encouragemen to some efforts of genius and industry, which are not now prompte by similar incitements

can we wonder that these efforts should be more brilliant in the former situation than they are found to be in the latter ? If *oratory, statuary, architecture*, and perhaps *poetry*, received superior countenance and patronage in Greece, than they found even in Rome, and much more than they have found in modern times, is it not natural to expect that their exhibitions should be more deserving of applause ?

3. If, on the other hand, *the moderns possess superior knowledge of the system of nature*, from the advantages which the progress of science has thrown into their hands ; if the improvements of government,' and the extension of refinement and knowledge, have led them to excel in *politics*, in *moral researches*, and in the greater part of the *useful arts*, can we be surprised at their superiority ? It was impossible that the moderns could rival the ancients in the former case ; it is equally impossible that we should not rival them in the latter. The superiority in the one case, or the inferiority in the other, neither compliments nor impeaches the genius of either ; it is the natural consequence of the different situations of human affairs, and, without a miracle, could not have been otherwise. Had the keen combatants in this controversy attended to this natural state of the case, they would have avoided their ill-founded and senseless recriminations. The patrons of modern literary merit unjustly measure the merits of ancient genius by a scale adopted from modern ideas and manners ; the patrons of ancient genius retaliate the same charge, and pretend to determine the eminence of modern genius by a scale derived from the ideas and manners of ancient times. Let these reasonable limitations be admitted, and the shadow of a controversy would vanish : the difference would at least be found to be so frivolous, as to satisfy every man of the absurdity of the contest. (*Chap. VI. Book III. Grammar of Rhetoric.*)

Note. A second rule, respecting the ambiguity of words, is couched in the following article.

VII. *Of Enumeration, Description, and Definition.*

462. *Rule* 2. After ascertaining the amount of a COMPLEX TERM by *enumeration*, by *description*, or by *definition*, employ it always in the *same sense*, without adding to, diminishing, or changing the Ideas it denotes.

Illus. 1. ENUMERATION, commonly called *division* by logicians, is a *recapitulation* of the *subordinate Ideas*, of which a *complex Idea* consists, and forms a very satisfactory method of explaining or ascertaining that complex Idea.

Example 1. The term GRATITUDE includes the following subordinate Ideas : a *consciousness* of favor received, a *disposition* to acknowledge it on every proper occasion, and a *resolution* to seize the first opportunity of returning a similar favor to the benefactor. HONOR, in like manner, includes an *unalterable regard to truth* in words, *humanity* and *generosity in actions, candor* and *forgiveness in thoughts*, and *resentment of insult* or *affront.*

Illus. 2. DESCRIPTION, also, is a sort of enumeration, but is applicable chiefly to objects of sight. It is used often to distinguish objects of *sight,* which have not obtained names, or of which the names are unknown. We describe a *landscape,* a *river,* a *house,* a *town,* a *ship,* a *horse,* a *tree,* a *robber,* in order to communicate Ideas of these objects to those who have not seen them, or to enable those to distinguish them when they do see them. Description is a recapitulation of the parts or properties of the object described.

Example 2. A LANDSCAPE contains *cornfields, plantations, water* running or stagnating, *hills, houses, villages, animals,* situate in such a manner as diversify it from all other landscapes. The *color, shape, strength, gentleness, fleetness,* and easy motion, which constitute the description of *my horse,* discriminate him from all other horses. A *deserter,* or a *robber,* is described by his *stature, figure, complexion, features,* and *dress,* or, in other words, by a recital of the *particulars,* which form his *appearance,* and which mark him out among other men.

Illus. 3. DEFINITION is the last method of ascertaining *complex Ideas* or general terms, and differs not essentially from the preceding methods. The chief difference is, the use of it on different occasions. It may be employed in fixing *complex Ideas* of all sorts, whether their *archetypes* are objects of the *external* senses, or are the *creatures* of *reflection ;* that is, whether they exist in *matter* or in *mind.* It is used, however, chiefly to ascertain *species, whose archetypes exist in the mind.*

A good definition consists of two parts ; by one part are marked those objects with which the *thing defined* has any *common qualities ;* by the other part are marked *those qualities which characterize the thing defined alone.* Nothing more can be done to ascertain the nature of any object, than to point out *those objects* with which it has *any common qualities,* and next to enumerate the *qualities peculiar to itself.* (*Art.* 288.)

Corol. 1. Hence the logical rule, that every definition should consist of a *genus* and a *specific difference* (*Art.* 179 and 168.), the GENUS denoting the *common qualities,* and the *specific difference* the *characteristic* or *peculiar ones.* (*Art.* 158.)

Example 3. Suppose it were required to define what the mathematicians call a *square,* or a *parallelogram,* these most accurate of all logicians will tell us that " a square is a figure which has four equal sides and four right angles," and that " a parallelogram is a four-sided figure, of which the opposite sides are parallel." (*Art.* 170. *Illus.* and *Corol.*)

Analysis. The things defined are *species ;* that is, the square and the parallelogram *are not a square and a parallelogram which exist in some book,* or are delineated on a particular board ; they stand for *the entire* species of squares and parallelograms, and mark the *properties common* to all the *individuals* of these species. (*Art.* 182. *Illus.* and *Corol.*)

The first part of the definition refers them to their *genus,* or characterizes them by the name of *figures,* by which it is signified that *they have something in common with all other mathematical species,* circles, triangles, rhombuses, ellipses ; namely, they include *space,* and are *bounded by lines.*

The second part of the definition exhibits their *specific difference*, or enumerates the • peculiar *properties which distinguish* them from all the other species of the same genus; SQUARES have *four right angles* and *four equal sides;* PARALLELOGRAMS have also *four angles* and *four sides;* but their specific difference consists in the *opposite* sides being equal and parallel, which no other species have but themselves.

Example 4. If we define ELOQUENCE to be the *art of speaking* or *writing well*—LOGIC the art of *reasoning well*—STATUARY the *art of forming an exact resemblance of the human shape in marble*—PAINTING the *art of delineating a resemblance of the same shape on canvass by means of oil colors*, we refer all these *species* to their *genus*, and mark *properties* in which *they all agree*, namely, in being *arts*, acquired by *industry* and *practice*, and then we mention the properties which distinguish *these arts* from *all other arts*, and from one another; ELOQUENCE by *speaking* or *writing well;* LOGIC by *reasoning well;* STATUARY by *forming a resemblance of the human shape in marble;* PAINTING by *delineating a similar resemblance on canvass.*

5. If, again, we define MORALITY to be the *science* which teaches to be *wise, virtuous*, and *happy*—POLITICS the *science* which teaches to *provide for the prosperity of communities*, or large bodies of men—MATHEMATICS the *science* which teaches to *compute quantity*—PNEUMATICS the *science* which teaches the *properties of spirits*, or the *doctrine of fluids*—OPTICS the *science* which teaches the *theory of vision and colors;* we refer, first, all these branches of knowledge to their next genus, science, by which we signify, that they *all agree* in presenting some *useful truths to the mind,* and that they are supported by *satisfactory evidence.* In the second place, we distinguish each science from the rest, and from all other sciences not mentioned, by specifying, as above, the particular truths which it inculcates. (*Example* 2. *Art.* 304.)

Illus. 4. DEFINITION might certainly be employed to discriminate *complex Ideas* on every occasion, and might supersede both enumeration and description; but in all such cases, the *specific difference would become either an enumeration or description.* Indeed, there is no material difference between these methods of ascertaining Ideas, except in the length of the specific difference. An *enumeration*, or a *description*, either *includes* or *supposes* a *genus*, to which the Idea explained refers; and the SPECIFIC DIFFERENCE of every DEFINITION is either an enumeration or a description.

Example 6. The enumeration formerly advanced, of the Ideas expressed by the word *honor* (*Example, Art.* 462.), may easily be converted into a definition, of which the specific difference will become the enumeration itself. " HONOR is a disposition which prompts us to regard *truth* in our *words, generosity* in our *actions, candor* in our *thoughts*, and to entertain *resentment* of *insult* or *affront*." In like manner, we may convert the *description* of a horse into a *definition*, of which the *description will constitute the specific difference.* We may call him an ANIMAL of a *cylindrical body*, long and taper legs, high neck, beautiful head, of gentle temper, easy motion, and fit for riding.

Illus. 5. It is to be observed, however, that when the *specific dif-*

18

ference resolves itself into an *enumeration*, or a *description*, it is of little consequence to distinguish the genus. On the other hand, when it is of consequence to distinguish the genus, the *specific difference* seldom consists of more than *one* or *two properties*. Definition is always used in the *last case*, and enumeration or description in the *two first*. *Enumeration* is commonly employed to explain *complex Ideas*, of which it is of little consequence to mention the genus; *description*, to ascertain *complex Ideas*, the *archetypes* of which are objects of *sight*; and *definition*, to ascertain the *abstract Ideas of species*.

Illus. 6. With respect to definition, it is proper further to observe, that we *must never attempt to apply it to simple Ideas*, because they are immediately derived from perception, prompted by the objects or operations which suggest them; and no definition or explication can render them more distinct or intelligible than they are. Even the mathematicians have not always been sufficiently attentive to this remark.

Example 7. The word *ratio* denotes the Idea of equality or inequality, which results from the comparison of two magnitudes of the same kind in point of quantity; as when one of the magnitudes is said to be equal to, greater or less than the other, or to hold to it some fixed proportion. (*Example* 1. *Art.* 304.)

Obs. The Idea appears to be simple; at least no words can make it plainer than the actual comparison of the magnitudes by which it is prompted. Yet some editions of Euclid, which we have seen, previous to the one published by Dr. Simpson of Glasgow, present the following definition of ratio. "Ratio," we are told, " is a habitude of magnitudes of the same kind, according to quantity." *Habitude* is a word, which, to say the least of it, is unintelligible as applied to *ratio;* yet it seems that no plainer word could be found. "Ratio," says Simpson, " is the mutual relation of two magnitudes, of the same kind, to one another, in respect of quantity." (See *Illus.* 3. *Art.* 304.)

Example 8. MOTION is another simple Idea, on which ARISTOTLE, and the SCHOOLMEN after him, have exercised their ingenuity, and have produced the following famous specimen of jargon. They tell us, that motion is "actus entis in potentia, quatenus in potentia," *the act of being in energy, as far as it is in energy.* Even later philosophers, who define motion by " a passage from one place to another," do not make the matter much plainer. They only substitute one word for another, and it is difficult to decide whether motion is better explained by passage, or passage by motion.

Corol. 2. As, then, COMPLEX IDEAS only are susceptible of explication in any of the ways which we have mentioned, if we would preserve perspicuity, careful attention must be paid, that the same meaning, thus settled, shall be invariably retained. The determination of this point is simple and easy, and may always be accomplished by substituting the explication in the place of the term defined. If this be practicable, and the sense be preserved, we may be confident we have not changed the meaning of the term. (*Art.* 167. *Illus.*)

Scholium. Before we relinquish this branch of the subject, it is proper to observe, that although, in compliance with the example of all logical writers, we have considered all knowledge as composed of Ideas, and feel even disposed to call every *impression* made on the mind, whether derived from an *external* or an *internal archetype*, by this name; yet these *impressions* have obtained other names than Ideas. Thus all *impressions*, prompted by *archetypes*, which have a *real existence without the mind*, are distinguished by the name of *perceptions*. (*Art.* 113.) All *impressions* of which the *archetypes* have *no real existence*, but are the *creatures of the imagination*, as a *mountain of gold*, a *sea of milk*, are denominated *conceptions*. (*Art.* 140. *Illus.*) Those *impressions* only are called Ideas, which have been formerly received into the mind, and are again recalled by Memory. You will find this explanation useful in reading this Grammar as well as some Metaphysical, and even some Critical Writers; but we may in general give the name of *Idea* to every impression, whether *simple* or *complex*, and from whatever source it may be derived.

Note. I am aware that in Chapter VI. Book II. some portion of the reasoning advanced in this chapter has been anticipated; but the subject matter of that chapter could not be discussed without anticipating some part of this; and as instruction, not pedantry, is the object of this Grammar, the logician, properly so called, will approve my plan, rather than join in its censure, with that illiberal spirit, falsely called criticism, so current among those, who, unacquainted with the discharge of scholastic duties, would "put old heads on young shoulders."

CHAPTER II.

OF PROPOSITIONS.

463. ALL that we have hitherto advanced in this Book, is a mere preparation of the materials of Logic; and we have to apply these materials to the investigation of truth and the acquisition of knowledge.

Illus. The investigation of truth and knowledge consists of two operations; one which compares two Ideas, or one pair of Ideas together, in order to perceive in them agreement or disagreement; another which compares two Ideas by the help of one or more intermediate Ideas. The truth or knowledge acquired by the first operation, is said to result from Judgment (see *Art.* 26.); the truth or knowledge acquired by the second operation, is said to result from Reasoning. (*Art.* 294.)

I. *Knowledge and Truth.*

464 What is knowledge? and, What is truth? We

are familiarized with these words, and are not disposed to suspect any mystery in their meaning. Their meaning, however, is not so obvious as is generally supposed; and it is of so much importance in our present inquiry, that we cannot proceed without attempting to ascertain it. (*Art.* 302. *I. II. Corol.*)

Illus. 1. KNOWLEDGE, then, in a logical sense, is the perception of the agreement or disagreement of Ideas with one another; TRUTH is the perception of the agreement or disagreement of Ideas with words. But what, it will again be asked, perhaps, is the signification of these words, *agreement* and *disagreement?* The signification of these words is not always the same, but varies according to the nature of the science, the art, or the subject, about which the Ideas are employed. (*Art.* 295. *Illus.*)

Example 1. In Arithmetic and Mathematics, the only *comparison* of Ideas which can take place, relates to the equality or inequality of the quantities; *agreement* denotes equality, *disagreement* inequality. Thus, when we compare the quantities four and five, we perceive that they are unequal, or that the Ideas of them disagree. We perceive, further, if we add *one* to *four*, that these two together form a compound quantity, which will be exactly equal to *five*, or that the Ideas *four* and *one*, conjoined, will agree with the Idea *five.*

Corol. 1. Our knowledge, then, that *four* is not equal to *five*, but that *four* and *one* are equal to *five*, is the INTUITIVE PERCEPTION which we have, that the Idea of *four* disagrees with the Idea of *five*, while the Idea of *four* and *one* together agrees with the Idea of *five.* (*Corol* 1. *Art.* 293.)

Example 2. In like manner, from the Ideas which we have of a *right angle*, or half a right angle, or from the Ideas which we have of an *acre*, and half an acre, which we know certainly, that the half right angle disagrees with, or is a less quantity than the whole right angle; that the half acre disagrees with, or is a less quantity than the whole acre; and that if we double the half right angle and the half acre, we shall form two compound quantities, the Ideas of which will *agree* respectively with those of the whole right angle and the whole acre.

Corol. 2. The perception of the agreement or disagreement of Ideas, in all these cases, is the same thing with the knowledge of the equality or inequality of the quantities compared.

Example 3. If, in natural philosophy, we compare body or matter with divisibility, we immediately discover that divisibility applies to matter, or is a property of it; in other words, we find that the Idea of matter and divisibility agree together, and we know that matter is divisible.

Obs. *Agreement*, in this case, signifies *property* or *relation*, not *equality*, as in the preceding cases.

Example 4. If we maintain in morals, that a good man is happy; or in politics, that a wise king is a blessing to his people; or in arts, that industry is commonly attended with success,—

Corol. 3. Our knowledge of all these maxims is perfectly the same thing with the agreement which we perceive between the Ideas of a good man. and happiness; of a wise king, and the happiness of his people; of industry, and the acquisition of wealth.

Illus. 2. (I.) TRUTH relates to the *enunciation of knowledge*, and is the *agreement* of Ideas with *words.* Thus, if we assert that the British is a free government, and that the English are more industrious than any other nation in Europe, we maintain truth, because our words actually correspond to accurate Ideas of the facts. If, again, we say, that the three angles of a triangle are equal to two right angles, we express a truth, because it is demonstrable that our *words* and our Ideas agree.

II. *Falsehood*, on the other hand, is the disagreement of *words* with Ideas; when it is asserted, that the British government is despotic, or that the three angles of a triangle are equal to three right angles.

III. A MISTAKE is the disagreement of *words* with Ideas, when we suppose that they agree.

IV. The *ignominious* falsehood called a *lie*, is the disagreement of *words* with Ideas, uttered with an intention to deceive. (See my *Grammar of Rhetoric, Ch. V. B. III.*)

Illus. 3. KNOWLEDGE, further, is of two kinds, *certain* and *probable.* *Certain knowledge* is that which the mind has when it is perfectly satisfied of the agreement or disagreement of Ideas. *Probable knowledge* is that which the mind has when the agreement or disagreement of Ideas is not so clear as to afford entire satisfaction. The degrees of probability are also greater or less, according as the satisfaction is more or less perfect. (*Art.* 310. *Illus.*)

II. *Different Kinds of Propositions.*

465. In judging of the agreement or disagreement of Ideas, we examine them in pairs, and the words in which we express that Judgment, form a sentence called a PROPOSITION. (*Illus. Art.* 29.)

Illus. For example, if the Idea of a *whole* be compared with the Idea of a *part*, it is immediately found that they disagree; and this Judgment is expressed by the following *proposition:* "The whole is greater than any of its parts." But, if the Idea of the *whole* be compared with the Idea of *all its parts taken together*, it is found that they agree; and this Judgment is expressed by the following proposition: "The whole is equal to all its parts taken together." (*Illus.* 2. *Art.* 306.)

466. If the agreement or disagreement be perceived by bare juxtaposition of the Ideas, without the intervention of any intermediate Idea, the *evidence* of the proposition is said to be *intuitive.* (*Corol. Example* 1. *Art.* 464.) But if the agreement or disagreement be perceived by means of some intermediate Idea, or train of Ideas, the mind then must proceed by steps. (*Art.* 298. *Obs.*)

18 *

Illus. It must compare the *first Idea* of the proposition with the *first intermediate Idea*, and pass a judgment on their agreement or disagreement. (*Art.* 464. *Illus.* 1.) It must next compare the *first intermediate Idea* with the *second intermediate Idea*, and pass a similar judgment. It must proceed, in like manner, through all the intermediate Ideas, and pass similar judgments, till it comes to compare the *last intermediate Idea* with the latter Idea of the proposition; and from all these intermediate judgments, the conclusive judgment is deduced, concerning the agreement or disagreement of the two primary Ideas of the proposition. (*Art.* 244. *Example.*) In this case, the evidence of the proposition, declarative of the agreement or disagreement of the two primary Ideas, is said to be founded on reasoning. (*Art.* 280. *Illus.* and *Examples.*)

Corol. It hence appears, that all knowledge, whether the offspring of intuition, or the result of reasoning, is denoted by *propositions*, which express the agreement or disagreement of Ideas; that each proposition contains two Ideas, simple or complex, besides the assertion of agreement or disagreement; and that the proposition which denotes agreement may be called *affirmative*, that which denotes disagreement may be called *negative*. "That the three angles of a triangle are equal to two right angles," is an *affirmative proposition;* and "that a part is not equal to the whole," is a *negative* proposition. (*Art.* 465. *Illus.*)

467. The *two capital Ideas* constitute *two parts* of a Proposition. The first Idea, or sometimes several Ideas considered as one, is that of which something is affirmed or denied, and is therefore called the *subject of the proposition* (*Art.* 159. *Illus.* 1.); the second Idea, or sometimes several Ideas considered as one, is the property, or quality, or attribute, which is either affirmed or denied to belong to, or to agree with, the first Idea, and is therefore called the *predicate of the Proposition.* (*Art.* 152. *Illus.* 2.)

Example. "The three angles of a triangle are equal to two right angles," is a proposition of which the *Idea of the three right angles forms the* SUBJECT, and the *Idea of equality to two right angles forms the* PREDICATE. The affirmation contained in the word *are* is commonly called by logicians the *copula*, or connective of the Proposition. (*Illus. Art.* 281.)

468. Propositions, further, are distinguished by different names, according to the clearness of the evidence by which the agreement or disagreement of the subject and predicate is evinced. (*Art.* 288.)

Illus. 1. If the evidence be perfectly satisfactory, the *proposition* is denominated *certain.* (*Illus.* 2. *Art.* 309.)

2. If the evidence be not perfectly satisfactory, it is denominated *probable;* and it is *more* or *less probable*, according as the evidence is *more* or *less satisfactory.* (*Art.* 309. *Illus.* 1.)

3. If the evidence for the agreement of the subject and predicate

balance the evidence for their disagreement, the *proposition is called doubtful.*

4. If the evidence be stronger on the side of disagreement, it gets the name of *improbable;* and the improbability will be the greater, as the evidence of disagreement shall increase.

5. If the proposition bear an affirmation contrary to Ideas, it obtains the name of *false.* (*Illus.* 3. *Art.* 278.)

6. If the affirmation be conformable to Ideas, it is denominated *true.*

469. Propositions, also, are divided into universal, particular, singular, indefinite, conditional, and relative. (See *Art.* 449, 450, 451.)

Illus. 1. An UNIVERSAL PROPOSITION is that whose subject comprehends an entire genus or species.

Example 1. Thus, " All animals are endowed with life and organization," is an universal proposition, because the *subject* of it includes, and the *predicate* applies to, *all living creatures,* or to *a whole genus.* (*Art.* 158. *Illus.*)

2. " All men are liable to err," is another universal proposition, because the *subject* includes, and the *predicate* applies to, a *whole species,* or every individual of the human race.

Illus. 2. A PARTICULAR PROPOSITION denotes a limited or partial meaning of the subject, or signifies that it does not include an entire genus or species; and, in this case, the restricting words, some, few, many, &c., usually *precede* the subject of the proposition. (*Art.* 159. *Illus.*)

Examples. " Few men spend their time to the best advantage,"— " Many men repent of their folly when it is too late,"—are both particular propositions, because they include a part only of the human species, to which they refer.

Illus. 3. A SINGULAR PROPOSITION has an *individual* for its *subject.*

Examples. " Alexander conquered the Persians,"—" Cæsar was assassinated in the senate-house."

4. An INDEFINITE PROPOSITION relates to *one* individual among many, and is commonly introduced by the indefinite article.

Examples. " A wise man guides his affairs with discretion;" " A fool is perpetually betraying his ignorance and impudence."

5. A CONDITIONAL PROPOSITION expresses condition or dependence.

Example 2. " If people break the laws, they will be punished."

6. A RELATIVE PROPOSITION denotes consequence or connection.

Example 3. " Though he fall, yet will he rise again." But the distinctions under *Illus.* 5 and 6, seem to belong rather to grammar than to logic.

470. PROPOSITIONS sometimes receive different names, according to the *kinds of evidence* by which they are supported. The chief of these kinds receive their names from the evidence furnished by *sensation, consciousness, intuition, reasoning,* and *testimony;* and it is of consequence to consider propositions with regard to these kinds of evidence, because they lead us to the chief sources of human knowledge.

Illus. By the external senses we are made acquainted with all the objects in nature, which can contribute either to our use or to our pleasure; and of all the propositions derived from the testimony of these senses and feelings, we never, in the intercourse of life, presume to entertain the slightest doubt. (*Art.* 100. *Illus.* 201.) We believe that the city, the house, the man, the horse, the tree, the fish, that we behold, really exist, and possess those properties or qualities which we perceive to belong to them. (*Art.* 120. *Illus.* and *Corol.*) We never hesitate whether the propositions containing the result of our perceptions respecting them are true. (*Art.* 116. *Illus.* 1 and 2.) We hesitate as little about propositions significant of the reality of our bodily feelings, and of our desires to gratify them; such as, that hunger, thirst, pain, are uneasy sensations, from which all men wish to be relieved, and that rest after fatigue is a source of pleasure. (*Art.* 112. *Illus.* 1, 2, 3, 4, 5, 6, 7.)

Corol. In all these cases, no means of conviction are presented to the mind, besides perceptions and feelings. The knowledge, accordingly, derived from this source, is often called the dictates of sense; and the sentences that denote this knowledge are sometimes termed *sensible propositions.* (*Art.* 290. *Illus.* 6. *Corol.*)

III. *Sources of Human Knowledge*

471. I. MENTAL FEELING, or CONSCIOUSNESS, is a copious source of knowledge, and furnishes evidence of the truth of a numerous class of propositions. By consciousness we gain an acquaintance with the human constitution, particularly with the important operations of the understanding, the imagination, and the passions. (See *Chapter I. Book II.*)

Illus. 1. If you affirm that your *imagination* is pleased with a fine prospect, a beautiful landscape, an elegant exhibition of art, whether in writing, painting, sculpture, or architecture; if you assert, that your understanding is delighted with the discovery of truth on all subjects, and in all degrees, from the lowest degree of probability to the most satisfactory evidence of *intuition* or *demonstration;* if you maintain that all your passions were given you for wise and good purposes; that all the gratifications of them, within the limits prescribed by reason and by virtue, are pleasant, salutary, and commendable; and that all irregular gratifications are in themselves not only improper, but also painful and destructive;—you have hardly any proof to produce of the numerous propositions, which express the various cases into which these views of the human mind may be resolved, except an appeal to the consciousness of the person whom you wish to convince. (See *Art.* 24.)

2. Should you affirm that your imagination is not captivated with a beautiful scene of nature or art; should you declare that your understanding receives no pleasure in the discovery of truth, or that the gratification of a regular passion yields you no joy, while the agitation of an irregular one fills you with satisfaction;—all I can

urge is, that you mistake your constitution, or that its structure is different from the constitution of most other men; and if you persist in maintaining the consciousness of the truth of what you assert, I can only oppose a contrary consciousness on my part. We must continue of opposite opinions, for I can advance no arguments to persuade you to adopt my notions.

Corol. 1. From this view of knowledge, it will appear, that many moral and political propositions, many too which communicate truth,. in oratory, poetry, criticism, and business, are principally, if not entirely, supported by consciousness.

Illus. 3. If you assert, that all men applaud a generous or a grateful action, and detest an unjust or a cruel one; that kings are prone to tyrannize over their subjects, or that the people are disposed to insult and oppose their rulers; that the beauties of eloquence and poetry are felt by all mankind, even the most unpolished and unlearned; that the rules of criticism are nothing more than the theories of emotions and passions; that prudence and industry are the best and surest means of attaining success in business, while folly and idleness are commonly attended with misfortune and contempt;— you appeal to consciousness concerning the truth of the propositions which you advance.

4. If you gain not immediate assent, all you can do to procure it is, to enumerate examples, by which the opinions which you maintain have been verified, and to hold forth these as documents of general concurrence, in support of the judgment which you have formed.

Corol. 2. In all these subjects, the most satisfactory evidence, and the best theories, are founded on the nature of the human constitution. The most sagacious and successful moralists, politicians, critics, and observers of human affairs, ground their maxims and their observations on the qualities of the mind, of which they are conscious themselves, or of which they discover that others are conscious.

472. II. INTUITION, another copious source of knowledge, communicates to us conviction of the truth of all those *propositions* which are denominated self-evident. *Intuition* is the perception of the agreement or disagreement of two Ideas on bare juxtaposition, without the intervention of any third Idea; and the proposition which expresses our judgment of that agreement or disagreement is said to be supported by *intuitive evidence.* (*Art.* 340 and 341.)

Illus. 1. All the axioms of mathematics and arithmetic; as, that " Two straight lines cannot contain a space,"—" Things equal to the same thing are equal to one another,"—" Two and three are equal to five,"—" Two and three are not equal to six;"—all the principles adopted in physical science; as, that " A body cannot be in two places at the same time,"—" Nothing can produce nothing,"—" It is impossible for the same thing to be and not to be;"— all the maxims relative to identity; as, that " Matter is matter," and, " Spirit is spirit" (which by the bye are truisms), form intuitive propositions.

2. All certain reasoning, commonly called *demonstration*, must begin with a comparison of two Ideas expressed by an intuitive proposition; and every proposition, expressive of the agreement of any two intermediate Ideas, or of every successive step of the demonstration, must be intuitive.

3. These are the chief cases of intuitive truth. But before we leave this topic, we must observe, that some axioms which philosophers seem to be so fond of holding forth as the foundations of all science, appear so far from being such, that no reasoning is ever founded on them, and that they are of no essential use in the course of reasoning. This leads us to ask, What is an axiom? It is evidently a general proposition, including a number of particular cases, and declarative of an *intuitive truth.* This truth must be as obvious, when surveyed in any of the particular cases, as it is in the general proposition. If this therefore be true, the axiom can be of little use, for its application to the particular case affords no light which the mind did not possess before that application.

Example 1. If you say that *two* and *three* are equal to *four* and *one*, I am perfectly satisfied of the equality of these two quantities, before the application of the axiom, that " Things equal to the same thing are equal to one another," and before I add, that they are both equal to five. The axiom adds no light to my conceptions. It merely repeats, in general terms, what was expressed more simply, if not more intelligibly, in particular terms.

2. If from two lines, each a mile long, you take away respectively two half miles, I cannot hesitate a moment, that the remaining half miles are equal to one another, although I had never heard of the axiom, " If equals are taken from equals, the remainders will be equal."

3. If from a field, of an acre in extent, you take away half an acre, and throw it into an adjacent field, I have the most entire conviction that the extent of the first field will be much less than it was before the division, without having recourse to the axiom, that " The whole is greater than a part."

4. If you infer that something must have existed from eternity, because something now exists, your conviction is complete, before you reflect on, or perhaps know, the scholastic maxim, " Ex nihilo nihil sit," *Nothing can produce nothing.*

5. If you are certain that the sun is above the horizon, you conclude, with entire confidence, that he is not also below it, although you may be unacquainted with the axiom, " Bodies cannot be in different places at the same time."

6. If, having two lines, one half a mile, and the other a quarter of a mile long, you add to each a whole mile, you are perfectly satisfied that the new line, composed of the mile and the half mile, is longer than that composed of the mile and the quarter. Nor do you procure any additional conviction whatever from the application of the axiom, " If equals be added to unequals, the wholes will be unequal."

Corol. From all these examples it is apparent, that axioms are general expressions of truths, obvious in particular cases included under general expressions. In a word, an axiom is applicable when we have found, by other means than by its aid, that under it is comprehended the particular case about which we are reasoning.

473. REASONING supports an exceedingly numerous class of propositions, more numerous than all the other kinds of evidence put together. But we do not now discuss its nature, nor explain the different degrees of evidence it supplies.

Obs. Almost all the propositions of science, most of those of the arts, and of business; in a word, those propositions of all cases in which the mind receives certain or probable conviction by the exercise of its rational faculties, belong to this class: but we have already explained the nature of these propositions under the different kinds of evidence by which they are supported, when we treated of the different kinds of evidence in Chapter XI. Book II.

474. TESTIMONY was the last source of knowledge, and the last species of evidence, which we purposed to explain. *Testimony*, founded in the trust which we repose in the veracity of our fellow creatures, and in their intercourse with one another, is of very extensive use.

Illus. All the credit of history, all the intelligence of places, men, and things, we cannot in person examine; all the security society can confer on life and property in courts of justice; all the information of business and social life; depend entirely on the opinion we have, that men will tell truth in their communications to one another. (See *Art.* 315 and 440.) In many cases, the evidence of testimony affords a high degree of satisfaction; but the degrees of satisfaction decrease, till they degenerate into that equivocal state, in which probability for and against truth are so equally poised, as to leave the mind in a state of suspense. (See *Art.* 315 and 439.)

475. Two causes chiefly induce us to distrust the credibility of testimony, 1*st. suspicion* that the relater was not fully informed; or, 2*dly.* that his *interest* might influence him to utter falsehood. The presence of either, or of both these causes, is a sufficient reason for hesitation. But where neither takes place, we seem to have no reason to distrust the information of testimony. Truth is congenial to the mind of man. It is more easy to tell truth than to utter falsehood. It is not easy to utter falsehood with success. Some time must elapse before the mind can acquire those habits, and that composure, which are necessary to secure falsehood from the inconsistency and embarrassment which instantly proclaim its baseness and its insincerity. (*Art.* 442.)

Illus. Though the evidence of testimony cannot be deemed equivalent to that of demonstration, or to that of the senses, yet in most cases it would be ridiculous to indulge the least suspicion.
Example. That there are such cities as Paris, Rome, or Pekin,

that Alexander conquered a great part of the western quarter of Asia, and that Julius Cæsar was killed in the senate-house, are all facts of which we cannot entertain the smallest doubt. (*Art.* 309. *Illus.* 2. and *Example.*)

Corol. The conviction which we have of the truth of such facts is called *certainty*, and the impression made on the mind by the evidence of testimony in general, is termed *belief*. The impression which results from *divine testimony*, or the evidence of *revelation*, has obtained the name of *faith*.

IV. *Of Mathematical, Moral, Political, and Prudential Reasoning.*

476. All knowledge is either *intuitive, demonstrative,* or *probable.* Intuitive knowledge is extremely circumscribed, and *reasoning* therefore begins where intuition ends, and consists in finding out the truth of a proposition, or the agreement or disagreement of its subject and predicate, by the help of intermediate ideas. The intermediate ideas form the steps, or links, by which the mind passes from the first of the primary ideas to the last, or from the subject of any proposition to its predicate; and finally perceives their relation.

Illus. 1. Reasoning assumes different names, according to the nature of the steps, or of the links, which display the relation between the primary ideas. Thus, if the mind attain complete satisfaction in every step of its progress, or in the successive comparison of every pair of ideas, it is said to acquire certainty of the agreement or disagreement of the two primary ideas; and the reasoning is called *demonstrative.* (See *Art.* 303, 304, and 305.)

2. If the agreement of the intermediate ideas with one another, and with the extremes, is not perfectly satisfactory, that is, if the steps of the reasoning leave the mind under some degree of hesitation, the reasoning is denominated *probable;* and the reasoner attains probability only of the truth of the proposition he investigates. Where certainty terminates, probability commences; and the latter admits numerous degrees, from the highest degree, which stands next to certainty, to the lowest, which makes so little impression, as to permit the mind to remain in a state of suspense. (See *Art.* 306 and 307, with their *Illustrations.*)

477. If a proposition, supported by probable evidence, relate to *speculation*, the judgment formed concerning it is often called *opinion;* if it relate to *facts*, chiefly supported by *testimony*, the judgment is generally called *belief*. (See *Art.* 278, with all its *Illustrations* and *Examples.*)

Illus. 1. In explaining, therefore, the branch of logic now before us, all we have to do, is, to reduce to practice, *first*, the analysis we have given of demonstrative reasoning (*Art.* 303); *secondly*, that of probable reasoning (*Art.* 306.) ; and point out the sciences and arts in which they are respectively employed.

2. All reasoning is either of the one kind or the other; and in every science or art, in which conviction does not come up to certainty, we must be content with probability (*Art.* 303.)

478. Mathematics and Arithmetic are the only sciences susceptible of *demonstrative* proof, which is so satisfactory and cogent as to exclude even the supposition of falsehood. (*Art.* 304.) Other sciences, in their principles, may perhaps furnish proofs nearly, if not completely demonstrative; but in the detail they exhibit nothing better than probability. The high evidence of the science of quantity, independent of the importance of the truths which it teaches, renders them good exemplifications of the rules of logic ; and one of the best methods of becoming a good reasoner, is, to be familiar with the processes of investigation which they supply. (See the *Illustrations* and *Examples* to *Art.* 304.)

Illus. To reduce to practice *demonstrative* reasoning, we shall now analyze some propositions of the Elements of Euclid. Reasoning is a successive comparison of every pair of ideas, from the *first* to the last, or from the *idea* which forms the *subject* of the proposition, to the *one* which forms the *predicate;* and in demonstration every comparison is intuitively certain. When these ideas are found to agree, the demonstration is finished, and the reasoning is concluded. (*Art.* 298.)

Example 1. Suppose we begin with the first proposition of the first book of the Elements, which proposes " To describe an equilateral triangle on a given straight line." Let us pass over the operations by which the triangle in the figure is described, because we mean to analyze only the reasoning of the proposition.

Argument. After the figure has been constructed on the given line, the proposition to be proved is, that " The triangle so constructed is equilateral, or has all its sides equal." The *subject* of the proposition, or the *first idea* of it, is, that of the *triangle described;* the *predicate* of the proposition, or the second idea of it, is, that of *the equality of the sides of the triangle.* Now, it is not intuitively certain that the three sides are all equal to one another; therefore some intermediate ideas must be placed between the *subject* and the *predicate* of the proposition, to show their agreement. The process consists of two steps; that is to say, *one intermediate idea* is necessary to prove the proposition. The first step is the comparison of the base A B* with one of the sides A C ; and of their equality we have intuitive certainty, because, by the description of the figure, they are radii of the same circle. The second step is the comparison of the same side A B, with the other side B C ; and of their equality, also, we have intuitive certainty, as they are both semi-diameters of another circle of the same radius with the former. This step finish-

---

* See the Figure in Simson's Euclid.

19

es the demonstration. The base is found to agree with both the sides; and the triangle must be equilateral, because all the sides are equal; the *subject* and *predicate* of the *proposition* are found *exactly to agree.*

Example 2. In the forty-seventh proposition of the first book of the Elements, the truth to be established is, "That in a right-angled triangle, the square of the side opposite to the right angle is equal in quantity to the sum of the squares of the other two sides." The square opposite to the right angle is the *subject*, the *sum* of the two other squares is the *predicate*, and the idea of the extent of the first square is to be compared with the idea of the sum of the other two squares.

Argument I. The first step is to prove, that G A C* is one straight line, and H A B another, in order to lay a foundation for demonstrating that the triangle F B C is equal to half the square F A, and the triangle A B D equal to half the parallelogram B L.

II. The next step is to prove the triangle A B D equal to the triangle F B C.

III. The third step is to prove the triangle A B D equal to half the parallelogram B L, and the triangle F B C equal to half the square F A; and hence to infer the equality of the square F A to the parallelogram B L.

IV. Three similar steps are necessary to find the square A K equal to the parallelogram C L; and hence to infer the equality of the whole square B E to the two squares F A and A K, which establishes the agreement of the *subject* and *predicate* of the proposition; or *that the square of the side opposite to the right angle, is equal to the squares of the two other sides.*

Corol. To complete this process, then, there are necessary these six capital steps, and each of these includes one or more subordinate steps, so that the sum of the subordinate steps amounts to no fewer than twelve; and if these are added to the six capital ones, it appears, that, to prove this proposition, there are requisite *eighteen intermediate ideas.* The mind has a clear and distinct perception of the agreement of every pair of ideas; and the effect is proportional to the cause, for the mind obtains the most complete certainty of the truth of the proposition.

479. All reasoning has this in common with demonstration, that the agreement or disagreement of the primary ideas must be proved by intermediate ideas; the difference is, that the agreement of the intermediate ideas with one another, and with their primary ideas, amounts not to certainty ; it is no more than probable.

Corol. From this view it will appear, that the far greater part of knowledge, and even the most interesting and important part, that which concerns morality, politics, the useful arts, and business, is not supported by better evidence than probability. (See *Art.* 211.) The probability, however, in many cases is highly convincing,

---

* See the Figure.

approaches very near to certainty, and affords good grund for acting upon it with perfect confidence and satisfaction. (See *Corol. Art.* 312.)

480. That all men should revere their Maker, and perform every duty which they conceive will be acceptable to him ; that they should do good to their fellow-creatures, and not wantonly hurt or injure them ; that they should live in temperance and moderation, in order to insure the highest happiness their constitutions can enjoy ; are all conclusions, the justness of which no one can doubt, any more, perhaps, than he can doubt that two and three make five ; or that the three angles of a triangle are equal to two right angles.

Argument. The agreement of the idea which we have of man, with those ideas which we have of his Creator, and of his fellow-creatures, infers these duties with an evidence which nearly approaches demonstration. But when we descend to investigate the nature of particular acts of regard to God, or of intercourse with our fellow-creatures, our scale applies inaccurately ; the agreement or disagreement of ideas is not perfectly clear ; and we are not certain (at least we do not agree) where regard to the Almighty terminates, and disregard begins ; where justice or charity ceases, and injustice or severity commences.

Corol. Till this can be done, we have no reason to expect that the precepts of morality shall be supported by the evidence of demonstration. (See *Art.* 353. *Corol.* 1 and 2.)

481. The same species of reasoning applies to the evidence of other sciences, of arts, and of business. In them all, the mind discovers only *moral certainty*, that is, different degrees of *probable evidence* (*Art.* 354.), according as the agreement of ideas is more or less clear and satisfactory.

Example 1. Suppose some reasoning were employed to recommend the love of God, or to prove this proposition—" MAN ought to love God." The agreement of ideas in moral reasoning, we have formerly observed, relates to *propriety, fitness, reasonableness.* (*Art.* 480.) The meaning, then, of the proposition will be, whether the idea we have of such an imperfect, dependent creature as man, agrees with the idea of his exerting love toward the great, wise, and good Being who made the universe, or whether it be fit, proper, and right, that man should love God. (See *Art.* 352. *Illus.* 1, 2, 3.)

Argument 1. To prove this proposition, a Theologian might employ several intermediate ideas ; he might first show that the Almighty is the most amiable Being in the universe, and that HE possesses all those attributes of goodness, wisdom, and power, most calculated to excite attachment. The amiableness of God would thus involve a large collection of particulars, of subordinate ideas, which together would constitute what, in the science of morals, is denominated an *argument.*

II. The Theologian might prove, secondly, that the love of God is the surest means of happiness to ourselves. It will communicate self-approbation, confidence in the wisdom of Providence, and the administration of human affairs; and will extirpate those anxieties and fears which haunt and distract weak and vicious men. The illustration of these topics, also, would include a great number of subordinate ideas, and would constitute another argument for the love of God.

III. The Theologian might further insist that love to God is reasonable and proper, in return for the numerous instances of kindness, mercy, and love, which the Deity daily exerts towards us. The illustration of these instances, likewise, would comprehend many subordinate ideas, and would furnish a third argument in support of the proposition. (See *Art.* 294. *Obs.* and *Example.*)

Example 2. Suppose, again, it were to be inferred from future punishment that " Men must be free agents," or that " The idea of future punishment agrees with that of self-determination, or the freedom of action." The following train of intermediate ideas will show that agreement.

Argument I. Future punishment must be inflicted by the Almighty; the Almighty can inflict no punishment that is not just; the punished of course must be guilty : they could, then, have done otherwise, and consequently must be free agents.

II. This train of ideas, more shortly expressed, will stand thus: Future punishment—God the punisher—punishment just—punished guilty—could have done otherwise—self-determination.

Corol. In this piece of reasoning there are four intermediate ideas, and five comparisons are made to discover the agreement with the extremes, and with one another. The agreement between the adjacent ideas in every step, appears with a high degree of conviction; and were each of the ideas illustrated at some length, according to the common mode of reasoning on moral topics, the whole would form an elegant deduction, and would communicate a very lively impression.

Example 3. Let us suppose, further, that the following political proposition were proposed to be proved; and let us consider the nature of the reasoning requisite to establish it. " Industry is the capital source of national prosperity." The ideas, or terms, as the Logicians express themselves, to be compared, are those of industry and national prosperity.

Argument I. We must here remark, that agreement of ideas in politics refers, not to reasonableness and fitness, as in morals, but to public utility, or national happiness. The meaning, then, of the proposition is this, that industry makes a nation prosperous, by extending its opulence, and exalting its reputation, in support of which we thus argue :—

1. Industry increases the population of a country, by providing subsistence for additional inhabitants.

2. An increase of inhabitants increases commerce and manufactures.

3. Commerce and manufactures procure riches from foreign nations of less industry.

4 These riches prompt a spirit of enterprise still further to ex-

tend commerce and manufactures. Hence new nerves to domestic industry.

5. The comforts, and many of the luxuries, of life are provided for all the members of the community.

6. Ample security is found for the continuance of these advantages by the national reputation which they procure, and the large resources of money and of men that they supply to maintain that reputation.

II. But national prosperity consists in these things which we have enumerated;—a wealthy, sober, industrious, and numerous people, respectable at home, and formidable abroad. Each of the steps might have been illustrated at considerable length, and might have formed a very pleasant and satisfactory discussion.

III. They may also be condensed into more narrow bounds, and may form the following series ready for the nearest comparison:— National industry—increase of people—improvements in commerce and manufactures—national riches—national enterprise—people at home, numerous and happy, respectable and formidable abroad— national prosperity.

Corol. This series presents five intermediate ideas; and six comparisons are requisite to afford conviction of the agreement of the first idea with the last, or of the subject of the proposition with its predicate.

482. In the Examples which we have advanced from Morals and Politics, the Evidence, you will observe, though highly satisfactory, is still no more than probable, and does not appear with that commanding tone which compels assent. Skeptical men may find reason to suspend their assent, and disputatious men may raise difficulties, which we must admit are not destitute of foundation. (*Art.* 439, and 440.)

Illus. Accordingly, against every step of the preceding *political series*, some doubt may be started. It may be argued, I. that industry is not always attended with an increase of people; it may even sometimes produce the contrary effect; it may induce the people to emigrate to other countries, where their labor will be better rewarded than at home. II. It may be urged, also, that the most warlike and powerful nations are often the poorest and the most hardy, while arts and industry only supply riches to tempt such adventurers to seize both the country and its wealth. III. It may, besides, be contended, that arts and industry enervate mankind, multiply their wants and vices, and render a people miserable in the midst of every provision for happiness; that they repress all the great and splendid, and, consequently, many of the most pleasant exertions of the mind.

Corol. It is the possibility of constructions of this sort, in all probable investigations, which diminishes their evidence, and renders the conviction which they produce inferior to demonstration.

483. But how susceptible soever of controversy these specimens of Reasoning may be, they are much more satis-

19 *

factory than are many of the conjectural estimations on which mankind every day act in some of the most important concerns of life.

Illus. Thus, many of the engagements which we form, and every new line of life on which we enter, involve numerous considerations to determine our conduct,—considerations which are scarcely supported by better evidence than speculation. The wisdom of the prudent man is seldom more meritorious than the sagacity which leads him to conjecture with most probability, or which teaches him to proceed with recollection and attention to surrounding objects, so as to avail himself of passing events.

484. In our Reasonings of Anticipation, we proceed chiefly by Analogy. We suppose that the future will resemble the past. (*Art.* 315. *Illus.* 1, 2.) In the negotiations of business, and in forecasting the probable consequences of any plan of conduct, we must conclude, that similar causes will produce similar effects; that men will act in time to come as they have done in time past; and that the course of nature will proceed by the established rules which have directed it since the world began.

Illus. We argue from the characters, the opinions, the interests, the passions, the weaknesses, and the caprices of men; and we endeavor to form systems of conduct for them, derived from the situations which they occupy. (*Art.* 349.) The trains of reasoning which we adopt in such cases, are in a great measure hypothetical; and the probability of the evidence frequently is of the lowest kind. Conjectures often so counterbalance one another, as to leave the mind in a state of total suspense. (*Art.* 317. *Illus.*, *Example*, and *Corol.*)

V. *Different Species of Reasoning.*

485. In the different methods, in common use, of distributing or arranging Ideas in different processes of reasoning, the Reasoning is said to be either direct or indirect. (*Art.* 305. *Illus.* 1, 2, and *Example.*) In *direct* Reasoning, we prove a proposition in the manner which we have now explained, by finding intermediate Ideas that show the agreement of the terms of which it consists. In *indirect* Reasoning, we do not trace the agreement of the terms of a proposition; it takes place only when the predicate of a proposition admits an *alternative*, and when either the predicate or the alternative must be true, or must agree with the subject of the proposition, because they exhaust every case that can exist. We prove that the alternative cannot be true; and therefore the predicate must be true.

Example 1. Euclid lays down this proposition, "That a straight line, drawn at right angles from the extremity of a diameter, falls without the circle."

Argument. No intermediate idea, it seems, occurred, by which he could deduce the proof directly from the nature of the circle, or of the perpendicular, or the extremity of the diameter. He proceeds, therefore, by *indirect* demonstration, and introduces an *alternative*. The perpendicular must fall either *without* the circle, or *within* it. No third supposition can be made, relative to the manner of its falling; for it cannot fall *upon* the circumference of the circle, except in *one* point. He proves that the *alternative* cannot be true, or that the perpendicular cannot fall *within* the circle.— The *predicate*, then, must be true, that the perpendicular falls *without* the circle.

Example 2. Again, " The moon is either an opaque or a transparent body."

Argument. It is not transparent, because, if it were, it would transmit the rays of the sun when it comes between the sun and the earth; and no eclipse of the sun could happen from the intervention of it between the sun and the earth. But this conclusion is contrary to truth, for such eclipse does happen. The *alternative*, therefore, that the moon is a transparent body, must be false, and consequently the *predicate* must be true, that *the moon is an opaque body.* The refutation of the alternative is always pursued, till it terminates in some contradiction, falsehood, or absurdity; and on this account indirect Reasoning is, by the Logicians, sometimes called " Reductio ad absurdum." (*Art.* 305. *Illus.* 1.)

486. It has often been disputed, whether indirect Reasoning be less elegant and less satisfactory than direct Reasoning; but we observe that both convey truth with perfect evidence; and when a reasoner has got possession of an indirect proof, he will not trouble himself much in searching for a direct one. It is, however, generally supposed, that Mathematicians never employ the former but in cases of necessity, and when they cannot have recourse to the latter.

Obs. 1. The great number of beautiful specimens of demonstration, of which their science is susceptible, may render them nice or delicate even about the elegance and manner of their reasonings; but on other subjects, and in other sciences, when the mind is glad to reach truth on any terms, it will be satisfied with good indirect proof. It may, perhaps, be doubted, whether the charge of inelegance is not the offspring of squeamishness and caprice, rather than of just taste.

2. An indirect train of ideas is often long, but may be conjoined with as much clearness and propriety as a direct train. The step from the *falsehood* of the *alternative* to the *truth* of the *predicate*, is perfectly satisfactory, if not elegant; and it may be added, that indirect reasoning imparts variety to the nature of the proof.

487. Reasoning, further, is said to proceed either *a priori*, or *a posteriori;* a distinction which relates entirely to *cause* and *effect*.

I. In reasoning *a priori*, we begin with the cause, and infer from it the reality, or the species of the effect.

II. In reasoning *a posteriori*, we reverse this progress; we begin with the effect, and reason backward from it to the establishment of the existence and the qualities of the cause.

VI. *Examples of Reasoning a Priori.*

488. Argument *a priori* proves or disproves the fact from the law, or the effect from the cause. Every argument *a priori* may be reduced to a perfect syllogism, consisting of three propositions; of which

One announces the law either positively or negatively.

Another compares the law with the fact to be proved; and

The third affirms or denies the fact, from its conformity with, or its opposition to, the law.

Example 1. If you maintain that the soul of man is a thinking principle, and therefore that it is immaterial, because matter cannot think; and hence again infer, that it is immortal, because what is immaterial cannot die or be destroyed, you reason *a priori;* you *deduce the effect from its cause,* and prove the soul to be immortal from the nature of its constitution. (*Art.* 99. *Corol.* 1, 2, 3.)

2. If, again, you argue, that the people who live fifteen degrees farther east than we, will have their day beginning and ending an hour sooner than ours; that navigators who have sailed fifteen degrees eastward will, of course, have lost an hour of our day, and will have gained an hour from the day of the people of that longitude; that these navigators will experience a similar loss and gain, in point of time, for every fifteen degrees eastward on the face of the globe; and that, as they must pass through four-and-twenty times fifteen degrees in sailing round the globe, so, on returning home, they will calculate time a day sooner than their countrymen, because they have lost twenty-four hours of the time of their countrymen, in their voyage. In this process, you reason *a priori*, because you deduce a curious fact, verified by experience from the figure of the earth, round which the navigation is performed.

VII. *Example of Reasoning a Posteriori.*

489. In reasoning *a posteriori*, we argue from the Effect to the Cause, and conclude from the former the nature or existence of the latter. In other words, arguments *a posteriori* prove, or disprove, the rule from the enumeration of particulars. Every argument *a posteriori* may be reduced to a syllogism, consisting of two propositions:

One is Induction, or enumeration of facts;

The other affirms or denies the law from the concurrence,

or want of concurrence, in the particulars brought to establish it.

Example 1. From the wisdom, power, and goodness, discernible in all the works of nature, you infer, that there must be some wise, benevolent, and omnipotent cause, from which these effects proceed. You cannot doubt of the effects, because you experience them every moment of your existence; you can as little doubt that these effects must proceed from some cause, and that the cause must possess the qualities conspicuous in the effects.

2. Again, you observe, that the shadow of the earth projected on the face of the moon in a lunar eclipse, is of a circular form; and from this effect you justly infer, that the figure of the earth is round, because this figure only could produce such a shadow.

490. In this volume there are numerous Specimens of both these methods of Reasoning; but the pupil will find that Reasonings *a priori* are much circumscribed, because causes are seldom so well known as their effects.

491. From effects, chiefly, we ascend to the knowledge of causes; and on this account Reasoning *a posteriori* is much more frequent. It is much employed in inquiries into nature; it is the ground-work of the famous method of induction for investigating natural knowledge, recommended in the " Novum Organum " of Lord Bacon; and it is of frequent use in politics and morals.

Illus. 1. The best way to obtain an acquaintance, both with the Author of nature and with the secondary causes which produce the effects we daily behold, is to survey with patience the effects themselves, because we have no means of information concerning the causes, except in this channel.

2. In like manner, to understand the duties a man owes to his country, or to his neighbor, we must scrutinize his constitution, what forms the happiness of such a being, both as a member of society, and a moral agent; what are his mental faculties, and his bodily powers; his attachments, and antipathies; his gratifications, and his wants. In all these inquiries we begin from the effect, and ascend to the cause, or we reason *a posteriori*.

VIII. *Analytic and Synthetic Reasoning.*

492. The last distinction of Reasoning divides it into ANALYTIC and SYNTHETIC, and refers chiefly to mathematical Reasonings.

I. ANALYSIS forms an elegant method of investigating the legitimacy of demonstrations.

II. SYNTHESIS puts together the different steps after investigation, so as to make out a proof.

III. ANALYSIS begins with the *predicate* of a proposition, and ascends from it to the subject. (*Art.* 493, and *Example.*)

IV. SYNTHESIS takes the opposite course, begins with the *subject*, and descends from it to the *predicate*, or it is the same thing with *direct reasoning*. (*Art.* 478. *Example* 1 and 2.)

Illus. 1. The ancients carried on analysis by means of mathematical figures; algebra is the great instrument of modern analysis. Many examples of the ancient analysis are to be found in Apollonius Pergæus, De Sectione Rationis. Every treatise of algebra, but particularly that of Sir Isaac Newton, will furnish specimens of the modern analysis by letters or symbols.

2. All the Demonstrations of the Elements of Euclid exhibit examples of *synthesis*, and we need not produce any of them.

IX. *Example of Analytic Reasoning.*

493. The purpose of the Analysis is to try the legitimacy of an investigation, or to discover whether the intermediate ideas, by which a mathematician suspects a demonstration may be accomplished, are sufficient for that purpose. He begins with supposing, that the ideas are good media for demonstrating the proposition in question, and constructs his figure on that hypothesis. He supposes, further, the thing done that the problem requires, or the truth established which a theorem proposes to prove. He sets out from the proposition, and reasons backward to the beginning of it; and if he encounter no contradiction, or terminate in no absurdity, he concludes the media to be pertinent and legitimate; if he terminate in an absurdity or contradiction, he infers, that the media are improper, and that the synthetical demonstration will be inconclusive.

Example. Were it required to analyze the first proposition of the first book of the Elements of Euclid, which proposes *to describe an equilateral triangle on a given straight line*, we would describe a triangle on the given line, and would suppose it equilateral. We would reason thus :—

I. If the triangle be *equilateral*, then the making one end of the base a centre, and describing a circle with the length of that base as a radius, the circle will pass through the other extremity of the base, and the extremity of one of the sides; so that the base and one of the sides must become radii of the same circle.

II. If another circle be described from the other end of the base, with the same base taken as a radius, this circle will pass through the other extremities of the base and of the other side. The two circles, therefore, are equal, because their radii are so. This step finishes the analysis, and proves the media to be legitimate, because the reasoning backward has reached its principle, the equality of the two circles, from which the synthesis begins, or from which the truth of the proposition, that the triangle is equilateral, is demonstrated.

494. Logicians mention some other distinctions of Rea-

soning, which we shall briefly define, because they sometimes occur in conversation, but more frequently in books.

495. When we argue from principles, or opinions, admitted by the person with whom we reason, whether they be true or not in themselves, we are said to employ an *argumentum ad hominem.*

496. When we urge in our defence some eminent authority, which an antagonist is ashamed to oppose, we are said to employ an *argumentum ad verecundiam.*

497. When we perplex or puzzle an adversary, we offer what is called *argumentum ad ignorantiam.*

CHAPTER III.

OF SOPHISTRY.

498. From Truth nothing can really.follow but what is *true:* whensoever, therefore, we find a *false conclusion* drawn from premises which seem to be true, there must be some fault in the deduction or inference; or else one of the premises is not true in the sense in which it is used in that argument.

When an *argument* carries the face of *truth* with it, and yet leads us into *mistake,* it is a sophism; and there is no need of a particular description of these fallacious arguments that we may, with more ease and readiness, detect and solve them.

499. Logicians have divided sophistry also into different kinds; the most remarkable of which it will be proper to specify, because they are very common.

500. The first is called Ignoratio Elenchi, and consists in *mistaking* or *misrepresenting* the state of the question under discussion. This species occurs in most controversies, but particularly in political ones, which now chiefly engage men of learning and ability. Religious and philosophical controversies have, fortunately for the peace of society, almost totally disappeared.

Illus. The moment a writer engages in controversy, in spite of all the attention he can maintain, partialities lay hold of his mind; his passions warp and mislead his understanding. (See *Art.* 427, and all its *Illustrations.*) He reads the performances of his antagonist under the influence of dispositions which induce him to mistake their

meaning. (*Art.* 449, and all its *Illustrations.*) He discovers malevolent or insidious designs, which are perceptible by nobody but himself; and he imputes principles and views to his opponent, which
the latter never entertained nor disavowed. (*Art.* 435, and its *Illustrations.*) He introduces principles and views of his own, and he reasons and speculates about them as if they were admitted by the
opposite party. (See *Art.* 437, and all its *Illustrations.*)

501. Another species of Sophistry is called PETITIO PRIN-
CIPII (*a supposition of what is not granted*), and consists in
assuming as true the proposition under debate.

Illus. Few men are so void of discernment, or so destitute of delicacy and regard to truth, as confidently to maintain what they have
not attempted to prove; and hence this species of sophistry is not
frequent in business. In philosophical and political investigations,
in which, on account of the intricacy or uncertainty of the subjects,
disputants take more liberty of obtruding their opinions upon their
antagonists, or presume more readily that assertion may be admitted
for a proof, the sophistry *petitio principii,* or " begging the question," is
exceedingly frequent.

502. The Peripatetics, by the following manifest *petitio
principii,* pretend to prove, that the centre of the earth is
the centre of the universe.

Sophism. " All bodies must move towards the centre of the universe; but we find from experience, that all bodies move towards the
centre of the earth; therefore the centre of the earth is the centre of
the universe."
Analysis. This argument proves nothing; for, although we allow
that all bodies with which we are acquainted, move towards the
centre of the earth, it does not thence follow that all bodies in the
universe move towards the centre of the earth. The truth is, that
a body near the surface of the earth moves towards it only by the
difference of attraction exerted by the earth above the other great
bodies in nature; that all the bodies in the solar system are attracted towards a point near the surface of the sun; and that all the
bodies of our solar system, and perhaps of all the systems of the
universe, are attracted towards some other point, which is the centre of the whole, but not surely the centre of the earth.

503. *Sophistry* frequently appears in arguing from one
particular to another, or inferring general conclusions from
particular cases. The Logicians call this species a " dicto
secundum quid, ad dictum simpliciter," as, That which is
bought in the shambles is eaten for dinner; raw meat is
bought in the shambles ; therefore raw meat is eaten for dinner. The argument of the Epicureans of old, to prove the
gods of human shape, will pertinently illustrate this sort of
sophistry.

Example 1. They maintained that the human form was the most
beautiful of all those with which men were acquainted, or of which

they had any conception, but the most beautiful form is always supposed to belong to the gods, the best of beings in the universe : it was, therefore, reasonable to conclude, that they were endued with the human form.

Analysis. ˙No connection subsists between the *nature of man* and that of the gods, to induce us to believe the gods must possess the shape of men; and we cannot infer, because the figure of man is the most beautiful with which we are acquainted, that, therefore, the form of the gods, admitting them to have some form, cannot be more beautiful than the human. The argument that the form of a pine-apple, being the most beautiful, perhaps, of vegetable forms, is also the form of the gods, would be equally conclusive, being a rare inference from one particular to another, between which there is no relation; or, in other words, between particulars which have nothing in common, whence such an inference can possibly be deduced.

Example 2. Should we, again, conclude, from the foolish or iniquitous behavior of some individuals, of a numerous order of men, that all the order are fools or rogues.

3. Or, from the unwholesomeness or bad taste of some sort of animal and vegetable food, that all sorts are unwholesome or unpleasant.

4. Or, because many bad kings and magistrates have been in the world, that all kings and magistrates are bad men; in each of these cases you would argue from premises insufficient to support your inference, because you extend the latter much farther than the former, and suppose that there are no exceptions where there may be thousands of exceptions.

504. This illegitimate and illiberal logic frequently appears in the intercourse of society, when all the connections, the family, the friends, and the order of an impudent or a criminal person are branded with the improprieties and the errors of which he only has been guilty; while they entertain, perhaps, a more lively disapprobation of his conduct than those who load them with reproach.

Illus. 1. Should you boldly declare that all the people of England in the time of Charles I. were murderers because a *junto* of bloody-minded men put him to death; that all the people of France were regicides because a few voted for the death of Louis XVI.; that all the people of the United States of America were unprincipled tyrants and assassins, because General Jackson put ARBUTHNOT and AMBRISTER, *British subjects,* to death on false accusations and principles of policy, which the laws of nations do not recognize;—you would display the spirit we have now in view.

2. It is, indeed, difficult to decide whether such a spirit is more characteristic of cruelty or want of candor. It is cruel, for it displays a strong disposition to criminate the innocent, and to pour into delicate and honorable minds that pungent vexation which results from the loss of reputation, under a consciousness of having done nothing to deserve such a misfortune. It is void of candor,

20

because no intercourse has subsisted between the culprit and the party accused, which can authorize any inference of blame from the one to the other; and it is not a little uncandid to deduce an inference without premises, or contrary to those laid down.

505. Numerous errors and much false reasoning result from forming hypotheses, to account for the phenomena of nature, or the actions of men, without endeavoring to investigate the true causes of these phenomena, and the motives of those actions from the effects which they produce. This species of sophistry the Logicians call *Causam assignare quæ causa non est, To assign that as a cause which is not the cause:* or, as Dr. Watts has it, *non causa pro causa* —or the *assignation of a false cause.* Philosophers and speculative politicians have been most prone to indulge in this kind of ratiocination, and many curious examples of it are to be found in physical books, and in real life. (See CHAP. III. BOOK I.)

Example 1. All the heavenly bodies, says Aristotle, in his Physics, must move in circles, *because a circle is the most perfect of all figures,* and because *bodies moving in such figures meet with least resistance.* The great philosopher does not tell us how he knew that the circle is the most perfect of all figures, and that bodies moving in circles meet with least resistance. Both these reasons are mere suppositions, contrary to truth, as well as the opinion that the heavenly bodies move in circles, which, by a little observation, he might have found to be erroneous.

2. To support the hypothesis he had adopted, concerning the eternity and perfection of the world, the same philosopher offers the following singular ratiocination. The world is a *perfect* production, because it is composed of *bodies*; and *bodies are perfect magnitudes*, because they consist of *three dimensions*, length, breadth, and thickness, and cannot admit of more. *Lines are not perfect magnitudes*, because they have length only, which may easily be made to move into a surface. *Surfaces are not perfect magnitudes*, because they have only length and breadth, which may easily be made to move into a solid." Now all this reasoning is mere conjecture, relating to the qualities only of magnitudes, and not in the least to their merits.

3. The *occult qualities* of the same author, and his followers, are not more satisfactory sources of natural knowledge. The pulse beats—the loadstone points to the pole—tartar is emetic—poppy produces sleep; because there is a beating *quality* in the pulse, an attractive *quality* in the loadstone, an emetic *quality* in tartar, and a soporific *quality* in poppy. Such philosophizing resembles the play of children, or the ridicule of empirics, rather than the serious investigation of grave inquirers after truth; and it furnishes an humiliating picture of the progress of natural philosophy among the ancients (See *Art.* 3, and *Corol.*)

506. The *moderns,* as well as the *ancients,* fall often into this fallacy, when they positively assign the reasons of natural appearances, without sufficient experiments to prove them.

Illus. 1. *Astrologers* are overrun with this species of fallacy, and they cheat the people grossly by pretending to *tell fortunes,* and to deduce the cause of the various occurrences in the lives of men from the *various positions of the stars and planets,* which they call *aspects.* When *comets* and *eclipses* of the *sun* and *moon* are construed to signify the fate of princes, the revolution of states, famine, wars, and calamities of all kinds, it is a fallacy that belongs to this rank of *sophisms.*

2. There is scarce any thing more common in human life than this sort of deceitful argument. If any two accidental events happen to occur, one is presently made the cause of the other.

Example. If Titius *wronged his neighbor of a guinea, and in six months after, he fell down and broke his leg,* weak men will impute it to the divine vengeance on *Titius* for his former injustice. This sophism was found also in the early days of the world ; for *when holy* Job *was surrounded with uncommon miseries,* his own friends inferred, that *he was a most heinous criminal,* and charged him *with aggravated guilt, as the cause of his calamities;* though God himself, by a voice from heaven, solved this uncharitable sophism, and cleared his servant *Job* of that charge.

Obs. How frequent is it among men to impute crimes to persons not actually chargeable with them ! We too often charge that upon the wicked contrivance and premeditated malice of a neighbor, which arose merely from ignorance, or from an unguarded temper. And on the other hand, when we have a mind to excuse ourselves, we practise the same sophism, and charge that upon our inadvertence or our ignorance, which, perhaps, was designed wickedness. What is really done by a necessity of circumstances, we sometimes impute to choice. And again, we charge that upon necessity which was really desired and chosen.

507. The next species of *sophism* is called *fallacia-accidentis,* or a sophism wherein we pronounce concerning the *nature and essential properties* of any subject according to something which is merely *accidental* to it. This is akin to the former, and is also very frequent in human life.

Example 1. So, if *opium* or the *Peruvian bark* has been used imprudently or unsuccessfully, whereby the patient has received injury, some weaker people absolutely pronounce against the use of the *bark* or the *opium* upon all occasions whatsoever, and are ready to call them *poison.*

2. So wine has been the accidental occasion of *drunkenness* and *quarrels; learning* and *printing* may have been the accidental cause of *sedition* in a state ; the *reading of the Bible,* by accident, has been abused to promote *heresies,* or *destructive errors;* and for these reasons they have all been pronounced *evil things. Muhomet* forbade

his followers the use of *wine;* the *Turks* discourage learning in their dominions; and at one time the *Scripture* was forbidden to be read by the *Laity.* But how very unreasonable are these inferences, and these prohibitions which are built upon them !

508. The next species of *sophistry* is REASONING IN A CIRCLE ; or the assuming of one proposition to prove another, and then resting the proof of the first on the evidence of the second. The Protestant theologians accuse the writers of the church of Rome of committing such blunders. " The Papal theologians " (say both the *Protestant logicians, Watts* and *Barron*) " first prove the divine authority of their church from the Holy Scriptures, and then they employ the infalli- bility of the Pope to confirm their interpretation of the Scriptures. They establish the infallibility of the Pope by the testimony of the senses, and they employ the same in- fallibility to destroy the testimony of the senses, when their antagonists remonstrate against the credibility of the doc- trine of transubstantiation."

509. The sophisms of *composition* and *division* come next to be mentioned.

Illus. 1. The *sophism* of composition is when we infer any thing concerning ideas in a *compounded sense,* which is only true in a *di- vided sense.*

Example 1. And when it is said in the gospel that *Christ made the blind to see,* and the *deaf to hear,* and the *lame to walk,* we ought not to infer hence that *Christ performed contradictions;* but those who *were blind before,* were made to see, and those who *were deaf before,* were made to hear, &c. So, when the Scripture assures us, *the worst of sinners may be saved,* it signifies only, that *they who have been the worst of sinners* may repent and be saved, not that they shall be saved in their sins. Or, if any one should argue thus, *Two and three are even and odd: five are two and three,* therefore *five are even and odd.* Here, that is very falsely inferred concerning *two or three in union,* which is only true of them *divided.*

Illus. 2. The *sophism* of *division* is when we infer the same thing concerning ideas in a *divided sense,* which is only true in a *com- pounded sense;* as if we should pretend to prove that *every soldier in the Grecian army put a hundred thousand Persians to flight,* because the *Grecian soldiers did so.* Or, if a man should argue thus, *Five is one number; two and three are five; therefore two and three are one number.*

Obs. This sort of sophism is committed when the word *all* is taken in a *collective* and a *distributive* sense, without a due distinction; as if any one should reason thus: *All the musical instruments of the* Jewish *temple made a noble concert;* the *harp was a musical instru- ment of the* Jewish *temple;* therefore *the harp made a noble concert.* Here the word *all,* in the major, is collective, whereas such a con- clusion requires that the word *all* should be distributive.

It is the same fallacy when the universal word *all* or *no* refers to *species* in one proposition, and to *individuals* in another ; as, *All animals were in* Noah's *ark ;* therefore *no animals perished in the flood ;* whereas in the premise *all animals* signifies *every kind of animals,* which does not exclude or deny the drowning of a thousand *individuals.*

510. The last sort of *sophisms* arises from our *abuse of the ambiguity of words,* which is the largest and most extensive kind of fallacy ; and indeed several of the former *fallacies* might be reduced to this head.

When the words or phrases are *plainly equivocal,* they are called *sophisms* of *equivocation;* as if we should argue thus : *He that sends forth a book into the light, desires it to be read: he that throws a book into the fire, sends it into the light;* therefore *he that throws a book into the fire desires it to be read.*

This sophism, as well as the foregoing, and all of the like nature, are solved by showing the different senses of the words, terms, or phrases. Here *light* in the major proposition signifies the *public view of the world;* in the minor it signifies the *brightness of flame and fire ;* and therefore the syllogism has four terms, or rather it has no *middle term,* and proves nothing.

But where such *gross equivocations* and *ambiguities* appear in arguments, there is little danger of imposing upon ourselves or others. The greatest danger, and which we are perpetually exposed to in reasoning, is where the two senses or significations of one term are near akin, and not plainly distinguished, and yet they are really sufficiently different in their sense to lead us into great mistakes if we are not watchful.

CHAPTER IV.

OF REASONING AND SYLLOGISM.

511. If the mere *conception* and *comparison* of two ideas would always show us whether they agree or disagree, then all rational propositions would be *matters* of *intelligence,* or *first principles,* and there would be no use of *reasoning,* or drawing any consequences. It is the narrowness of the human mind which introduces the necessity of *reasoning.*

20 *

When we are unable to judge of the truth or falsehood of a proposition in an *immediate* manner, by the mere contemplation of its subject and predicate, we are then constrained to use a *medium*, and to compare each of·them with some *third idea*, that, by seeing how far they agree or disagree with it, we may be able to judge how far they agree or disagree among themselves.

Example 1. If there are two lines, *A* and *B*, and I know not whether they are *equal* or not, I take a third line *C*, or an *inch*, and apply it to each of them ; if it agree with them both, then I infer that *A and B are equal ;* but if it agree with the one and not with the other, then I conclude that *A* and *B are unequal :* if it agree with neither of them, there can be no comparison.

2. So, if the question be, *whether God must be worshipped,* we seek a *third idea*, suppose the idea of a Creator, and say,

> *Our Creator must be worshipped ;*
> *God is our Creator ;*
> *Therefore, God must be worshipped.*

Illus. 1. The comparison of this *third idea* with the two distinct parts of the question, usually requires two propositions, which are called the *premises ;* the third proposition which is drawn from them is the *conclusion,* wherein the *question* itself is answered, and the subject and predicate joined either in the *negative* or the *affirmative.*

2. The *foundation of all affirmative conclusions* is laid in this general truth, That so far as two proposed ideas agree to any third idea, they agree also among themselves. The character of *Creator* agrees to *God,* and *worship* agrees to a *Creator ;* therefore *worship* agrees to *God.*

3. The *foundation of all negative conclusions* is this, That where one of the two proposed ideas agrees with the third idea, and the other disagrees with it, they must needs disagree so far also with one another ; as, if no *sinners are happy,* and if *angels are happy,* then *angels are not sinners.*

Corol. Thus it appears what is the strict and just notion of a *syllogism :* it is a sentence or argument, or a step of an argument, made up of three propositions, so disposed, as that the last is necessarily inferred from those which go before, as in the instances which have been just mentioned.

I. *Of the Constitution of Syllogisms.*

512. In the *constitution of a syllogism* two things may be considered, *viz.* the *matter* and the *form* of it.

I. The *matter* of which a syllogism is made up, is, *three propositions ;* and these three propositions are made up of *three ideas* or *terms* variously joined.

II. The *three terms* are called the *remote matter* of a syllogism ; and the *three propositions* the *proxime* or *immediate matter* of it.

513. The three terms are named the *major*, the *minor*, and the *middle*.

I. The predicate of the conclusion is called the *major term*, because it is generally of a larger extension than the *minor term*, or the *subject*. The *major* and *minor terms* are called the *extremes*.

II. The *middle term* is the *third* idea, invented and disposed in two propositions, in such a manner as to show the connection between the *major* and *minor term* in the conclusion ; for which reason the *middle term* itself is sometimes called the argument.

514. That proposition which contains the predicate of the conclusion, connected with the middle term, is usually called the *major proposition*, whereas the *minor proposition* connects the middle term with the subject of the conclusion, and is sometimes called the *assumption*.

Note 1. This exact distinction of the several parts of a syllogism, and of the major and minor terms connected with the middle term in the major and minor propositions, belongs chiefly to *simple* or *categorical syllogisms*, of which we shall speak by and bye (*Art.* 522.), though all syllogisms whatsoever have something analogical to it.

2. That the *major* proposition is generally placed first, and the *minor* second, and the *conclusion* in the last place, where the syllogism is regularly composed and represented.

515. The *form of a syllogism* is the framing and disposing of the premises according to art, or just principles of reasoning, and the regular inference of the conclusion from them.

516. The *act of reasoning*, or inferring one thing from another, is generally expressed and known by the particle *therefore*, when the argument is formed according to the rules of art ; though, in common discourse or writing, such *causal* particles as *for*, *because*, manifest the act of reasoning as well as the *illative* particles *then* and *therefore* ; and wheresoever any of these words is used, there is a perfect syllogism expressed or implied, though perhaps the three propositions do not appear, or are not placed in regular form.

517. Each proposition possesses *quantity* and *quality*. By quantity is meant, that it is universal or particular ; by quality, that it is an affirmative or negative.

Illus. 1. An universal proposition (*Art.* 469. *Illus.* 1.) includes a whole genus, or a whole species, and affirms or denies something of them. The major proposition of the following syllogism is an example ; as,

> " All animals are mortal ;
> Man is an animal ;
> Therefore, man is mortal."

" All animals are mortal," is an universal affirmative proposition. Mortality is affirmed of the whole genus of animals.

" No animal can live without food," is an universal negative proposition.

2. A *particular proposition* includes only a part of a genus or of a species, and affirms or denies something of it. (*Illus.* 2. *Art.* 469.) Accordingly, " Some animals are long lived," is a *particular affirmative proposition.* " Some animals are not endowed with reason," is a particular negative proposition.

Corol. 1. Hence it appears that four sorts of propositions only can enter a syllogism ; or, in other words, that syllogisms are divided into four kinds, either according to the question which is proved by them, according to their own nature and composition, or according to the middle term, which is used to prove the question. They must be either *universal affirmatives*, or *universal negatives*, *particular affirmatives*, or *particular negatives*.

2. The *general principle* upon which these universal and particular syllogisms are founded, is this, Whatsoever is affirmed or denied universally of any idea, may be affirmed or denied of all the particular kinds or beings, which are contained in the extension of that universal idea.

Note. In the doctrine of syllogisms, a *singular* and an *indefinite* proposition are ranked among *universals*.

518. These four sorts of propositions, for the convenience of distinguishing them, are denominated by the four following vowels, *a, e, i, o.* (*Art.* 536.)

A signifies universal affirmative ; *e*, universal negative ; *i*, particular affirmative ; and *o*, particular negative. To assist the memory, these vowels and their properties are formed into the two following monkish verses :

> Asserit E negat A, sed universaliter ambæ.
> Asserit I negat O, sed particulariter ambæ.

Scholia 1. We have now seen, that although a syllogism consists of three propositions, it contains only three ideas, which are called terms, each of which is twice repeated, to make up the propositions. (*Art.* 511.)

2. That one of these ideas, which is always the predicate of the conclusion, is called the *major term ;* another, the *minor term,* which is always the *subject* of the conclusion ; and the third, the *middle term.* (*Art.* 513.)

3. The *reasoning* of the syllogism lies in pointing out the *agreement* or *disagreement* of the *major* and *minor* terms, by comparing them with the *middle term.* (*Art.* 517.)

4. The *middle term* never appears in the conclusion, or third proposition ;—it is compared successively with the *major* and *minor* terms in the *two first propositions*, or premises, as they are sometimes called. It is *twice* repeated in the premises ; it may be either the *predicate* of the *major* premise, and the *subject* of the *minor ;* or it may be the *subject* of the *major* premise, and *predicate* of the *minor.*

In like manner, both the major and minor terms stand once in each premise, and they are both repeated in the conclusion.

Example. In the syllogism formerly quoted (*Art.* 517.), the *minor* term is MAN, the *major* term is MORTAL, the *middle term* is ANIMAL. In the *first* premise, " all animals are mortal," the *middle* term, ANIMAL, is compared with the *major* term, MORTAL. *Animal* is the SUBJECT; *mortal* is the PREDICATE; and it is affirmed or predicated of all animals, that *they are mortal*. In the *second* premise, " man is an animal," MAN, the *minor* term, is compared with ANIMAL, the *middle* term; and it is affirmed or predicated of man, that he is *an animal*. The *middle* term, ANIMAL, is the *subject* of the *former* premise, and the *predicate* of the *latter*. In the conclusion, " man is mortal," the *minor* term, MAN, is inferred to agree with the *major* term, MORTAL, because, in the premises, they were *both* found to agree with the same *middle term*, ANIMAL.

II. *Of plain, simple Syllogisms, and their Rules.*

519. THE next division of syllogisms is into *single* and *compound*. This is drawn from their *nature* and *composition*.

520. *Single syllogisms* are made up of three propositions: *compound* syllogisms contain more than three propositions, and may be formed into two or more syllogisms.

· 521. *Single syllogisms*, for distinction's sake, may be divided into* *simple, complex,* and *conjunctive.*

522. Those are properly called *simple* or *categorical syllogisms*, which are made up of three *plain, single* or *categorical propositions*, wherein the middle term is evidently and regularly joined with one part of the question in the major proposition, and with the other in the minor, whence there follows a plain single conclusion; as, *every human virtue is to be sought with diligence; prudence is human virtue; therefore prudence is to be sought diligently.*

Obs. Though the terms of propositions may be *complex*, yet, where the composition of the whole argument is thus *plain, simple,* and *regular*, it is properly called a *simple syllogism*, since the *complexion* does not belong to the syllogistic form of it.

523. *Simple syllogisms* have several *rules* belonging to them, which, being observed, will generally secure us from false inferences: but these *rules* are founded on four *general axioms*.

524. *Axiom* 1. Particular propositions are contained in universals, and may be inferred from them; but universals

---

* As ideas and propositions are divided into *single* and *compound*, and *single* are subdivided into *simple* and *complex*, so there are the same divisions and subdivisions applied to syllogisms.

are not contained in particulars, nor can they be inferred from them.

525. *Axiom* 2. In all universal propositions, the subject is universal : in all particular propositions, the subject is particular.

526. *Axiom* 3. In all affirmative propositions, the predicate has no greater extension than the subject ; for its extension is restrained by the subject, and therefore it is always to be esteemed as a particular idea. It is by mere accident, if it be ever taken universally, and cannot happen but in such universal or singular propositions as are *reciprocal.*

527. *Axiom* 4. The predicate of a negative proposition is always taken universally, for in its whole extension it is denied of the subject. If we say, *no stone is vegetable,* we deny all sorts of *vegetation* concerning *stones.*

The Rules of *simple, regular* Syllogisms are these :

528. *Rule* I. *The middle term must not be taken twice particularly, but once at least universally.* For if the middle term be taken from two different parts or kinds of the same universal idea, then the subject of the conclusion is compared with one of these parts, and the predicate with another part, and this will never show whether that subject and predicate agree or disagree : there will then be *four distinct terms* in the syllogism, and the two parts of the question will not be compared with the *same third idea;* as, if I say, *some men are pious,* and *some men are robbers,* I can never infer that *some robbers are pious,* for the middle 'erm, *men,* being taken twice particularly, it is not the *same men* who are spoken of in the major and minor propositions.

529. *Rule* II. *The terms in the conclusion must never be taken more universally than they are in the premises.* The reason is derived from the first axiom (*Art.* 524.), that *generals can never be inferred from particulars.*

530. *Rule* III. *A negative conclusion cannot be proved by two affirmative premises.* For when the two terms of the conclusion are united, or agree to the middle term, it does not follow by any means that they disagree from one another.

531. *Rule* IV. *If one of the premises be negative, the conclusion must be negative.* For if the middle term be denied of either part of the conclusion, it may show that the terms of the conclusion disagree, but it can never show that they agree.

532. *Rule* V. *If either of the premises be particular, the conclusion must be particular.* This may be proved for the most part from the first axiom.

Obs. These two last *rules* are sometimes united in this single sentence—*The conclusion always follows the weaker part of the premises.* Now negatives and particulars are counted inferior to affirmatives and universals.

533. *Rule* VI. *From two Negative Premises nothing can be concluded.* For they separate the middle term both from the subject and predicate of the conclusion, and when two ideas disagree to a third, we cannot infer that they either agree or disagree with each other.

Obs. Yet where the *negative* is a part of the *middle term*, the two premises may look like *negatives* according to the words, but one of them is *affirmative* in sense; as, *What has no thought cannot reason;* but *a worm has no thought;* therefore *a worm cannot reason.* The minor proposition does really affirm the middle term concerning the subject, namely, *a worm is what has no thought*, and, thus, it is, properly, in this syllogism, an *affirmative* proposition.

534. *Rule* VII. *From two Particular Premises nothing can be concluded.* This rule depends chiefly on the first axiom.

III. *Of the Modes and Figures of Simple Syllogisms.*

535. The FIGURE of a syllogism is the proper disposition of the *middle term*, with the parts of the question.

Illus. The middle term may be the *subject* of the major premise, and the predicate of the minor, when the syllogism is of the *first figure* (see *Art.* 543);
Or it may be the predicate of both premises, which makes the syllogism of the *second figure* (see *Art.* 544);
Or it may be the subject of both premises, when the syllogism will be of the *third figure* (see *Art.* 545);
Or it may be the *predicate* of the major premise, and the subject of the minor, when the syllogism will be of the *fourth figure.*
Corol. As the middle term never appears in the conclusion, and must appear *twice* in the premises, it will appear, that these four are all the positions of which it is susceptible; and consequently that the number of figures must also be *four.*
Note. The examples of each figure are deferred till we shall have explained the meaning of *mode*, when the same examples will serve to illustrate both figures and modes.

536. All syllogisms are composed of four sorts of propositions; *universal affirmatives*, or *universal negatives*; *particular affirmatives*, or *particular negatives;* and these propositions are discriminated by the vowels *a, e, i, o.* (*Art.*

518.) Now the MODE of a syllogism is determined by the species of the propositions of which it is composed.

Illus. 1. These species may be THREE *universal affirmatives*, marked by THREE *a*'s ;
Or THREE *universal negatives*, marked by THREE *e*'s ;
Or THREE *particular affirmatives*, marked by THREE *i*'s ;
Or THREE *particular negatives*, marked by THREE *o*'s ;
Or they may be TWO *universal affirmatives*, and ONE *universal negative*, marked by TWO *a*'s and ONE *e ;*
Or TWO *universal affirmatives*, and ONE *particular affirmative*, marked by TWO *a*'s and ONE *i ;*
Or TWO *universal affirmatives*, and ONE *particular negative*, marked by TWO *a*'s and ONE *o.*

2. Each of these combinations makes a Mode ; and there may be as many modes in each figure, as there are possible combinations of the four vowels. It is found by computation, that the number of possible combinations is no fewer than sixty-four for each figure, so that all the four figures will furnish two hundred and fifty-six modes.

537. But of these possible modes, a few only form legitimate syllogisms. The FIRST FIGURE has no more than four conclusive modes ; one consisting of three universal propositions, denoted by three *a*'s, to which the schoolmen have given the name of *Barbara*, because it contains the vowel *a* three times.

538. A second, consisting of an universal major proposition, an universal affirmative minor proposition, and an universal negative conclusion, denoted by the vowels *e, a, e,* to which has been given the name of *Celarent*, because the vowels of this mode form the vowels of that word.

539. A third, containing an universal affirmative major proposition, a particular affirmative minor proposition, and a particular affirmative conclusion, denoted by the letters *a, i, i,* out of which is formed the word *Darii*, for the name of this mode.

540. A fourth, consisting of an universal negative major premise, and a particular affirmative minor premise, and a particular negative conclusion, marked by the vowels *e, i, o,* of which has been formed the word *Ferio*, for the name of the last mode.

541. In the SECOND FIGURE are found also four conclusive modes ; and the quantity and quality of their proportions will be readily comprehended from their names, in which, as in the preceding figure, the vowels only are significant. *Cesare* is the name of the first mode ; *Camestres*, of the second ; *Festino*, of the third ; *Baroco*, of the fourth

542. The THIRD FIGURE has six modes, denoted by the hard words, *Darapti, Felapton, Disamis, Datisi, Bocardo, Ferison*.

Corol. Hence it appears that all the legitimate modes of the three first figures are no more than fourteen. The names of these modes and figures were, to aid the memory, formed by the schoolmen into the following barbarous hexameters :—

Barbara, Celarent, Darii, Ferio, dato primæ ;
Cesare, Camestres, Festino, Baroco, secundæ ;
Tertia grande sonans recitat *Darapti, Felapton ;*
Adjungens *Disamis, Datisi, Bocardo, Ferison*.

Note. Aristotle has not treated separately of the modes of the fourth figure, because he found they could be reduced to those of the former figures. We follow his example.

543. We shall now offer some examples to illustrate the theories which we have endeavored to explain. The following example is a syllogism of the FIRST FIGURE, and of the mode *Barbara :*—

BAR All bad men are miserable ;
BA All tyrants are bad men ;
RA Therefore, all tyrants are miserable.

Analysis. The major term is " miserable," the minor term is " tyrants," and the middle term is " bad men." The middle term is the subject of the major premise, " all bad men are miserable," and the predicate of the minor premise, " all tyrants are bad men." The syllogism is therefore of the first figure, which requires these positions of the middle term. The propositions are all universal affirmatives ; consequently the mode is *Barbara*. (*Art.* 537.)

544. The next shall be an example of the SECOND FIGURE, and of the mode *Cesare*.

CE No deceitful man merits confidence ;
SA All honest men merit confidence ;
RE Therefore, no honest man is deceitful.

Analysis. " Deceitful" is the major term ; " honest man " is the minor term ; and " merits confidence " is the middle term. The middle term is the predicate of both the premises, " no deceitful man merits confidence," " all honest men merit confidence," which are the situations of the middle term required by the second figure. The first premise is universal negative, marked by the letter *e*, " no deceitful man merits confidence ;" the second universal affirmative, marked by the letter *a*, " all honest men merit confidence ;" the conclusion universal negative, marked again by the letter *e*, " no honest man is deceitful." These letters constitute the mode *Cesare*. (*Art.* 541.)

545. The subsequent syllogism is of the THIRD FIGURE, and of the mode *Darapti*.

21

DA   All good men are happy;
RAP   All good men hate the devil;
TI   Therefore, some men who hate the devil are happy.

Analysis. The major term is "happy;" the minor term is "hate the devil;" and the middle term is "good men." The middle term is the subject of both premises, "all good men are happy," "all good men hate the devil," which constitutes a syllogism of the third figure. The major premise, "all good men are happy," is an universal affirmative; the minor premise, "all good men hate the devil," is the same; the conclusion, "some men who hate the devil are happy," is a particular affirmative. The two premises are noted by the two *u*'s, the conclusion by *i*, and these letters form the mode *Durapti*. (*Art.* 542.)

We have now produced an example of a mode of each figure. It would be tedious to exemplify all the modes; but, to prevent suspicion of unfair dealing in this branch of logic, we shall, from the different figures and modes, add a few instances promiscuously, to illustrate further the nature of this famous instrument of reasoning.

546. The following syllogism is of the mode *Bocardo*, which belongs to the third figure. The name shows that the first premise, *o*, must be a particular negative; the second premise, *a*, an universal affirmative; and the conclusion, *o*, a particular negative. The third figure requires the middle term to be the subject of both premises; all these requisites are thus fulfilled.

BO   Some good men are not rich;
CAR   All good men are happy;
DO   Therefore, some happy men are not rich men.

547. The next example is of *Camestres*, a mode of the second figure.

CAM   All men are animals;
EST   No stone is an animal;
RES   Therefore, no stone is a man.

Analysis. "Animal" is the middle term, and is the predicate of both premises, as required by the second figure. The first premise is *a*, universal affirmative; the second, *e*, universal negative; the conclusion, *e*, also universal negative. Hence the mode *Camestres*.

548. The mode *Darii* shall furnish another example.

DA   Every thing base should be avoided;
RI   Some pleasures are base;
I   Therefore, some pleasures should be avoided.

Analysis. "Avoided" is the major term; "pleasures," the minor term; "base," the middle term. Base, is the subject of the major premise, and the predicate of the minor, which refers the syllogism to the first figure. The first premise, marked *a*, is universal affirma-

tive ; the second premise and the conclusion are marked *i, i,* particular affirmatives ; hence the mode *Darii.* (*Art.* 589.)

549. In each figure there are singular syllogisms, or syllogisms relative to individuals, which cannot be reduced to
any of the modes. They are allowed, however, to be legitimate syllogisms, and they are constructed on the same principle with the rest. The only difference is, that all the
established modes refer to genus and species : these refer to
species and individuals.

> Every traitor deserves death ;
> Judas was a traitor ;
> Therefore, Judas deserved death.

This syllogism is of the first figure, where the middle term " trai-
tor " is the subject of the major premise, and the predicate of the
minor premise.

550. The following is a particular example of the second
figure :—

> Socrates was an ugly man :
> Plato was not an ugly man ;
> Therefore, Plato was not Socrates.

The middle term, " ugly," is the predicate of both premises.

551. A particular example of the third figure :—

> Judas did not obtain salvation ;
> Judas was an apostle ;
> Therefore, every apostle did not obtain salvation.

" Judas," is the *middle* term, and the *subject* of *both premises,* according to the requisitions of the third figure.

IV. *Of Complex Syllogisms.*

552. It is not the mere use of *complex terms* in a syllogism that gives it this name, though one of the terms is
usually *complex ;* but those are properly called *complex
syllogisms,* in which the middle term is not connected with
the whole subject, or the whole predicate in two distinct
propositions, but is intermingled and compared with them
by parts, or in a more confused manner, in different forms
of speech ; as,

> The sun is a senseless being ;
> The Persians worshipped the sun ;
> Therefore, the Persians worshipped a senseless being.

Here the predicate of the conclusion is " *worshipped a senseless
being,*" part, of which, " a senseless being," is joined with the middle
term, *sun,* in the major proposition, and the other part, " worshipped,"
in the minor.

Obs. Though this sort of argument is confessed to be *entangled,* or
confused, and *irregular,* if examined by the rules of *simple syllogisms,*

yet there is a great variety of arguments used in books of learning, and in common life, whose consequence is strong and evident, and which must be ranked under this head ; as in the five following cases :—

553. (I.) *Exclusive* propositions will form a complex argument ; as,

> Pious men are the only favorites of heaven ;
> True Christians are favorites of heaven ;
> Therefore, true Christians are pious men.

Or thus : Hypocrites are not pious men ;
> Therefore, hypocrites are not favorites of heaven.

554. (II.) *Exceptive* propositions will make such complex syllogisms ; as,

> None but physicians came to the consultation ;
> The nurse is no physician ;
> Therefore, the nurse came not to the consultation.

555. (III.) Or *comparative* propositions ; as,

> Knowledge is better than riches ;
> Virtue is better than knowledge ;
> Therefore, virtue is better than riches.

Or thus : A dove will fly a mile in a minute ;
> A swallow flies swifter than a dove ;
> Therefore, a swallow will fly more than a mile in a minute.

556. (IV.) *Inceptive* and *desitive* propositions ; as,

> The fogs vanish as the sun rises ;
> But the fogs have not yet begun to vanish ;
> Therefore, the sun is not yet risen.

557. (V.) Or *modal* propositions ; as,

It is necessary that a general understand the art of war ;
But Caius does not understand the art of war ;
Therefore, it is necessary Caius should not be a general.

Or thus : A total eclipse of the sun would cause darkness at noon ;
It is possible that the moon, at that time, may totally eclipse the sun ;
Therefore, it is possible that the moon may cause darkness at noon.

558. Besides all these, there is a greater number of *complex syllogisms* which can hardly be reduced under any particular titles, because the forms of human language are so exceedingly various ; as,

Example 1. Christianity requires us to believe what the Apostles wrote ;
> St. Paul is an Apostle ;
> Therefore, Christianity requires us to believe what St. Paul wrote.

2. No human artist can make an animal ;
> A fly or a worm is an animal ;
> Therefore, no human artist can make a fly or a worm.

3. The father always lived in London;
The son always lived with the father;
Therefore, the son always lived in London.

4. The blossom soon follows the full bud;
This pear-tree hath many full buds;
Therefore, it will shortly have many blossoms

5. One hailstone never falls alone;
But a hailstone fell just now;
Therefore, others fell with it.

6. Thunder seldom comes without lightning;
But it thundered yesterday;
Therefore, probably, it lightened also.

7. Moses wrote before the Trojan war;
The first Greek historians wrote after the Trojan war;
Therefore, the first Greek historians wrote after Moses.

Note. Perhaps some of these syllogisms may be reduced to those which are called *connective* (*Art.* 566.); but it is of little moment to what *species* they belong; for it is not any formal set of rules, so much as the evidence and force of reason, that must determine the truth or falsehood of all such syllogisms.

Corol. Now, the force of all these arguments is so evident and conclusive, that though the form of the syllogism be irregular, we are sure the inferences are just and true; for the *premises*, according to the reason of things, do *really contain the conclusion that is deduced from them*, which is a never-failing test of a true syllogism, as shall be shown hereafter.

559. The truth of most of these *complex syllogisms* may also be made to appear, if needful, by reducing them either to *regular, simple syllogisms*, or to some of the *conjunctive syllogisms*, which are described in the next section. We will give an instance only in the first, and leave the rest to exercise the ingenuity of the reader.

Example 1. The first argument may be reduced to a syllogism in *Barbara*; thus,

The sun is a senseless being;
What the Persians worshipped is the sun;
Therefore, what the Persians worshipped is a senseless being.

Though the conclusive force of this argument is evident without the reduction.

V. *Of Conjunctive Syllogisms.*

560. Those are called *conjunctive syllogisms*, wherein one of the premises, namely, the major, has distinct parts, which are joined by a conjunction, or some such particle of speech. Most times the major or minor, or both, are *explicitly compound propositions;* and generally the *major* prop-

21 *

osition is made up of two distinct parts or propositions, in such a manner, as that by the assertion of one in the *minor*, the other is either asserted or denied in the *conclusion;* or, by the denial of one in the *minor*, the other is either asserted or denied in the *conclusion*. It is hardly possible, indeed, to fit any short definition to include all the kinds of these ; but the chief amongst them are the *conditional* syllogism, the *disjunctive*, the *relative*, and the *connective*.

561. (I.) The *conditional* or *hypothetical* syllogism is that whose major or minor, or both, are *conditional* propositions; as,

> If there be a God, the world is governed by Providence ;
> But there is a God ;
> Therefore, the world is governed by Providence.

Illus. 1. These syllogisms admit two sorts of true argumentation, whether the major is *conditional* or not.

I. When the antecedent is asserted in the minor, that the consequent may be asserted in the conclusion : such is the preceding example. This is called *arguing from the position of the antecedent to the position of the consequent.*

II. When the consequent is contradicted in the minor proposition, that the antecedent may be contradicted in the conclusion ; as,

> If atheists are in the right, then the world exists without a cause ;
> But the world does not exist without a cause ;
> Therefore, atheists are not in the right.

This is called arguing *from the removing of the consequent to the removing of the antecedent.*

Illus. 2. To *remove* the antecedent or consequent here, does not merely signify the *denial* of it, but the *contradiction* of it, for the mere *denial* of it by a *contrary* proposition will not make a true syllogism, as appears thus :

> If every creature be reasonable, every brute is reasonable ;
> But no brute is reasonable ;
> Therefore, no creature is reasonable.

Whereas, if you say in the minor, *every brute is not reasonable,* then it would follow truly in the conclusion, therefore *every creatur is not reasonable.*

Illus. 3. When the antecedent or consequent are *negative* propositions, they are removed by an affirmative ; as,

> If there be no God, then the world does not discover creative wisdom ;
> But the world does discover creative wisdom ;
> Therefore, there is a God.

In this instance, the consequent is removed or contradicted in the minor, that the antecedent may be contradicted in the conclusion So in this argument of St. Paul, 1 Cor xv.

> If the dead rise not, Christ died in vain ;
> But Christ did not die in vain ;
> Therefore, the dead shall rise.

562. There are also two sorts of false arguing.

I. From the removing of the antecedent to the removing of the consequent ;

Or, II. From the position of the consequent to the position of the antecedent.

Examples of these are easily framed ; as,

1. If a minister were a prince, he must be honored ;
   But a minister is not a prince ;
   Therefore, he must not be honored.

2. If a minister were a prince, he must be honored ;
   But a minister must be honored ;
   Therefore, he is a prince.

Who sees not the falsehood of both these syllogisms ?

Obs. 1. If the subject of the antecedent and the consequent be the same, then the *hypothetical* syllogism may be turned into a *categorical* one ; as, If Cæsar be a king, he must be honored ; but Cæsar is a king ; therefore, &c. This may be changed thus : Every king must be honored ; but Cæsar is a king ; therefore, &c.

2. If the *major* proposition only be *conditional*, the conclusion is *categorical* ; but if the *minor* or *both* be *conditional*, the conclusion is also *conditional* ; as,

The worshippers of images are idolaters ;
If the Romans worship a crucifix, they are worshippers of an image ;
Therefore, if the Romans worship a crucifix, they are idolaters.

But this sort of syllogism should be avoided as much as possible in disputation, because it greatly embarrasses a cause. The syllogisms whose major only is *hypothetical*, are very frequent, and used with great advantage.

563. (II.) A *disjunctive syllogism* is when the major proposition is disjunctive ; as,

The earth moves in a circle or an ellipsis ;
But it does not move in a circle ;
Therefore, it moves in an ellipsis.

564. A *disjunctive syllogism* may have many members, or parts ; thus,

It is either spring, summer, autumn, or winter ;
But it is not spring, autumn, nor summer ;
Therefore, it is winter.

Obs. The true method of arguing here, is, *from the assertion of one, to the denial of the rest,* or *from the denial of one or more, to the assertion of what remains;* but the major should be so framed, that the several parts of it cannot be true together, though one of them is evidently true.

565. (III.) A *relative syllogism* requires the major proposition to be relative ; as,

> Where the general is, there shall his soldiers be ;
> But the general is in winter quarters ;
> Therefore, his soldiers shall be there also.

Or : As is the captain, so are his soldiers ;
> But the captain is a coward ;
> Therefore, his soldiers are so too.

Obs. 1. Arguments that relate to the doctrine of proportion must be referred to this head; as,

As two are to four, so are three to six; but two make the half of four; therefore, three make the half of six.

2. Besides these, there is another sort of syllogism, which is very natural and common, and yet authors take very little notice of it, call it by an improper name, and describe it very defectively; and that is,

566. (IV.) A *connective syllogism.* This some have called *copulative*, but it by no means requires the major to be either a *copulative* or a *compound* proposition, according to the definition given of it (*Art.* 560 and 568.) ; but it requires that two or more ideas be so connected, either in the complex subject or predicate of the major, that if one of them be affirmed or denied in the minor, common sense will naturally show us what will be the consequence.

Example 1. Meekness and humility always go together ;
> Moses was a man of meekness ;
> Therefore, Moses was also humble.
Or we may form this minor :
> Pharaoh was no humble man ; therefore, he was not meek.

2. No man can serve God and Mammon ;
> The covetous man serves Mammon ;
> Therefore, he cannot serve God.
Or the minor may run thus :
> The true Christian serves God ;
> Therefore, he cannot serve Mammon.

3. Genius must join with study to make a great man ;
> Florino has genius, but he cannot study ;
> Therefore, Florino will never be a great man.
Or thus : Quintus studies hard, but has no genius ;
> Therefore, Quintus will never be a great man.

4. Gulo cannot make a dinner without flesh and fish ;
> There was no fish to be gotten to-day ;
> Therefore, Gulo this day cannot make a dinner.

5. London and Paris are in different latitudes ;
> The latitude of London is $51\frac{1}{2}$ degrees ;
> Therefore, this cannot be the latitude of Paris.

6. Joseph and Benjamin had one mother ;
> Rachel was the mother of Joseph ;
> Therefore, she was Benjamin's mother too.

7. The father and the son are of equal stature ;
   The father is six feet high ;
   Therefore, the son is six feet high also.

8. Pride is inconsistent with innocence ;
   Angels have innocence ;
   Therefore, they have no pride ;
Or thus : Devils have pride ;
   Therefore, they have not innocence.

567. We might multiply other instances of these *connective* syllogisms, by bringing in all sorts of *exceptive, excusive, comparative,* and *modal* propositions into the composition of them ; for all these may be wrought into *conjunctive,* as well as into *simple* syllogisms, and we may thereby render them *complex.*

Obs. 1. Most of these may be transformed into *categorical* syllogisms, by the student who has a mind to prove their truth that way ; or they may be easily converted into each other by changing the forms of speech.

2. These *conjunctive* syllogisms are seldom deficient or faulty in their form ; for such a deficiency would generally be discovered at first glance, by common reason, without any artificial rules of logic ; the chief care, therefore, is to see that the *major* proposition be true, upon which the whole force of the argument usually depends.

VI. *Of Compound, Imperfect, or Irregular Syllogisms.*

568. COMPOUND SYLLOGISMS are made up of two or more *single syllogisms,* and may be resolved into them. IMPERFECT, or IRREGULAR SYLLOGISMS cannot be reduced to the rules of *mode* and *figure.*

Example. Should we argue thus,—
      Every man is mortal ;
      Therefore, every king is mortal,—
the syllogism appears to be *imperfect,* as it consists but of two propositions. Yet is it complete, only the *minor,*
      Every king is a man,
is omitted, and left to be supplied by the reader, as being a proposition so familiar and evident, that it cannot escape his observation and judgment of the conclusion.

569. ENTHYMEME, the first seemingly imperfect syllogism we shall handle, occurs frequently in reasoning, especially where it makes a part of common conversation. (*Example, Art.* 294.)

Illus. The example just given is an *enthymeme ;* and in the following example one of the propositions which constitute the premises is omitted, and the conclusion is drawn from the other premise, as if the syllogism were regular and complete.

Example. Whatever thinks is a spiritual substance ;
      Therefore the mind of man is a spiritual substance ·—

Or thus : The mind thinks ;
           Therefore, the mind is a spiritual substance
In the former case, we omit the minor proposition,
           The mind of man thinks,
and infer the conclusion from the major. In the latter case, we omit
the major proposition,
           Whatever thinks is a spiritual substance,
and infer the same conclusion from the minor. It is supposed, in both
cases, that the connection of the conclusion with either premise, is
so apparent, as to render unnecessary the presence of the other
premise.

The *premise* in this case is called the ANTECEDENT ; and the *conclusion* the SEQUELA, or the INFERENCE.

Scholium. In enthymemes there is a particular elegance, especially
in common conversation, because, not displaying the argument in all
its parts, they leave to the exercise and invention of the mind that
scope which it delights to take. Besides, by this means, it is put upon
that exercise that makes it a partaker in the discovery of what is proposed to it. And, in fine writing, this is the great secret, so to frame
and put together our thoughts as to give full play to the reader's imagination, and draw him insensibly into our views and course of reasoning. This, says Duncan, gives a pleasure not unlike to that which
the author feels himself in composing. It, besides, shortens discourse,
and adds a certain force and liveliness to our arguments, when the
words in which they are conveyed favor the natural quickness of the
mind in its operations, and a single expression is left to exhibit the
whole train of thoughts.

570. But there is another species of reasoning with two
propositions, which seems to be complete in itself, and where
we admit the conclusion without supposing any tacit or suppressed judgment in the mind, from which it follows syllogistically. We should term this *the ground of reasoning in
immediate consequences.*

Illus. 1. This so appears, when between propositions where the
connection is such, that the admission of the one, necessarily, and at
the first sight, implies the admission of the other. For, if it so falls
out that the proposition on which the other depends is self-evident,
we content ourselves with barely affirming it, and infer that other by
a direct conclusion.

2. Thus, by admitting an *universal proposition*, we are forced to
admit of all the particular propositions comprehended under it, this
being the very condition that constitutes a proposition universal.
(*Art.* 469. *Illus.* 1.) If, then, that universal proposition chances to be
self-evident, the particular ones follow of course, without any further
train of reasoning.

Example 1. Whoever allows, for instance, that things *equal to one
and the same thing are equal to one another*, must at the same time allow, *that two triangles, each equal to a square whose side is three inches,
are also equal between themselves*. This argument therefore—*Things
equal to one and the same thing are equal to one another ; Therefore,
these two triangles, each equal to the square of a line of three inches, are
equal between themselves—*

is complete in its kind, and contains all that is necessary towards a just and legitimate conclusion ; for the first or universal proposition is self-evident, and therefore requires no farther proof; and as the truth of the particular is inseparably connected with that of the universal, it follows from it by an obvious and unavoidable consequence.

571. Now, in all cases of this kind, where propositions are deduced one from another, on account of a known and evident connection, we are said to reason by *immediate consequence.* Such a coherence of propositions, manifest at first sight, and forcing itself upon the mind, frequently occurs in reasoning. Logicians have explained the several suppositions upon which it takes place, and allow of all *immediate consequences* that follow in conformity to them.

Obs. These arguments (*Art.* 570 and 571.), though seemingly complete, because the conclusion follows necessarily from the single proposition that goes before, may yet be considered as real *enthymemes*, whose *major*, which is a conditional proposition, is wanting.

Example 1. The syllogism just mentioned, when represented according to this view, will run thus :

Things equal to one and the same thing are equal to one another ;
These two triangles, each equal to a square whose side is three inches,
    are also equal between themselves.
But things equal to one and the same thing, are equal to one another ;
Therefore, also, these triangles, &c. are equal between themselves.

Illus. 1. The foregoing observation and example will be found to hold in all *immediate consequences* whatsoever, insomuch that they are in fact no more than *enthymemes* of hypothetical syllogisms. But then it is particular to them, that the ground on which the conclusion rests, namely, its coherence with the *minor*, is of itself apparent, and seen immediately to flow from the rules of logic. As it is, therefore, entirely unnecessary to express a self-evident connection, the *major*, whose office that is, is constantly omitted ; nay. and seems so very little needful to enforce the conclusion, as to be accounted commonly no part of the argument.

2. It must indeed be owned, that the foregoing *immediate consequence* might have been reduced to a *simple* as well as an *hypothetical syllogism.* This will be evident to any one who gives himself the trouble to make the experiment. But it is not my design to enter farther into these niceties : what has been said shows, That all arguments consisting of but two propositions are real *enthymemes*, and reducible to complete syllogisms of some one form or other.

Corol. As, therefore, the ground on which the conclusion rests, must needs be always the same with that of the syllogisms to which it belongs, we have here an universal criterion whereby at all times to ascertain the justness and validity of our reasonings in this way.

572. *A sorites of plain, simple syllogisms,* is a way of arguing, in which a great number of propositions are so linked

together, that the predicate of one becomes continually the subject of the next following, until at last a conclusion is formed, by bringing together the subject of the first proposition and the predicate of the last.

Example. Of this kind is the following argument :

> *God is omnipotent.*
> *An omnipotent being can do every thing possible.*
> *He that can do every thing possible, can do whatever involves not a contradiction.*   •
> *Therefore, God can do whatever involves not a contradiction.*

Illus. 1. This particular combination of propositions may be continued to any length we please, without in the least weakening the ground upon which the conclusion rests. The reason is, because the *sorites* itself may be resolved into as many simple syllogisms as there are middle terms in it; where this is found universally to hold, that when such a resolution is made, and the syllogisms are placed in train, the conclusion of the last in the series is also the conclusion of the *sorites.*

2. This kind of argument, therefore, as it serves to unite several syllogisms into one, must stand upon the same foundation with the syllogisms of which it consists, and is, indeed, properly speaking, no other than a compendious way of reasoning syllogistically. Any one may be satisfied of this at pleasure, if he but takes the trouble of resolving the foregoing sorites into two distinct syllogisms ; for he will there find, that he arrives at the same conclusion ; and that too by the very same train of thinking, but with abundantly more words, and the addition of two superfluous propositions.

573. *A sorites of hypothetical syllogisms.* What is here said of plain, simple propositions, may be well applied to those that are conditional ; that is, any number of them may be so joined together in a series, that the consequent of one shall become continually the antecedent of the next following ; in which case, by establishing the antecedent of the first proposition, we establish the consequent of the last, or by removing the last consequent, remove also the first antecedent.

Example 1. This way of reasoning is exemplified in the following argument :

> *If we love any person, all emotions of hatred towards him cease.*
> *If all emotions of hatred towards a person cease, we cannot rejoice in his misfortunes.*
> *If we rejoice not in his misfortunes, we certainly wish him no injury.*
> *Therefore, if we love a person, we wish him no injury.*

Illus. It is evident that these *sorites,* as well as the last, may be resolved into a *series* of distinct syllogisms, with this difference only, that here the syllogisms are all conditional. But as the conclusion of the last syllogism in the series is the same with the conclusion of the *sorites,* it is plain, that this also is a compendious way of reasoning, whose evidence arises from the evidence of the several single syllogisms into which it may be resolved.

Example 2. The mind is a thinking substance. A thinking substance is a spirit. A spirit has no extension. What has no extension has no parts. What has no parts is indissoluble. What is indissoluble is immortal. Therefore, the mind is immortal. (*Corol.* 1, 2, and 3. *Art.* 99.)

This species, like the former, is only a train of syllogisms abridged, into which it may easily be resolved in the following manner :—

All thinking substances are spirits ;
The mind is a thinking substance ;
Therefore, the mind is a spirit.

Spirits have no extension ;
The mind is a spirit ;
Therefore, the mind has no extension.

Things having no extension have no parts ;
The mind has no extension ;
Therefore, the mind has no parts.

Things having no parts are indissoluble ;
The mind has no parts ;
Therefore, the mind is indissoluble.

Things indissoluble are immortal ;
The mind is indissoluble ;
Therefore, the mind is immortal.

Analysis. Here, also, it appears, that all the intermediate propositions between the first and the last of a *sorites* may be formed into separate syllogisms ; and that it is equivalent to an argument formed of as many syllogisms as the argument contains intermediate propositions. It may also be observed, that every idea of the *sorites* is twice repeated, and that it might be farther abridged without any detriment to the evidence it communicates. Had it stood as follows, the agreement of its ideas would have been as clear, and its evidence as satisfactory, as in any other form. Mind—thinking substance—spirit—without extension—without parts—indissoluble—immortal.

574. *Ground of reasoning by Induction.* We come now to that kind of argument which Logicians call *induction ;* in order to the right understanding of which, it will be necessary to observe, that our general ideas are, for the most part, capable of various subdivisions.

Illus. Thus, the idea of the lowest species may be subdivided into its several individuals ; the idea of any genus into the different species it comprehends ; and so of the rest. If, then, we suppose this distribution to be duly made, and so as to take in the whole extent of the idea to which it belongs, then it is plain that all the subdivisions or parts of any idea taken together constitute that whole idea. Thus the several individuals of any species taken together constitute the whole species, and all the various species comprehended under any genus make up the whole genus. This being allowed, it is apparent, that whatsoever may be affirmed of all the several subdiv...ons and classes of any idea ought to be affirmed of the whole general idea to which these subdivisions belong. What may be affirmed of all the individuals of any species, may be affirmed of the whole species; and what may be affirmed of all the species of any genus, may also be affirmed of the whole genus; because all the individuals taken together are the same with the species; and all the species taken together the same with the genus.

575. *The form and structure of an argument by induction.* This way of arguing, where we infer universally concerning any idea, what we had before affirmed or denied separately of all its several subdivisions and parts, is called reasoning by *induction.*

Example. Thus, if we suppose the whole tribe of animals subdivided into men, beasts, birds, insects, and fishes, and then reason concerning them after this manner;—

All men have a power of beginning motion;
All beasts, birds, and insects have a power of beginning motion;
All fishes have a power of beginning motion;
Therefore, all animals have a power of beginning motion;—

the argument is an *induction.* When the subdivisions are just, so as to take in the whole general idea, and the enumeration is perfect, that is, extends to all and to every one of the inferior classes or parts, there the *induction* is complete, and the manner of reasoning by *induction* is apparently conclusive.

576. *The ground of argumentation in a dilemma.* A *dilemma* is an argument by which we endeavor to prove the absurdity or falsehood of some assertion.

Illus. In order to this, we assume a conditional proposition, the antecedent of which is, the assertion to be disproved, and the consequent a disjunctive proposition, enumerating all the possible suppositions upon which that assertion can take place. If, then, it appears that all these several suppositions ought to be rejected, it is plain that the antecedent or assertion itself must be so too. When, therefore, such a proposition as that before mentioned is made the *major* of any syllogism, if the *minor* rejects all the suppositions contained in the consequent, it follows necessarily that the conclusion ought to reject the antecedent. which, as we have said, is the very assertion to be disproved. This particular way of arguing is that which Logicians call a *dilemma ;* and from the account here given of it, it appears that we may, in general, define it to be an *hypothetical syllogism where the consequent of the major is a disjunctive proposition, which is wholly taken away or removed in the minor.*

Example. Of this kind is the following :

If God did not create the world perfect in its kind, it must either proceed from want of inclination, or from want of power;

But it could not proceed either from want of inclination or from want of power.

Therefore, God created the world perfect in its kind ; Or, which is the same thing, it is absurd to say that he did not create the world perfect in its kind.

577. *An universal description of a dilemma.* The nature, then, of a *dilemma*, is universally this. The *major* is a conditional proposition, whose consequent contains all the several propositions upon which the antecedent can take place. As, therefore, these suppositions are wholly removed into the *minor*, it is evident that the. antecedent must be so too; insomuch that we here always argue from the removal of the consequent to the removal of the antecedent. That is, a *dilemma* is an argument in the *modus tollens* of hypothetical syllogisms, as logicians love to speak. Hence, it is plain, that if the antecedent of the *major* is an affirmative proposition, the conclusion of the *dilemma* will be negative ; but if it is a negative proposition, the conclusion will be affirmative.

578. A *dilemma* becomes *faulty or ineffectual three* ways : *First,* When the members of the division are not well opposed, or not fully enumerated ; for then the major is false. *Secondly,* When what is asserted concerning each part is not just; for then the minor is not true. *Thirdly,* When it may be retorted with equal force upon him who utters it.

Example. There was a famous ancient instance of this case, wherein a *dilemma* was retorted. *Euathlus* promised *Protagorus* a reward when he had taught him the *art of pleading*, and it was to be paid the first day that he gained any cause in the court. After a considerable time *Protagorus* goes to law with *Euathlus* for the reward, and uses this dilemma :

Either the cause will go on my side or on yours ;
If the cause goes on my side, you must pay me according to the sentence of the judge ;
If the cause goes on your side, you must pay me according to your bargain ;
Therefore, whether the cause goes for me or against me, you must pay me the reward.

But *Euathlus* retorted this dilemma, thus :

Either I shall gain the cause or lose it ;
If I gain the cause, then nothing will be due to you according to the sentence of the judge ;
But if I lose the cause, nothing will be due to you according to my bargain ;
Therefore, whether I lose or gain the cause, I will not pay you. for nothing will be due to you.

Obs. 1. A *dilemma* is usually described as though it always proved the absurdity, inconvenience, or unreasonableness of some opinion or practice; and this is the most common design of it; but it is plain, that it may also be used to prove the truth or advantage of any thing proposed; as, in heaven we shall either have desires or not; if we have no desires, then we have full satisfaction; if we have desires, they shall be satisfied as fast as they rise; therefore, in heaven we shall be completely satisfied.

2. This sort of argument may be composed of three or more members, and may be called a *trilemma.*

579 I cannot dismiss this subject without observing, that as there is something very curious and entertaining in the structure of a *dilemma,* so it is a manner of reasoning that occurs frequently in mathematical demonstrations.

Illus. Nothing is more common with *Euclid,* when about to show the equality of two given figures, or, which is the same thing, to prove the absurdity of asserting them unequal; nothing, I say, is more common with him than to assume, *that if the one is not equal to the other, it must be either greater or less;* and, having destroyed both these suppositions, upon which alone the assertion can stand, he thence very naturally infers, that the assertion itself is false. Now, this is precisely the reasoning of a *dilemma,* and in every step coincides with the frame and composition of that argument, as we have described it above.

VII. *Of the Merit of Syllogistic Reasoning.*

580. That we may do it no injustice in the course of the discussion, it may be necessary to observe, that every syllogism must not be considered as containing a complete argument, or a train of reasoning, if the argument requires more than one intermediate idea. One syllogism, on the contrary, contains only one step of a train of reasoning; and, in arranging a train of reasoning in the syllogistic form, as many syllogisms must be made as there are steps or comparisons in that train. We must also observe, that by proceeding in this manner, any train of reasoning, in arts, in science, or in business, may be converted into syllogisms. These remarks may be illustrated by exhibiting the first demonstration of the first book of Euclid in this form.

Illus. The object of the proposition is to prove that, The triangle described on the given line AB, by means of the two circles, the semi-diameter of each of which is the line AB, is equilateral. From the properties of the circle, each of the sides of the triangle is found equal to the base, and the inference is drawn necessarily, that all the sides are equal. This train of reasoning, expressed by syllogisms, will stand as follows:

1. All the semi-diameters of the same circle are equal ;
   The lines AB, AC,* are semi-diameters of the same circle ;
   Therefore, these lines are equal.

2. All the semi-diameters of the same circle are equal ;
   The lines BA, BC, are semi-diameters of the same circle ;
   Therefore, these lines are equal.

3. Whatever things are equal to the same thing, are equal to one
      another ;
   The lines AC and BC are equal to the line AB,
   Therefore, the lines AC, BC, are equal to one another.

4. Triangles, having their sides equal, are called equilateral ;
   The triangle ABC has all its sides equal ;
   Therefore, it is equilateral.

581. Now, the point to be investigated is, Whether the syllogistic method of exhibiting this demonstration, or any other train of reasoning, is preferable to that adopted by Euclid, or to the method which places the successive ideas in the nearest juxtaposition, and expresses them in the fewest and plainest words.

Illus. From the example which we have given, it will appear, that the syllogistic form is not nearly so concise as that of Euclid ; for all the ideas of Euclid's demonstration are expressed in one half of the words which are requisite to constitute these four syllogisms. Even Euclid's manner of expression is copious and full ; and the evidence of his demonstration would not perhaps have been impaired, had he communicated it as follows :—The semi-diameters AB and AC of the one circle are equal ; the semi-diameters of AB and BC of the other circle are equal also ; therefore, the triangle is equilateral, and described on the given line.

582. But, besides being more prolix, the syllogistic method adds no light to the evidence by which the ideas of the train of reasoning are perceived, which light the ideas possess not in their natural state of juxtaposition. Every syllogism consists of three terms, and the reasoner must have discovered the middle term, and observed the agreement of it with the extremes, before he can form the terms into a syllogism. After the syllogism is formed, the mind acquires no satisfaction from the contemplation of it, which the terms did not suggest in the state of juxtaposition.

Illus. Suppose we were to prove, that Socrates was content with his condition, because he was a wise man ; we should have three terms, of which a syllogism may be formed, and which, in their natural order, would stand thus : Socrates—a wise man—content with his condition. We affirm, that the agreement between Socrates

---

* See the figure in Simson's Euclid.

and contentment, is as obvious and satisfactory in the simple juxta
position of the terms, as it is after these terms are formed into the
following syllogism :

> All wise men are content with their condition ;
> Socrates was a wise man ;
> Therefore, Socrates was content with his condition.

583. Farther, as the syllogistic form communicates no
additional light, so neither does it assist in discovering middle terms.   The principal operations of any investigation
are the invention of intermediate ideas, and the comparison
of them with one another, and with the extremes.   The invention of middle terms is the chief operation ; and excellence in it is the most important qualification any inquirer
can possess.   It seems to depend on natural sagacity and
acuteness, fortified and improved by exercise.   From syllogism, in particular, no aid can be derived.   It does not
even pretend to give any aid.   Its only object is to assist in
the second operation, the comparison of ideas ; and we have
seen that the syllogistic exhibition is not more perspicuous
than the natural one.

584. But the most singular phenomenon of syllogism is,
that the conclusion is often a self-evident proposition, sometimes even trifling and insignificant.   The discussion of
this point will unfold the whole mystery and merit of the
method.

Illus. In converting a train of ideas into the syllogistic form, there
must be made as many syllogisms as there are steps or comparisons
in the train, and as many as there are ideas in the train, except one.
Each idea of the train, beginning with the second, is the major term
of its respective syllogism : the other two terms of the same syllogism are, one a genus, and the other a species of that genus.   The
major term is compared first with the one, and then with the other,
and must be found either to agree or disagree with both.

Example.   Take, for example, the train of reasoning formerly mentioned.   (*Art.* 573.)   Human mind—thinking substance immaterial—
indissoluble—immortal, and convert it into syllogisms.

> *First.*   Whatever perceives, judges, and reasons, is a thinking sub-
> stance ;
> The human mind perceives, judges, and reasons ;
> Therefore, the human mind is a thinking substance.

Analysis. In this syllogism, the major term, " thinking substance,'
and the second idea of the train, is compared with the genus, " whatever perceives, judges, and reasons," in the first premise, and is found
to agree with it.   The same major term is compared again with the
species, " the human mind," in the conclusion, and is found also to
agree with it.   Now, the genus, " whatever perceives, judges and

reasons," the species, " the mind of man," and " thinking substance," are all the terms of this syllogism.

Secondly.   Whatever thinks is immaterial ;
The human mind thinks ;
Therefore, the human mind is immaterial.

Analysis. " Immaterial," the third idea of the train, and the major term of this syllogism, is compared first with the genus, " whatever thinks," and next with the species, " the human mind," and is found to agree with both.

Thirdly.   Whatever is immaterial is indissoluble ;
The mind of man is immaterial ;
Therefore, the mind of man is indissoluble.

Analysis. " Indissoluble," the fourth idea of the train, and the major term of this syllogism, is compared first with the genus, " whatever is immaterial," and next with the species, " the mind of man," and is found to agree with both.

Fourthly.   Whatever is indissoluble is immortal ;
The mind of man is indissoluble ;
Therefore, the mind of man is immortal.

Analysis. " Immortal," the last idea of the train, and the major term of this syllogism, is compared first with the genus, " whatever is indissoluble," and then with the species, " the mind of man," and is found to agree with both.

585. From these examples it appears, that the *major* term of every syllogism is one *of the ideas of the train, beginning with the second;* that the *minor* term of every syllogism is the *first idea* of the *train ;* and that the *middle term* of every syllogism is a *genus of the minor.* The syllogisms which we have formed are all of the first figure ; but this circumstance is no objection against the remarks which we have to make, because all the other figures and modes proceed on the same principle ; namely, the comparison of the major term, first, with the *genus* of the *minor,* and, next, with the *minor* as a *species ;* or the syllogisms of the other figures may be reduced to those of the first in which these conditions take place.

586. What, then, is the mystery of this mighty syllogistic art, which has so long engaged the attention of learned men, and is still accounted by many of that description to contain something meritorious, or to be an analysis of the art of reasoning ? It is no more than this, " Whatever agrees with any genus, will agree with every species of that genus; or whatever disagrees with any genus, will disagree with every species of that genus." If this be the principle of the art, can we wonder at the self-evidence of all the conclusions of

all its syllogisms, or that it never gratified science or business with the discovery of any useful truth?

587. When we reflect how genus and species are formed, it is impossible but what agrees or disagrees with the one, must agree or disagree with the other. What is a genus? It is a collection of all the qualities common to the species it includes. What agrees then with the *common qualities* of any species, must agree with the *species itself*, as far as these qualities extend; and syllogism carries the agreement of the major term with the minor and middle terms no farther than these qualities. What agrees with the *genus* must agree with the *species;* it is only an agreement with the same thing in different situations; the major term agrees or disagrees with perfectly the same qualities in the genus with which it agrees or disagrees in the species.

Corol. Hence it appears, that after finding the agreement of the major term with the genus of the minor term, the conclusion, which asserts the agreement of the major term with the species, or the minor term itself, must be self-evident. To arrange things into species and genera, is extremely convenient for the purposes of language, and some of the purposes of philosophy; but to pretend to reason from the one to the other, seems to be the quintessence of vanity or folly.

588. Examine any *demonstration* of Euclid, any investigation of *morals, politics,* or *affairs* of common life, and you will find, that no man in earnest reasons from a genus to a species.

Illus. 1. A *mathematical demonstration* consists of the comparison of quantities of the same species; figures are compared with figures; angles with angles; and lines with lines.

2. An inquiry concerning *justice* or *charity,* compares these virtues with the principles of reason, equity, the laws of the community, and the situations of persons.

3. A process in the *arts* refers to the theory of the art, and to the example of the most reputable and successful practitioners.

589. It is of little consequence to maintain, that the syllogistic art sometimes makes its way into the most serious business, and that every indictment for a crime, for instance, is a syllogism; of which the major premise contains the description of the crime, and its punishment appointed by the law; the minor premise, the application of the law to the case of the criminal; and the conclusion, an assertion that the criminal merits the punishment appointed by the law.

Illus. 1. That an indictment stands in the form of a syllogism, no

doubt can exist. The major term is the punishment; the crime committed is the minor term and the species; the description of the crime
in the law is the middle term and the genus.

Corol. The *major term*, or the *punishment*, agrees with the *genus*,
or *the law;* and it agrees also, perhaps, with the *minor term* and the
species, or the *crime* of the *prisoner*. But there is not here, strictly
speaking, any reasoning.

Illus. 2. A trial is no more than a scrutiny, whether a *particu'ar
crime* is included under a *general law*, or whether the *indictment accords* with truth, when it asserts, that the *prisoner*, in taking away the
property or the *l:fe* of his fellow-creature, has committed *the crime* of
theft or *murder*, of which crimes the perpetrators are declared by the
law to *deserve punishment.*

Corol. There is no more reasoning in this case, than in every application of the principles of science to the particular cases they
include.

Illus. 3. The assertion that a particular field consists of a certain
number of acres, is equally a syllogism with an indictment charging a
culprit with the commission of a crime punishable by law.

Example. The number of acres, suppose *ten*, is the *major term ;* the
length and *breadth* of the fields, is the *minor term* and the *species ;* the
number of acres of which all fields of the length and breadth of the
one under consideration consists, is the *middle term* and *the genus.*
The *major term*, ten acres, agrees with the dimensions of all fields of
the extent of the one under consideration; it agrees, also, with the
dimensions of the one under consideration ; and, therefore, it agrees
both with the genus and the species of the syllogism.

Conclusion.

But, though the syllogistic method be nugatory and insignificant as
an instrument of reasoning, it possesses high merit as an engine of
wrangling and controversy. It was the happiest contrivance that
could have been devised for conducting those public disputations and
comparative trials, which for ages prevailed in Europe, and in which
the discovery of truth was no part of the ambition of the combatants.
The most ready and acute framer of syllogisms was sure to retire tri-
umphant. The grand contest was not whether the syllogism contained any useful truth. The object of one party was to maintain its
legitimacy ; of the other, to controvert or deny one of its propositions.
Wrangling thus became a science ; and the mind of man, apparently
enthusiastic in the discovery of truth and knowledge, never wandered
farther from their paths.

BOOK V.

THE PHILOSOPHY OF HUMAN KNOWLEDGE.

——◆——

CHAPTER I.

HUMAN KNOWLEDGE ADDRESSED TO THE MEMORY.

590. In *Art.* 464. *Illus.* we inquired, generally, what knowledge is ; but it is now necessary to show that all HU- MAN KNOWLEDGE is conceived to consist of sciences and arts, between which it is difficult to fix the distinction with accuracy ; and, accordingly, we sometimes find the same branch of knowledge denominated, promiscuously, a science and an art. All the principles of science have some reference to practice, and the theory of every art may merit the appellation of a science.

Illus. 1. Some difference, however, there is between them, which, as far as it is of any importance, may be characterized in the following manner :—A SCIENCE is a system of general truths relative to some branch of useful knowledge, and supported by evidence, either demonstrative or highly probable. An ART is the application of the organs of the body, or the faculties of the mind, to the execution of some design, directed by the best principles and rules of practice.
2. A SCIENCE is addressed entirely to the *understanding ;* an ART generally occupies both the *understanding* and the *members* of the body. A science is acquired by study alone ; an art cannot be acquired without much practice of the operations it contains. Accurate knowledge is all that is necessary in science ; eminence in art demands, besides, an acquaintance with rules, and the habit of dextrous and ready performance.

591. Human knowledge divides itself into three great compartments, adapted to the *memory,* the *understanding,* and the *imagination.* To the MEMORY may be addressed HISTORY ; to the UNDERSTANDING, PHILOSOPHY ; and to the IMAGINATION, POETRY.

Obs. 1. These words, history, philosophy, poetry, taken in their most extensive meanings, may comprehend every branch of human knowledge.

Illus. I. Under HISTORY are included all *facts* relative to *nature* or *society*, of which we can obtain intelligence, and which we can commit to record.

2. Under PHILOSOPHY is contained all information relative to *sciences* or *arts*, attainable by the exercise of the *understanding*, or by *experience* and *practice*.

3. Under POETRY are implied all those branches of knowledge, which in any form contribute chiefly to engage or interest the imagination.

Obs. 2. These great divisions will be perceived to run into one another, because different branches of knowledge are generally addressed to more of those faculties than one.

592. History is divided into three parts, *Sacred, Civil,* and *Natural.*

Illus. SACRED HISTORY comprehends the narrative parts of revelation, and the history of the church, commonly called Ecclesiastical History; embracing the history of the Jews, both political and ecclesiastical; the history of the propagation and progress of Christianity, as far as they were carried on by Jesus Christ, and his immediate successors the apostles; and the history of the Christian churches, from the era of the apostles to the present time.

593. CIVIL, or, as some writers call it, *profane history,* in opposition to sacred, contains an account of the governments, and of the civil and military transactions of nations; and displays those great exhibitions of human nature, which the preservation of the happiness of large communities of men, and the convulsions of societies, frequently produce.

Illus. The most instructive lessons in morality and in politics, those most useful sciences, which provide for the felicity and comfort of individuals and nations, are presented to our view in civil history. It recounts the noble deeds of the patriot and the hero, and insinuates, by their example, the most salutary instruction, while it holds forth the cruelty of the oppressor, or the irregularities and crimes of bad men, as the causes of their misery. All civilized nations have exhibited specimens of their progress in this branch of knowledge.

594. Another branch of civil, is *literary history;* or details of the origin and progress of learning, with the revolutions it has undergone in different ages and situations. Though the incidents of this branch are not so splendid as those of the former, they are entitled to regard.

Illus. Civil history displays the qualities of the statesman and the warrior. Literary history unfolds the productions of the imagination, of the heart, and of the understanding, and illustrates the effects of external circumstances, in calling forth or repressing the exertions of the man of genius, and of the philosopher. Next to provision for the safety and happiness of individuals and communities, the most meritorious objects of general attention, are those pursuits which advance the character of human nature, and promote its civilization, its refinement, and its dignity.

595. Profane history includes, further, MEMOIRS, ANNALS, BIOGRAPHY, and is intimately connected with *antiquities, chronology,* and *geography.*

Illus. A *memoir* is a familiar narration, in which the author attempts not the profound discussion, nor the dignity of style employed by the historian. The writer of memoirs presents a simple and plain relation of facts, and leaves reflections and comments to the reader.

Obs. A work of this sort, executed with ability, possesses many attractions, sufficient to gain admirers. It is generally more circumstantial and more picturesque than regular history, and by admitting the reader into more intimate familiarity with the author, communicates instruction with the ease of conversation, without assuming the austere and less pleasant tone of teaching

596. ANNALS are a history constructed in the form of a journal, and bind it sometimes so closely in the trammels of chronology, that the author cannot depart from the order of time, nor anticipate any part of his narrative, to connect the several incidents of an event. The transactions that occur within the year must appear in their proper places ; and if the events extend over several years before their completion, their annual portions are detached and related apart.

Obs The annalist seldom attempts to throw much interest into his work, or to convey any knowledge besides a distinct and accurate view of facts. He seldom endeavors to adorn his relation, or to interweave in it moral or political information. He undertakes the humble task of delineating with accuracy the naked facts, and leaves the historian to embellish them. He is properly the pioneer of the historian, and contributes greatly to shorten his labor, and to accelerate his progress.

Example. Both Thucydides and Tacitus have given to their highly-finished histories the form, and the latter even the name, of annals. Thucydides imposed harder conditions upon himself than are demanded by the rigid rules of annals. His narrative is divided into periods of half a year, and he scruples not to mince his transactions into fragments, to make them correspond to this minute distribution of his time. The annals of Scotland, published by Sir David Dalrymple, realize the idea we have given of this species of writing.

597. BIOGRAPHY records the lives of eminent individuals, and is susceptible of much interest, as the personages may be selected from any order of society—They may be *men of letters,* of *pleasure,* of *business*—They may be *kings, statesmen, politicians, artists, warriors.*

Obs. The relation of their lives may comprehend entertaining strictures on the character and conduct of those with whom they have been connected, and important discoveries into the history of the times in which they have lived.

598. ANTIQUITIES, CHRONOLOGY, and GEOGRAPHY, are the handmaids of history.

599. ANTIQUITIES contain discussions concerning *monuments, political, military, sepulchral,* or *etymological,* that transcend the limits of history, and relate to events, customs, or opinions, about which no other documents exist. The early transactions of all nations are involved in obscurity, because the composition and preservation of records hardly appear but in an advanced state of civilization. There is, however, in mankind, a desire to perpetuate the memory of important events, as well as to investigate the meaning of manners, practices, and opinions, the origin of which is obscure. Hence, *stones,* and *coins,* and *columns,* the most durable materials with which men are acquainted, before the use of writing, are naturally selected to gratify this desire.

Obs. The most important branch, however, of antiquities, relates to the obscurities of *history, manners,* and *laws.* " Antiquitates," says Lord Bacon, in this sense, " historiæ deformatæ sunt, sive reliquiæ historiæ, quæ casu e naufragio temporum ereptæ sunt." Without some knowledge of antiquities, neither old laws, nor many important usages in languages, in the affairs of nations, and in public rites and ceremonies, can be understood. The explanation of these is grateful to numerous individuals, and productive of useful discoveries, relative to titles, to honors, and to property.

600. CHRONOLOGY assigns to events the *order of time* in which they happened, and, therefore, without it, a relation of facts must be a mass of confusion, which the memory cannot retain, nor the understanding apply to any useful purpose. Chronology forms into a system the transactions of nations, and distinguishes the progress of science, of manners, and of arts. The revolutions of the heavenly bodies are allowed to be the best, and the most universal measures of time ; but the practice of observing these revolutions with accuracy is of late acquisition, and appears not till considerable progress has been made in mathematics and astronomy.

Obs. The chronology of ancient history is, for this reason, not a little imperfect, because it is difficult to reduce to any fixed point the eras from which the authors reckon. Even the commencement of the Olympiads, and the building of Rome, are not perfectly determined ; while the chronology of the Jews, and of the early Greeks, is hardly supported by better evidence than *conjecture.*

Illus. The chronology, then, of history, is ascertained for a period extending backward two thousand six hundred years from the commencement of the Olympiads (about eight hundred years before the birth of Christ) to the present time. *The only written* records which exist previous to the commencement of the Olympiads, are the books of the Old Testament; and as the authors either could not, or did not fix their chronology, many systems have been formed to supply that defect. The most rational and satisfactory of these systems is that advanced by Sir Isaac Newton.

601. As the design of Chronology is to determine the time, the purpose of GEOGRAPHY is to fix the place of the transactions recorded in history. Geography exhibits in miniature the positions of all the places on the surface of the globe, with their bearings or relative situations. It brings the surface of the earth in some measure under the eye of the spectator, and communicates a more perfect idea of its form, and of its parts, than could be conveyed by an actual survey.

Illus. It is commonly divided into two parts, general and particular. The former treats of the figure of the earth, and the theory of winds, tides, and currents. *Particular geography,* delineates the situations of kingdoms, cities, rivers, mountains, coasts, and seas. When the situations of these are understood, the reader more easily comprehends the transactions of which these form the field ; the marches and operations of armies ; the navigations and encounters of fleets ; the effects of climate, and the produce of soils.

602. The third branch of history is termed NATURAL, and includes a large field of knowledge, both useful and entertaining ; especially as it comprehends an account of all the phenomena in the heavens, and the productions on the earth, which are or which may be the objects of our senses, together with the changes that may be made on these phenomena and productions by physical causes, or the means of art. This part of natural history, which Lord Bacon calls Narrative, addresses itself to the memory. The use which may be made of it by induction, towards ascertaining the laws of nature, belongs to natural philosophy and chemistry.

Obs. Natural History, then, in this view, is divided into two branches ; one containing the *productions of nature,* whether ordinary and regular, or extraordinary and monstrous ; and the other, the *productions of art.* The natural historian recounts every fact and circumstance relative to these productions.

603. The PRODUCTIONS OF NATURE are divided into those of the heavens, those of the atmosphere, and those of the earth.

604. The PRODUCTIONS OF THE HEAVENS are the phenomena of the solar system and of the fixed stars. The phenomena of the solar system are numerous and brilliant; those of the fixed stars scarce contain more particulars than their names and positions. The phenomena of the solar system are copiously recorded by several popular writers, particularly by Keil, Fergusson, Vince, La Place, and Herschel; and from them it appears that much progress has been made by the moderns in this curious branch of knowledge, beyond what was attained by the ancients.

Obs. The Ptolemaic system, which placed the earth in the centre, was generally received by the ancients; but it was reserved for Newton, in the end of the seventeenth century, to apply to the true system which places the sun in the centre, the most enlightened theory ever devised by the mind of man, and to establish it by evidence which leaves no doubt of its truth, while it communicates such ample information as scarcely permits a desire to know more on the subject. (See my edition of *Adams's Elements of Useful Knowledge, Book II.*'

605. The PHENOMENA OF THE ATMOSPHERE relate to the elasticity, the altitude and weight of the air; to meteors, lightning, thunder, clouds, aurora borealis, snow, hail, rain; to the reflection and refraction of the rays of the sun, the rainbow, evaporation, dews, winds, &c., all which form curious and interesting subjects of investigation, and of the greater part of which modern philosophy has collected the history, and has endeavored to ascertain the theory. (See *Books IV.* and *V.* of *Adams's Elements of Useful Knowledge*, fifth edition.)

606. The PHENOMENA OF THE EARTH relates to its figure, to its division into land and water, and to the productions which are found above and below its surface.

Illus. 1. Its spherical figure first merits attention, which, though contrary to appearance, and to the opinions of the vulgar, yet is so completely established by physical arguments and experiments, that no doctrine in philosophy is better supported.

2. Its division into land and water next attracts curiosity, and the large proportion which the surface of the water bears to that of the land.

3. The most remarkable phenomena of the water are the tides and currents, together with the innumerable varieties of animals and vegetables to which it affords life.

607. With regard to LAND, the first phenomena which summon observation, are *the figures of the two great continents*, extending far, from south to north, and affording many

varieties of climates, of soils, and of productions ; the direction and magnitude of rivers ; the extent, the altitude, and the figure of mountains ; the great lakes of fresh water, the sands and rocks with which they are interspersed.

608. The *situations* and *figures* of ISLANDS next attract our notice, with their immense distances from one another, and afford curious and interesting inquiries concerning the manner in which they have been replenished with the animals and vegetables they contain.

Obs. All these phenomena belong to the geographer to recount and to explain ; those we shall enumerate fall within the province of the natural historian.

609. The natural historian divides the productions of the earth into *animals, vegetables,* and *minerals.*

Illus. 1. Under animals, he comprehends all living creatures, from man to the meanest insect ; and of every species he attempts to deliver the history, as far as observation or information can afford him materials.

2. From animals, the natural historian proceeds to *vegetables.* He examines, and reduces into classes, all the plants which the earth produces.

3. From the surface, he descends into the bowels of the earth, examines the nature and position of the *strata* of which it is composed, and all the varieties of *minerals* which it presents to his observation. But natural historians have too often spent their time in idle disputes about classification, rather than in adding to the general stock of knowledge, and enlarging our acquaintance with the objects that exist.

Obs. The history of nature is, for these reasons, far from being complete ; and the whole theory of general principles, which Lord Bacon calls the inductive part, and which he declares was totally wanting in his time, may still be affirmed to have advanced but a small space.

610. The *history of the* MECHANIC ARTS, or of those experiments and operations which are performed on the materials furnished by nature, forms the last branch of knowledge addressed to the memory.

Obs. 1. The phenomena of the-fine arts will be better introduced under the branch addressed to the imagination.

2. It is vain, in this volume, to attempt a specification of the operations of the mechanic or useful arts. The materials about which they are exerted, are almost as numerous and various as are the different substances and combinations of substances which this earth presents. Should you desire more accurate information, you will have recourse to the works that treat exclusively on those arts, or to the practitioners, who can give you, in one half hour, a better insight into any particular art, than from books you could gain in the half of a year.

CHAPTER II.

HUMAN KNOWLEDGE—ADDRESSED TO THE UNDER-STANDING.

611. Human knowledge, as addressed to the under-standing, is more extensive than that addressed to the memory, as it comprehends all the sciences, and the theories of all the arts.   If we divide it according to its objects, it will resolve itself into two departments, the knowledge of mind, and the knowledge of body.

Obs. This division would be very convenient, if mind and body were always found disunited, or were we not frequently obliged to contemplate them conjointly.   But in all inquiries concerning human nature and human acquisitions, which constitute a large portion of this department of knowledge, mind and body are connected by the closest relations, and must be surveyed and examined in that compounded state.   We are necessitated, for this reason, to adopt another division, more adapted to the actual arrangement of the objects in nature ; and to consider knowledge as referring to mind unconnected with body, or to mind and body connected, or to body unconnected with mind ; in other words, to consider it as referring to God and spirits, to man and human nature, to irrational animals, to vegetables, and to inanimate matter.

612. Of the *world of spirits* we know nothing, except what we learn from the experience of the operations of our minds, and from the general analogy which we are apt to infer subsists among spirits of all orders.

Obs. Between us and the great Spirit that made the universe, whom we cannot suppose to have any connection with matter, there may be, for any thing we know, infinite gradations of spirits, who may be more or less connected with body, according to their elevation in the scale of being.   But of their natures, their endowments, their predilections, or their antipathies, we are altogether ignorant, and perhaps incapable of receiving information.

613. We are no less ignorant of the nature of the first Spirit, particularly of what are called his incommunicable attributes, self-existence, eternity, omnipotence, and infinity.   Though we must admit that these attributes constitute ingredients of the character of a perfect being, yet what the ingredients are, we can now form no adequate conception ; and perhaps we never shall be competent to the task.   The moral attributes of the Almighty, goodness, mercy, judgment, and veracity, are more adapted to human comprehen-

23 *

sion, and form the ground-work of all the science we deduce
from his nature.

Obs. We possess, indeed, no adequate idea even of these attributes; but theologians have deemed it fair to presume, that these attributes resemble in quality, though very different in degree, the virtues which are distinguished by the same names among men. The
delineation of the doctrines and principles which result from these attributes, forms the science of natural religion, and part of the science
of metaphysics.

614. NATURAL RELIGION comprehend the *proofs* for the
existence of God, which result from the order, the beauty,
and the design conspicuous in the works of nature. We
cannot controvert the reality of these qualities, nor suppose
that the works of nature came into existence without a cause.
No other solution can be admitted, than that they originated
from some great, good, and wise Being, who made all beings,
and who governs all nature; who can act from no motive,
and upon no system, which embrace not general happiness;
who has a right to command the obedience of every creature, and in obeying whom only a rational agent can expect
happiness.

Obs. The metaphysical part of knowledge relative to God, contains
discussions concerning the necessity of his existence, independence,
infinity, eternity, omnipotence, which are usually reckoned a branch
of Pneumatics. All these topics have been often and fully canvassed,
and little now remains to be advanced upon them. The pneumatical
branch, in particular, has afforded ample field for profound investigation, in which several writers of bold genius have indulged themselves
in speculations, which transcend, perhaps, the compass of human
powers, and which, therefore, should be relinquished as unprofitable.
But they deserve a more severe censure, if they contribute, as they
sometimes do, to controvert the principles of truth, and to defend the
cause of skepticism.

615. The branches of knowledge relative to MAN, respect
either the *faculties of his mind,* or the use he makes of these
faculties, first, in acquiring and communicating knowledge;
and, secondly, in acquiring happiness. The science which
explains the *faculties* is a branch of Pneumatics; the sciences which teach the *modes of acquiring and communicating
knowledge,* are denominated Logic and Rhetoric; and the
science which delineates the road to happiness, has obtained
the name of Morality.

616. PNEUMATICS form a general history of the faculties
of the mind. The exertions of these faculties constitute the
sciences of *logic, rhetoric,* and *morality.*

Obs. PNEUMATICS, and these sciences, for this reason, run into one another; and in general views of human knowledge, it is unnecessary and inconvenient to contemplate them apart. We shall, therefore, proceed to the latter sciences, the survey of which will afford a place for exhibiting every thing valuable in the science of pneumatics.

617. LOGIC, or the art which delineates the progress of the understanding in the investigation of truth, contains, as we have seen, three parts—the doctrine of ideas, of propositions, of reasoning or proof. But on all these we have delivered our opinion pretty fully in the preceding Books, and shall not, therefore, now enlarge.

618. RHETORIC includes, at least presupposes, the arts subservient to retention and recollection ; but its proper business is to unfold the art of communication.

Illus. The arts subservient to retention and recollection, are those of writing and printing ; by which general knowledge is accumulated, present inquirers are made acquainted with the acquisitions of preceding ages, and may transmit their stores to posterity. The art of communication is conversant about *grammar, composition,* and *criticism.*

619. GRAMMAR divides words into classes, and treats of their inflections, their syntax, and their prosody.

620. COMPOSITION teaches us to communicate our thoughts with perspicuity and proper ornament.

621. CRITICISM informs us whether we have been successful. It qualifies us to read with discernment and improvement, and to determine the literary merit of the performances we peruse. (*See my* GRAMMAR *of* RHETORIC, Chap. II. Book V.)

622. MORALITY, or the science of happiness, may be divided into two great branches, one relative to *individuals,* and the other relative to *communities.*

Illus. 1. The branch respecting INDIVIDUALS comprehends many important topics of investigation ; namely, that the inhabitants of such a compound constitution as is the human, consisting of reason, conscience, many passions and appetites, must result from an arrangement which permits gratification to each of these parts, in proportion to its dignity and consequence, and that this arrangement is recommended by the principles of virtue ; that the laws of human conduct are manifestly marked by the nature of man ; and that his constitution points out the will of his Creator, with the obligations to integrity which arise from this will ; that the performance of the duties which man owes to his Maker, his neighbor, and himself, is not only dictated by obligation, but also by interest, because, in proportion as he deviates from these duties, he deviates from happiness ; and that the *best man is,* and must be, *the happiest,* as virtue is the truest wisdom, the best knowledge, and the most solid consolation; while vice is folly, ignorance, and misery! (See *Chapter XII. Book II. Moral Perception.*)

2. The morality that regards the happiness of communities, constitutes the science of politics, which resolves itself into three branches.

The first, containing the laws of peace and war, or the rules which guide the intercourse of communities, founded on the practice of civilized nations, and the dictates of equity.

The second, delineating the different civil governments which have been contrived or adopted to secure the safety of states, with the prosperity and comfort of individuals.

And *the third*, exhibiting economical arrangements, or the laws which punish crimes, and encourage industry, protect and cherish commerce and arts.

Corol. From the topics which constitute the sciences of morality and politics, it appears, that they are of the greatest importance both to individuals and communities. As soon, therefore, as human nature acquired any degree of refinement, and virtue and industry were found to be subservient to its felicity, these sciences could not fail to attract the attention both of the man of speculation and the man of business. They must have been found to be the best guides of the statesman and of the private citizen. Theories and discussions concerning them are accordingly discovered in early periods of society; to which have been added such copious improvements, by the enlightened genius of later times, that few branches of knowledge seem more completely investigated. It is pleasant to think, that the mind of man has been adequate to any satisfactory investigation. In very few sciences has it been more successful.

623. Human knowledge, relative to BODY, *animated* or *inanimated*, is divided into three branches.

The *first*, containing the *metaphysics of body*, or an account of its general *properties, extension, solidity, impenetrability, motion, vacuum*, &c.

The *second*, regarding the *surfaces of bodies*, or the *computation* of the quantities of which these surfaces consist.

And the *third*, respecting the *internal parts* of bodies, or their structure and constitution. Every inquiry relative to body must be comprehended under some one of these branches.

Illus. 1. In discussing the *metaphysics* or general properties of body, we discover that *extension* is an essential quality, and that it is the chief quality which distinguishes body from spirit.

2. We inquire, further, whether all matter be *solid* and *impenetrable*, that is, whether it resists the entrance of extraneous matter into the place it occupies, however impelled by any force; and we find, that though some matter is compressible, yet that all matter resists the entrance of extraneous matter into the place it occupies, till it be permitted to retire, and that in this sense it is *solid* and *impenetrable*.

3. We discover, also, that *motion* is an occasional property of body, though it seems incapable of assuming that property to itself. It must receive motion from some external power, but when received, it retains motion till it is deprived of that property by some other, or by the same external power.

4. We inquire, next, whether all space is *filled* with *matter*, or whether nature admits a *vacuum*, that is, space void of body. This question has been the cause of long and bitter controversy, one sect of philosophers maintaining, that all space is full of matter, and that *nature abhors a vacuum*, which were the sentiments of the *Cartesian school;* while the greater part of the followers of *Newton* have embraced the doctrine of a *vacuum*, and have been of opinion, that the *phenomena of the air-pump* alone are sufficient to establish that doctrine.

624. The sciences concerned about the surfaces of bodies are three, ARITHMETIC, GEOMETRY, and NATURAL PHILOSOPHY, which were called by the ancients *Mathemata*, or "the most illustrious knowledge," on account of the importance of the truths they contain, and the complete evidence by which they are supported.

Illus. 1. *Arithmetic*, which, in an extended sense, includes algebra, is the science of computation. Its object is quantity discrete, or divided into parts, and the design of all its operations is, to ascertain the numbers of these parts, as far as the knowledge of them may be subservient to the purposes of human life.

2. All we can wish to know relative to numbers, is, to determine the amount of particular sums of units, which is obtained by the operation called *addition;* or to ascertain their difference, which is performed by the operation called *subtraction*.

3. Into these operations, therefore, all the operations of arithmetic and algebra, however intricate and remote, are resolvable.

4. Multiplication and division are nothing but abridgments of addition and subtraction.

5. Many of the operations of arithmetic and algebra depend upon the doctrine of proportion; and in all these operations, if three of the terms be known, the fourth may be found, by the rule of three in arithmetic, or by an algebraic equation. The foundation of both methods is, that the product of the extremes is equal to that of the means.

625. The *investigations* of ALGEBRA differ not essentially from those of arithmetic, except in these three particulars. Algebraic Investigations proceed by equations, in which the quantity sought is included; they are expressed by letters instead of figures; and they may be applied to continuous quantity as well as to discrete.

Illus. In all arithmetical and algebraical questions, something is given, and something sought; or something is known, and something unknown. Between these, some ratio may generally be discovered, so that if both the given and the sought quantities be denoted by symbols or letters, an equation may be deduced from that ratio, which will involve the value of the unknown quantity. When the equation is found, the sequel of the operation is easy; for it is always practicable, by means of addition and subtraction, to place the known quantities on one side of the equation, and the unknown quantity on the other, from which position its value will be apparent.

626. The SYMBOLS or *letters* of an *equation* may express either *numerical* or *mathematical quantities;* they may signify *lines* as well as *numbers*. The addition, then, of two letters, may denote the sum of two numbers, or the length of two lines ; and the multiplication of two letters may signify the product of two numbers, or the rectangle contained by two lines.

Obs. It is this capacity of denoting quantities of all sorts, which has procured to algebra the name of universal arithmetic, and from its capacity of operating with unknown quantities, as if they were known, it has obtained the name of *analysis*, and has superseded, in a great measure, the *analytic method* of the ancients.

627. ALGEBRA has been particularly useful in explaining the operations of *arithmetic*, the *extraction of roots*, and the *properties of curve lines*. In all which cases it has communicated the most important information, and has facilitated exceedingly the progress of science.

Obs. But the application of it to numerical questions, which was the chief use of it previous to the middle of the seventeenth century, was rather a matter of amusement than of utility. Des Cartes first employed it in geometrical questions, since which time it has been the favorite mode of investigation. The ancient method of analysis may excel it in simplicity and elegance, but in point of expedition, and extensive use, in the most difficult physical researches, the resources of algebra are important, and its superiority is decisive.

628. The ancient and elegant method of computing *continuous quantity*, or the *extent of the surfaces* and the *solidity of bodies*, is GEOMETRY, the science of superficies and of solids. The elements of this science are divided into three parts; the first, treating of the *properties of plain figures;* the second, of those of *solids;* and the third, of those of the curve lines, called CONIC SECTIONS.

Illus. 1. Euclid has discussed the first in his first six books; the second, in his eleventh and twelfth; and Apollonius, the third, in his elaborate treatise on the subject. In all these works, the merit of the ancient geometers is very great.

2. The Elements of Euclid, it seems, are the most perfect productions in science, for all the ingenuity of modern times has not

added to their merit, nor superseded their use. They appear to have sprung nearly as complete and satisfactory from the hands of their author, as we still survey them.

3. The cones of Apollonius display profound knowledge, and great industry, but they are not so finished as the Elements. The arrangement of them has been improved, several of the demonstrations have been abridged and generalized, and many useful corollaries have been subjoined by the additional attention of modern mathematicians.

Obs. But if we except some progress made in the doctrine of the sphere, and of eclipses, by Proclus; in the investigation of the mechanical powers, hydrostatics, and the art of calculating curvilineal spaces, from the method of approximation, by Archimedes; we have enumerated all the advancements achieved by the ancients in this most illustrious of sciences. They had acquired little knowledge of mixed mathematics, or the application of them to physical purposes, now called Natural Philosophy. They knew nothing of the true solar system, nor of the laws that direct its motions, which Sir Isaac Newton has investigated with so much success and universal applause. They knew something of the doctrine of reflected light, as we learn from the famous contrivance of Archimedes, for setting fire to the Roman ships at the siege of Syracuse, by means of burning-glasses. But they seem to have understood little of the theory of optics, and nothing of the curious doctrine of light and colors.

629. The refined and abstract nature of the higher parts of mathematics will prevent them from being objects of general attention; but all philosophers and artists may, notwithstanding, avail themselves of the practical principles they present; and every inquirer who can pretend to the advantages of a liberal education, should study the elementary branches of the Mathematics.

630. Independent of forming a part of polite education, and of the advantage derived from the salutary exercise of the reasoning faculty, the study of Euclid demands attention on account of the necessary connection which Geometry has with many of the common and useful arts.

Illus. 1. The principles of all sorts of *machinery* are derived from his Elements, together with the laws which direct the most profitable application of force, whether of animals, of water, or of air.

2. The art of *surveying* is an immediate practice of the most simple deductions of this science, and of course the arts of delineating maps and charts, which convey, in a manner satisfactory and expeditious, the knowledge of the situations and bearings of places on the earth which we have never seen.

3. The whole *theory of longitude and latitude* is deduced from the same source, without which neither the construction of maps, charts, nor globes, could have existed. The face of the earth would have remained unknown, as navigation must have been confined to the ancient dangerous an' circumscribed method of coasting.

4. The useful and ingenious *art of ship-building* owes all, or the greater part, of its merits to the principles of mathematics.

5. *Fortification* and *gunnery*, these dreadful, but, it seems, necessary arts, have derived almost all their improvements from the same origin. In a word, in whatever light we survey the Elements of Euclid, whether as an useful or an ornamental study, they merit highly the attention of every person who is ambitious of distinguishing himself, either as a philosopher or as a man of business.

631. The *third division* of knowledge respecting MATTER explains the branches that regard the *nature*, the *structure*, and the *composition of bodies*.

632. This compartment is subdivided into three parts; *first,* the general laws or properties of bodies; *secondly*, the internal structure of animals, with their diseases and cures; and *thirdly,* the ingredients or component parts of bodies.

The first constitutes the science, or the *philosophy of natural history ;* the second, *medicine;* and the third, *chemistry*. We formerly mentioned natural history as a record of facts; we now speak of it as a branch of philosophy.

Obs. Lord Bacon anxiously and repeatedly recommends the study of natural history as necessary to furnish materials for erecting the great temple of natural knowledge. The philosopher investigates, compares, compounds, and separates these materials, till he deduces the general laws of agreement and of disagreement among the works of God, and establishes the doctrine of an enlightened and a satisfactory science. Lord Bacon himself led the way in this new and noble path to fame ; and though the progress of that eminent inquirer could not be great, yet he had the merit of foreseeing and predicting the achievements of posterity.

633. Of the three classes of NATURAL HISTORY—*animals*, *vegetables*, and *minerals*—that of animals exhibits the most illustrious marks of wisdom and design, though the other two are not destitute of conspicuous specimens of the same qualities. (*Art.* 609. *Illus.* 1, 2, 3, and *Obs.*)

Obs. 1. Not to mention the instincts, or mental powers which all animals possess in some degree, and which man in great eminence possesses; their external form, the construction of their bodies, and the final causes, or uses to which their members are subservient, display marks of contrivance superior to those found in any other classes of the works of nature.

Illus. 1. ANIMALS possess the power of *self-motion*, of *sensation*, of seeking and appropriating *nourishment*. Their organs are more complicated, and their changes more rapid, than those of vegetables. Some vegetables possess a degree of irritability. They contract on the application of stimuli. Few, however, are gifted with this power, far the greater number being susceptible of no movement, except what results from the elasticity of their roots, branches, and leaves. They have not, like animals, any feeling of pleasure or pain; and they can only imbibe nourishment from those parts of matter with which they are in permanent contact.

2. But though these differences are conspicuous in the greater part of animals and vegetables, yet in the lower species of the former, and in the higher species of the latter, they in a great measure disappear; and it is difficult to determine where the class of animals terminates, and that of vegetables begins. The polypus, which generates as many animals of its kind, as are the parts into which it may be divided, seems not to be endowed with a much higher degree of vitality, than that which is possessed by many vegetables.

3. Both in the animal and vegetable kingdom, the smaller species are more numerous than the larger. Thus, there are many more insects than there are men; the plants of grass are more numerous than the trees; and the number of flies surpasses that of horses.

4. As animals descend to vegetables, so the latter approach minerals. Minerals are called inorganized, or inanimate bodies. They seem to compose the mass of the globe; certainly, at least, its external crust. They increase in volume; but this seems to arise entirely from the juxtaposition of parts, and the force of attraction, or that assimilating power of nature which generates from different combinations of the same materials, parts of such different constitutions and uses. The ascent of juices in vegetables seems to depend on the principles by which water rises in capillary tubes. Vegetables grow with a rapidity palpable and conspicuous. In a short space of time many of them reach perfection, after which they suffer decay, and finally dissolution. The growth and decay of minerals is so slow and imperceptible, as to render it sometimes doubtful whether they are susceptible of these qualities. Vegetables have organs by which they elaborate the nourishment attracted from the earth and the air Minerals seem to undergo no change but what arises from the chemical action of bodies on one another.

Obs. 2. Commercial intercourse, and voyages of discovery, added to literary peregrinations and correspondence, have left unknown to modern naturalists no important region almost on the face of the globe, and have communicated very satisfactory accounts of the greater part of the countries it contains. The kingdoms of animals and plants have been pretty fully investigated, and minerals of late have been favored with a large share of attention.

634. The *second branch* of knowledge relative to the structure of bodies, is MEDICINE, whose chief object is to explain the nature of the human constitution, the *diseases* to which men are *liable*, and the *remedies* by which they may be *cured*.

Obs. The human body is one of the most curious pieces of mechanism which nature can present, and furnishes a most important subject of philosophical investigation; yet necessity, not curiosity, produced the science of medicine, and led to its various improvements. A similar attachment to utility still confines the researches of the physician almost entirely to the human body; but there is much useful knowledge to be obtained also from an attentive examination of

24

the structure of other animals, whose org . is and vital functions are, in many respects, analogous to those of man.

635. The bodies of men, like those of other animals, naturally accommodate themselves to their situation. If exposed to the severities of climate, if accustomed to exercise, and inured to wholesome, though coarse fare, they acquire a firmness of texture and a soundness of constitution, which either repel the encroachments of disease, or set its attacks at defiance till an advanced age. But when the efforts of art pretend to set at defiance the operations of nature; when men attempt to adapt the climate to the constitution, instead of accommodating the constitution to the climate, nature makes ample reprisals, and loads with maladies those who seek indulgences reprobated by health. The art of medicine, accordingly, has been employed chiefly to counteract the inroads of luxury, and much ingenuity and industry have been exerted to accomplish this important design.

Obs. 1. The human body has been examined, and all its vital motions have been studied with the utmost care. The knife of the anatomist has been sedulously and sometimes successfully employed in investigating the structure and functions of the different parts of the body. The effects of thousands of medicines have been tried, and the influence of air, exercise, and climate, has been observed. Much learning, sagacity, and experience, have been exerted with assiduity and perseverance, to bring the healing art to perfection.

2. But, notwithstanding the combined industry of ancient and modern physicians, the structure and uses of many parts of the body are still involved in such impenetrable darkness, that the nature of the changes which take place in disease, and the means by which these morbid changes are to be removed, are in many cases perfectly unknown. From these causes, the science must naturally be imperfect. From them also have probably originated those absurd conjectures and theories which so long disgraced the healing art. Notwithstanding these disadvantages, the exertions of the physician, properly directed, are capable of affording the most essential services to mankind.

636. CHEMISTRY, the last branch of knowledge which regards the structure of bodies, presents a large field of instruction and amusement. The object of chemistry is to discover the qualities of bodies by means of analysis and composition, and to observe the results that take place from these operations. With this view, it investigates the effects of *air, light, heat,* &c. on the bodies in nature, and all the changes which these undergo, whether from their spontaneous action on each other, or from the operations of art.

Illus. 1. By *analysis* the chemist endeavors to discover the component parts of bodies, or to reduce them to their elementary principles. *Composition*, or *synthesis*, reverses this process, and forms new compounds by the union of bodies which were formerly distinct. The latter furnishes the greatest number of truths, and those of greatest importance, as in chemistry, there are few, if any operations, in which some combinations do not take place. Perhaps it is scarcely possible in any case to determine what bodies are elementary, and what are not so, many being now discovered to be compounded which were formerly considered as simple.

2. To discover *elementary principles*, however, is not the most important part of the science. The exertions of the chemist should always be directed to discover the laws on which the operations of his art depend, the order of the different combinations of bodies with one another, and the attractions which regulate these combinations.

3. While chemistry confines its inquiries to these operations, it deserves every commendation, and repays, with much emolument, the labors of the philosopher. But this, like other branches of science, has been disgraced by the projects of empirics, who pretended not to investigate, but to rival nature. Of late the proper objects of chemistry have sometimes been mistaken, and many have endeavored to extend its principles to the explanation of phenomena to which they could not apply;—but chemistry, however, has already done much, and promises to do much more, in elucidating and explaining many laws of nature, and in simplifying many processes in the arts.

CHAPTER III.

HUMAN KNOWLEDGE, ADDRESSED TO THE IMAGINATION.

637. THOUGH the UNDERSTANDING is the noblest faculty of the human mind, yet its exercise is not always attended with the most pleasure. Many of its exertions are extremely fatiguing, sometimes even painful; they are recommended chiefly by the importance of the consequences which they involve, and the ascendency that they procure. This remark, however, applies chiefly to those exertions which are purely *scientific*, and which are occupied about long and intricate trains of reasoning. The most popular, the most familiar, and certainly not the least useful exertions, are engaged about the objects of the other faculties to which knowledge is addressed,—the MEMORY and the IMAGINA-TION

638. MEMORY is the faculty whose exercise yields least employment, its chief use being to furnish materials for the operations of the understanding. (*Art.* 247.) But the IMAGINATION partakes deeply of the pleasure resulting from the contemplation of all the works of genius; and is that faculty whose exertions convey the most exquisite satisfaction that can be received, independent of moral sentiment and the affections of the heart. (*Art.* 264.)

Illus. 1. In the most captivating objects of the imagination, however, there is always intermixed a large portion of those qualities which recommend the objects to the understanding, and gain its approbation. Without this intermixture, the objects of *imagination* may excite a transient surprise, or momentary gratification; but they will never please upon reflection, nor will they long engage the attention of correct taste. (*Art.* 265.)

2. Even POETRY must present *sound sense,* and a *legitimate logic,* and PAINTING must exhibit *design, propriety,* and *utility,* before they can obtain a more favorable appellation than the offspring of a disordered or distempered fancy. (*Art.* 267 and 268.)

639. These remarks show how the objects of one faculty solicit the attention of another, and circumscribe the objects which we are now to represent as addressed immediately to the *imagination.*

640. The word POETRY (*Art.* 591. *Illus.* 3.) was appropriated to characterize these objects; but in this case it must be extended much beyond its common acceptation. It must receive a sense not restricted to metrical composition, but extended to ALL ELEGANT PRODUCTIONS OF ART, whether communicated by *language,* by the *pencil,* or the *graving tool.* It must comprehend, in a word, all ORNAMENTED or FIGURATIVE COMPOSITION, whether in prose or VERSE; the exertions of the STATUARY, of the PAINTER, and of the ENGRAVER; and the most meritorious exhibitions of the ARCHITECT, of the MUSICIAN, and of the GARDENER.

Obs. As far as the objects of the Imagination can be expressed by language, I have anticipated the view of them in my Grammar of Rhetoric, in which it has been my endeavor, not only to introduce the reader to an acquaintance with poetic compositions, but to render him a judge of their merit, and to guide his exertions in similar attempts. It remains, then, only that we conclude this survey by some remarks on the other branches of knowledge which we have mentioned.

641. GREECE is not the country in which we are to look for the greatest and most useful improvements in the necessary arts of life; for in agriculture, manufactures, and commerce, it was behind Egypt and Phœnicia; but, in all

that respects the *fine arts*—POETRY, RHETORIC, SCULPTURE, and ARCHITECTURE, no nation of antiquity rivalled *Greece;* and the models which yet remain of these are not only models of imitation, but standards of excellence to the moderns, in the judgment of the most civilized nations of our own times.   In sketching the outline of the exertions of the statuary and the architect, we shall, therefore, view Greece at the period when the active spirit of the Athenians, which, after the defeat of Xerxes, would have languished, but for the new direction that luxury gave it, began to display itself, and the arts broke out at once with surprising lustre.

642. The age of Pericles, the era of luxury and splendor, was the golden age of the arts in Greece. The acquisition of fame was then the capital inducement to exertions of genius; but as a secondary excitement, we must assign a large portion to the *Theology* of the Greeks, which furnished ample exercises for the genius of the architect and the sculptor.

Obs. But that which enabled the Grecian artist to excel in sculpture was the advantage he enjoyed of studying the human figure naked, in all its various attitudes in the Palæstra, and in the public games. The antique statues have, thence, a superior grandeur united with perfect simplicity, because the attitude is not the result of an artificial disposition of the figure, as in the modern academies, but is an exhibition of unconstrained nature.

Example. Thus, in the *dying gladiator*, we observe both the relaxation of the muscles, and the visible failure of strength and life; we cannot thence doubt, that nature was the sculptor's immediate model of imitation.

643. The *Grecian Architecture* universally allowed to be the most perfect, consists of the DORIC, the IONIC, and the CORINTHIAN orders; and these three several orders are respectively adapted to three different kinds of buildings.

Illus. 1. Thus, the DORIC, possessing masculine grandeur, and a superior degree of strength over both the Ionic and Corinthian, is admirably adapted to buildings of great magnitude and of a sublime character; for with chasteness and simplicity the character of sublimity is essentially connected.

Example 1. The temple of THESEUS, at *Athens,* constructed ten years after the battle of Marathon, is of this order, and at this day almost entire.

Illus. 2. The Ionic order possesses lightness and elegance. As the Doric boasts masculine grandeur, the Ionic values itself on its feminine *elegance:* it is besides *simple;* for simplicity is an essential requisite of genuine beauty.

Example 2. The *Temple* of APOLLO, at Miletus, was built after this order; as were also that of the Delphian Oracle, and of Diana, at Ephesus.

24 *

Illus. 3. The CORINTHIAN order, possessing an exuberance of rich-ness, marks an age of luxury and magnificence, when pomp and splendor, without extinguishing the taste for the sublime and beauti-ful, had become the ruling passions. But this union of these charac-ters satisfies not the chastened judgment; nor does it please, except where the taste has been corrupted by the ingredients of luxury and magnificence.

644. The TUSCAN and COMPOSITE orders are both of Ital-ian origin ; the former, nearly allied to the Grecian style, possesses an inferior degree of elegance ; and the latter, as its name imports, shows that in the three original orders the Greeks had exhausted all the principles of grandeur and of beauty ; and that it was not possible to form a fourth order without a combination of the former.

645. The GOTHIC Architecture presents no contradic-tions to the foregoing definitions and illustrations. It must, however, be allowed, that the effect which it produces cannot be entirely accounted for by the rules of symmetry or har-mony in the proportion between the several parts ; but de-pends chiefly on certain ideas of vastness, gloominess, and solemnity, which are reckoned powerful ingredients in the sublime.

646. GARDENING is now improved into a *fine art* (*Art.* 264. *Illus.* 1 and 2.) ; and when we talk of a GARDEN, without any epithet, we mean not the garden of Alcinous, described by Homer, but a *pleasure garden ;* a spot of ground which the " prophetic eye of taste" (*Art.* 269. and its *Illustrations*) has laid out for beauty solely, and which, beside the emo-tions of beauty from regularity, order, proportion, color, and utility, can raise the emotions of grandeur, of sweetness, of gayety, of melancholy, of wildness, and even of surprise or wonder. But we have anticipated, under the head of IM-AGINATION, Chapter IX. Book II., what might here become the materials of a train of reasoning on gardening.

647. As to PAINTING and ENGRAVING, the best service I can here render the reader will be to sketch the state of those arts in the age of Leo X.

648. The human mind seems to take, in certain periods, a strong bent to one class of pursuits in preference to all others, as in the age of Leo X. to the fine arts of painting, sculpture, and architecture. This direction of the human mind may be, in part, accounted for from moral causes ; such as the peaceful state of a country, the genius or taste of its sovereigns, their liberal encouragement of those arts, the

general emulation that arises where one or two artists are of confessed eminence, and the aid which they derive from the studies and works of each other.

649. Under the ruins of the Roman empire, the arts of painting and sculpture were buried in the west, and gradually declined in the later ages, as we may perceive by the series of the coins of the lower empire. The Ostrogoths, instead of destroying, sought to preserve the monuments of taste and genius, and became the inventors of some of the arts dependent on design, as the composition of Mosaic. But, in the middle ages, those arts were at a very low ebb in Europe. They began, however, to revive a little towards the end of the thirteenth century. A Florentine, named Cimabue, beheld the paintings of some Greek artists in one of the churches, and began to attempt similar performances. He soon excelled his models, and his scholars, Ghiotto, Gaddi, Tasi, Cavallini, and Stephano Fiorentino, formed an academy at Florence, in 1350.

650. But the works of these early painters, with some fidelity of imitation, had not a spark of grace or elegance; and such continued to be the state of the art till towards the end of the fifteenth century, when it arose at once to perfection. Raphael at first painted in the hard style of his master Perugino; but soon deserted it, and at once struck into the noble, elegant, and graceful, imitation of the genuine *antique*. This change was the result of genius alone; for the ancient sculptors were familiar to the early painters, though they had looked on them with cold indifference. But they were now surveyed by the eyes of Michael Angelo, Raphael, and Leonardo da Vinci, geniuses animated by a similar spirit of taste, and a similar solidity of judgment, that formed the Grecian Apelles, Xeuxis, Glycon, Phidias, and Praxiteles.

651. Italy, however, was not alone thus distinguished; for Germany, Flanders, and Switzerland, produced in the same age artists of consummate merit.

652. Before we notice these, we shall briefly characterize the schools of Italy. *First* in order is the school of Florence, of which the most eminent master was Michael Angelo, born in 1474. His works are distinguished by a profound knowledge of the anatomy of the human figure, perhaps chiefly formed on the contemplation of the ancient sculptures. His paintings exhibit the grand, the sublime, and the terri-

ble, but he drew not its simple grace and beauty from the antique.

Second.—Raphael d'Urbino, born 1483, founded the Roman school. This great painter stands unrivalled in invention, grace, majestic simplicity, and forcible expression of the passions: he united almost every excellence of the art, far beyond all competition. .From the antique he borrowed liberally, but without servility.

Third.—The most eminent artists of the school of Lombardy, or the Venetian, were Titian, Giorgione, Corregio, and Parmeggiano.

Illus. 1. Titian is most eminent as a portrait-painter, and chiefly in the painting of female beauty. Such is the truth of his coloring, that his figures look nature itself. It was the testimony of Michael Angelo to the merits of Titian, that, if he had studied at Rome or Florence, amidst the masterpieces of antiquity, he would have eclipsed all the painters in the world. Giorgione, with similar merits, was cut off in the flower of his youth. Titian lived to the age of an hundred. Corregio, superior in coloring, and knowledge of light and shade, to all that have preceded or followed him, owed every thing to study. In other painters, those effects are frequently accidental, as we observe they are not uniform: thus, Parmeggiano, imitating the graceful manner of Raphael, carried it to a degree of affectation.

2. In these three original Italian schools—the character of the Florentine is grandeur and sublimity, with great excellence of design, but a want of grace, of skill in coloring, and effect of light and shade—the character of the Roman is equal excellence of design, grandeur, tempered with moderation and simplicity, a high degree of grace and elegance, and a superior knowledge, though not an excellence, in coloring—the character of the Venetian is the perfection of coloring, and the utmost force of light and shade, with an inferiority in every other particular.

653. The second Roman school succeeded the school of Raphael, and was called the school of the Caraccis, three brothers, the most excellent of whom was Annibal. His scholars were, Guercino, Albano, Lanfranc, Dominichino, and Guido. Though all eminent painters, the first and last of these were the most excellent. The elegant contours of Guercino, and the strength, the sweetness, and the majesty of Guido, are the admiration of all true judges of painting.

654. The Flemish school, in the same age, was of a quite different character, and inferior to the Italian; but it shone with great lustre.

655. In the fifteenth century, oil-painting was invented by the Flemings; and, in that age, Heemskirk, Frans Floris, Quintin Matsys, and the German, Albert Durer, are very

deservedly distinguished. Of the Flemish school Rubens is the chief ornament, though a painter of a much later age. His figures, though too corpulent, are drawn with great truth and strict observance of nature, and he possesses inexhaustible invention, and great skill in the expression of the passions. Switzerland produced Hans Holbein, an artist of great eminence in portrait-painting, and remarkable for truth of coloring. Of his works, from his residence at the court of Henry VIII., there are more specimens in Britain than of any other foreign painter. Holland had likewise its painters, whose chief merit was the faithful representation of vulgar nature, a perfect knowledge of the mechanism of the art, the power of colors, and the effect of light and shade.

656. But with the art of painting, sculpture and architecture were likewise revived in the same age, and brought to high perfection; and Michael Angelo's universal genius shone equally conspicuous in all the three departments. Michael's statue of Bacchus, Raphael judged to be the work of Phidias or Praxiteles.

657. The Grecian architecture was first revived by the Florentines, in the fourteenth century; and the cathedral of Pisa was partly constructed from the materials of an ancient Greek temple. The art reached the highest perfection in the age of Leo X., when the church of St. Peter's at Rome, under the direction of Bramante, San Gallo, Raphael, and Michael Angelo, exhibited the noblest specimen of architecture in the universe.

658. We date the invention of the art of engraving on copper by Tomaso Finiguerra, a goldsmith of Florence, about 1460; and from Italy it travelled into Flanders, where it was first practised by Martin Scoen, of Antwerp. Albert Dürer, his celebrated scholar, engraved with excellence both on copper and on wood. Etching on copper, by means of aquafortis, was discovered by Parmeggiano, who executed in that manner his own beautiful designs.

Illus. 1. No art underwent, in its early stages, so rapid an improvement as that of engraving; for, in the course of 150 years from its invention, it nearly attained perfection; and there has been but little proportional improvement in the last century, since the days of Audran, Poilly, and Edelinck.

2. The art of engraving in mezzotinto is, however, of much later date than the ordinary mode of engraving on copper, and was the invention of Prince Rupert, about 1650. It is characterized by a soft

ness equal to that of the pencil, and a happy blending of light and shade, and is therefore, peculiarly adapted to portraits, in which those requisites are highly essential.

Obs. The age of Leo X. was likewise an era of very high literary splendor; but to take notice of the writers of distinguished merit in that period, would compel us to launch forward into a View of the Progress of Literature and of the Sciences during the sixteenth and seventeenth centuries.

659. MUSIC has a place among the fine arts, and 'tis fit it should, from its commanding influence over the human mind, in conjunction with words.

Illus. Objects of sight may indeed contribute to the same end, but more faintly, as where a love poem is rehearsed in a shady grove, or on the bank of a purling stream; but SOUNDS, which are vastly more ductile and various, readily accompany all the social affections expressed in a poem, especially emotions of *love* and *pity.*

660. MUSIC may, no doubt, be made to promote luxury and effeminacy; but with respect to its pure and refined pleasures, music goes hand in hand with gardening, architecture, and sculpture, her sister arts, in humanizing and polishing the mind. They may doubt this who have never felt their charms; but the soldier, whose courage has been roused by music performed upon instruments without a voice, knows the all-powerful charms of music; the lover, whose grief and pity have been raised by melancholy music, or by association of sounds, reminded of the mistress whose siren voice once ravished his soul, does not require the authority of Polybius to believe how dear was music to the Arcadians, under those great teachers, Timotheus and Philoxenus.*

Illus. 1. But no disagreeable combination of sounds is entitled to the name of music; for all music is resolvable into melody and harmony, which imply agreeableness in their very conception.

2. The agreeableness of vocal music differs from that of instrumental; the former, being intended to accompany words, ought to be expressive of the sentiment which they convey; but the latter, having no connection with words, may be agreeable without any relation to sentiment. Harmony, properly so called, though delightful when in perfection, hath no relation to sentiment; and we often find melody without the least tincture of it.

3. In vocal music, the intimate connection of sense and sound rejects dissimilar emotions, those especially that are opposite. Similar emotions, produced by the sense and the sound, go generally into union; and at the same time are concordant or harmonious; but dissimilar emotions, forced into union by these causes intimately connected, obscure each other, and are also unpleasant by discordance.

---

* Polyb. Lib. IV. Cap. III.

661. These illustrations make it easy to determine what sort of poetical compositions are fitted for music.

Illus. 1. As music, in all its tones, ought to be agreeable, it can never be concordant with any compositions in language expressing a disagreeable passion, or describing a disagreeable object, for here the emotions raised by the sense and by the sound are not only dissimilar, but opposite; and such emotions, forced into union, produce always an unpleasant mixture.

Example 1. Music, accordingly, is a very improper companion for sentiments of malice, cruelty, envy, peevishness, or any other dissocial passion; witness, among a thousand, King John's speech in Shakspeare, soliciting Hubert to murder Prince Arthur, which, even in the most cursory view, will appear incompatible with any sort of music.

2. Music is a companion no less improper for the description of any disagreeable object, such as that of Polyphemus, in the 3d Book of the Æneid; or that of Sin, in the 2d Book of Paradise Lost—the horror of the object described, and the pleasure of the music, would be highly discordant.

Illus. 2. With regard to *vocal music*, there is an additional reason against associating it with disagreeable passions. The external signs of such passions are painful; the looks and gestures to the eye, and the tone of pronunciation to the ear: such tones, therefore, can never be expressed musically, for music must be pleasant, or it is not music.

3. On the other hand, *Music* associates finely with poems that tend to inspire pleasant emotions: music, for example, in a cheerful tone, is perfectly concordant with every emotion in the same tone; hence our taste for airs expressive of mirth and jollity.

4. Sympathetic joy associates finely with cheerful music; and sympathetic pain no less finely with music that is tender and melancholy. All the different emotions of love, namely, *tenderness, concern, anxiety, pain of absence, hope, fear*, accord delightfully with music; and, accordingly, a person in love, even when unkindly treated, is soothed by music; for the tenderness of love, still prevailing, accords with a melancholy strain.

Example 3. This is finely exemplified by SHAKSPEARE in the 4th Act of *Othello*, where Desdemona calls for a song expressive of her distress. Wonderful, indeed, is the delicacy of that Poet's taste, which never fails him, not even in the most refined emotions of human nature!

Obs. Melancholy music is suited to slight grief, which requires or admits consolation; but deep grief, which refuses all consolation, rejects, for that reason, even melancholy music.

Illus. 5. Where the same person is both the actor and the singer, as in an opera, there is a separate reason why Music should not be associated with the sentiments of any disagreeable passion, nor with the description of any disagreeable object: this separate reason is, that such an association is altogether unnatural.

Example 4. The pain which a man feels who is agitated with malice or unjust revenge, disqualifies him for relishing music, or any thing that is pleasing; and, therefore, to represent such a man, contrary to nature, expressing his sentiments in a song, cannot be agreeable to any audience of taste.

Example 5. Whatever may be the opinion of the public, or of contemporary critics, this Illustration appositely applies to " Macheath," in the " Beggars' Opera"—a character between whom, or rather whose principles, and the endurance of those principles by any audience, there is but one step to *the faith of the materialist—the character is bold and reckless mirth, that with the desperate must be the mask of despair;* and as is the character, so is the horror inspired in every mind of pure and refined sensibility, by Macheath's mixing music, and his companions mingling the dance, with the agitated feelings which all their sophistry can never conquer.

Illus. 6. For a different reason, Music is improper for accompanying pleasant emotions of the more important kind; because these totally engross the mind, and leave no place for music, nor for any sort of amusement.

Example 6. In a perilous enterprise to dethrone a tyrant, music would be impertinent, even where hope prevails, and the prospect of success is great. Alexander, attacking the Indian town, and mounting the wall, had certainly no impulse to exert his prowess in a song.

662. It is true, that not the least regard is paid to these rules either in the French or Italian Opera; and the attachment which we Britons have to operas, may, at first, be considered as an argument against the doctrine I have endeavored to establish. But the general taste for *operas*, and what are called *melo-dramas*, is no argument; for in these compositions the passions are so imperfectly expressed, as to leave the mind free for relishing music of any sort indifferently; and it cannot be denied, that the pleasure of an opera is derived chiefly from the music, and scarcely at all from the sentiments—a happy concordance raised by the music and by the song is extremely rare; and I agree with Lord Kaimes, that there is no example of it, unless where the emotion raised by the former is agreeable, as well as that raised by the latter.*

---

* A censure of the same kind is pleasantly applied to the French *ballettes* by a celebrated writer: " Si le Prince est joyeux, on prend part à sa joye, et l'on danse: s'il est triste, on veut l'egayer, et l'on danse. Mais il y a bien d'autres sujets de danses: le plus graves actions de la vie se font en dansent. Les prêtres dansent, les soldats dansent, les dieux dansent, les diables dansent, on danse jusques dans les enterremens, et tout danse à propos de tout."

THE END.

www.ingramcontent.com/pod-product-compliance
Lightning Source LLC
Chambersburg PA
CBHW060558030726
47498CB00005B/1448